The Silence is
BROKEN

Cathy,
Thank you! –
Anne Elden
2023

Charleston, SC
www.PalmettoPublishing.com

The Silence is Broken

Copyright © 2023 by Anne Elder

Paperback ISBN: 978-1-7367479-1-9

The Silence is

BROKEN

ANNE ELDER

Preface

It's Crazy! Crazy in a way you can't believe it is happening, not just in one way, but many ways. It has to do with those things you take for granted. Then you realize those things are not even close to how you think they are, and not even in your imagination could you have ever believed any of it is the way it really was. It all began with my father, Carl Jenkins.

So, his story and mine continues, as well as the story of my mother, my brother Jonathan, Nick, Whitney, Seth and Olivia, Brett, Elizabeth, Jack, and the small town of Millersville near the Jersey Shore. This is a tale of lives woven together in love, mystery, deception, loss, discovery, ambition, betrayal, strength, lies, and truth.

Abby

For a moment I sit stunned, looking at Brett, tears wetting his face as he stands at the car window.

"When?" I manage to speak through the sudden ache of sadness which gathers in my chest. "Little Abigail?" I whisper the words barely audible as they leave my heart.

"Last night," he says. "Seth just called me." I lay my head on the steering wheel and weep. He reaches for me and gently edges me into his arms. "I know, Morgan. I know." Finally able to gather myself to move, I climbed into his truck.

Looking over at him I ask, "What in the world are we going to say to them? They have just lost their granddaughter. The pain they feel from their loss, and for Cissy and Josh has to be excruciating." He was quiet, but I could see his mind deliberating by the expression on his face. Waiting patiently for him to express his feelings, I look out the truck window at the landscape moving rapidly past me. Fields of corn run for miles and miles. The smell of freshly mowed hay is permeating my senses.

The ride was mostly in silence, both of us lost in our thoughts. There were several cars at Cissy's house, and we had to maneuver our way off the side of the road to find a parking spot.

Grabbing Brett's hand, I smile tentatively and say, "Are you ready for this?"

"Outside, I believe, yes. Inside, I confess, I am not sure. Brett looks around at the cars and trucks parked along the driveway.

"Hey, isn't that your brother's work truck parked over there?" Looking toward where he was pointing, I see Jonathan's truck. For a moment, I smiled. It is so good to see that he is here.

———————— • ————————

The beautiful light of the sun shines through the stained-glass window. It took me weeks, every minute worth it, to create and position it perfectly right in my bedroom. Sometimes I lie there watching the colors change as the sun makes its way up over the horizon, and I think how its journey resembles mine. I think about Jonathan and what his thoughts are this morning. No cows to milk but a choice to save our parents' legacy. Jonathan's life was spiraling downhill and with it, the farm. By the time I came back, it was on a runaway train to ruin. The memories, disappointment, and resentment I felt finally succumbed to time and its power of healing. Now with a lot of hard work and help from another local businessman, he would be farming again. The bank finally put together a proposal and sent it to Jonathan. I need to go over it with him and plan to go see him early this afternoon.

In addition to reestablishing farm production, a part of the land will be subdivided. The upper acres on the hillside will be surveyed into two-acre residential lots with beautiful views. The proposal from the bank is supposed to provide financing to any qualified prospect who is interested in building on the property and help with all the subdivision approvals and infrastructure improvements required.

Knowing the bank and Tom Fraser, nothing about this deal is going to be transparent, so every condition and term must be scrutinized. For now, they have said that they will give him enough money to continue farming.

It has been two weeks since Abigail's funeral, and I decided to wander over to Seth and Olivia's where I see them having coffee on their deck.

"I've been worrying about the two of you," I say as I hug Olivia. "After Abby's funeral, I really wanted to spend time with you, but Brett assured me you needed to be by yourselves for a time."

"Oh Morgan, we don't know how to console Cissy. It is such a helpless feeling. Every day I wake up thinking how I am going to take Abigail for ice cream, and then reality comes crashing in." Seth puts his arm around Olivia pulling her close.

"Morgan, somehow, we need to unravel what happened to Abby," exclaims Seth.

Raising her head from Seth's chest, Olivia pleads, "Will solving what happened to Abby bring her back, Seth? She's dead, don't you realize nothing can ever change that?"

"I know my love," Seth whispers as he cradles her.

"Oh, Olivia." As my tears begin to well and spill over, I take her hand. "We can't bring her back. But we can, together, vow to make sure no other child will be lost this way."

"Please Morgan, we must!" she declares. Hugging each other, she whispers, "We will. We will do it for you, Abby."

Heidi

Leaving Seth and Olivia's, I check my phone and see a missed call from Heidi. The relief I feel settles over me, and picturing Heidi with her beautiful wavy hair made me smile. Nothing will make me happier than to see her beautiful blue eyes looking back at me. Walking back to my house, I tried Heidi's cell phone again. Standing on my porch, I listen to the rings wondering if she is going to answer.

Finally, I hear, "Mom, I've been trying to reach you. I called earlier but you didn't answer."

Laughing with relief, I say, "Heidi, I tried to call you when your flight landed, and now that I look at my watch, it's three hours later. Where have you been?"

"Mom, I stopped in town to get something to eat. My stomach was loudly letting me know it needed nourishment. I have to tell you the food was absolutely delicious, and the waitress there was so friendly," Heidi says through her laugh.

"Heidi, you stopped at the Millersville Diner, and I'm sure your waitress was Susie Mitchell. How close are you?"

"My GPS says fifteen minutes. I can't wait to see you, Mom. I can't believe I am finally here. I have missed you."

Smiling, I agree, "Me too, just be careful, and I'll be waiting for you in the front yard so you will be sure not to miss the house."

Hanging up from Heidi, I busy myself with straightening up and finishing the last- minute touches to the bedroom I had set up for her. The colors she loves were integrated into every aspect of the room—from the pictures on the wall to the bedspread and carpet. I wanted my new home to be as welcoming to her as it could be, especially with all the changes approaching us.

During Heidi's childhood we were inseparable. It was not just because I was raising her by myself. It was also because we were so much the same. We could finish each other's sentences. We loved the same movies and would sing as loud as we could in the car to the latest songs dancing in our seats. I can't wait for her to get here. So much has happened since I decided to come back. The decision to return to Millersville was difficult for me and choosing to stay was still an ever-changing thought. I am sure Heidi must question why I have chosen to stay away from our home so long.

Standing in the front yard, I watch the road not wanting to miss her coming. I see a car coming and slowing down and suddenly realize it's Heidi. Waiting for her to pull in, I can hardly contain myself. Running over to the car, I threw the door open, and we jumped into each other's arms.

"Heidi, I am so happy to see you."

"Mom, I'm so happy to see you too. I've missed you," Heidi responds, laughing with joy. Together, arm in arm, we walk into the kitchen and sit down at the kitchen table beside a window with a view of a welcoming Willow tree in the back yard.

"How was your flight, Heidi?"

"It was smooth as silk, Mom. No turbulence at all. I slept for most of the flight. Hunger pains were beginning when I got here though. They only had snacks on the flight. "You know, those peanuts you can't open," she chuckles as she makes motions of the attempt. "As I was listening to my phone telling me which way to turn, I was trying to look around as much as I could without running off the road. The diner downtown looked so welcoming. I had to stop and grab something. I am so glad I stopped because, I must say, the food was nothing like we ever had at home. The server brought me their special which was a flat piece of dough in sauce with scrumptious chicken, mashed potatoes, and apple pie for dessert. It was out of this world." Smiling, I reach to hold her hands, barely believing she is finally here.

"It was the chicken pot pie Susie served you, Heidi. It is a local favorite. I would agree that it is delicious. But, enough about food, you have had a long flight, and I know you must be tired. I can't wait for you to see the bedroom I decorated for you."

"So, what are we waiting for? I am anxious to see this bedroom, knowing you, is gorgeously decorated," says Heidi. Laughing out loud, I grabbed her hand, and we walked upstairs.

"I made the last room on the left your room because it looks right out to the backyard."

"Oh my, Mom, you have out done yourself," Heidi exclaims when she opens the door. "Look at the paint color and the bedspread, all in my favorite colors." Her eyes traveled to the elegantly framed photographs above the bed. "Where did you get those pictures on the wall? They are so beautiful," she exclaims again.

Smiling, I answer, "I took those pictures here in Millersville not too far from here. There were so many days that I rode around the area shooting photos, and out of all of them, these two were the ones I loved the most."

"You will have to take me to these places while I am here. I love the room Mom, but I can hardly keep my eyes open," Heidi says, stifling a yawn.

"It's ok, Heidi, go ahead and climb into bed. We have all day tomorrow to talk."

Heading back downstairs, I walk into the kitchen and sit down. Thinking about the day, I breathe a deep sigh accompanied by a wide grateful smile. Leaning my head back against the chair, I close my eyes. *There is so much I need to tell Heidi; I think to myself. Tomorrow, Morgan, tomorrow. Tonight, you need to get some rest as well.*

Deciding to try to get a hold of Brett one more time, I called his cell. After several rings, he picks up.

"Hi Morgan, what have you been doing with yourself all day? I thought you might stop by the tavern, but with all the customers and problems I had today, something tells me I must have missed you."

"Missed me? Now Brett," I laugh. "You know I would not have left until finding and talking to you."

Sighing into the phone, he says, "I guess not, but I wish you had stopped by. You can brighten any day. So, did you see Seth and Olivia at all today?"

"Oh Brett, I did, and it was heartbreaking. Olivia looks like the life has been sucked out of her, and Seth is trying to be the strong one."

"Morgan, we need to be there for them as much as we can."

"I know, and we will be. They are strong, and their faith will keep them grounded. Cissy needs them, and I know this is what is on their mind right now." Feeling myself getting anxious, I beg off the conversation, "I'm heading to bed now, call me tomorrow when you get a minute." Brett agrees and hanging up, I found myself tearing up and thinking to myself, *What the hell am I going to do? There is nothing you can do right now, so go to bed.*

As I climb the stairs to my bedroom, I stop for a moment in front of Heidi's room, put my hand softly on her closed door and whisper, "Good night my darling." Exhausted but happy, I nestle myself in bed and sleep soundly until the rising sun peeks through my window to wake me.

———— • ————

Throwing my covers off trying to cool myself down, I wonder what time it is. Seeing how light it is, I know it's probably time to get up. Every morning during my youth if you weren't up by daylight, someone was at the bottom of the stairs yelling for you to get up. Rolling to my side and throwing my legs to the floor, I get up and slowly walk to the bathroom. Sitting down on the toilet, I lay my head in my hands and think about the roller coaster of the last few weeks.

Abby, just seven years old, has died! The devastation of the loss of a child is forever, and my heart aches for Seth and Olivia. I am aware of the silent killer that is responsible, but the time for that discussion needs to be later. Standing up and finishing my toiletries for the day, I decided it's time to talk to Jonathan. Heidi will be sleeping for quite a while, and I want to talk to Jonathan before she wakes up.

Driving out to the farm, I wonder what kind of progress Jonathan has made in the restoration of the farm. I need to talk to him about the bank's proposal before he makes any decisions of consequence. Right now, it's about us as a family and Jonathan's ability to get back to farming. Deciding this as I am driving up Jenkins Lane, I pull into the farmyard instead of the house driveway which is across the road. I decided to park there because it is a better vantage point to see again the condition of the farm. It's like the remnants of an accident. You know it's bad. At first you turn away, and then you can't help yourself but to look back at it.

Until recently, when I saw for the first time what had become of our family's farm, the past had been in my rearview mirror, only demanding a glance every now and then. Since then, the events and Jonathan's actions which caused the demise of our farm have troubled me. After much consideration, I am determined to assemble the pieces, help Jonathan in the salvage of the farm, his life, his reputation, and restore my family's rightful place in the community.

Getting out of my car, I walk around the yard. Weeds and debris are still everywhere. I see a dumpster sitting off to the side. Walking over to it, I find a ledge on the side to climb up and look in. Seeing a large quantity of trash in it makes me feel a little better. Climbing down, I turn to head up to the house. Just as I am crossing the road, Jonathan walks out of the kitchen door. For a moment, I see my brother, the man who was just a young farmer when I left, with a constant hesitation in his gate and shoulders weighted down with stress.

Walking up the driveway, I yell out, "Hey I know it's early, but I couldn't wait this morning to see you."

Reaching out to hug me, Jonathan says as he laughs, "Misty, it doesn't matter what time you come here, just keep coming." Sliding out of his embrace, I take a closer look at him. He looks different this morning. His eyes are brighter, the slump of his shoulders has disappeared, and he is walking with determination that is different from before. His countenance is confident.

"Well, we need to talk about the bank's proposal. Have they sent it to you yet?" Frowning slightly, Jonathan turns to look out over the fields.

"No, there has been nothing as of yet. I put a call into Tom Fraser yesterday to remind him." Nodding, I turn around and walk toward the farmyard.

"Let's go and look at the milking parlor and make sure that there are no repairs needing to be done before you start milking."

Casting a sidelong glance at Jonathan as we walk toward the milk house, I notice a slight slump has returned in his shoulders which was not evident just minutes ago. He moves ahead of me to open the milk house door. Turning back to look at me, I noticed the tears forming in his eyes.

Touching his arm, I murmur, "It's alright, we will figure it out." Nothing, however, prepared me for what I saw next. The area where Dad's desk sat, well let's just say I couldn't see the desk. Walking into the tank room, the smell was enough to knock me over. Apparently, the tank was never chlorinated and cleaned when Jonathan had finished milking for good. I had to cover my nose and concentrate on breathing through my mouth until we left the area. Jonathan was watching me quietly.

Moving toward the swinging door which took us into the actual milking parlor, Jonathan grabs my arm and says, "Misty, it is bad. I ran out of money and couldn't keep up the maintenance on the milking machines and the pipeline needed so many repairs. It would have been ridiculous to do it. I really needed to replace the whole pipeline, but the cost was more than I could handle. So, I patched it where I could until there wasn't any milking being done anymore."

Walking in the memory, the smell assaults me. It's hard to explain but imagine the smell of sour milk, along with the odor of cow manure, then top it with the smell of iodine and hard water. The difference now was a shroud of mustiness permeating the air. Walking down the ramp to the pit, I close my eyes for just a second or two, and I can almost hear the vacuum cadence of the milking machines. When milking, the sound was almost reassuring and would become the sign that something was wrong when the cadence would change.

Feeling Jonathan at my shoulder, I say, "You know, something tells me this is all going to work out. If we have faith in everything we do, that faith will carry us through this difficult time. Always remember Jonathan, good things happen to good people, and we are those people. Have we missed a beat here and there? Of course, we have! But Jonathan, we are the cream and remember, as Mom would always say before making ice cream, cream always rises to the top. We must always be diligent, though, when dealing with Tom Fraser and the bank. Their actions over the past few weeks have been somewhat suspect."

Sitting down on the step leading up to the platform where the cows were milked, Jonathan tentatively smiles adding, "Misty, I dreaded this day when you might finally come home and see what a mess I've made of everything. Nothing I can say or do will ever make up for the time lost and the idiotic way I acted toward you before you left home. Not realizing how strong and determined you were or the weight of the pain you must have felt while being away from here is unimaginable. This land is in your blood."

Smiling sadly, I touch his arm as I answer, "We have to move on and look forward. There is nothing we can do about the past except embrace what we have learned from it. We need to learn from our mistakes, and that means we must be on our game when it comes to the bank."

Leaning against the gate that lets the cows out of the parlor, Jonathan mumbles under his breath, "What do you think, Misty, I am going to let them walk all over me?"

Casting a glance at him, I say, "Jonathan, did you just say something? I didn't quite hear you."

Keeping his head down, he speaks louder, "I said, what do you think I am going to do?" Struggling with my emotions I think to myself, *apparently, his blinders have been on since he seems to think he has everything under control.* Funny, people change when they gain a little bit of confidence and money, suddenly feeling like they have the world by the tail.

"Jonathan, I know you are fully aware of the ramifications of this agreement with the bank, but I am here to make sure that you don't get 'farmer happy' and agree to whatever Tom Fraser and the bank say. We both know the bank has had another plan all along about this project, and now because I'm back, it all has changed."

Rolling his eyes, Jonathan says, "Really Misty, what does 'farmer happy' mean anyway? Is that one of your famous euphemisms?"

Moving past me to walk back out to the milk house, he turns and retorts over his shoulder, "You know, Misty, I appreciate what you are trying to say, but believe me no one is going into this agreement blindly. You weren't here when I initially went to the bank for help. It was one of the worst days I can remember having in a long time. The scrutiny and the ambiguous attitude Tom Fraser had toward me was humiliating." Jumping up from the step I was resting against, I spin around with my arms in the air.

"Why do you think they acted like that, Jonathan? Do you see this in here," and pointing outside, I say, "and out there? What happened, did you just stop looking at it after a while?"

Clenching his fists at his side, he mumbles, "Don't Misty, can we just look forward like you said? I am ashamed of what happened here, ok?"

Walking up to him, I gentle my tone, "You are right, let's go up to the house and look over the proposal and make sure the bank is not trying to pull the wool over our eyes." Shutting off the lights in the parlor, we move through the office part of the milk house. Stopping him for a minute, I say, "Won't it be a great moment to finally hear the milk running through the pipes again?"

Morgan & Heidi

Linn Creek has been relatively uneventful for us. Somehow, I have managed to keep our life there as quiet as possible for no other reason than because I had such an eventful life before. Heidi and I became a part of the mountains that loomed above us. We moved quietly within our community. The townspeople accepted us as part of their community, and we both blossomed slowly. Heidi grew into a beautiful teenager. There were some trying times during her early years because there was never mention of where her dad was. She questioned where and when he was coming back to see her from time to time. Each time she asked, I struggled to find the right and painless answer for her. I never could and somehow managed to avoid the difficult answer.

Eventually, I was going to have to tell her about him, home, and how I settled in a town much like where I grew up. It was small and quiet with a lot of history in the buildings, the land, and the community's love for the area. It reminded me so much of my home that missing my family became less of a burden. As Heidi grew up, her desire to see where we came from became less important to her. She grew to love what was her home if not mine.

Over the years, Heidi formed close bonds with friends that became like family and a community that belonged to her and to me. Linn Creek had always been home. Her personality and her beauty exceeded all my expectations. She was loving, happy, funny, curious, friendly, energetic, and kind. We were content with our life. Heidi was popular and well liked in school, and I felt valued at my job with the paper. After Dad died and Jonathan's spiral downward with the farm, I became less homesick. That's when I truly wanted to belong to the home that Heidi and I had made together. It wasn't until much later that the idea of going back to Millersville began to form in my mind. So, I pitched an idea to my editor, and he agreed. The editor in chief was all about what was going on in other regions so we could stay competitive and get people to visit our area. I pitched a tour of the Eastern part of the United States to find a place as close to our area in size with a draw of nature to bring visitors.

Convincing Heidi proved to be more difficult. She couldn't understand why the trip would take so long, and I struggled with what to say about the many unknowns. As the day got closer to my leaving, she became very quiet and withdrawn. Assuring her it wouldn't seem that long and reminding her of all her friends and her overseeing the house for a while quickly changed her attitude. Suddenly, she was happily helping me pack, and we spent a weekend cooking so she would have some dinner to eat.

The Farm

None of what has happened during the last five weeks could have been more of a surprise to me than what happened to Jonathan with the farm. Seeing the farm's decline up close, at first, made me sad and angry at myself that I didn't come back sooner to help him, however, knowing Jonathan, I knew it would take something more eventful than my efforts to wake him from his nightmare.

The bank's intensive drive to push him into signing over the farm was very suspicious. Something just didn't seem right to me. My bullshit antennas were firing rapidly every time I saw and talked with Tom Fraser. His entire demeanor did not sit well with me or Jonathan, albeit for different reasons.

"Jonathan, we need to go over the contract from the bank as soon as we can."

"Yes, I know, Tom Fraser keeps leaving voicemails wanting to know when I will be bringing it in signed. I haven't called him back because you and I need to but have not gone over it, as you would say, with a fine-tooth comb. So, what are we waiting for, Misty?" Realizing it might be time to let Jonathan know he has a niece and that she is here in Millersville, I take a deep breath.

"Jonathan, I know we need to get this done, but I have been a little busy in the last couple of days." Pulling him to me, I held both of his hands and looked at him simply smiling. "Jonathan, I know you have had several life changing events in the last few weeks. There is something I need to tell you." Quickly, I notice a slight tilt in his head which brings memories flooding back to my mind of my dad who would do the same thing when just a touch annoyed.

"Hey, it's nothing bad, so I'm not sure why you are looking at me this way. I just wanted to tell you that…" and I hesitate, deciding it might be too hard to see his expression when I tell him. I lean in to hug him and then whisper, "You have a beautiful niece named Heidi, and she is here in Millersville." Pushing me back, Jonathan has such a quizzical look on his face that I burst out laughing. Jonathan had kneeled down as if the weight of what he just heard was too much for him.

Looking up at me, he says, "What are you laughing at? You have managed to shock me again. It's not enough that you return from God knows where, and now you are telling me that while you were gone you had a daughter. What the hell, Misty?"

Aware of old feelings rising to the surface, I say, "What difference does it make now? Come on, Jonathan, break the mold, don't do this again. You were never good at listening, especially to me. Look at me, Jonathan, I'm not the little sister that was the annoyance to you. Time, strangely enough, does unexpected but great things. It changes people, brings them up, makes them better, and most of all makes them realize they are loved. Please, tell me you want to get to know her and have her be a part of your life."

Lowering his head, his shoulders sagging, he mumbles, "Misty, I will never be able to tell you how sorry I am. You are right. I need to break my old habits. You came home, and that should be enough to change anyone. The sister I thought was gone forever has come home. The day we saw each other at the cemetery in front of Mom and Dad's grave was the best day of my life. Something broke in me that day, but it wasn't a bad thing, it changed me." Finding the words to respond was difficult because my throat was so constricted with tears.

"Jonathan, I don't know what to say, except I'm sorry it had to be this way. We have both changed from our past. Family means everything, and it is time we understand."

Walking together up to the house, Jonathan playfully punches my arm asking, "So when do I get to meet this daughter of yours?"

Reaching my car, I laugh and answer, "Well, she was sleeping when I left, so let me get home and see how she is feeling after a good night's sleep. Besides, I need to come back over later to read the bank contract."

Grimacing, Jonathan shakes his head, "It doesn't feel right to me. Now looking back on when I went to the bank, they didn't seem surprised that I was there. It was too orchestrated like they were just waiting for me." I stop in my tracks.

"What? The bank knew you were coming for help? How can that be?"

Jonathan starts cracking his knuckles before answering me, "I don't know, I thought it was odd they were so readily willing to help me when it's known fact, they don't like to invest money into farmers."

Throwing my hands up, I all but shout, "Jonathan, when do banks become the savior to a struggling farmer without so much as a blink of an eye? There is more to this than we are aware of. I think we need to figure this out quickly, so if we need to pursue another avenue we can."

"Misty, what do you mean by that? They have assured me the money will be deposited as soon as I sign the contract. I've already committed myself to purchasing forty head of cattle." Deciding it was not worth continuing in this vein, I reassured Jonathan, nothing would stop him from starting to farm again.

Backing out of the driveway, I roll my window down and say, "Heidi and I will be back later to see you. I'll call you when we are on our way out."

Heidi

Rolling over and covering her head with the pillow, Heidi moans and says to herself, "Why does the sun, no matter where you are, shine right in your window when you are trying to sleep late?" The pillow covering only lasts a few minutes. Swinging her legs to the floor, which propels her body upright, she stands up. Thinking back to her childhood, she laughs to herself. All her friends used to make fun of her when she would spend the night at their house.

Lindsay, her best friend, would push her back down in bed claiming, "I want you to sit up first then put your feet down." Making all kinds of noises, Heidi would try it and then lay back cracking up.

"I can't do it, there is only one way to get out of bed. You roll over, spin your legs to the floor and stand up."

Smirking, Lindsay would say, "Heidi you are so weird. I know that's how your mom does it, so I guess it is ok." Smiling to herself, she decides it's time to see what her mom is doing.

Walking downstairs, she realizes it is very quiet. Entering the kitchen, the smell of coffee is lingering in the air. The coffee maker looks as if it shut off, but maybe the coffee is still warm. Pouring herself a cup, she walks over to the refrigerator hoping beyond hope that her mom has French Vanilla. Opening the door, the familiar blue container with the red top was standing right in front. Sitting down at the table, sipping her coffee, she knows no one is home.

"It is fine, I need some time to think about my journey so far and what might be in store for me today," she says to herself. Mom seemed very excited yesterday when we were making our plans for today, so I probably ought to finish up my coffee and head to the shower. There is one thing that hasn't changed in her—she does not like to wait."

Coming out of the bathroom after her shower, she walks into her mom's bedroom and looks around. There is a kind of vibe in the room which makes her consider they might be staying here for a while. Everything looks exactly like her bedroom at home. All her jewelry is strewn over the bureau, and her creams and perfume are standing like soldiers watching over all the other trinkets she has taking up space. Walking over to the window, she sees a couple outside tending their bird feeders.

"They must be the neighbors she talks about all the time." Finishing her makeup and putting the last touches to her hair, she walks downstairs. "Mom always says I am outgoing, so I hope she doesn't get mad at me for going over there without her," she tells herself as she reaches the side door.

Seth & Olivia

Seth turns to look at his wife, Olivia. It had only been days since Abby's funeral, but every day Olivia seems more engaged than the day before. Today, her wanting to come outside and tend to her bird feeders was a good sign. Losing a child is crushing, and when it's one of your own, it is earth shattering. Olivia had put her sorrow and loss away so she could cloak their daughter with love, protection, and strength.

Looking over toward Misty's house, Seth sees a young woman walking out the side door. At the sight of this young woman, Seth remembers Olivia telling him about a phone call, he realizes it must be Heidi. Putting two and two together, he knows this young woman must be Heidi. Throwing his hand up in a friendly wave, he sees Heidi enthusiastically wave back and start walking over.

"Hey Olivia, honey! It looks like we have a visitor." Standing up from her flower bed, Olivia sees a pretty girl walking over, stepping delicately through the flowerbeds.

Moving toward Olivia, Heidi extends her hand, "I hope I'm not interrupting anything, I just wanted to say, hello." Hearing Seth cough, Olivia turns and looks at him. She sees him raising his eyebrows questioning. Nodding in her silent communication, it was fine. This was Misty's daughter.

"Well, hello there, you must be Heidi. It's so nice to finally meet. Your Mom, Seth, and I have become great friends. We are the Palmers, Seth and Olivia."

Grinning Heidi says, "It is nice to meet you Seth and Olivia. I did not want to intrude, but I came downstairs and realized Mom wasn't home. I was getting myself together and saw the two of you, so here I am."

Standing next to Olivia, Seth offers his hand to Heidi beginning, "We are incredibly happy to meet you Heidi and hope you find your stay here in Millersville full of adventure. We have thoroughly enjoyed spending time with your mom since she has been here. It was by chance we met her and since then, she has been spending some time with us." A red cardinal lands on the birdfeeder near where Heidi was standing. Seeing the bird perch on the feeder makes Heidi smile. Seeing this, Seth motions to the cardinal.

"Do you have birdfeeders around your home? Olivia and I enjoy watching them when we are eating breakfast since a couple of our feeders are hanging near our breakfast nook."

Nodding in agreement, Heidi says, "We always had a cardinal come every day at the same time. It would hover right by Mom's truck door looking at itself in the side mirror. She always said it was my grandmother coming to check on us. A wistful look of longing would dart across her face, and it always made me feel sad for her." Wanting to tell Heidi things about her grandmother was practically bursting from Olivia, but it wasn't fair to Misty to say anything to Heidi.

Instead, she says, "Cardinals are messengers from heaven bringing comfort from a loved one. So, your mom was probably right. It was your grandmother sending her a message of love."

"I hope so. Sometimes Mom seems sad and then becomes very preoccupied. It happened a lot right before she left on this job assignment. Millersville seems to have been the right atmosphere for her because now she seems confident and content. Thank you both for becoming such good friends to my mom." Seth moves to Olivia and puts his arm around her.

"Heidi, you are welcome here whenever you want, but I think I see your mom's car coming down the road. Tell her we said hello and stop back over later. We will have cocktails on our deck and get to know you a little better." Waving goodbye, Heidi walks across their yard and opens the garden gate to her mom's home. Somewhere, her senses tell her, *If Mom is happy here, maybe I should stay for a while.*

"Oh my, I need to get a grip, I just got here."

Pulling into the driveway is none other than the subject of Heidi's thoughts. As her mom gets out of the car, Heidi admires her mom's beauty which has always amazed her. Looking at her, she is so proud that she is her mother. Nothing would please Heidi more than if her mom could be totally happy.

———— • ————

"Hey Mom, where were you so early this morning?"

Turning to lock the car, I laugh hysterically, "Early, Heidi, do you know what time it is? We could be planning on eating lunch by now."

Shamefully, Heidi lowers her head and responds, "I know, cut me a break, I had a long flight yesterday, and the bed was so comfortable. It wouldn't let me get out of it. Something kept telling me to snuggle down a little more until the sun just wouldn't stop shining." Walking away from the car, I grabbed ahold of my daughter and hugged her tightly.

"Don't stress about sleeping a little late. Obviously, you have been up for a while. I saw you walking through the garden gate when I pulled up."

"Just did a short visit with your neighbors, Seth and Olivia. They are very nice people, and I know why you are all friends. Mom, they think the world of you. You must have had an impact on them." Laughing, Heidi throws her hands up in a magical sign and says, "Did you cast some kind of spell over them?"

Taking a sidelong glance over to Seth and Olivia's, I see them working around their yard which is good to see. It is still hard to believe that Abby passed away, and it probably would be a good time to tell Heidi about it before she spends any more time with them.

"How was your visit? They are very nice people and have been so good to me since I came here. It was such a nice thing to do, going over there and introducing yourself."

Tapping me on the shoulder, Heidi laughs and says, "Mom I am almost twenty-one years old, and you did bring me up with manners. They are your neighbors, so I thought it was important for me to visit them. They were so friendly. They told me about how much they liked you, and we talked about their garden. There was a cardinal feeding on their bird feeder, and it reminded me so much of the cardinal who came every day and looked in your truck mirror. I told them we thought it was my grandmother coming as an angel." Surprised at Heidi's comment, I try not to sound irritated.

"What did they say when you were talking about your grand-mother?" Turning to look at me, Heidi pastes a quizzical look on her face which lets me know that I didn't disguise the tone of my voice well.

Moving on, she responds, "They just listened. What did you think they were going to say?"

"Heidi, I don't know what in the world I was thinking. So, how hungry are you because I am starving? Let's go in and see what we can throw together for lunch." Putting my arm around my daughter, we head inside to eat.

Morgan

Along the street outside of my new home, there were towering trees, and now, standing at my kitchen window, I could see them waving. Shadows were dancing along the grass with the leaves floating down from their place within the trees. In the distance, I could hear a fire whistle blowing. A moment of unease came over me wondering what family was going to experience a tragedy.

"Mom, where were you just then? You looked like you were a million miles away." Snapping out of my gloomy reverie, I turn to look at my beautiful daughter. Her hair was pulled up in a messy bun which was her favorite style. Eyes, almost navy in color, twinkled at me as she came over to sling her arm over my shoulder. "What's going on with you today? You don't seem yourself." I wonder how so many nights I thought I would know all the right things to say to her about Millersville and my childhood home, but now that it was time, I wasn't sure how to begin.

Now, though, it is time. I've waited so long to tell her about her family. Through her adolescence and then her teenage years, I found myself fantasizing about how it would all play out. Nothing prepared me for today. Who would have thought she would be here in Millersville? Today I would get the chance to tell her, amongst the smells and noises of the town that Jonathan and I grew up in. The people and friends of the past and the future helped me come to grips with the dynamics of my family. It was time to tell Heidi about her family—while I could still control the narrative.

As for her father, she doesn't need to spend time worrying about who he is right now. The information I made available about her father was minimal at best. We were navigating life just fine, and it didn't seem important to her until she got to high school. Up until then, life was moving along at a normal pace, and it was my decision to keep her moving in a forward direction. Walking over to the window that looks over the backyard, I sigh, wondering how I am going to begin. The life I created for us was sacred to Heidi and me, and I am about to upset her equilibrium by telling her about my past. Somehow, I need to find my voice. It's been long enough.

"Heidi, when we finish lunch, let's take a ride, and I'll show you around Millersville. There are some places that I want you to see. Before coming here for this assignment for work, I realized you noticed I was somewhat distracted. We have never talked much about my childhood and my family, and I know you have always been curious about my life growing up. It's shameful the way I acted toward you whenever you wanted to know more about your grandparents. I spun excuses to keep you from delving too deep into our family history. For years I wanted our family to be you and me and all the friends we have back home. Upsetting you or the life we have in Linn Creek was not my intention." Watching Heidi absorb and process what she just heard makes me smile.

She thought for a moment before responding, "Mom, I love our friends and the family feeling we have, plus we don't need anyone else but you and me. So, what is going on with you?" Taking a deep breath, I begin to explain hoping that she will understand why it took me so long to tell her.

"When I was around your age, I left home and went to college. You know I went to college in Arizona and how much I liked it there. It was during my time in college that my mom passed away. She had been sick for a long time, and there was nothing I could do to make her better."

Reaching out to squeeze my hand, Heidi says, "I can't imagine, Mom, what that must have been like for you. My life would be devastated if I lost you."

Shaking my head, I implore, "Please don't even think about something so terrible." Reaching over, I give her a quick hug and smile. "I assure you I'm not going anywhere but let me continue. This is way overdue! Those nights you would come in before going to bed and I was on my computer, those nights I was searching for information about my home." The thoughts swirling around in my brain were starting to spin out of control. There was so much to tell her. I wasn't quite sure where to begin, so I decided the best thing would be to start from the beginning.

"It all began with my father, Carl Jenkins. Like most daughters, I held a special reverence for him, thinking he could do anything and knew almost as much." Heidi moves to lean against the counter and crosses her arms. "At least, that is what I believed until the age of thirteen. Glasses rode low on his nose, always giving the feeling he was peering at you over them. Somehow it never felt encouraging, and it infused unease when talking with him. He was often quick to anger. As a little girl, I can remember being frightened of him whenever he would ask me to go get something in his shop. There were so many tools in his shop, Heidi, bringing back the wrong one was paramount to a tongue lashing at the least. It wasn't until much later, I learned of the loving man who dwelled behind the displays of impatience, frustration, and anger." Smiling gently at Heidi, I go on, "We lived very modestly on a dairy farm and work came first before any other fun activity was allowed." The expression on Heidi's face was one of interest but with an expectation of something worrisome to come next.

Finding her voice, she inquires, "Mom, who is the 'we' you are talking about? Did you have siblings who are my aunts and uncles?"

Grabbing a hold of her hands smiling, I confess, "You have an uncle, Heidi, and his name is Jonathan." Dropping my hands, she walks away from me to stare out at the backyard.

"Mom, is this why you left home? Were you looking for your family?" Choosing my words carefully, I moved to stand beside her and put my arm around her waist.

"Heidi, it has been so long, and now that I have the chance to tell you, I'm not sure what words to use. Never in a million years do I want you to think our life and home in Linn Creek is still not a place where you will always call home. It will always be your home because you grew up there. You and I had our best years there—your job, friends, and maybe something more is waiting there for you. I needed to re-connect with my family here in Millersville. The need to come back was occupying every waking moment and the fear everything your grandfather and grandmother worked so hard for was going to disappear."

Tears streaming down my cheeks, I turn to face her as I continue, "Part of me longed to see my brother, the farm and those who, in the years between, had vanished from my life. Heidi, this is my family's home, where I was born, grew up and left to become my own woman and raise my beautiful daughter. Except now, it is time for me to come home and renew my heritage for you and for me. Nothing is more important to me right now than to right all the wrongs that were done to your grandparents, and somehow through all of this, possibly make this your home too." Pulling away from me, I see she is crying which is breaking my heart.

"Heidi, please don't cry." Wiping her nose with the back of her hand and standing so straight, I realize the tears were of anger not sadness. It didn't surprise me, so I just waited for her to unleash it. Trying to hold herself together she turns to look at me.

"Mom, why, why didn't you tell me this? All those times we talked about my grandparents you never said that you left them." The volume of her voice was rising now. "Why would you do that? I could have known them instead of just hearing stories about them. It seems so unfair, it's as if you had a whole other life, you never wanted to share with me. Why?" I realize she wanted justification from me so she could understand why her mother, her best friend, would be so devious.

"Heidi, there were several reasons why I left home when I did but believe me, your grandparents were wonderful people, and their lives were cut short. Your grandmother became very sick with a horrible disease which took her memory of her life, her kids, and her husband. After she died, leaving seemed the only option, your grandfather was angry and disillusioned about life and what it had dealt him. He loved my mom very much, and they had spent most of their life together. Losing her was like having his heart turned off. Believe me this isn't an excuse for keeping you away from your family, but my goal was to keep you as safe as possible."

She bows her head. I could see the turmoil swirling above her like God was touching her and telling her life wasn't always perfect but to seize it and make it her own. Reaching for her, I try to hug her, but she pulls away. Not wanting to pressure her, I stepped away and went into the other room to give her some space. Confrontation was not either one of our strong suits. I need to leave her to think for a little while and let her process this new information. Hearing a vibration in my pocket, I realize my cell phone is ringing. Looking at the display, I see its Jonathan. Knowing he is wondering when I am coming over to go over the bank's proposal, I hit the decline button. There was something I needed to do before we made any decisions.

Walking back into the living room, I touch Heidi on the shoulder saying, "Heidi, I know this is a lot to process. Nothing is stopping you from taking whatever time you need to figure it out. We will work this out and come out on the other side together. However, for now I need to take care of something. When I'm finished my errand, we can talk some more. Ok?"

Heidi glanced up at me briefly nodding, yes, but casting her eyes downward again. Her shoulders were slumped and shaking. Moving toward her, I went to hug her, and she pulled away again. Trying to keep my composure, I stepped back realizing there was so much going on in her mind. At that moment, there was nothing I could do but give her space and time.

Quickly, Heidi squeezed me and says, "I will be here when you come back."

Getting in my car, I bow my head on my steering wheel, tears streaming down my face. What have I done to Heidi? All this time I have been worrying about Jonathan and my parents' legacy. Really, was it worth it to me if Heidi can't embrace it?

Starting my car, I pull out of my driveway and turn toward town. Finding out what Tom Fraser is up to is something I need to do without Jonathan. Seth is out by the road and flags me down.

"Hey Misty, or is it, Morgan? I'm not sure what to call you these days."

Sadly, knowing what Seth must be feeling right now, I smile tentatively, "Seth, I want you to know I'm going to be Morgan from now on. It's time I left Misty behind, begin a new life here in Millersville as Morgan. I hope Olivia and you are ok with this." For the first time in a few days, Seth gets a big smile on his face. Reaching into my car window, he hugged me.

"Morgan, I know what all of this has meant to you—getting back home and finding a place here. I also know there is so much more to be done. Olivia and I are so happy you are home. Just remember, we are on your side, and we love you."

Smiling, I say, "Seth, tell Olivia that I will be back, and I will stop over and see her. Heidi will, hopefully, come with me." Waving goodbye, I drive off toward town. Pulling into the public parking, I find a spot to park. Laughing to myself, I realize having a public parking lot was so odd for Millersville. Who would have thought we would have such a thing? So much of downtown had changed with the brewery open and new life being bred into the Hotel that the parking had become a necessity.

Walking into the bank, I see Whitney in line waiting for a teller. Heading back toward the offices, I see her glancing in my direction. Smiling and giving a small wave, I waited for the receptionist to notice me.

"I'm looking for Tom Fraser, is he in today?" With an automatic smile, she tells me she will check and see. "Please tell him Misty Jenkins is here to see him. I'm sure he will make himself available."

Looking as though she doubts me, she dials his extension and begins, "Mr. Fraser, Misty Jenkins is here to see you. Yes, she is sir. Ok, I'll bring her back." Hanging up the phone, she starts to stand up.

With a firm but respectful tone, I say, "I know my way, thank you." Advancing to the back hallway, I wonder how Tom Fraser is going to react. I was prepared for every avenue he might want to head down while manipulating the bank's proposal. Just as I put my hand up to knock, the door opens.

"Misty, it's nice to see you again. I've been meaning to give you a call to see if we could get together and get to know each other. There has been such an atmosphere surrounding your disappearance. It makes me curious to know you better. Come on in and sit down," says Tom smiling. Moving into his office, I take a seat at his small conversation table. I feel this would level the playing field because sitting across from him at his desk would give him the illusion of having the upper hand.

Figuring it would be best if I start the conversation instead of Tom, I begin, "Tom, I agree we were due to get together and yes, it has been a whirlwind of excitement since I have come back. Jonathan and I have a lot of catching up to do, but I'm staying here in Millersville, so we can take our time. Nothing means more to me than setting straight the things that have affected our family." Frowning slightly, Tom makes a motion with his hand as if he was dismissing what I just said. I turn the conversation toward the agreement with Jonathan. "Tom, the agreement the bank has put together for Jonathan has some real problems which will delay his signing, any part of it, until he and I have dissected all of it."

"Misty, I understand completely. Please take as much time as is reasonable. We don't want the investors to get impatient, so try to sit with Jonathan soon," Tom says quietly. Standing up to take my leave, I look at Tom.

"I hear you Tom, but rest assured the investors will wait. This property has so much potential and could make them and you a lot of money if I'm not mistaken. What is important to Jonathan is having the ability to work on a farm again. Beyond that, I don't think he cares about the rest of it. The problem facing you and the investors is, I do care, and my plan is to make sure this sale is something which is beneficial for all of us."

Frowning slightly, Tom nods and says, "Everything is being managed correctly, our legal team worked overtime on making sure all the bases were covered."

Opening his door to take my leave, I look back and say, "Let's hope so!"

Back in my car, I think to myself, there is nothing that bugs the hell out of me more than people who think they are superior. Tom must think I just came out from under a rock with how condescending he sounds. Reaching my car, I dig around in my pocketbook for my car keys.

"Looking for something are we?" Straightening up, I turn and see Nick Darlington standing just a little too close. Nick Darlington, someone I have spent most of my adult life damming to hell and back. He was, or at least I thought, the love of my life, but sometimes life creates a tailspin, and I was tossed right in the middle of it.

"Really Nick, what are you doing sneaking up on me like that? And why are you standing so close to me?"

Stepping back slightly, Nick smiles devilishly and says, "Misty, you looked as though you were having some trouble, and I wanted to help."

"Did you now?" Dangling my keys, I continue, "I have every-thing under control, thank you! The clock is ticking, and I am late getting to my appointment. So, if you'll excuse me." Opening my car door and sliding in, I look up and Nick is still standing there. Rolling down my window, I stared at him. "Nick, unless you are planning to get run over, I suggest you move out of the way. And by the way, don't call me Misty anymore. I've been Morgan for the last twenty years, and I like her, so please start calling me by that name." Visibly annoyed, he moves toward the sidewalk, and I pull out of my parking spot. Sitting at the light, I look in my rearview mirror and see him staring after me.

Nick & Whitney

Whitney and Nick are struggling with how to handle their new-found knowledge about Misty being home. Spending these past few days together has helped them emotionally. Knowing they might have a chance to put their past away in a better place has given the two of them a reprieve from their constant nightmare.

"Nick, what are we going to do now? You do realize, don't you? We are going to be seeing her all over this town. Once it gets out that she's back, what will happen then?" Nothing was further from Nick's mind at that moment. He could still hear Misty telling him she wanted to continue using Morgan as her name. *Why? Are her memories of the time growing up here so disturbing she is willing to give up her family name? Or is there another reason hidden from everyone?*

Looking over at Whitney, he smiles before reassuring her, "Don't worry about it, Whitney. She assured both of us we would all work it out somehow, and I believed her."

Trying to keep the impatience out of her voice, "Of course you do, but I'm not so sure. You weren't there that day when I talked to her. She was so angry, and then became so calm. Which honestly Nick, bothered me more than anger. This whole thing has really un-nerved me, although I feel like we've grown slightly closer, right?"

Realizing he needs to tread lightly, Nick says, "Yes, Whitney, we have but don't get ahead of yourself. We still have a lot of healing to do. I'm feeling as good as you are about everything, and we need not worry about Misty or Morgan if that's what she wants to be called. We better go. The boys are about to get done camp." As they were walking out the door, Nick draped his arm over Whitney's shoulders. Whitney smiles to herself.

Jonathan

Jonathan decides it is time to sit down and look over the contract from the bank before Misty gets back. He loves his sister, but she could be aggressive when she had something or someone in her sights. It appears what she is focused on right now is Tom Fraser and the bank.

If I truly want to make a change in my life, then I need to be as prepared as possible and try to be one step ahead of her, Jonathan thought. Sitting down at the kitchen table, he flips open the contract. Reading through the first couple of pages reveals nothing of any importance. Most of it was laying out the scope of the land and all the surveyor's findings. A couple of pages further on, he sees an italicized paragraph saying the fields on either side of the pond were excluded from the site plan due to unknown environmental issues. *What in the world could they think was harmful enough to be called an environmental issue?*

Making a note on the page, he continues through the rest of the contract and realizes maybe he really does need Misty to look it over. In a couple of hours, she would be coming over with Heidi. Thinking of Heidi brought a smile to his face. Standing up and stretching, he realizes how stiff his knees are becoming. Age was catching up to him, and it became more obvious to him that farming small was in his future.

Pulling into the driveway at Jonathan's, I see Sara coming around the corner with her clothes basket. Joining her, we walk in the backdoor where old jackets are hanging hooks, and a mop leans in a bucket as if to say, *I'm tired, let me rest.* Standing at the back door, I see clothes hanging on the clothesline bringing back so many memories. Mom stopped us before we walked into the kitchen, telling us to take off our smelly jackets and boots, yelling to me to get the clothes off the line and fold them, and asking Jonathan if he remembered to bring in milk. I had to keep myself from breaking down into tears. Sara turns, sees my face, and comes quickly to my side.

Touching my arm, she says, "Misty, it's ok to be upset. There are so many memories here, and it's been a long time for you. Take it all in. We haven't changed it much since your parents lived here. Jonathan never wanted to change things whenever I wanted to alter the house. So, I eventually stopped trying. It became apparent to me his need to keep things the same was an attempt to convince himself, and me, life was going to standstill."

Sitting down at the kitchen table, I look at my sister-in-law who I barely knew. When she married Jonathan, I was already gone so my memories of her were as Jonathan's girlfriend. Except now, I realize she has become one of us over the last twenty years and has experienced all the good and bad times of being part of our family. In that moment, I knew we were going to be formidable because we all had our lives and happiness at stake.

"Sara, the three of us will overcome all of this. Nothing will stop me now that I am home. It may take some time, but the Jenkins family will regain its family's reputation and we will create a new legacy our parents would have been proud of. Right now, Jonathan and I have to look over the bank agreement. But before we do, I need to ask you something before Jonathan comes back in." Frowning slightly, Sara nodded. Knowing this was going to be hard for her to admit, I venture the question, "Do you want to milk cows again?"

Sara at once reacts, "Of course we do." Expressions move across her face like storm clouds ever-changing their intensity. Bowing her head dejectedly, I feel a pang of remorse for asking the question, but I had to know. This was their chance to change the outcome of their life, but they had to be in it together, and I just wasn't sure.

"Oh Misty, I don't know. It's been so hard, and Jonathan hasn't been good for several years. The farming industry has changed so much in the last five years and there isn't any movement to make it any better. I'm afraid if he starts to milk again, we will head right down the same path and that would be deadly. I sincerely want him to farm again, but milking cows again almost makes me feel sick. Other farms in the area have expanded their business by raising beef cattle, pigs, and in some cases even chickens. If he would only consider this alternative to milking, I would be ecstatic. Doing something different would make him happy and keep him feeling valued."

Laughing, I comforted her, "Oh my Sara, I think my parents would turn over in their graves if Jonathan started raising chickens. Something tells me you won't be collecting eggs any time soon. Work on Jonathan, though, because changing how he farms could be just the right medicine to heal his wounded ego." Hearing the back door open, I smiled at Sara. "Let's figure out this agreement, and then we can work on the rest of the plan."

"Hey, Misty. I thought you were bringing Heidi with you?"

"Jonathan, she is still processing the news, so I thought it best to leave her alone for a little while. There is the agreement we need to look at and I didn't think we should talk about all of it with Heidi here. Did you get a chance to look at the agreement?"

Nodding, Jonathan says, "Earlier, I took a quick look, and it was so confusing. Something tells me it was written that way purposely."

"Jonathan, it seems as if they were assuming you were becoming so desperate with selling the farm, they decided to complicate the agreement with a bunch of legal ease. This is exactly why we need to lay it all out and go over it page by page. Tom Fraser is wanting you to sign this soon, so let's get to it."

During the next hour or so we went through over half of it, high-lighting areas that came into question. Nothing abnormal stood out, but I understood why Jonathan was getting frustrated. "Jonathan, we need to get some help with the interpretation of this document, there is no way the three of us can do this without help. Do you have a lawyer you have used in the past?" Sara and Jonathan shared a look with each other.

Sara spoke first, "No, we don't—at least not one we would use again." At this, Jonathan motions to Sara to stop.

"Misty, what Sara is trying to say is we had Mom and Dad's lawyers help us when we had something small to do, but this definitely is nothing we would have done by his firm. We need some help from someone else."

Staring down at the table for a minute, I decide, "Jonathan, I will figure this out. Just give me some time, and I will get us a lawyer." Standing up, I walk toward the back door turning back toward the two of them, I hesitate. "What the two of you need to do is have some serious discussions with each other." Jonathan pushes back his chair and stands up.

"What are you trying to say, Misty? You just got home, and I'm getting the feeling that you are assuming too much responsibility with this project. Sara and I have been the ones suffering here with milk prices, sick animals, and high veterinarian bills. We will decide what happens here after we sign the agreement."

A little sarcastically, I say, "Is that right? Do you honestly think the bank is going to make it easy to farm again? I know they keep saying there is going to be something for you to farm, but we need to make sure the rest of the contract is correct because without that, you won't have enough money to farm. So, why don't we all sit back down and talk sensibly about the plan for this farm's future." After the small outburst, we went over everything again, and I highlighted the problem areas for a while until realizing it's time I needed to get back to Heidi.

Standing up, I lean down to give Sara a hug and whisper, "Don't worry, together, we will figure this out." Moving toward the door, I turn back and look at Jonathan and say, "I think I will talk to Seth about finding a lawyer. He will lead us in the right direction, and we all know he and Olivia will do whatever they can to help us."

Heidi

Heidi went outside to sit on the front porch in search of fresh air and some peace of mind. Thinking about everything she's found out since getting here has her mind wandering. Part of her was excited she now had family she could actually see and talk to, but her thoughts could not stop drifting to her father. Was he from here and could he still be living here in Millersville? She needs her mom to get back so they can talk more. Hearing a car coming down the road, she looks until she has the car in sight. Sighing in relief that it's her mom's car, she stands up and waves. Heidi feels tears forming and a sense of relief comes over her.

———————•—•———————

Hopefully, Heidi is feeling better about the bombshell I dropped on her. It needed to be done quickly so we could move on with our lives. There is so much I needed to tell her, and it feels good to finally have our family together in one place. Pulling into my driveway, I put my car in park and got out.

Heidi runs down the steps, "Mom, I thought you would never get back here. It seems like you have been gone a long time. Where were you all this time?"

Not wanting to tell her about the sale of the farm, I say, "What have you been doing since I've been gone? Have you been sitting out here the whole time?" Heidi laughs as if this comment was the most ridiculous thing she'd heard.

"Mom, of course not. I got something to eat and then honestly, I can't stop thinking about what you told me. I know my reaction wasn't very good when you first told me, but it was a lot to take in, and I really didn't know how to react. It's like our family grew overnight." Understanding her trepidation and uneasiness with the situation, I put my arms around her to hug her.

"Heidi, I know it has been quite a revelation, and it took me a very long time to come to grips with the life I left here, but over the next few days we will talk about it all. I don't want to put any more on you right now. Finding out you have an uncle and aunt living right here in Millersville is enough for one day, don't you think?"

Smiling tentatively, she says, "I have so many questions for you, but I know how hard this was for you to tell me, and I'm ok. Mom, I love you, and all I want is for you to be happy. There is a glow about you which wasn't there at home, and it obviously sets well with you being here. So, what are we waiting for? Let's go see my uncle and aunt. By the way what are their names?" I couldn't help but smile.

"Jonathan, and his wife is Sara." Grabbing a hold of her and twirling around dancing with her, I tearfully proclaim, "I love you for all you are and how much you love me as your friend and mother. So, let's get in the car and ride out there. I believe they might be waiting for us."

Morgan & Heidi

Brett finished up tallying last night's sales and needed to get to the bank before the afternoon rush came in the bar. Letting the bartender know he was leaving for a little while, he gets in his truck and starts heading downtown. Pulling into a parking place alongside the curb outside of the bank, he looks in his side view mirror making sure it was safe to open his door. Seeing that the car stopped in his blind spot was Morgan's, he quickly gets out. Waving to get her attention, he walks back to her car. The window came down and a young woman with the bluest eyes was smiling at him.

———— • ————

A slight panic came over me at the sight of Brett with Heidi by my side.

"Well look at these two beauties. Where are you off to this fine day?" Thankfully, at the same moment he began to approach the light changed saving me from explaining Heidi right at this moment.

"We are taking a little ride. The light's changing, Brett. I will call you later," I offered quickly. Pulling away, I could see the quizzical look on Brett's face causing me to make a mental note that we would have to have the Heidi talk sooner rather than later.

Heidi takes a sideways glance at me, and I could feel her eyes on my hands, which I now see have turned white from my tense grip on the steering wheel.

"Mom, what's the matter, who was that guy? He is really handsome, don't you think?"

Releasing the tension in my hands, I give a small laugh and inform her, "Yes, he is quite handsome and no nothing is the matter. I must be just nervous about you meeting your aunt and uncle, that's all." Hoping she wouldn't ask any more questions about Brett, I started pointing out landmarks along the way to the farm. "Look over there, Heidi, there is the bowling alley where I bowled when in high school. And down the street is a western store that sells cowboy boots and hats, fancy belt buckles, and all sorts of cowboy paraphernalia." Heidi's head was turning back and forth trying to take in all the scenery.

"Wow, look how big that rocking chair is."

Laughing, I say, "It used to be a furniture store, but now it's this really cool place selling furniture made out of wine barrels, and all kinds of antiques are displayed there. The chair has always been one of the famous landmarks of our area, and I hope it never leaves its perch."

"Really? We will have to stop there, so I can look around. You could buy something for your house since we might be staying here. How much further do we have to go before we are there?" This was a monumental moment for her and me as well. Nothing can prepare you for the onslaught of emotion when faced with the past and present coming together. Taking a deep breath, I point out to my left.

"Heidi, look up there, see the small house in the distance? That was Grandmom and Grandpop's house. The farmhouse is in front behind the grove of trees to the right. We will be turning on the next road coming up on the left. Everything is going to be fine, they can't wait to meet you, so no worries, ok?" I turn on to Jenkins Lane and slow down so Heidi could look around. Grabbing her hand, I squeezed it tightly.

"All of this ground you see was your grandparents and it gave them a good life. Uncle Jonathan and I learned a lot of life lessons here." We came up to the farmhouse, and I slowed down to turn in. Before I even got the car turned off, Jonathan and Sara were out the door smiling.

I turn to look at Heidi and tell her, "It's time, honey, don't be nervous, they are so happy to see you." Opening up the door, Heidi steps out and tentatively walks around the front of the car. Jonathan is grabbing a hold of her and hugging her so tightly I think she might be struggling to breathe. Releasing her, he looks into her face, and I see the tears leaking out of his eyes.

"Oh, my goodness child, you look so much like your mom did when she was young." He starts to touch her face as if he was tracing her features so they would be etched into his brain. "Tell me every-thing about yourself, Heidi." Stepping back, Heidi looks over toward me with a look of panic.

Seeing the familiar look, I tap Jonathan on the arm and say, "Hey give her some space. This is still so new. Before a few hours ago, she didn't even know the extent of her family."

Realizing the intensity he was showing toward Heidi, he smiles at his sister and his newfound niece pleading, "I'm sorry if I

51

overwhelmed you just then. I can't contain my excitement that your mom is home."

Moving to stand next to his wife, Sara, he goes on, "Heidi, we weren't sure we were ever going to see your mom again, and then not only does she come home but brings her daughter here as well. Within a few days, I gained my sister back and a niece on top of it. Life couldn't be any better than right at this moment." Understanding how much it meant to Jonathan that I was home, I knew the reaction coming from him right now was not quite what he was feeling. More like screaming from the rooftops would be what he wanted to do but knowing the whole situation with Heidi and my life before, he definitely toned it down a bit.

We spent the next few hours talking and sharing our life with the two of them. Sara was so interested in our life in Linn Creek. With the farm, getting a chance to travel was not something either one of them had done much of. Hearing about life in another town appealed to her sense of adventure. Heidi was so in tune with people, their expressions, and body language—it wasn't long before she was entertaining Sara and Jonathan with events from our life. Every now and again, Jonathan would cast a sideways glance at me and wink. Seeing the interaction unfolding in front of me made the last twenty years away not so horrible to stomach anymore. After a few more stories, I caught Heidi's attention and gave her a look. It was time we got ready to go back home.

Heidi stood up, "Uncle Jonathan and Aunt Sara, it's been great to finally meet you. I see now why my mom wanted to come back here. Apparently, there are reasons, which I don't know yet, as to why we didn't come back sooner, but I'm sure they were important to her." I watch Jonathan pause for a moment as if considering his next words.

"Well, whatever those reasons were or still are, I'm sure when she is ready, they will be shared with you. No matter what, we are so happy you are both here." With that, I touch her arm to go, and we say our goodbyes.

On the way back home, Heidi was full of enthusiasm for her time with Jonathan and Sara. I listen to her and smile to myself. It was great to hear how happy she was now that the initial shock had worn off from the bombshell I dropped on her earlier.

Brett

Knowing he had some time to kill before heading back to the bar, Brett decides to go over to his mother's. Elizabeth, Brett's mother, is on a vacation for another two weeks—or as she would say, "a holiday." She's already been gone for a few weeks, and he had promised her he would check on her house and her flowers. He definitely didn't want any wilting or deadheads on his watch.

Pulling up to the house, he notices her flowers are looking as though they want to lie down. Too much heat and their energy to bloom has worn them out. He smiles to himself and thinks *Mother would be so annoyed to see her beloved dahlias struggling.* Walking through her gardens, he bends down here and there and plucks off some dead leaves and dead-heads her Gerber daisies. After spending about an hour working in her gardens, he stands back and looks at his work and realizes everything was back to his mother's expectation. Walking up to the house, he leans down and removes the loose paver on her backstep and grabs the key. Her kitchen is spotless and still has a lemony scent lingering in the air as if someone had just cleaned.

Walking down the hall to her sitting room, he takes a small step into the sitting room, a room off-limits when he was a kid. Mother spent a lot of her nights alone here, reading a book or writing in her journal. Suddenly, he notices her journal sitting on the small table by her chair. Sitting down, he notices the fragrance she always wore seeping out of her chair. Brett tries to remember the perfume.

She had worn the same fragrance for as long as he could remember. Staring at her journal for several minutes he could envision her hand moving across the page. Hesitating, he picks it up and turns it to the last few pages.

Today was somewhat of a disturbing day. Brett came to see me and was very abrupt in his manner toward me. I really don't know what has gotten into him. All this talk about bringing this woman over to see me. It is apparently important to him, which I really don't know why. Nothing lately has been going well; it seems like I can't get Jack out of my mind. Suddenly, it's like a lightbulb went off in my brain and all the memories of the last few years have been running like a movie through my mind. All those visits to the farmer who was messing with the stray current really changed him during those years. His normal ruthlessness and determination to be successful had waned dramatically, and it made me so angry. His whole demeanor became softer and kinder, which was fine, but it was his ruthlessness that drove him and now he seems like he doesn't care about much anymore. I needed to figure out a way to make this new Jack revert back to his former self. In the end, I had to take things into my own hands, and I knew then someday it was going to rear its ugly head again.

Laying his head back on her chair, he closes his eyes trying to remember. Nothing in his memory told him his mother was so involved in Jack's work. His memory of then was definitely nothing of what he was reading on these pages. His mother had always seemed too worried about the parties going on or the latest pair of shoes she bought to go with the new dress for the latest event. Sometimes, I would wonder what made her tick. She spent all week figuring out what their weekends were going to entail, and the other part of her day was planning the next vacation they would take. Her day started out with a little coffee, because you know, too much coffee is not good for you. Then came her walk. She could never understand why people didn't exercise.

Brett constantly had to tell her the world was not like hers. People had lives, work, kids and so many more important things to their everyday life. She looked down her nose at those people. Her life was all about Jack, so much so that Brett felt he had become an annoyance. She never had a motherly attitude towards him, which hurt him deeply when he was younger because he saw how his friends' parents acted towards them. Flipping the pages, he read on.

I didn't want to discourage Brett with bringing his woman friend over, but I really was not in the mood for some passing fling that he might be having. His constant need to show me his independence has become trying. I never wanted him to buy that bar. The image of being a bar owner is so above him and his name. He is a Compton, and his father would never have accepted his role as a bar manager. Jack, on the other hand, thought it was thinking outside of the box. Becoming a bar owner in the town, in his eyes, was so smart. He believed Brett was providing a safe haven from the world at large. The people who frequented his bar were trying to escape the outside circle of people who were flooding them with their issues.

Shaking his head, Brett wonders what his mother was really about. Why in the world would she be so callous about someone he was bringing over to meet her? Her attitude was as if he was seventeen again and asking for her approval. Surprised at her feelings about the bar, Brett grew angry. He recalls coming to Jack and her for advice before he made the offer, and nothing was ever alluded to their adverse feeling about the project. He felt betrayed because the bar was successful, and his patrons were his friends. Did they have some issues, yeah but if nothing else, he agreed with Jack. It was a safe haven to talk, laugh, and sometimes cry with people who cared but were outside of your circle of concern. They were there for the same reason you were—to have an escape from reality. Continuing on, he read more.

He brought her over today. It was not as bad as I thought it was going to be. Actually, she was very interesting, the awareness she displayed for my flowers and the décor of my home was very pleasing. Especially her admiration of my piano, although it made me slightly uncomfortable. Everything was fine until she came back again by herself. What was Brett thinking?

Brett lays back his head and thinks about that day. Mother was on her best behavior, and he recalls Morgan was very quiet until Mother started talking about Jack and his obsession with the farmer he was constantly hanging around. Thinking back to that day, Brett suddenly realizes Morgan seemed very interested when Mother was telling the story about the birth of the calf at the Jenkins farm. *Why would that be?* Wondering if he should read on, he puts the journal down worrying somehow his mother would know he read it. This was crazy. She seemed almost obsessed with Morgan. His mother was never obsessed about anything or anyone unless it had something to do with her. *So, what was it about Morgan which made Mother so interested?* Standing up, he puts his hands on the mantle and lays his head down for a moment.

Hearing a noise, he jerks up suddenly and knocks a picture of their many vacations off the mantle. It falls to the floor and cracks the glass. Bending down to pick up the pieces, he notices a piece of paper that must have been stuck behind the picture. The paper was yellowed with age and had writing which was barely legible. Wondering what the importance was, he walks back into the kitchen.

Laying the paper down on the counter under the cabinet lighting, he could now see there were numbers listed in what looked like some kind of combination. Not all of the numbers were legible, so trying to figure out what they meant was going to be difficult and take some time. Brett realizes he was delving into his mother's personal space but knew something wasn't right about this and what he read in her journal. Pocketing the scrap of paper, he goes back into the sitting room and cleans up the glass from the broken frame then goes into the hall closet where he knew his mother kept extra picture frames. Finding one very similar, he puts the picture in the new frame and sets it back on the mantle. Sitting back down, he picks up the journal to continue reading. He could almost hear his mother's voice laced with disdain.

She seemed so interested in my flowers even to the point of asking if she could come back, but I definitely didn't like the direction the conversation was going when talking about Jack and Carl Jenkins. I guess I will find out more about her when she comes back, and it seems like Brett is smitten with her.

Slamming the journal shut, Brett puts the journal back to exactly where it was sitting when he had gotten there earlier. Pulling the piece of paper out of his pocket, he grabs his mother's magnifying glass out of her cross-stitch basket. Turning the lights on under the cabinets, he looks more closely to the paper. It was very apparent the numbers appear to be some kind of combination. The numbers were 28, 31,13 and what looked like 11. Now the question becomes, a combination to what and where?

Pocketing the paper again and putting the magnifying glass back in her basket, he moves to the solarium where he went about watering her flowers and plants. Somehow, he needs to figure out what was going on with his mother and her feelings for Morgan. It was obvious there was an aura surrounding the two of them. He felt it the whole time they were together, and the interest Morgan displayed in Jack's relationship with Carl Jenkins was abnormal. Deciding it was time to leave, he closes up everything and headed for his truck. Realizing he had more time available before getting back to the tavern, he turned toward Olivia and Seth's house knowing he also wanted to see if Morgan was back home. It was driving him crazy who the girl was with her earlier today.

Brett, Morgan, & Heidi

Passing Seth and Olivia's on our way home from the farm, I see Brett's truck parked in their driveway. Knowing Brett, he probably is asking Seth and Olivia if I have a visitor.

Making a quick decision, I look over at Heidi and say, "How about we stop in and see Seth and Olivia?"

Heidi hesitates with a face that clearly suggests she didn't feel like going before finally answering, "Sure, but it looks like they have company. Maybe we should come back over later."

Swallowing down my trepidation, I touch her arm offering, "It's fine, Seth and Olivia love to have company, and right now it might be a good thing for them. I don't know if I told you or not, but they just lost their granddaughter to a terrible illness. We don't have to stay long." Now, Heidi touches my arm.

"Oh Mom, this is terrible. What was her name?"

Keeping my voice steady, I say, "Abby." Pulling into my driveway, I shut the car off and looked over at Heidi thinking, after all, she had quite an experience today. Maybe I should let her be by herself for a while.

"Are you ok with going over there? If you aren't, it is fine. We have plenty of time to visit them another day."

"Mom, I would love to visit, but it's been a long day, and I'm expecting a phone call from my work. They are asking when I'm going to be back. Why don't you go on over? I will see them later." As we were getting out of the car, I looked over to Seth and Olivia's and saw Brett is heading our way.

"Hey Morgan, I stopped over to see Seth and Olivia, and luck is with me. I get to see you too."

"Hey Brett, how are you? I've been so busy lately. I haven't been able to stop into the tavern." Heidi was walking up the front steps, so I stopped her. "Honey, I want to introduce you to someone. Brett, I would like to introduce you to my daughter, Heidi."

Watching Brett's expression change from utter surprise to interest to his normal polite demeanor made me laugh.

"What a surprise, Morgan, I didn't know you had a daughter. Hello Heidi. It's very nice to meet you."

Heidi with her good manners, put out her hand to shake Brett's while saying, "Brett, it is very nice to meet you as well. Please excuse me though, after my flight here and other things, I need to sit down and chill."

Smiling at both Heidi and me, Brett agrees, "Please go and get some rest, Heidi. There will be plenty of time to get to know you."

"Let me go in with Heidi for a minute to show her where the remotes are and how to turn on the surround sound, then I'll come back out, and we can talk." Nodding, Brett moves to sit down on one of my porch chairs.

Once inside, Heidi's subtle interrogation began, "Mom, you didn't tell me that you were hanging out with such a handsome man."

Smiling devilishly at her, I reply, "He is handsome, isn't he? Brett is very good friends with Seth and Olivia. He also owns the Town Tavern where I met Seth and Olivia. We have become friends."

"Ok, whatever you say Mom, but it looks like he has made himself comfortable in one of your chairs as if he has sat on your porch a few times." Moving toward the window and looking out, I smile. There was Brett with his feet propped up on the railing looking as handsome as ever. Feeling that familiar feeling in my gut whenever I was around him, I turn toward the door.

Over my shoulder, I say to Heidi, "I won't be too long, but I need to talk to Brett."

Walking out to the porch I realize Brett is snoozing, I can hear a small snore. Not wanting to wake him, I sat down in the chair next to him and laid my head back thinking about today. Having Heidi come here to visit me made me realize how important it was to me for Jonathan and Sara, along with the two of us, to become a family again. There is so much to tell Heidi, but it will have to wait.

My encounter with Whitney at the bank affirmed that Whitney and Nick are two people I need to deal with right now. We need to find a way to forgive each other and move on. The actions of the past happened when we were young and unaware of the consequences of such reckless decisions. Looking at Brett, I realize there is much we have to discuss about the suspicions I have of his mother but not now. Touching his hand to wake him gently, I look at him and see the strength in his face with the worry lines and realize I don't want to make them any deeper. Deep down, I knew there was something about Brett which tugged at my womanhood. When I am around him, it is difficult not to touch him.

Feeling his eyes on me I turn and smile, "Hey, do you feel rested? You looked so content I didn't want to wake you." Taking my hand, he sits up in the chair and looks at me.

"Morgan, it's so great to finally see you, and I have to tell you it was a surprise when you introduced your daughter, Heidi. Is this something you forgot about or was I not important enough for you to share this information?" Understanding his frustration, I decided to proceed slowly.

"No, you are very important to me. It wasn't something I felt comfortable talking about not having known you for very long. Recently, we have gotten closer, and I realized it might be time to tell you about Heidi. Then she decided to come here. I thought I would have time to tell you before you got to meet her. Nothing was meant by not telling you earlier. I know I should have told you more about myself, but I have a lot going on. In a short time, I have found myself aware of a closeness to you. It is a feeling I have not experienced in a long time and has caught me by surprise." Realizing I am rambling on, I look at Brett. He is looking at me with the biggest smile on his face.

"I am so happy to meet her and can't wait to get to know her. Now, though, please come and sit on my lap so I can hold you. The scent of you drives me crazy, and I've missed you during the last few hectic days. We haven't seen each other since Abby's funeral." I am happy to hear his response because explaining Heidi wasn't something I was ready to do yet. Moving to his chair, I tentatively sat on his lap. Immediately, his arms surround me and squeeze me tightly. Turning to face him, I lean in to give him a kiss. He tenderly takes my head in his hands and kisses me long and deep. "I've missed you, Morgan." Leaning into him I touch him, smell his scent, and feel myself burn with desire for him. All I wanted to do at that moment was feel him against me. I haven't seen Brett in a few days, and now I realize how much I missed him.

"Brett, I know you probably have questions about Heidi. I had her when I was very young. I'll admit it was a struggle for a while, but we have been living happily and thriving in Linn Creek, Missouri." I can see him listening intently and processing the words I just said. Not sure what his reaction was going to be, I go on.

"It's just the two of us there, in case you are wondering. Heidi doesn't have any contact with her father. For reasons I don't want to share right now, it was then and is now, better this way. As you know, my job brought me here to Millersville, and I found myself feeling really good about life, my being here, and my work, so I asked Heidi to come and visit me." My anticipation of waiting for Brett to say something was unsettling because I wanted him to understand. Brett stands up and leans on the railing looking out toward Seth and Olivia's.

"Morgan, I'm happy Heidi has come to visit, but I am puzzled why you never said anything about her. We were becoming so close right before Abby died. Why didn't you say anything about Heidi, then?" Getting up to stand with Brett, I take his hands and hold them tightly. Looking up at him, I smile gently.

"I'm not sure, Brett, why I didn't say anything. At first, I knew it was because I didn't think I wanted to stay, let alone get involved with anyone in the town. After we met, I resisted my feelings for you and, again, didn't want to get involved. I realized how close we were becoming, and it seemed right to tell you. Then, we found out how sick Abby was. I didn't want to talk about my daughter when Seth and Olivia were going through so much. Time has gotten away from me, and now, she is here." Letting go of Brett's hands, I raise my hands and motion to the area around us. "This, beyond any expectation of mine, has now become my home, and I want you to be a part of all of this with me. I hope that you can forgive me for not telling you of Heidi."

Pulling me back into his arms, Brett leans down and whispers in my ear, "I want to be part of your life here, and I'm looking forward to getting to know Heidi." Gently kissing my lips, he steps away from me and looks over to Seth and Olivia's house. "Do they know about Heidi?"

Laughing, I say, "They sure do, but not because I told them or introduced her to them. She went over there and introduced herself when I wasn't here earlier. I was planning on taking her over there right before you stopped over, but she went on her own. We had a lot going on today, and she still hasn't caught up on her sleep. She worked a double before flying here, so I'm going to leave her to rest."

Brett nods and grabs my hand as we went and sat down on the loveseat and enjoys the rest of the early evening light listening to the crickets and the coming to life of the creatures of the night.

Seth & Olivia

Sitting on their patio, Seth and Olivia could see Brett and Morgan sitting on the front porch of Morgan's house.

"Olivia, wouldn't you like to be a fly on the wall to hear that conversation. It must be somewhat awkward with Heidi arriving here since I'm sure Morgan never mentioned Heidi to Brett."

Smiling at her husband of twenty-five years, Olivia agrees, "You can be sure on that one, my dear. It was just a few weeks ago we found out, and then it was only by chance when I answered her phone. I am almost positive she didn't tell him before today."

Shaking his head, Seth says grimly, "I really hope Brett understands but without all of the facts it might be disconcerting, and he doesn't like controversy."

"I think you might be wrong about Brett," Olivia responds. "Knowing his feelings for Morgan, I'm confident he will be ok with it. She never told me anything about Heidi's father, and I know from other conversations with her that there was never a male figure in their life in Linn Creek." They realize suddenly Whitney's car is slowing down as if she is going to Morgan's driveway.

Olivia gets up and runs across the grass yelling, "Morgan, why don't you and Brett walk over and have a glass of wine?" All the time Olivia is watching Whitney's car. Seeing Brett and Morgan move off the porch and start to walk over to Seth and Olivia's must have made her drive past. Olivia knew if Whitney slowed down to stop at Morgan's, it couldn't be good.

———————— · ————————

Confused by Olivia's abrupt and adamant request, Brett and I make our way across the lawn where Olivia meets us halfway.

Grabbing my arm, she quietly informs me, "That was Whitney's car slowing down to pull into your driveway." I look back toward the road and notice the taillights of a car.

Squeezing Olivia's hand, I whisper in her ear, "I will talk to you tomorrow about everything. Let's just make the conversation as neutral as possible for now. I told Brett about Heidi, and I want to give him time to absorb the information."

"What are you two girls whispering about up there?" Brett jokes. "I can see your heads tipped together, so there is nothing good coming out of a conversation between you two, right Seth?"

Hitting Brett on the back and laughing, Seth tells Brett, "You know those two always talking and planning their next move." Together, the four of them walk onto Seth and Olivia's patio to sit down. The rest of the evening was spent making small talk, and me casting sidelong glances at Brett to gauge his mood. From what I could tell, there was only an inkling of unrest detectable, and since nobody else seemed to pick up on this stray from his usual mood, I decided to enjoy the rest of the night with our friends.

Whitney

Standing and looking out at her property made Whitney understand, and at the same time wonder, why she had stayed here. As she gazes at the pool and the garden pond along with the screenhouse, she realizes they had become her solitude—even though Nick had pushed her into doing the pond. *Nothing like cutting a tree down, pulling the root, and realizing you have a hole big enough to become a garden pond, with a waterfall no less*, she thought. Now, the upkeep and the time spent keeping all of it to look just so had become an albatross around her neck. Nick has always become so annoyed when things aren't cleaned up and orderly.

Now Misty is back, his attention is on her. He has become obsessed with Misty being back in Millersville and the theory that we will be able to go back in time. It is laughable to think Misty, Morgan, or whatever she wants to call herself, would ever become best friends with me again. Nick is conveniently forgetting all the actions of the past and the impact they had on Misty. Seeing Misty standing there that day on the porch, looking so different but sounding the same, her anger, and her sadness had been enough to ensure my silence.

The bitterness in her voice made Whitney want to curl up in horror for what Nick and she did. Whitney knew, though, that all of it needed to stay in the past. Punishment has been handed out to all of them over the past twenty years. Now, somehow life needs to go on. Whitney knew Nick and her must forgive themselves for what they did and find a way to help Misty release the lingering pain that their actions caused her to bear all these years.

Feeling such remorse, Whitney realizes the only way to clear her heart and mind is to go and see Misty again. This time, maybe they could have a normal conversation, not one fraught with shock or anger and regret. Grabbing her handbag, she heads into the garage to leave. Remembering the box that Nick was so intent on finding, she grabs a ladder and stands on the very top rung to reach the box she had propped up in the rafters. Steadying herself with one hand, she reaches up and grabs the box, tipping it toward her so she can look inside and grab the envelope with all the old pictures. Pushing the box back up into the rafters, she works her way back down the ladder and gets in the car.

Despite realizing driving to Misty's unannounced might not be the best course of action to take, the urgency Whitney feels in her heart is enough to convince herself it is ok. Maybe a gentler conversation and sharing the photos of the two of them when they were young would render some fond memories that they could build upon to regain a measure of the understanding they had as friends.

On the way over to Misty's house, thoughts from their past together keep running through Whitney's mind. She thinks about the times they spent together at each other's houses and the times they cried together when their parents were fighting so violently that they feared for themselves. She remembers how much Misty struggled with the passion her parents showed for each other, both good and bad. She recalls their rides to school and the rush to make it to class on time, the late-night talks about boys, friends, and dreams they both had—except somewhere along the way, Whitney's dreams changed. There came a point where all she could do was think about Nick and want him to look at her the same way he looked at Misty. Whitney shakes her head at the thought. Even then she had known, and still, somehow knew, Misty was his one true love.

As she was coming up to Misty's house, she could see Brett and Misty walking off her porch heading over to Seth and Olivia's house. Wanting to stop at Misty's house so badly, Whitney slows down, but then she realizes now isn't the time. She didn't want to have this conversation with Misty in front of Brett or Seth and Olivia. So, stepping on the gas, she drives on by and decides it would be best to go back home. Patting the pictures on the seat beside her, she realizes it could all wait for another day. Seth and Olivia have been through so much lately. Instead of following her normal antagonistic personality and causing havoc, maybe it was time to try to change and mend the relationships in her life. *I will begin with Nick*, she thinks. Speeding up, she realized for the first time in a long time, she was looking forward to going home.

But first, there were some errands she needed to run, so she went downtown and parks. Walking around town always reminded her of Misty. They spent a lot of their youth walking downtown and eating at the diner. French fries with brown gravy and cherry 7-ups were all the rage, and the diner had the best brown gravy. It was quite a bit different downtown now. Main Street was a bustling street now with people going in and out of the storefronts. The brewery is doing well and has a constant run of people. The deli is busy with students and businesspeople getting lunch while the shake shop is making nutritional shakes and teas for breakfast and lunch.

Whitney feels calmer, or maybe more hopeful, than she has for a long time, and it is all because Misty has come back. Even though their relationship wasn't anything like before and her husband seemed focused on his past with Misty, she knew it could hopefully become better if all could be forgiven. So much had changed in both of their lives.

"What am I thinking?" Whitney says out loud to herself. "Misty left Millersville because of me, her best friend, who plotted and pursued Misty's boyfriend, the guy all of Millersville thought she was going to marry. And I didn't just sleep with her boyfriend but ended up marrying him." Somehow, Whitney was pretty sure twenty years may have only dimmed Misty's anger and hurt.

Parking her car near the bank, she sees Tom Fraser talking to a man very animatedly and patting him on the back. Next thing she knew, Tom and he gave each other a hug. Whitney frowns to herself. Tom never seemed jovial, let alone capable of standing out in front of the bank being so demonstrative. Crossing the street, she looks back, and the man is getting into a black Audi with a New York license plate. Something looks familiar about the man, but Whitney couldn't figure out why. Realizing it was getting close to when the boys would be home from football camp, she hurries up and finishes her errands temporarily forgetting about the mysterious New Yorker.

Brett

After the visit with Seth and Olivia, Morgan and Brett spend some time talking about Abby's services and how beautiful the weather and flowers were. The outpouring of love shown for Cissy and Josh, Seth and Olivia, and actually many of their friends was so endearing to see. So many of them were close to Cissy's family, and Brett felt like he had known them forever, even though he had only been back in Millersville for the last ten years. Before coming back to Millersville, he had lived in California. So much of his time there was spent trying to come to terms with his childhood and the relationship he had with his stepfather, Jack.

Jack was a unique individual, and his fatherly traits were completely absent. His world was his work, and Brett's mother did everything she could to ingratiate herself into Jack's career so he would pay attention to her. Her days were spent trying to figure out what she could do to make herself invaluable to his career and his success. In those days, it seemed Brett was less important to her than Jack. Attending private school in California, so far from Millersville, made it nearly impossible to have friends locally. Seth had become his only friend, and it didn't become a strong bond until coming back home.

———— • ————

My eyes were becoming heavy, so Brett and I talked about when we were going to get together again and decide we would touch base the next day. Standing up to leave, he puts his arms around me.

"Morgan, if you have time tomorrow, I would like to come back and visit with you and Heidi. It's very important for me to get to know her and have her comfortable with me."

Smiling up at him, I assure him, "It's fine Brett, don't feel any kind of pressure. We have plenty of time to develop a relationship between all of us."

Leaning down, Brett touches my lips so tenderly whispering, "That sounds like a plan. By the way, did you notice Whitney driving by earlier? It seemed as if she was going to pull in and then changed her mind. Do you know Whitney?"

"I saw Whitney when I was living at the Hotel. Edmond and I were playing pool one night, and she was at the bar arguing with Nick. You remember Edmond?"

Frowning slightly, Brett nods and says, "Don't tell me you have forgotten already. He was one of the main reasons I wanted you to find another place to stay. Edmond has far too many issues surrounding him."

Keeping my voice neutral, I say, "Yes, I remember how picky you were about my living space, and I respected your opinion. You are wrong about Edmond. He is a good person. He has become disillusioned with his life and honestly, in some ways, I feel sorry for him. Even though I know most of it has been self-inflicted over years." Quizzically, Brett looks at me.

"How would you know anything about his past when you just moved here a month ago?"

Realizing my mistake, I quickly recovered explaining, "It was all he talked about when we were together. He couldn't understand why I was so upbeat and honestly, Brett, I think it annoyed him most of the time. However, he befriended me when I first came to town, so I appreciate his friendship despite his reputation and attitude."

In response to my diatribe, he smiles and says, "Well thank heavens you moved to this nice quiet neighborhood with Seth and Olivia as your neighbors." Stepping in as close as I could get, I reached up and kissed him deeply.

"Brett, I'm so glad I met you when I came here, and time will tell all for us." Getting into his truck, he looks up at me and smiles.

"Morgan, when the sun rises tomorrow, my first thought will be of you." Smiling, I reached in to hug him.

Seth & Olivia

Seth and Olivia found themselves worrying about Cissy and her family now that a month had passed since Abby's death. Trying to be there for their daughter, they became outsiders to her grief. Cissy was struggling with seeing anyone including her parents. Her devastation over the loss of her child was almost more than she could bear. Seth and Olivia felt helpless in their role as parents. Waking up, Olivia rolls over and taps Seth's shoulder.

"Hey, are you awake?"

Smiling sleepily, he says, "I am now. Tell me."

"I'm sorry, I know it's early, but I can't sleep anymore. All I can see when I close my eyes is the torment Cissy is going through when she walks by Abby's room. I hear her screams when she realizes there won't be a little girl sitting up at the counter asking for her cereal."

Leaning on his elbow, he looks over at his wife and tells her, "Olivia, I know, and I see the same things, but we need to remember something. We raised Cissy with strength and most of all, faith. She will come through this. We need to give her as much space as we can. Remember one thing. She knows we are here, and when she is ready for our support and love, we will be here waiting."

Giving Seth a look of frustration, she then nods saying, "I know except I'm not going to sit around and wait. I have to do something. The first thing I'm going to do is talk to Morgan and Jonathan Jenkins. They were both a part of their dad's mission to control the stray current emanating from the old towers. She already told us on the day of Abby's funeral we were all going to work together to find out why those currents are so dangerous." Trying to keep Olivia's angst to a low roar, Seth gives her a tight hug.

"Olivia, I'm sure Morgan will be more than willing to share whatever she knows with us. She's struggling, as well, with all the problems caused by the electromagnetic fields infiltrating the animals and humans. We will talk to her. You haven't forgotten who is coming here today, have you? I know you woke up pretty upset, but did you forget what day this is?" Olivia laughs.

"How could I forget? Your illustrious younger brother is showing his handsome face today. Do you know when Jackson is supposed to get in?"

"Olivia, you know Jackson. He will stop at ten places on his way here. I thought he was just going to take the train from New York, but he decided to drive. Apparently, he just bought a new Audi and wants to show it off. So, he could show up here at any moment but more than likely, he will be here just in time for dinner."

Jackson

Jackson was driving around Millersville familiarizing himself again with his hometown, waving back to people who waved at him, not knowing if he knew them or not. He smiles to himself. It had been quite a few years since he had been back in Millersville, but one place that had always held a special place in his heart was the Town Tavern. Swinging into the driveway, he parks and steps out of his car. Locking it and looking back at it as he walks toward the entrance, he smiles with pride. His sporty new car was black, with sleek lines, characteristic of his success—so he thought.

Jillian, Brett's bartender, is coming out of the kitchen with a food tray when Jackson walks through the tavern door. Looking toward the door, Jillian stops dead in her tracks almost losing the food tray. The man who just came through the door was the most gorgeous man she had ever seen. As he moved toward the bar, the aura around him was one of importance, confidence, and strength. She could almost feel the atmosphere in the tavern change with his entrance. After delivering the food to her table, she wanders back behind the bar and heads in the gentlemen's direction.

"Welcome to the Town Tavern, my name is Jillian." Emerald eyes mimicking the deep, shimmering, newly grown spring grass looked back at her, and for a moment she is transfixed, unable to respond. Then she hears the words, "May I get you a drink?" fall from her lips.

Shaking herself out of her trance, she hears his silken voice say, "It's very nice to meet you, Jillian. If you wouldn't mind, I would like a vodka tonic made with Grey Goose and oh add a lime, please, thank you." Smiling to herself, she wonders where she had heard that before. Someone else she knew said the double entendre when speaking. It would come to her later, but for now she needs to get him a vodka tonic.

"Here you go, one vodka tonic with lime. And by the way, we only make our vodka tonics with Grey Goose vodka. It's a pet peeve with the owner. He makes all his drinks with top shelf liquor. By the way, what is your name, sir?"

Smiling broadly with his pearly whites gleaming, he puts out his hand and says, "Hi, I'm Jackson, and it's nice to be back at the tavern."

With a look of surprise, Jillian asks, "You have been here before? I don't recall ever seeing you." Laughing, Jackson leans in toward Jillian.

"I haven't been here for quite a while, Jillian, but a long time ago I sat on these stools drinking beer with my older brother and his buddies." Suddenly, Jillian hears her name called and with a tap on his hand, she politely moves away from her mysterious customer. Jackson sips his drink and looks around the tavern. Subtle changes had been made, but it still had the same feeling it did all those years ago. Peanut shells strewn all over the floor, the jukebox playing '80s music, and a cacophony of voices in the background. He sits back and can almost hear Seth laughing and Olivia chirping with her girl-friends. After a time, he calls Jillian back over and asks to get his bill.

Putting his hand out as if he was going to shake Jillian's hand, he instead kisses the back of her hand and says, "It's been great meeting you Jillian, and I'm sure I will see you again."

Jackson figures he still has a little bit of time before getting to Seth's house, so instead of turning down their road, he continues out of town. Driving along, he thinks about his brother Seth. Their childhood was unique because Jackson didn't have an older brother until he was five. Jackson clearly remembers the first day he came to his new home to meet the rest of his new family. His adoptive parents spent a lot of time with him before bringing him home. Flashing back to that day, he can remember how excited Seth was.

Seth had the biggest smile on his face and was saying over and over again, "I have a brother, a brand-new little brother." Grabbing Jackson, he hugged him and says, "We are going to have so much fun together."

And for the most part, they did. In grammar school, they ate lunch together, played at recess together, and then after school, did their homework together. Seth is only nine months older than Jackson. His mother, for some reason, could not have any more children. Both parents, coming from big families, felt very strongly Seth should not be an only child. Jackson excelled in school, so he was able to skip a grade by testing out, and therefore, was in the same class as Seth. Seth was truly a good person and even when their competitiveness with each other got in the way, somehow, they always talked it out, which was mostly due to Seth. It wasn't until their junior year when their relationship became strained. Olivia had entered the picture, and Seth was enamored of her. He was never home anymore. When all of the college letters started to come in for Jackson, Seth tried to act like it didn't bother him—except it did.

Jackson could feel the same hurt feelings well up all of these years later. He found himself resenting Olivia and was pretty open about his feeling for her, which Seth wanted to hear none of. The arguments and hurtful words made for a bittersweet senior year. When the full scholarship came for University of Arizona, Jackson went. The way things became between the two of them made it very easy for him to stay in Arizona during the summers.

Coming out of his thoughts, Jackson realizes he has driven by the Jenkins farm. He remembered hearing something about the farm falling on hard times, but by the looks of things, someone was starting to breathe new life into the property. Dumpsters were sitting in the farmyard, and he could see activity through one of the open doors of the machine shed. Slowing down so he can get a good look at what was going on, he sees Jonathan Jenkins coming out of the farmhouse. Giving a friendly wave, Jackson goes down the road further and pulls into a gravel driveway to turn around to head back toward Seth and Olivia's house. Before backing out, he looks to his right toward the grove of trees that borders the field's edge and smiles at his memory of the summer he graduated from college.

Seth, Olivia, & Jackson

"I told you, Seth. He hasn't seen us in a couple of years, and he can't get here a little early? Believe it or not, I would like to visit with him before I have to be in the kitchen."

Knowing Olivia was right, Seth says, "Olivia, I'm sure he will be here soon. Maybe he stopped at the tavern for a drink. He always liked going there during the summer after he graduated from college. Stop fretting about Jackson." Olivia laughs hysterically.

"Fretting? Is that what you think I'm doing? It's quite the opposite. Have you forgotten how competitive Jackson is with you? I sometimes wonder if everything he does has something to do with you." Not wanting to work Olivia up anymore, he keeps his comment to himself. It was something which he was ashamed of and remembering it now made him uneasy. Jackson was competitive, but it was coming from a place of discontent. Seth knew deep down inside how much Jackson was hurt during their last year in high school.

Looking back, Seth knew he managed his relationship between Olivia and Jackson all wrong. Olivia's family life wasn't the best and as a result, she became a constant in the house. It was hard for Jackson, and he should have recognized the signs, but they were young and stupid. Jackson had felt deserted as he had been as a child. It didn't matter how many years had passed where he was loved and cared for—those early memories are the ones that can rear up at the worst time.

Olivia starts in again, "Honestly, Seth it would have been different if he had only talked to you during those times and asked for your friendship. His lack of communication with you in the last few years made it very surprising when he said he was visiting. Seth, I know you are happy he is coming here especially after Abby's death." No sooner did those words leave Olivia's mouth, Jackson pulls in and blows his car horn.

"Hey, is anyone home? Where is my big brother?" Seth opens the door and steps out. Jackson walks toward him as if he was going to shake his hand. As he got closer, Seth hears him say under his breath, "Oh Hell!" Seth recognizes Jackson's demeanor and, in that instance, decides to welcome his brother as if it was the day he first came into his life. They reach for each other at the same time.

"Hi brother," both exclaim.

"Jackson, it is so good to see you, how the hell have you been and is that your new car? She's a beauty for sure."

"Hey Seth, it's great to see you too. It's been a long time." Stepping back from his brother, and moving into the doorway, Jackson shouts, "Where is my crazy sister-in-law?"

"You best watch it brother, she has a wicked left." Seth warns with a laugh. Olivia comes out of the kitchen and with only a slight hesitation in her approach, gives Jackson a big hug.

"It's great to see you, Jackson." Looking into her face, Jackson could see the evidence of loss on her face but mostly in her eyes. Olivia always had animated, and sparkling eyes, but today they were a testimony of grief.

Giving her an extra squeeze, Jackson whispers in her ear, "Olivia, I'm here to stay for a while. Seth and you can lean on me for anything, you hear me." Moving away from Jackson and dipping her head, Olivia, balancing her composure, wipes the beginning of tears from her eyes.

"Come on in and get comfortable. Seth, please get Jackson something to drink. We have wine and beer, but Seth will have to let you in on where he keeps his other stash."

"He knows where it is. It's still in the same place I have always kept it," he laughs. "What can I get you? I have Grey Goose. Is that still your favorite?" Jackson took his overcoat off and draped it over a dining room chair. Moving into Seth and Olivia's family room, he stands for a moment. Memories come assaulting him from when he had been home during the summer after college.

Smiling to himself, he looks at Seth, "Wow, it's great to be home. This house was so much like my second home. I remember how much I was here that summer after college."

Seth laughs and teases, "Yeah, Olivia and I couldn't get rid of you. If I remember correctly, you were hanging out with a girl that summer." Just then Olivia comes in with a glass of wine.

"Seth, did you get Jackson something to drink?"

Jackson held up his glass answering, "My old standby Grey Goose on the rocks." Thankful nothing else was said between Seth and him, he asked the hard question which was on all of their minds. "How are you two doing? I'm so sorry to hear about Abigail. How are Cissy and Josh doing?" Seth moves to stand next to Olivia and puts his arm around her.

"We are trying hard Jackson. Every day that goes by brings us closer to a normal life. Except, what is a normal life after such a loss?" Olivia bows her head to hide her tears.

"Our anguish is devastating, and the fact that she died unnecessarily..." continues Seth.

"What do you mean, Seth, she died unnecessarily?"

"The environment around her was contaminating her body during the years of her young life. The continuous assault weakened her system over time. Cancer found a breeding ground and finally took her life. Cissy was unsure about moving there, but the house was perfect for them. Jackson, we didn't know. If we did, we would have told her not to buy the house," exclaims Seth. Olivia is getting so upset, she has to leave the room to get herself together.

"If you knew what, Seth?" Seth, struggling with his emotions, nods toward the door where Olivia went. Jackson puts his hand on Seth's shoulder, "Seth, its ok, talk to me. I will talk to both of you eventually, but Olivia is still too emotional. I need to know what you are talking about."

Tom Fraser

Seeing Jackson Palmer today really threw him. Jackson was always a great kid and grew up to be a phenomenal lawyer except seeing him back in Millersville today had unnerved him. He had become an environmental lawyer which evolved into his taking on more criminal cases with environmental impact than the typical EPA cases. Walking back into his office, Tom sits down and thinks about the early days of his career. Tom had come to Millersville as a young, recently graduated accounting major. The memory of the first day at work stood out in his mind as one of the most profound events in his life.

Becoming a loan officer early in one's career is a great accomplishment, and here Tom is, as a twenty-five-year-old sitting in judgement and deciding people's destiny. Feeling butterflies in his stomach in the morning, he arrives at work very early. Getting in and sitting down at his new desk while orienting himself to the bank's procedures, he hears a customer showing some irritation with a teller. Feeling empowered, he walks over to see if he can help the customer with whatever was going on. Suddenly, he feels a tug on his pants. Looking down he sees a little boy with eyes so green they remind him of newly mowed grass.

"Mister, can you help my Mamma? She is very upset right now because there is no money in her account, and we have to pay our bills, or my brother and I are going to have to sell our toy trucks and tractors." Wondering how to respond to the boy, he realizes this might be the

beginning of his career at the bank. Motioning to the teller his intentions, he touches the mother's arm.

"Madam, may I see you over in my office for a moment?" The woman and her son are part of the Palmer family. The Palmer family is part of the fabric of Millersville. If memory serves him correctly, the woman in front of him is a descendant of the founder of Millersville. Her father was the son of the man who founded the town where he had decided he would make his living and raise his family. Looking at the little boy who is clinging to his mother's leg, he realizes he didn't resemble a Palmer at all. He was of a different ethnicity entirely, and the attention and love coming from his mother's eyes made it a moment that couldn't be overlooked.

"Mrs. Palmer?" As she turns herself around to look at him, he finds himself mesmerized by the beauty of the woman standing in front of him. The bone structure of her face, the sensual curve to her lips, and her hair curling around her face as if framing it for a painting left him speechless for a moment. Somehow the effect of her shabby dress worn around the edges was diminished by her stately beauty and a stature of a woman who knows who she is. Noticing all of this, he realizes he would have to tread carefully.

"Would you come into my office for a moment, please? I would like to talk with you, and by the way, who is this handsome boy you have with you?"

Smiling down at her son, she says, "Why this is my son, Jackson. Say hello Jackson, to the nice young man."

Looking up at Tom, Jackson says, "Hi, my name is Jackson Palmer, and it's my new name. Do you like it? I have a new brother and new parents who are all my new family." Slightly embarrassed, Mrs. Palmer smiles at Tom.

"Jackson is so outgoing, and we are very happy about his addition to our family." Walking into his office where they are away from prying eyes, Mrs. Palmer removes her confident façade, sits slowly down in the chair, and closes her eyes. Recovering from her previous demeanor, she sits straight up on the edge of her chair.

"Mr. Fraser, I'm not exactly sure why you have asked me here, but I can assure you, Palmers do not except charity." Trying to maintain his composure, he speaks quickly and quietly.

"Mrs. Palmer, we are here to help our community, and your family is no exception. If there is anything we can do for you, I sincerely hope you would come to us." Sitting back in his seat, he smiles at her and says, "We at the bank take care of our own." Several minutes go by in which the only sound is Jackson playing with a marble maze on his desk. Tom watches her closely as emotions are playing across her face as if she is coming to a decision. Slowly, she stands up and he can visibly see the façade come back down over her face. As she reaches out with her hand, Tom quickly stands and shakes it. She holds onto his hand for a moment and covers it with her other hand.

"Mr. Fraser, I appreciate what you are suggesting, but it's unnecessary. We are going to be fine. We are navigating this bump in our life, but I will never forget what you offered to do for us. I will never forget!"

From that day on, Tom Fraser followed everything Jackson Palmer did. All the awards and academic accomplishments Jackson received along with all the baseball reports in the local paper. Tom was invested in the success of the little adopted boy who loved his adoptive family so much. The commitment and care of this little boy stayed with Fraser for a long time, and he did whatever he could for the Millersville community until he met Jack Callahan.

Sara

Sara couldn't stop thinking about what Misty said about changing the farm's end use. She had done some investigation and wineries were popping up all over the county. It became very obvious to her that land was what they needed. Most of the wineries were not set up on a large property, so renting land for their grape production was going to be crucial. Somehow, she needs to broach the subject to Jonathan.

Today, he was so distracted. There were all kinds of people here helping to clean up the property. Dumpsters showed up early this morning, and a backhoe was pulling in the yard as she looked outside. Tears falling over her lashes, she feels such belonging to a community. Sometimes people just need to ask for help, and if they do, their community will be there for them. Jonathan had not let go of all the inflammatory comments about their whole family, but today's activities will start the healing.

She moves to look out the front window which looks over a lot of the farm acreage on either side of the road. There was a truck pulled over on the side of the road with two guys walking down the road. Sara realizes there is a surveying transit set up in front of the one person. *Why were they here surveying this part of the property?* If her memory served her correctly, this part of the farm was going to stay intact for them to raise their new calves, so it now seemed the time had come for Misty and her to tackle the bank's motives. Something wasn't right about the proposal. Jonathan wouldn't share it with her, and Misty seemed uneasy about it when she looked over it. Jonathan was coming in the back door, and she meets him in the shed where he is taking off his work shoes.

"Hey, it's great to see all the people here helping us clean up. Who was the company that sent the dumpsters?" Sighing, Jonathan pulls out a kitchen chair and flops down.

"Sara, you know who they are, Robert Parsons Construction Company sent them over, and they are the ones with the backhoe. I am so tired. Question after question about what I want to keep and what is trash is making me crazy. Honestly, I don't want to admit this, but it was easier turning a blind eye to the mess out there, but then Misty showed back up." Looking at her husband in shock, Sara slaps her hand down on the table.

"What is wrong with you? You have been talking in your sleep during the last few months, and I could hear you crying out for her. So, don't try to bullshit me about your sister. Maybe when you were younger things weren't so great, but time heals all kinds of wounds. You have to forgive her for leaving and do you understand why? You were as responsible for her leaving as Nick and Whitney." Feeling defeated, Jonathan lays his head down on his arms. Feeling the grittiness of the table and the smell of the onions cooking irritated him. Standing up and leaning against the sink, he looks at his wife of twenty years.

"Sara, why are you awake listening to me?"

"I don't know Jonathan. There has been so many sleepless nights in our marriage."

"Sara, I'm sorry for all the conversations and the irritation of our family. Misty and the drama which went on before she left caused a domino effect on our whole family. She became an albatross around me wondering where she was and if she was ok."

Sara shakes her head disgusted explaining, "The relationship she has with you is so understated, and it has become hurtful to you, but you realize now it was because of everything that happened here. She left because she couldn't take it anymore. Having all of this weighing on both of us, yet separately, became so hard for me. The effect it has had on you lingers every day, and I see your aggravation about the smallest things. Your patience with people has dwindled so much it hurts me to see. You always saw the good in people before all of this happened. It needs to end Jonathan. We need to move on and let all of this anger go. Misty is home now. So whatever feelings you harbored about her, both good and bad, need to dissolve. It's now time for the two of you to start over again. You have been given a new chance and something tells me this will be what you need to feel at peace." Moving toward Sara, Jonathan pulls her to him.

"Sara, you are right except there are a few things needing to be done before any of us can put away the past. The first thing is I need to truly look into what happened to Dad the day he died. Something was off about that day, and Misty is sure there was something underhanded going on."

Hugging her husband tightly, she says, "We will figure it out. Now that Misty is home, the two of you can figure out what happened to your dad that day. I agree something was off, but in the end, Jonathan, he died. What are we going to do about it now?" In this moment, Jonathan thinks to himself, *maybe it was time to talk candidly to Sara. She had become such an integral part of the new plan for the farm that it was time to share with her Misty's suspicions.*

Their father was a robust, healthy, and dedicated farmer and father. Randomly he was in a field working one day and dropped dead. Except the problem is there were people watching every move he made while he was determining what and why the stray currents were hurting people. Jack Callahan, Brett's stepfather, became a constant visitor to the farm investigating the theory of why people were dying and sick with incurable diseases. He dissected every move their father made trying to determine his method and if it was destroying the electrical current emanating from the towers. Jack Callahan worked for the electric company and his role with them was undefined. Something wasn't right about his visits and the camaraderie he displayed to their father, especially when Jack's army friend came to help him with whatever the electric company was attempting to cover up. Charlie! A very scary person!

Jackson & Seth

Jackson and Seth share some small talk and get caught up on what their parents were up to these days. Jackson had been out of the country on a big legal debate regarding a mask mandate in schools due to a pandemic that had hit Europe. Although the case was stalled because of the political mire of the European Union debacle, the intensity of the case was still enough to cause him to lose contact with his parents. Sitting back in Seth's favorite chair, Jackson looks over at this brother.

"Seth, talk to me. What happened to Abby? The last time I talked to you, she was doing better. What changed?" It takes all of Seth's control to keep from saying more time had passed than Jackson realized. They hadn't talked for at least two years, and Abby was doing fine then because they hadn't been in their new house for very long.

"Jackson, it all started when they moved to their new home in Alloway. She started having a lot of days when she was going to the nurse at school. It then moved to having several days absent during the month. We got concerned, but it is a slippery slope when you need to tell your adult children there is something they need to pay attention to with their children. Olivia and I decided we would be as supportive as we could, and then she began to get worse. Jackson, she was hospitalized during Christmas last year. Do you know what that does to a six-year-old?" Jackson finds himself lacking any words to say let alone words that would comfort Seth.

Finding his voice, he speaks, "Seth, I can't imagine what all of you have been going through the last couple of years, and Seth, we both are very analytical. So, I know you have a theory of why she was constantly sick. What is it?"

"This is going to take a while to explain, and I need to see how Olivia is doing because she has a feast cooking in the kitchen which is being neglected right now." Standing up and moving toward the kitchen, Seth looks back at Jackson. "Hey, if I've ever needed something from you, Jackson, now is the time. I need your expertise and your level head to help me find out why this happened to Abby. By the way, Olivia has made a phenomenal dinner for you. She is such a great cook. I constantly tell everyone I have an iron chef in my house."

Jackson is overwhelmed with emotion. The last few years were not good with his brother, and now tragedy had touched his family. Seth had always been there for him when they were young. Now it was time for him to repay the debt. Jackson didn't like to think about what his life would have been like if the Palmers hadn't adopted him.

Jackson begins, "Great because I am so hungry. We will eat ourselves full just like we did when we were kids asking Mom if there was more." Grabbing his brother's arm, Seth motions toward the back of the house.

"Her cooking has been her salvation during this time. It's been like this for quite a while. She moves around our kitchen like a conductor moves through his orchestra. Night after night, she never ceases to amaze me with her culinary skills. So, Jackson, if you ask her for more to eat you will have started to thaw her heart. Because right now she is struggling terribly, and I can't seem to bring her out of it."

Olivia listens to Seth and Jackson talking and is taken aback by the bond of family. No matter what has happened in the past, if just one positive thing happens, the whole dynamic changes. But remembering the pain Seth felt with the criticism coming from his sister-in-law, Jackson's wife, Katrina, still had the ability to spur anger. Her uncanny timing of asking serious questions was amazing—like the phone call they received from her when they were in the hospital telling Seth what he should be doing about Cissy—as if it was any of Katrina's business. Jackson's blatant exclusion of our family and his arrogant, chameleon-like actions drove Seth crazy because he knew too many people were caught up in it, especially his mother. Calming down, she mentally acknowledges the strength of each man individually and the way their relationship had changed over the years. Each one of them is working toward a different goal and driving both to be successful.

Now, though, it seems Jackson may have become reacquainted with his feelings for his brother. This could only be a good thing for Seth. If she really thought about it, the same would be for her as well. Jackson was a decent, loving, maybe a little egotistic, but wonderful human being. The things she saw on the internet about the charity work he was doing warmed her heart. Nothing would make her happier right now, during this dark time, than for Jackson to stay home for a while. She knew his intellect and his determination would be such an asset to finding out what happened to Abby. It's important to get Jackson and Morgan together. She could give him so much information about the towers.

Drawing her mind back to the present, she needs to get dinner served and enjoy Jackson's company, and then it will be time to explain about the contaminating giant monsters that killed their granddaughter.

Brett

Rolling over realizing there was no more time for more sleep, Brett starts thinking about his day. Right now, though, all he could think about was Morgan and his mother. Based on his past and his mother's attitude, he never imagined he would be thinking about the woman he was falling in love with and his mother within the same thought. His mother's journal was very upsetting, as was the piece of paper he found behind the picture frame. After looking at the paper over and over again, he was sure the numbers represented a combination of some sort. It warranted a discussion with his mother which he wasn't looking forward to but felt was necessary.

Nothing in recent days would have led him to believe Morgan had some other agenda. She was very apologetic about the omission of Heidi and thinking back on it, he realized he was hurt but couldn't blame her. Their relationship was now evolving and just intensified after Abby died. Her death had a strong impact on Morgan which still resonated with him as being odd. She hadn't been here long enough to feel that kind of connection to Seth and Olivia let alone Cissy, Josh, and Abigail.

Shaking his head, he decides that was enough thinking about all this right now. It was time to get up and start his day. He had a big day ahead of him. Jillian wanted to start a couple new IPAs, and he wanted to get the information out on social media so the turnout tonight would be good. With all the breweries opening in the area, the local bar had to be able to compete, so Jillian was on the lookout for the latest breweries who were at the canning stage. Jillian was so enthused about bringing in the new beers, she would probably be early to work. Maybe later he would be able to make the connection, and seeing Morgan might be just the trick. He was supposed to stop over there later and get some more time to talk with her daughter, Heidi.

Morgan

Walking out on the deck this morning made me realize how much had changed in just a few weeks. Thinking back to the day I came back to Millersville, I can still see the trees casting shadows onto Main Street giving it such a picturesque view. Seeing all the new businesses occupying the old storefronts had given me such joy knowing the community had evolved into the future. The old bank became a brewery, and the music store had found a home in the old insurance office. The town's cultural community was taking hold with festivals and First Friday events happening throughout the seasons.

The events that had survived all the changes in our social existence amazed me. The Festival of Homes was still going strong working on its thirtieth year. This consisted of visiting homes in the area, viewing their unique accoutrements and Christmas decorations and was scheduled the first Friday of December. Memories came flooding back of Mom, Sara, and I walking through those houses looking at all of the beautiful greeneries and Christmas trees in the houses along Main Street.

Laughing to myself, I distinctly remember the annoyance during a couple of years when I had plans but Mom insisted I go because Sara was new to the family, and she wanted us all to do things together. I was more interested in spending time with Nick. Nick Darlington, yes that's right, is now Whitney's husband. Nick was my high school boyfriend and was seriously being touted throughout the community as my future husband.

You need to understand Millersville then. The community lived for high school football. The team would eat dinner at the home of the family whose raffle was drawn on Sunday. The community would run a raffle every Sunday at the churches in the area, and whoever was picked on Tuesday morning would host the dinner. Later, I remember hearing it changed to Thursday night because the high school put up lights for the football stadium, so Friday night games were being played.

Everyone was invested in the football team, and Nick was the star quarterback. Whitney and I stood cheering Nick on from the sideline watching him create his magic. He put our school on the map and received lots of attention from the Big 10. Films were sent to Michigan and all kinds of pressure was put on Nick, which I believe led to the end of our relationship along with a little help from my best friend. That's right, Whitney.

Remember your first love, when you take the frantic walk down the hall by his class hoping he will still be outside the door? Wondering, will he see you when he is hanging out with his buddies at the courts as you are sitting in the bleachers watching and waiting for just a glance or a smile or the times you walk by his locker, wanting him to follow you? The ugly jeers coming from his friends about how you look at him are music to your ears because now you know he understands. You want him to touch you just to feel his hand on your arm or the hug that gives you a feeling deep down. The new feeling which is spurring into a deep tingling down inside you, accelerating the desire to spend more time with him and become his everything.

This was everything I felt when I first saw Nick Darlington. Our time together blossomed into a serious relationship except somehow it all fell apart. Why, you ask? I honestly don't know. It seemed to be about my family, but really was this why? Looking back all these years later, it seems to be more about timing and lust. I know it may seem naïve to ask this, but why would Nick give in to Whitney if it wasn't any more than lust? He said he loved me. He "loved me." It is so immense—the impact of this as a seventeen-year-old. It was going to be the wedding of Millersville. Their shining knight was getting married to the hometown girl. But yet, was it the wrong girl? So now you know, he betrayed me in the worst possible way. He slept with Whitney two days before our Senior Prom and guess what happened. Whitney came to see me and made sure I knew it.

In time, it became a distant memory—you know the one you keep hidden deep down in your subconscious. Then something goes wrong one day. You have a bad day at work, your daughter gets into a spat with her boyfriend and all of a sudden, it's there again. The problem is I couldn't get over it no matter how hard I tried. Somehow, I couldn't process the intensity of my feelings and then there were all of the other factors which impacted so many people because of their actions. It became a constant nag in my subconscious worming its way into my conscious mind telling me to fix all the things which drove me away from my home. Shaking off the memories, I get ready for the day.

Jonathan & Sara

Another day was starting out with the noise of heavy machinery. Sara spent early mornings catching up on her emails and some days catching up on whatever book she was reading. Realizing it was getting near the time Jonathan would be coming in for breakfast, she closed her computer. Wanting to see the progress being made in the yard, she walks out on the front porch and looks across the farm. A backhoe was digging and moving dirt, a dump truck was parked nearby, and a couple of men were standing near the machinery drinking coffee. Just as she was wondering whether she should put an extra pot of coffee on, she saw one of the gentlemen turn and wave. Straining to see who it is, she waves back tentatively.

Later she would take out a thermos of coffee and figure out who it was. Jonathan was being tightlipped about who was actually helping out. He kept saying it was a few guys from Parson Construction, but I'm sure it is someone we know because half the county works there. Standing there looking at the farm brought back a memory of Jonathan's mother. One day when there was a horrible thunderstorm brewing, Mom was telling her how Jonathan and Misty's father would stand on the porch and watch over the barns in fear of a lightning strike. Such an event could destroy a barn if it were to start a fire. Suddenly hearing her name called, she realizes Jonathan had come into the house. Rushing back in, she sees Jonathan leaning against the kitchen counter with a cup of coffee.

"Sara, where were you? I called out to you a couple of times, were you upstairs?" Knowing how annoyed Jonathan would get if he had to wait for breakfast, she hurries into the kitchen.

"I was standing out on the front porch looking out over the farm. Sorry breakfast isn't ready yet, but I got distracted earlier. Also, it is such a nice morning. I took a minute to enjoy the beginning of the day," says Sara.

Coming over and gently touching his wife's arm, he smiles and assures her, "Sara, its fine. Remember I don't have to hurry to get back out there." Laughing, he adds, "We have people."

Giggling at Jonathan's remark, Sara responds, "Oh, that's right, you are orchestrating the cleanup with 'your people.'"

"Yeah, something like that. All joking aside, if it weren't for Robert Parson lending his equipment and his men, we would be doing this ourselves which, as you know, would take forever and be awful. Thanks to Seth's friend, Brett, for getting in touch with Robert. I know him, but I didn't feel comfortable asking for help."

Smiling to herself, she adds dryly, "Well that's for sure because if you did, we would have already started cleaning up. It's been like this for years, Jonathan. So, let's be honest, Misty's return home is the reason why. I had forgotten how assertive she can be, which I know annoys you some, but this is what we need right now. Someone to take the bull by the horns and help us get this done quickly, so we can decide which way we are going to take this farm into the future." Moving away from her to sit down at the kitchen table, Jonathan sips his coffee. Sara starts the bacon and gets the toaster out of the cabinet moving quickly out of habit. "Do you want scrambled or fried eggs this morning, Jonathan?"

Turning to look at his wife of thirty years, he says, "Surprise me." Frowning, Sara goes to the refrigerator and stands before it looking as if it was going to throw the ingredients out to "surprise" him. Seeing last night's vegetable mix, she decides on an omelet.

Busying herself with making the food, she nonchalantly says, "Hey, I was talking with Misty the other day, and the idea came up about possibly utilizing the farm for something other than milking cows."

With impatience lacing his voice, Jonathan responds quickly, "So what exactly do you and Misty think I should be doing now with the farm. And was this you and Misty talking or was this Misty's idea?" Feeling some anxiety welling up inside her, Sara took a breath before answering her husband. This might be the only chance she would have to plant the idea of utilizing the ground for grapes.

"Well, we were talking about how many wineries were starting up in the county and their need for land. Our ground is perfect for growing grapes. Misty was very enthusiastic about the idea." Seeing the sincerity in his wife's eyes, he bit back his first retort.

"Have you and Misty done any other research for this idea?"

Attempting to navigate the minefield of her husband's mind was always fun, so taking a deep breath, Sara says, "No, it wasn't Misty's idea about the wineries. Her stance is more about utilizing the farm for some other end use, whether it be to grow more grain or corn to sell or something else entirely. This is what got me thinking. You and

I both know we have the exact kind of soil needed to grow grapes. Don't you remember a few months ago when we were taking a ride we talked about this exact thing? You might have said it in passing, but Jonathan, it could be a reality. There is nothing in the bank contract which states how you go back to farming. They were going to leave a portion of the land under our control." Finishing the omelet and bringing the rest of the food to the table, she sits down.

Tapping her husband's arm, she goes on, "Jonathan, just think about it. No one is pressuring us yet. We need to get all this property cleaned up. However, you must admit, it is a good idea and one which is doable. There are so many people we could count on for help and guidance to set up the vineyard. You have someone right in your own family. Your dad's brother Anson has grown grapes for forty years out in California. Call him and bounce the idea off of him." Then, laughing, she adds, "You never know, we could be the east Napa Valley."

Realizing Sara might be on to something, he puts away his irritation for Misty's involvement. Deep down he knows his sister is only trying to help. It's just hard getting used to her being around again, and realizing she has grown up. She's not the seventeen-year-old whose heart was broken over that piece of shit, Nick Darlington.

Smiling at Sara, Jonathan says, "Maybe later this week, I'll give Uncle Anson a call and see what he thinks about the idea." Jumping up from the table and hugging him, Sara can't control her happiness.

"Thank you for listening. It's a good idea, you'll see." Jonathan stands up.

"Ok but promise me we will think this all the way through. We don't want to fail again, Sara. I've got to get back out there." Sara smiles at this.

"I'm going to bring out more coffee to refill the workers' thermoses." Jonathan leaves and Sara does a little dance around the kitchen. "I've got to go see Misty later and tell her about the conversation."

Brett

Sitting down drinking his coffee, Brett decides he better call the bar and see if Jillian has come in yet. He really didn't want to make her wait for him to get there because she wanted to get the order in for the new IPAs. The phone rings once, and Jillian doesn't even say hello.

"Hey boss, are you on your way? I've been here for an hour." Smiling at Jillian's enthusiasm, he tells her he will be there in a half hour. He hangs up, gets up, throws the rest of his coffee out, and rinses his cup in the sink to make sure there were no coffee spots. Straightening his chair, fixing the wrinkle in the tablecloth where his coffee mug sat, and refolding the kitchen towel to be perfectly centered on his stove handle, he finally decides everything is good. Backing out of his driveway, he thinks riding by his mother's house would be a good idea. He was pretty sure she told him she would be home sometime this week from her trip abroad. Feeling conflicted about her return would prove to be right or wrong after talking with her, but for now, he just needs to make sure everything is in order there if she wasn't home yet.

Thinking back to the day he took Morgan to meet his mother, he remembers there was an immediate connection between them—except this is not one which his mother is comfortable with or Morgan either for that matter. Something or someone had put the two of them in a conundrum, and he was going to find out what or who it was. His mother invited her back by herself, which was the day Abby died. Brett never found out from either one of them how the visit went. Since then, everything has been focused on Seth and Olivia, Cissy and Josh, and their healing after such a tragedy. It was time, he found out exactly what happened between the two of them, and he was going to start with his mother as soon as she got home.

Swinging onto his mother's street, he sees a dark colored van sitting across the street from her house. Turning into her driveway, he looks in his rearview mirror to see if anyone is in the van. All he can see is one person but nothing other than mirrored sunglasses reflecting the sun. Pulling all the way back to the garage, he notices her trashcans are knocked over. Picking up the cans and righting them, he sees the bags are torn as if some animal had been rooting around for food. Making sure everything is in order, he unlocks the back door and walks in as the telephone is ringing. Hurrying into the hallway for the phone, he notices dirt on the floor near the front door.

Distracted, he grabs the phone, "Hello?"

After a hesitation, he then hears, "Is Elizabeth at home?"

Focusing, he says, "I'm sorry, no she is not. May I take a message?" Another hesitation and then the caller says the strangest thing.

"Tell her Carl knows what she did."

Stunned, Brett remarks, "I'm sorry, can you repeat that please?"

"No, you heard me. Just tell your mother when she returns. She will understand." Click. Brett stood there for a moment in disbelief. *What the hell just happened and who the hell was Carl?* Putting the phone back down, he walks back to the kitchen and sits down. He suddenly realizes the caller recognized his voice on the phone.

"He knows who I am," he says aloud. First a van parked out front, the phone call, an accusation, and then the recognition. At the turn on a dime, things no longer made sense. The minute hand on the clock in the kitchen only moves three times before he leaps from the chair and runs to the window. But the van is gone.

"Damn! How could I have been so stupid not to get the license plate number?" Sitting back down, he lays his head down on his arms trying to make sense of it all. Then, he hears the most familiar but intimidating voice ever.

"Brett, what in the world are you doing sitting here with your head lying on my table? Have you forgotten people sit down at that table and eat food? What are you doing here? I never texted or called you to say I was coming home today." Standing up and feeling like he needed to be taller, he walks to her and gives her a hug.

"Mother, it's great to see you. I came to check on your house before heading to work today. Figuring your month was close to ending, I wanted to make sure everything was in order in case you were to get home this week." Releasing her and standing back, he looks at her. "Oh my, Mother you look wonderful. What did you do while you were away? You look ten years younger."

Twirling around and coming to a stop reaching out to her only child, she hugs him and says, "Brett, I had the most glorious time. I traveled through Italy and Spain eating and drinking. Spending immense time with the locals and understanding their customs. It was the best time I have ever had. There were so many events I wished you could have seen with me. I feel great and am happy to be home."

Wrapping his arms around her, he gives her another hug, and if he was going to analyze, it was the hug he should have given her before she left on her trip. Except now, he had all of this other drama circulating in his mind about her journals, the paper with the combination, the phone call, and the van. *Where am I going to start or should I just wait*, he thinks.

Taking the high road, he says, "Mother, it's so wonderful to see you home safely. I hate to run, but I didn't expect you home today, and there are people waiting for me at the tavern. Your mail is inside the foyer table, and all the phone messages are by the phone. The phone was ringing today when I came in to check on everything. I went to grab it, but there was no one there." He hated lying to her about the call, but he needed to find out more about Morgan's visit here those many weeks ago and somehow, he didn't think the van was there for no reason.

———•———

Meanwhile, the occupant of the van decides he better check in. Dialing the number and then entering his access code, he waits for a connection.

"Sir, yes, I'm here now… Yes, she has returned, however, her son was just there and answered when I called. So, the effect we wanted it to have on her was wasted. …No, sir, I did not know he was going to answer her phone. I did not know he was even there. … Yes, sir, I realize I need to pay more attention." Listening for a few more minutes, he responds, "I'm fully aware what is at stake, but how were we supposed to know Jenkins' daughter was ever going to return? I know we cannot fail again. I will get the evidence, and no one will ever be the wiser." Hanging up, he bangs his fist on the steering wheel. *How is this farmer still giving us problems after twenty years of silence? We took care of him and now his daughter, who no one ever thought would return to Millersville, is back and causing problems. I need to find out what Misty Jenkins knows. Now, nothing is off the table about how this will come to an end.*

Jackson, Seth, & Olivia

After dinner, Seth helps Olivia clear the table and put the leftovers away. Jackson stands up and comes to stand between Seth and Olivia. He drapes his arms across both their shoulders.

"How about the two of you get our after-dinner drinks ready, and I'll get the rest of this mess cleaned up."

"Oh Jackson, you don't need to do this, I'll have it done in no time flat. Go sit down and visit with Seth," Olivia says smiling.

Guiding Olivia gently into the living room, Jackson turns to look at Seth insisting, "You too, brother! I'll take a finger of whiskey. Jameson if you have it."

Laughing at his brother who already disappeared back into the kitchen, Seth now grabs his wife's hand and says, "You got it!" Sitting down in her chair, Olivia looks over at her husband working behind their small bar.

"It's obvious you are happy he's here. I have to say dinner was very enjoyable. He is so entertaining and seems excited to be visiting. Something tells me Katrina and he are having problems because he hasn't mentioned her once." Putting ice into two small glasses, Seth then pours whiskey into them.

"What would you like to drink babe? Wine, or do you want to join Jackson and I and have some whiskey?"

"Actually Seth, I'm going to check on Jackson really quick, and I'll grab some cold wine out of the refrigerator." Walking back into the kitchen, she stops at the doorway. Jackson had her kitchen sparkling from ceiling to floor. She clears her throat, and Jackson turns at the sound.

"Olivia, I hope I haven't overstepped my bounds. The memories of this kitchen overwhelmed me and before I knew it, I was cleaning everything in sight. Although there wasn't much to clean, I wanted to help, that's all. You aren't upset are you about me invading your kitchen?" Walking toward Jackson, she grabs hold of him and hugs him tightly.

"I am so glad you are here. Seth and I need family right now and you are our family, Jackson."

Returning the hug, Jackson whispers, "Olivia, I will be here for whatever you need and for as long as you want. I've taken some well-deserved time off so Jackson Palmer, Attorney at Law, at your service."

Breaking the contact, Olivia says, "Oh Jackson, I'm not sure what we will need, but it's so kind of you to offer your help."

"Olivia, remember we are family and family sticks together."

Seth calls from the living room, "Hey, you two I'm feeling parched. How about joining me?"

Looking up at Jackson, Olivia says, "Let's go sit down and catch up." Together they walk into the room and sit down. For the next couple of hours, Jackson entertains them with stories of cases he had won and the corruption of corporate America. Olivia was torn with the desire to talk about Abby and her illness, but listening to

Seth and Jackson laugh made her realize tomorrow would be soon enough. Then maybe she could ask Morgan to stop over.

Morgan

Coming down the steps, the smell and the crackle of bacon were permeating the air. Going into the kitchen, I see Heidi standing in front of the stove cracking an egg.

Hearing me, she turns and smiles cheerfully greeting, "Good morning, Mom. Breakfast will be ready, and if you like, there is fresh coffee in the pot."

With a quiet look of surprise, I walk over and squeeze her shoulder as I offer my thanks, "Well this is quite a surprise, and one I am happy to enjoy. What time did you get up this morning, Heidi?"

Laughing, she defends herself, "Mom, have you forgotten the early times I have to be at work? My internal clock is having me rise early these days. So, I decided to put my time to good use and cook my mom breakfast." Sitting down at the table with my coffee, I watch my daughter move around the kitchen like a seasoned chef.

"How much cooking have you been doing since I have been away?"

Adding salt and pepper to the eggs and flipping the pancakes, Heidi turns and answers, "Well it was getting expensive eating take-outs and fast food all the time, so I decided it was time I learned to cook something. Thanks to the Food Network, I've learned a few dishes, so at least I wouldn't starve or go broke first." Plating the food and putting it down at each of their places at the table, she leans in and gives me a kiss on the cheek. "It's the least I can do for you after the few weeks you have had since you arrived here. All these years being away from your family and now regaining a relationship with Uncle Jonathan and Aunt Sara, it's been intense. Something tells me there will be more things to come, so while I'm here let me cook for you. With a little help of course."

Between mouthfuls, I suggest, "You can cook all the time if it's going to taste as good as this. What seasoning did you put in the eggs?"

Acting as though she was going to tell me the biggest secret, she leans in and with a serious expression, she whispers, "It's called everything bagel seasoning. Isn't it the best?" Then, she burst out laughing. We continued our breakfast making small talk and then cleaned up together.

"What would you like to do today, Heidi? I am at your disposal."

Leaning back in her chair, Heidi gets a devilish look in her eyes and asks, "Is there a mall nearby? Shopping, as you know, is always high on my list." Nothing appealed to me less than going to the mall, however, Millersville is known for its western stores, and Heidi loves her cowboy boots.

"There is a mall about 45 minutes away, but Millersville has a couple good western stores where I know you would like to shop. One is on the way to the farm, so we can stop there afterwards to visit if you want." Giving me a thumbs up, she runs upstairs to get showered. Knowing everything was in an uproar at the farm, I decided it might be a good idea to call Sara and see what is going on. Jonathan could be somewhat stressed right now so showing up unexpectedly, even if I did just get back home, would throw my brother into a tailspin.

Hearing Sara's voice, I begin, "Hey, what's going on today? Heidi and I were going to stop out in a little while. Is everything going as planned?"

Sounding a little tired, Sara says, "Well, besides all kinds of land moving equipment showing up every day and Jonathan stressing over what to throw out and what to keep, it's going great. Plus, I mentioned what we talked about the last time you were here."

Thinking about our last conversation, suddenly, I smile and say, "So what was the response? Let me guess, he blamed me for the idea?"

"Oh, my God, Misty! How did you know?"

Laughing a little too hard, I say, "It just doesn't surprise me. Jonathan has always dismissed my ideas and old habits die hard. It's ok though because Sara, it's a great idea."

Hearing a sigh on the other end of the phone, Sara replies, "I know and honestly so does he. It's just hard for him to think of something else besides milking cows. Cows are not going to be our solution though, Misty. So, when are you coming over again because I can't wait to come up with a plan." Heidi had finished getting ready and was walking into the kitchen.

Putting Sara on speaker, I say, "Sara, tell Heidi what you just said."

Making a crazy sound, she says, "Heidi, your mom and I are going to change the farming world in this county. So, you two need to get out here right away."

"Wow, Aunt Sara, after that enthusiasm, you can be sure we will be there as soon as we can. I can't wait to dive into whatever crazy idea the two of you have." Getting my pocketbook and keys, we headed out to the car. Looking over to Seth and Olivia's, I notice a black Audi sitting in their driveway. For a moment, I wonder who is visiting, but getting out to Jonathan's is preoccupying my mind, so the car is dismissed.

There is a feeling of excitement building in my stomach with the hope of future success for our family farm. Dad always said we need to think outside of the box to be successful, and this idea was on the way to progress. But whether or not Jonathan will become invested is the question now. We need him to buy into the idea because it is the only way it will truly be successful. We need his soil knowledge and the understanding of his ground to facilitate any plan.

Heidi is scanning the countryside humming a popular tune. Humming had become a habit of Heidi's. Whenever we were going to the doctor, dentist, or to school for one of those meetings, she would hum. As she entered her teenager years, it became annoying. Now listening to her, it was music to my ears. However, it made me wonder what exactly was going on in her mind right now. We soon arrive at the farm, and Sara comes out the back door to meet us.

"Hey, you two, I'm so happy you are here. Jonathan just went back out to help everyone. Morgan, do you see what is going on out there?"

Looking toward the farm, I smile broadly and answer, "Sara, I sure do, and it is a wonderful view! Nothing makes me happier than to see all of this stuff, or should I say trash and debris, removed from this property." Looking over at Heidi, I say, "When Sara first met your Uncle Jonathan, PopPop was very intense. Nothing was too hard for him to do. Machinery repairs, breeding animals, burning horns off of bulls were just a few of the things he was doing. He worked twenty-four seven on this farm and expected all of us to do the same." Swallowing thickly, Heidi looks as though she is going to be sick.

"Burning off horns, breeding animals? I must confess, after getting here and seeing the farm, I went on YouTube to see how farmers work. The things I saw were awful. Arms going up into cows, you know, it must have been their private parts, men tackling beautiful black and white cows using branding irons and searing off parts of their head. Mom, it was absolutely awful." Sara and I started laughing hysterically. My sides are hurting so bad that I have to bend over and take a breath. Finding Sara in the same condition made me laugh even harder. Looking up from my bent over position, there is my daughter, her arms crossed with the biggest frown on her face, and her voice is becoming higher pitched than normal.

"What are the two of you doing right now? Do you both think this is funny? I was traumatized. Did PopPop really do these things to his cows?" The two of us getting together, standing upright.

"Oh Heidi, it's not entirely like you saw on YouTube. There is a reason why farmers do those things, and honestly, it's not considered cruel by farmers. Other people might view it differently, but they aren't farmers, so they wouldn't understand. These events need to be done periodically on a farm, and believe me when I tell you, PopPop did it as humanely as he could. As far as the breeding goes, this was how our farm grew and became prosperous. There was nothing cruel being done. It was purely just to ensure the integrity of the lineage of the sire."

Sara put her arm around Heidi's shoulder and provided additional explanation, "Believe me Heidi, I felt the same way you are feeling when I first met Jonathan and he would tell me some of the things that went on here. However, after working on the farm with your uncle, I have found all of those things are just part of running a farm. Now, though, things are very different, and it has become very hard for the farmer to make any money. Therefore, your mom and I want to change how the farm works—to use the ground for other things to make the farm successful." The three of us sit down at the kitchen table to discuss what should happen next.

"Sara, we should start with the County Extension office of Rutgers and ask if there is any information available to begin soil preparation. Also, see if there is contact with the state for licensing and any other state permits we may need. Call them, or better yet, go out to the office and get all the information available. In the meantime, I am going to call our Uncle Anson and pick his brain about getting vines and which ones to start with. He grew up here, so he understands the climate plus we are on the same latitude as California, and he has had a very successful winery out there for many, many years. However, we all know this is contingent on Jonathan's cooperation. I can get the bank's agreement on this plan. All they want is their portion of the land to develop. What we do with the remaining ground is not their concern. Sara, let's get together again in a couple of days and see what we have pulled together. Then we will present it to Jonathan."

Smiling at me, Sara says, "This is going to work, Morgan, we are going to have the most fun getting this winery going. Jonathan mentioned calling Uncle Anson as well, so he is not totally against it. He just wants to be prepared. All of us are going to be sure the farm prospers again."

Seemingly pleased listening to her mom and aunt, Heidi sits back and says, "It's amazing hearing the two of you talk. Are you two thinking about starting a winery? Is this possible?" Sara responds quickly, "Heidi, we believe it is possible. There are still a lot of variables, but we are going to work through it and hope by the spring we will be planting root stock. Then in a few years, we will have grapes to pick and sell to a winery for their wine production."

Standing up, I go to look out the window toward the farm. I can see and hear the heavy machinery moving around knocking down old, dilapidated sheds. Realizing Dad's shop looks like it is falling down, I spring into action because it needed to stay standing, so I could look through there again.

"Sara, I need to run out there and make sure they don't take down Dad's shop. Is Jonathan out there with them?"

Sara grabs her phone and says, "Don't worry, I will call him. He is on one of the backhoes running it for Parsons." While she was getting a hold of Jonathan, I think back to the day Jonathan found the envelope that was left for us by Dad. Nothing in the world would have prepared me for the information written on those pages. He wasn't articulate but the message was clear—something is not right in this town.

"Morgan, Jonathan wants you to come out there. He said he has time now to go through the shop if you do. There can't be too much left in there because Jonathan cleaned a lot of it out a while ago." Heidi is getting antsy, and I knew it was because she wanted to go shopping.

Understanding her impatience, I look over at her and say, "Heidi, I'm going to be a little while with Uncle Jonathan. Do you want to go back home, or do you want to go shopping? I will have Sara bring me home."

Seemingly appreciative of my awareness, Heidi hops up, gives Sara a hug and me a kiss and says while walking out the door, "If you are going to be awhile, I'll stop and look around the mall and pick you up on the way home. Then, if there's time, can we go to those stores where they have the boots? It will still be early enough, won't it?"

Laughing, I say, "I won't be too long, and yes we will get there before they close for the day." Before walking out to Jonathan, Sara put her hand on my arm and looked at me closely.

"Morgan don't come on too strong with Jonathan if it comes up about the winery idea. We have to be more prepared when we talk to him about this."

"Sara, have no worries. There is something I must look for in Dad's shop, and it's possible it might be something valuable. Jonathan will probably think it's pointless to look for anything in there because he always thought Dad was crazy about the electromagnetic field issues. I feel as though there may be something more in there which will clarify things for us." Walking over to the farmyard, several men waved which was nice even though none of us knew who each other was. I see Jonathan stepping off of backhoe. Waving to him, I pick up my step to get over to him quickly.

Smiling at him, I say through a laugh, "Having fun yet?"

Giving me a sideways look, he retorts, "Real funny, Misty. In case you have forgotten, this is pretty painful for me." Waving his arms around, he adds, "All of this looks like this because I had my head in the sand."

Staying optimistic, I smile and remind him, "I know you are having trouble calling me Morgan, but please understand using Morgan as my name is a testament to the new life Heidi and I made in Linn Creek. Morgan Kiernan is who I am now, but to you, I know I will always be Misty. Just try, ok?" Once Jonathan nods in agreement, I continue, "Jonathan, I need to go through Dad's shop one more time before a backhoe knocks the roof in." Grabbing my arm, a little too aggressively, he pulls me toward the shop.

"Misty, what do you think you are going to find? Wasn't all the information you needed in the envelope I found? Which by the way, you never told me exactly what was in there."

Opening the door of the shop proves to be more difficult than the last time we were in there. The door had fallen off its hinges and was just hanging on by a literal thread. It looks as though someone had tried to reattach the door with nylon thread. Examining it closer, I saw it was nylon fishing line.

Turning around to Jonathan and pointing to the hinge, I inquire, "Did you do that?"

Going up to the hinge and pulling on the line, he turns to me answering, "No I did not which now brings up the question, who did?"

Frowning and moving further into the shop, I reply, "I don't know, and right now I'm not going to stress over it. However, I'm sure there is something in here. Why else would someone be sneaking in here? Dad must have written something down. He saw so many people trying to figure out why stray current was more prevalent in certain areas. Besides his notebook, there has to be more notes. Mom would have been sure to write down who he was seeing. This is the book or whatever we need to find, Jonathan."

Moving around in the shop, I pick up things and try to open drawers that were sitting lopsided full of mouse dirt and other disgusting items. Putting my hands into these drawers was making me uneasy, but it had to be done. Cobwebs were glistening in the sun-light, and I could hear scurrying which gave me the willies. Swiping away a cobweb, which annoyed its occupant, I walked toward the back of the shop where there was a writing table. I began inspecting the top of the table, scanning all the papers which were yellowed. The print faded from years of sun exposure. I noticed a change in the dust pattern. Looking closer, I can see a handprint as if someone had leaned on the table while they were looking for something. Trying to hide my excitement, I turned to Jonathan.

"You don't need to stay here with me if you have other things to do. Heidi will be picking me up, so I won't be here for very long. All I ask is you make sure no one knocks down this building. I'm sure there is something here since we've had a visitor," I say pointing to the handprint.

Brett

Leaving his mother's, Brett wonders if Morgan is home. Nothing would be better right now than to see and talk to her. He had so many questions in his mind that only she could answer. It was time he found out what became of Morgan's visit with his mother. Slowing down in front of her house, he notices Heidi getting out of Morgan's car. Pulling into the driveway, he waves to Heidi. Seeing her hesitate, he gets out of his car quickly, so she would see who he was.

"Heidi, how are you? I'm sorry if I scared you pulling in so quickly. It simply was a last-minute decision on my part because I saw you in your mom's car."

Laughing, Heidi says, "Oh, Brett it's ok. When I realized it was you, I figured you thought it was Mom." Understanding her next words needed to be chosen well, she says, "Mom is visiting someone she met recently, but she won't be much longer. I can let her know you stopped by." Seeing the look of astonishment on Brett's face, Heidi smiles to herself. *I'm not sure what he is thinking, but it can't hurt if he thinks he might have some competition.*

Hesitating for a moment, he nods and says, "Heidi, she's visiting a friend? I didn't realize she knew many people here in Millersville."

Shrugging her shoulders, she admits, "Sorry, I really don't know." Walking back toward his car, he turns to look at Heidi.

"When you see your mom later, please let her know to call me. I have to get to the tavern." Backing out of their driveway, Brett's mind goes rogue. *Who in the world would she be visiting today? Besides Seth, Olivia, and irritatingly Nick, there wasn't anyone else she would feel comfortable enough to visit, or at least as far as I know. Could she have met someone?* These thoughts were swarming through his mind and intensifying his desire to find out more about her. Something didn't add up, and he was going to find out what and why. The last few weeks had been so intriguing with her, but stepping away from it, he realizes there are many discrepancies.

Arriving at the tavern, Brett is able to get in through the back-door just as Jillian is coming through the kitchen door.

"Hey boss, I didn't know you were here. We are so busy out there, and one of the girls called out. Can you help me behind the bar for a little while?"

Taking a deep breath and getting his mind on track, he looks at his best employee and tells her, "Damn right I can help you. Tell me what side of the bar you need the most help."

Looking at his face, Jillian realizes he might not be himself, so showing doubt, she says "I'll take the busy side, and the other side will be the best for you."

Knowing his bartender very well, he says, "Jillian, we will make it an event. Who can give the boss the hardest drink to make? It will be fine, chin up my girl, we've got this."

Jackson, Seth, & Olivia

Rolling over and pulling the covers over his face, Jackson groans loudly. It had been a long time since he had stayed up late like last night. Plus, he is pretty sure Seth and he killed a bottle of Jameson. Smiling despite the pounding in the back of his head, he understood how important it was that he finally came to see his brother and his wife. After talking with Seth and Olivia last night, he realized how much they were struggling with the death of Abby. Cissy and Josh had taken time off from work because their grief was overcoming them. A tornado of questions of why Abby died swirled around them, intensifying in strength each day, as it was consuming their life. Olivia became so angry during their conversation last night, while Seth remained very calm. Hearing some movement downstairs, he gets up and heads to the bathroom to get a quick shower hoping the warm water will help to assuage the pounding in his head.

Heading down the hallway, he overhears Olivia talking to Seth, "Seth, I'm sorry I acted the way I did last night. It definitely wasn't the time or place to react like I did when Jackson had just gotten here."

Seth smiles and comforts her, "Olivia, don't worry about it, by the time you were getting angry, Jackson and I were not feeling any pain. I'm sure if he does remember, he understands the anguish we are experiencing." Feeling uneasy about eavesdropping, Jackson continues to the bathroom.

Waiting for the water to get hot, he looks at himself in the mirror. Gray hair was beginning to discreetly make its way around his temple, but his hair still remained mostly dark. His green eyes stare back at him although today they were slightly bloodshot. Wondering again what his birth mother looked like, he smiles. She must have had good genes because besides his hair not graying too early, his light brown skin looked as healthy as it always had. Smiling to himself, Jackson has a flashback of Seth telling him he was the color of a black and white milkshake and that he loved black and white milkshakes. Much later, he figured out it probably wasn't politically correct to talk in such a way, but it was Seth, and he loved his brother unconditionally. Jumping in the shower, he enjoyed the hot water beating on his shoulders.

Finishing up and stepping out, he hears a knock on the door and then Seth's voice shouting, "Hey, Jackson, breakfast in ten, ok?"

"Thanks, I will be out of here in a few minutes and downstairs in five." Seth smiles. Jackson always wanted to be the best, and apparently it hadn't changed. Seth told him ten minutes, but he will be sure to be downstairs in five. About five minutes later, Jackson comes strolling into the kitchen, walks over and gives Olivia a kiss on the cheek, and a hug to Seth.

"How are my two favorite people this fine morning? Are either one of you feeling as bad as I did when I woke up this morning?"

Olivia speaks up, "Well not pointing any fingers, but this guy," looking at her husband, "took a few trips to the bathroom during the night and there was a god-awful sound coming from somewhere."

Smiling at her husband, she goes on, "Jackson, it makes me happy to have you here with us. Too much time has gone by since we were all together."

Hesitating for just a second, Jackson moves his eyes between his sister-in-law and his brother and says, "You're so right Olivia, and it's time we move on from whatever childish resentments we had in the past. I, for one, am so happy to be back here visiting with you guys. It feels so much like home."

Walking over and pulling Seth out of his chair and grabbing Jackson, Olivia put her arms around the two of them and says, "We are family, and family stays together always no matter what has happened in the past. So, let's eat, shall we?" Sitting down together, they enjoy a healthy hangover breakfast. While they are eating, Olivia clears her throat.

"I just want to let you both know, you aren't the only two who are suffering after last night. I could barely get myself out of bed this morning. My eyes were all puffy, and it was scary looking in the mirror." Jackson can't help himself. He breaks out into a full-blown laughing attack. "Really, Jackson!"

Trying to get himself under control, he finally catches his breath and says, "Olivia, I'm sorry. It was just this morning, in the bathroom when looking at my face, I told myself it looked good. Especially after a night of drinking."

Seth looks incredulously at his brother exclaiming, "You're kidding us right now, what did you have on blinders because you look almost as bad as we do. So, get over yourself, Jackson." All of them laughing together is music to all of their ears. Quietly, they finish eating breakfast and clear the dishes from the table. Seth and Jackson wash everything up while Olivia goes outside to water some of her hanging plants.

Coming back in, Olivia says, "Can we all go in and sit down for a bit? We need to talk to you, Jackson." After everyone gets comfortable, Olivia struggles for a moment and then says, "Jackson, we really need your help. Something caused Abby's death. Seth and I know it, someone else knows it, but we truly need your expertise." Jackson subtly agrees. Olivia continues, "I don't know how much Seth told you, but Cissy and Josh moved to a really nice area, and their home was exactly what they were looking for. Not too long after they moved there, Abby started getting sick. Nothing terrible at first, just not feeling good and then it started affecting her schooling. She was constantly going to the nurse, and honestly, I'm beginning to think the school became part of the problem." Listening to Olivia and giving her time to talk, Jackson decides now was the time to intervene.

"What do you mean, Olivia? How is the school complicit in Abby's death? I want you to really think about this because this has legal impact if you are right."

Thinking for a minute, Olivia looks over at Seth, "Anytime you would like to speak up would be good."

Frowning at his wife yet understanding her frustration, he says, "Jackson, what Olivia is trying to convey is Abby constantly went to the nurse. It was often that her teacher reached out to Cissy and wanted to know if everything was ok at home. Josh's job requires him to work long hours, so his involvement was never great, but when this happened, he marched right down to the school and confronted the principal. After resolving the nurse's question, Josh and Cissy became more aware of Abby's behavior when she was home. Over several months, her condition worsened. Josh's job enabled him to travel quite a bit, so Cissy and Abby would go with him on trips. Sometimes they would be gone for several weeks, and Cissy would home-school Abby while they were away."

Jackson interjects, "How did Abby feel when they were on their trips?" *Was it possible something was going on in school which was causing the constant visits to the nurse?*

Seth speaks up, "Jackson, it was crazy. The longer she was away from home, the healthier she became. That's when we finally talked to Cissy and Josh about their house. Honestly, we had no idea what was wrong, but something was, and neither of us could figure it out. We struggled talking with them because obviously this was really none of our business. Abby is our granddaughter, and we were very careful about not stepping out of bounds when it came to her up-bringing." Listening to Seth, Jackson contemplates his next words carefully.

"Seth and Olivia, I am very good at my job and my record is spotless. The two of you need to understand I will need more information about the environment around Cissy's home. Also, I need to talk with this other individual you have referred to a couple of times now." Eyeing Seth, Olivia raises her eyebrows in question. Seth understands Olivia's look and takes a deep breath.

"Jackson, I need you to keep an open mind about what I am going to tell you. There is so much to tell you it's hard to know where to start." Staring at his brother, Jackson realizes right away Seth's soul has been bruised by Abby's death. No matter what he was about to hear, he knew helping them was in his future no matter how long it would take.

"How about starting at the beginning? I have all day to listen to both of you. Talk to me!"

"Ok, Olivia I'm sure you will fill in anything I might miss, right?" With a small smile, Olivia nods.

"Jackson, I don't know if you remember my friend, Jonathan Jenkins, he lived on a farm just outside of town. He had a younger sister, Misty, who dated Nick Darlington through high school. Is any of this ringing a bell with you?"

"Yes, it does, but what do they have to do with this?"

"Do you remember all the talk around town about their dad and his trying to help people who were getting sick?" Seth was really going back in time. Jackson tries to remember what was going on with Mr. Jenkins since he spent a lot of time around their house one summer.

Seth continues, "Anyway, Mr. Jenkins was sure the decline in health of some people in the county was due to the stray current emanating from the electrical towers which are scattered throughout the area. He concluded the stray current was turning into electromagnetic fields which could possibly cause cancers and other terminal diseases." Olivia decides it is time for her own interjection.

"Jonathan wasn't on board with any of his dad's beliefs, while Misty was in high school trying to navigate her teenage years. All the small-minded people in the community made it very hard on their family. Seth and I have recently been reminded of just how hard it was for them."

Before Olivia or Seth can continue, Jackson asks, "What does all of this have to do with Abby?"

Seth speaks first, "Cissy and Josh's house is located within a mile of electrical towers."

Olivia buts in, "And the towers are deteriorating, however, the electric company is still utilizing them. Tell me how in the world these old towers can be safe. They must be dropping stray voltage all over the place. People have been getting seriously ill or dying who live in close proximity to these old towers. The county health official was contacted but has done nothing." Lowering his head for several seconds, Jackson quickly processes everything Seth and Olivia told him.

Raising his head, Jackson confirms, "So what you are telling me is you both think Abby's sickness was caused by antiquated electrical towers. With more information, I believe I can help you. The resources I have at my disposal are significant and nothing stops me when I have credence in it. Now though, I need to know everything you know, including whatever information others know. Let me make some phone calls, and if you don't mind, I am going to be your houseguest for the next several weeks." Talking together for the next half hour or so, Jackson decides to table any more conversation until he could talk to this mysterious person they had mentioned.

Morgan

Seeing the handprint, Jonathan shakes his head and looks over at me.

"What is going on Misty? No one has been in here since the day you and I found the envelope." Casting an eye around the interior of the shop, I try to discern whether someone had been rummaging around in the shop. I watch a spider slowly move toward an insect which was caught in its web. Mesmerized, I think of how all the events of the last few weeks are weaving themselves together into a web full of lies and deceit.

Jonathan taps me on the shoulder and questions, "Hey did you hear anything I just said?"

"Yes, I did and how sure are you no one has been in here? It seems to me there has been a lot of activity around here the last couple of days. Maybe someone came in here snooping around." Jonathan walks further into the shop as if he needed space to remain calm. He picks up an old "LIFE" magazine which was still intact and readable.

Slowly turning the pages, he says, "Misty, take a look out there. Do you really think anyone of those guys running those big rigs are interested in anything in here? From the outside, it appears this building is about to fall down, so I really don't think anybody working here left that handprint." While Jonathan is talking, I look around Dad's desk. It appears someone had tried to force a drawer open. The desk is in such bad shape—the drawers had warped, yet each of the drawers looked tampered with.

"Jonathan, come look at this. Someone thinks there is something important in this desk. Apparently, they were unsuccessful because it doesn't appear these drawers were opened. What in the world could they be looking for?" Peering over my shoulder, Jonathan notices the disturbance of dirt and a mark indicating someone was trying to pry the drawer open. Hearing a lot of noise outside of the broken-down door, Jonathan turns and sees one of the riggers standing in the doorway.

"Are you Jonathan?"

"Yes, I am. What's going on?" Shaking his head in frustration, he motions to the yard behind him.

"Dude, you need to get out here. We need some guidance on what to demolish. Some of these buildings are in really bad shape, like this one, and the boss is telling us to take down everything that looks unstable." Sending a look of apology, Jonathan walks out with the rigger to address his concerns.

I hear Jonathan say, "I will show you what to take down, but for now this building needs to stay standing." Walking out of the shop and directing the rigger to the other buildings in decay, Jonathan turns and looks back at me standing in the shop doorway. I notice a smirk appear on his face as his eyes fall to my hands which I have defiantly placed on my hips. Memories come flooding back to all the jokes my family would make about this comfort stance I would resort to every time I sought to gain control of a situation.

Watching Jonathan walk away with the rigger, I wonder if I should have told him about my visit to Elizabeth's house. Finding the canister in Elizabeth's guest bathroom was so disturbing. Thinking of it now brings me back to how much has happened since then—especially with the farm. Sara's enthusiasm makes me so excited about the future for the farm. However, keeping the information away from Jonathan is not right. I really want to get back to Elizabeth's house with Brett so I can look around, but so far, the opportunity has not presented itself. I am concerned too much time has gone by, and it will seem like I was hiding something from him. As soon as I can, I need to share the information with Jonathan.

Finding myself scanning the walls, the benches, and all the containers Dad utilized during his prime, it became overwhelming wondering where his data was stored. I am sure he kept it in here. Something tells me he hid it so only those close to him would be able to find it. Rummaging around the shelves, looking in old paint cans, finding containers of old nails and screws, I begin to wonder if all of this is useless. Then I find myself thinking about Abby, seeing her casket covered with flowers and watching her parents fall apart while looking at each other struggling with the loss. The anger bubbling inside overwhelms me, and my thoughts turn back to my mission to find the papers my dad had hidden.

"I know Dad wrote everything down and hid it somewhere in this shop," I hear myself say. The canister found at Brett's mother's house connects Dad, Jack Callahan, Elizabeth, and Tom Fraser. It is glaring right in front of me—the relationship they had was boiling over with contempt, deceit, and greed, and the Jenkins family became the target. Stepping away from the desk, I look around some more. There were so many drawers, some sealed shut with age and others hanging by their hinges trying to breathe new life into their contents. It became daunting.

Walking back toward the door, I see backhoes and front loaders moving trash and parts of buildings toward a huge container hooked to a tractor trailer. All of a sudden, it comes to me how fast this all is moving. The priority to find whatever Dad left in here stares me in the face.

Glancing down at my watch makes me panic for a moment. Heidi will be heading back here to pick me up if I don't get a ride from Sara. I really don't want to accept a ride from someone else, so waiting for Heidi seems to be my best option. Knowing Heidi, I decided it might be a good idea to text her and find out what her timeframe is on picking me up.

Nick & Whitney

Riding by Morgan's house today, or whoever she was calling herself now, was not a good idea. Whatever Nick's plan was it didn't work out the way he wanted it to. He was hoping to see Morgan outside so he could stop and talk to her. Thinking back on it, he could feel his face blushing. He was acting like he was a teenager hoping for a glance of some girl he wanted to notice him. Driving toward his home, he wonders whether or not Whitney is home. He finds himself wanting to see her, surprising himself but smiling all the same. As he turns onto his street, he sees his boys outside throwing a football laughing and tackling each other. The closer he gets to his house, he realizes Whitney is standing at the door watching the boys or maybe waiting for him to get home.

Laughing, he says to himself, "Let's not get to ahead of yourself buddy." As he is slowing down to pull in his driveway, the boys see him. They begin yelling and jumping up and down—emotions that Nick realizes they have not exhibited in a while. His boys were very happy to see him, and Nick smiles at this small act. Positivity between their parents was showing its effect. During the last couple of years, the negativity had played havoc with their emotions and self-esteem. Getting out of the car, he is assaulted by the two of them hugging him and talking over each other wanting him to throw the football to them.

"Hey, you two, let me go in and see Mom, and then I will come out and throw passes to the two of you." The two of them were high fiving each other as he walked up to the front door where Whitney was waiting. Opening the door, Nick stands for a moment and looks at his wife.

"Hello," he says quietly. "How are you feeling today?" Whitney opens the door wider and stands to the side, so he can walk in.

"Better, I've been thinking a lot today about the past few months. My drinking and the paranoia became detrimental to all of us, especially the boys. I realize now the constant doubt and skepticism of your actions was affecting my psyche. Now, though, I believe things are going to work out for both of us. Whether that is together or separate, I'm sure we will be better people."

Nick smiles and says with relief, "Agreed. I couldn't have said it better. Whether intentionally or not, we spent a lot of wasted time making each other miserable. I don't know about you, but I would rather use my time to work on my relationship with our family." Whitney nods in agreement, and points outside to their boys. They were both sitting on the grass patiently waiting for their dad to come out and play ball with them.

"I think you are in high demand, or they are just tired. Pretty sure it's the first thing I said, so you better get out there before they start arguing who is going to get your first throw." Briefly squeezing her hand, Nick heads out to work on his boys' catching abilities. Whitney stands at the door watching the three of them play wondering what is going to become of her and Nick. She wasn't going to fool herself into thinking it was going to be great between them because there was still Misty.

Her sudden appearance in Millersville has brought their problems to the surface, and Whitney figures maybe she should thank her. Deep down Whitney has always loved Nick and keeping their family together is very important to her. She was going to do something she should have done a long time ago and that was work at having Nick try to love her. Facing Morgan together was something the two of them needed to do even though Morgan made her feel somewhat doubtful. She feels it is necessary for all three of them to talk. Feeling uneasy about seeing Morgan, she thinks back to their high school years.

Morgan and I were inseparable, but something always stood between us as friends, and it was Misty's knack of always being one step ahead of everybody else. Her grades were always on point, all the teachers loved her, and most of the time she was working so hard to include even the most unpopular person in conversation. It was so annoying, but she was my best friend. Nick Darlington was Misty's everything, and it quickly became apparent they were destined to be together forever. Nick was the star quarterback and was known as one of the best football players Millersville ever produced. Misty was the bookworm of the senior class, and I was deemed the partier of the class.

During our senior year, the feelings I had toward Nick were becoming so intense it was hard to conceal the resentment I felt with Misty. Why? Because I wanted Nick, no I loved Nick, and nothing was going to stop me from getting him. Suddenly, she could feel nausea overcoming her, but the memory persisted.

One day, I decided nothing would stop me from having Nick as my future husband, and I calculated the events which ended my friendship with my best friend just so I could have someone who really wasn't mine.

Hearing one of the boys yelling to her to get them all some water, Whitney realizes nothing from the past does anything for the future. She knows that she and Nick need to move forward and take ownership of their issues, and then, only then, would they be able to heal. Going to the garage refrigerator to get water for everybody, Whitney flashes back one more time.

Misty and I were hanging out in her bedroom, painting our fingernails and trying out all kinds of makeup anticipating our debut in high school. Misty was a farm girl and wearing makeup and doing hair wasn't on the top of her list. Trying to convince her to wear just mascara was a monumental task. This day, however, Misty had met Nick, and all of sudden, it was important to her to look pretty. She wanted to spend the day trying on clothes and putting on makeup.

Whitney realizes now, Misty's friendship was the most beautiful thing she had, but sometimes, people are so single-minded nothing can deter them from their thoughts. This is why she had executed a devious plan against her best friend. Now, twenty years later, she has the chance to fix it. And maybe Nick and her will do what is right and begin to heal, or perhaps someday forgive.

Brett

Jillian is running around the bar like a crazy woman because the orders for drinks tonight are so exotic. She continually has to run back to the cooler.

At one point, when she and Brett were able to stand next to each other for a second, she laid her hand on his arm and says, "Boss, I take back all my doubts. This was a fabulous idea. We should do this every month. Word must have gotten around because there are so many people here, and I don't know about you, but this is nothing I thought would happen. Look at the number of people here, its nuts."

Squeezing her arm and smiling, Brett leaned in saying, "We got this, Jillian, and this is why this bar is so popular. We know how to make things work."

In the background they heard, "Hey you two, let's go, we need drinks over here. The best you can make, the vote is out, bring it on!" For the next three hours, Jillian and Brett make drink after drink. Some they were pretty sure they had never made before and would probably never make again. Finally, the crowd diminishes, and both are able to sit down for a minute. Looking at his phone, Brett sees there are several missed calls from Morgan and Seth.

"Jillian, are you ok handling the rest of the crowd by yourself? I need to make some calls."

"No problem, Boss. The people who are left here wouldn't know who was serving them drinks anyway. I need to find them all rides home, so when you are done, please come back out here and help me navigate all of the intoxicated customers." Laughing, he grabs and hugs her.

"Jillian, what would I do without you? We are a great team you and I, and this was a phenomenal night for our bar."

Hugging him back, she leans back and smiles, "Our bar?" Taking a deep breath, he looks at his employee who has always had his back and has never let him down since he bought the place.

"Jillian, I want to make you a partner if that's ok? Something told me a few weeks ago you were so right for our future here, and I need to make sure it's worth your while. Please tell me being here with me for the indeterminable future is what you want to do. We can work out all the details by the end of the year, just tell me you are ready for this responsibility." Before he could say anymore, Jillian practically leaps into his arms.

"Boss, you have no idea how happy you have made me right now. I've dreamed of being part of this business since I came here to work. You and I connect, which is rare between a boss and employee. Thank you so much for having the confidence in me to extend this offer."

Smiling at her, he replies, "Well, I believe we are all in this together, and to be successful, we need to work together, not you work for me. So, this just makes it official. I will get the paperwork drawn up this week, so you can go over all the details." Jillian, with tears in her eyes, puts her arms around him and hugs him tightly.

"We will be the best place in a hundred-mile radius to stop, have a drink, and eat great food among nice and friendly people." Looking around at their tavern, Brett sees the bar beginning to fill up again.

"It seems by the amount of people who are coming in we are going to be able to start executing our plan tonight—the best place to come and relax with good friends and make new ones." Jillian goes off to start working the bar, and Brett heads to the package goods side to make sure everyone is taken care of as well. Working hard during the next couple of hours, Jillian and Brett managed to handle the crowd until there was only a small group of people hanging over by the jukebox. There was some ordering he needed to do before they closed, so Brett tells Jillian if she needed him, he would be in the office.

Brett heads back to his office, closes the door, and sits down. Working up the order took longer than he thought it would, so by the time he was finished, Jillian was cashing out and closing things up. Wondering where Morgan was at this moment, he makes a mental note, *tomorrow I will go and see her.*

Jillian sticks her head in and inquires, "Hey are you almost done because I am going to head out if that's ok?"

"Really Jillian? Remember, you aren't going to be asking permission from me anymore." With a broad smile, Jillian tilts an imaginary hat and says goodnight. Working just a few more minutes, Brett decides it is time to leave as well. Anything left can always be done tomorrow. Standing and shutting all the lights off, he locks up and heads out. Driving home, he decides to take a detour and drive by Morgan's house.

Morgan & Heidi

Shadows were getting long and realizing several hours had passed, I looked around the shop at all of the nooks and crannies knowing there is still more time needed in here. Dad must have known how important this information would be eventually because it appears he really chose a unique place to put it. Obviously, somewhere I hadn't found yet, and after all day rummaging in here, I know a shower is in my future. Cobwebs and the smell of decay cling to me making me feel slightly ill. The notebooks he wrote everything down in about the farm were always kept in the container given to him by his father—except now, that container is sitting in a cabinet in the bathroom of Brett's mother, Elizabeth Callahan.

Elizabeth's husband, Jack Callahan, who befriended my dad, became a constant visitor to the farm. Thinking back, I remember the anxiety and worry wreaking havoc on my mother's face when she realized Jack was cultivating his relationship with dad for nefarious reasons. It became clearer something deceitful was going on when Charlie, Jack's army buddy, showed up. I can almost hear my dad's voice when he was telling us Charlie was a sniper in the army. My parents were very patriotic, and anyone who served in our military was elevated in their view.

Thinking back on that time, I realize this admiration may have led to their unsuspecting view of both Jack and Charlie. Jack, especially, asked way too many questions about Dad's methods of detecting the electromagnetic fields, constantly wanting proof of what

Dad was collecting concerning the illnesses and deaths of people who lived near the towers. Hearing my cellphone ring, I come back to the present.

Seeing it's Heidi calling me, I answer, "Hey, were you wondering if I went missing or have you been sleeping?"

Sounding as though she was stifling her laugh, she answers "Is it that obvious, Mom? You know me too well because I just laid my head back for a few minutes and next thing I knew, several hours had passed. I panicked because I was sure you had been trying to call me to pick you up."

Walking outside the shop to stand in the waning light of the day admiring the beautiful sunset forming toward the west, I tell her, "Heidi, I lost track of time, so no worries. If you are ready come and pick me up, we will grab a bite to eat at the diner on the way home. I'm suddenly starving, and I have a hunch Susie Mitchell has some kind of great special tonight on the menu."

"Ok, I'll be right out to get you, but I'm ashamed to ask. How do I get there again?"

"Oh my, I never thought about it. Ok, come out of the driveway and make a left. When you get to the stop sign, turn right, and follow that road all the way down until you come to a four-way stop. Turn left and make a quick right, follow this road until you come to a stop street. You will see the farm up on the left as you come through the stop street. Better yet, Heidi, I will text you the address, and then you can just bring it up on your phone."

"Mom, perfect because the directions you just told me, well, I would have gotten lost on the first turn."

Amused, I tell her, "I get it, unfamiliar terrain for sure. Just pull into the farmyard. Uncle Jonathan and Aunt Sara had a big day, so I don't want to bother them. I stayed here a long time, but Uncle Jonathan went in a while ago." Hearing Heidi shut her car door and then her smile showing through her voice, I smile too.

"Mom, I think it is so cool I am picking you up from your brother's, my uncle. Nothing has surprised me more in my life than hearing about my mother's family in the East."

Understanding there might be some unease in this comment, I respond, "Heidi, I know it's a lot to take in, but I hope you understand there was never a moment during your life where it wasn't up front and present in my mind."

"It's ok, Mom. Listen, we can talk more about all of this at dinner. I need to pay attention to my GPS, or you are going to be walking to the diner."

Laughing, I reply, "Ok, I'll be waiting." Walking back into the shop, I look around. Somewhere in here there must be evidence of the electric company's neglect of their killing machines. Dad knew in his soul there was stray current contaminating water, and in turn, hurting people and animals. In my heart, I knew nothing would deter him from his mission to help our community. He was a healthy man—robust, energetic, and dedicated to his mission of helping out his fellow man, and I'm sure his death was not from natural causes. Dying in a field for no apparent reason was just too hard to accept.

I might have accepted it when it happened because my mind wasn't ready, but now it is screaming at me to find the truth.

Jonathan's memory of that time is dim because the guilt he has harbored keeps him from remembering any details of the day Dad died. Now, however, with all the changes being made to the farm and with the outlook for the future much brighter, maybe his guilt will wane. Then those repressed memories will come to the surface, and I will be there to hear all the events of that fateful day.

Suddenly, I see headlights pull into the yard. With a sigh of relief, I see Heidi has made it to pick me up. Walking out of the shop, I automatically move to shut the door and then realize there is no door. Oh well, tomorrow is a new day, and I am coming back to look some more before this building is demolished. Waving to Heidi, I walk to the car and get in.

"Hey, I guess you made it here ok. Do you still want to hit the western stores in the area because I believe they are still open."

Heidi looks over at me, "Does a leopard have spots? Of course, I do!"

Whitney & Nick

The light was starting to fade, so Nick hauled the boys inside, much to their chagrin.

"Come on you two, we can't keep playing. It's getting too dark to see. Put the football back in the garage, and make sure you take your shoes off before coming in. I'm sure they are packed with mud and grass, and I don't want your mom to get mad. She just mopped the kitchen floors this morning." Moaning and groaning, they walk to the garage and do what he asked. Stepping inside the kitchen, Nick sees Whitney standing in front of the refrigerator with a perplexed look on her face.

"Hey, what's the matter?" Shaking her head in disgust, she says, "I keep looking in here thinking something is going to jump out and say, 'Cook me for dinner,' except so far that has not happened."

With a chuckle, he walks over to her and suggests, "Hey, the boys can have peanut butter and jelly sandwiches with chips. They don't care, especially if we tell them they can eat and watch TV in the family room. Why don't we head over to the diner and get something? Maybe Susie has some tasty pie we can have for dessert. What do you say, do you want to go?" Hesitating for just a moment, Whitney looks up and smiles.

"Sure, can you get the boys what they need while I go clean up a little?" Giving her a small hug, he agrees. When Whitney left the kitchen, Nick calls the boys to come and get their sandwiches. Once he gets them settled in the family room, he walks back to his bedroom. Pushing open the door, he smiles. Whitney was sitting at her makeup table, which she hadn't used for a long time, fixing her hair.

Looking at her reflection, Whitney see the lines around her mouth and the frown lines on her forehead. Tracing her finger over the lines, she knows each of them is filled with stories of love, deceit, happiness, anxiety, but most of all guilt. Whitney's best friend, and really her only friend, had her life destroyed because of Whitney's own actions. Shaking off the memories, she dabs a little lip gloss on her lips. It is time for it all to end.

Seeing Nick at the door, she turns off the light of her mirror and stands up smiling when Nick says, "Well don't you look nice? I guess I better get cleaned up, so I don't look like a bum."

Whitney laughs and assures him, "Listen, no matter what you did, it would be fine with me. I'm just trying to do something with my hair. I can't use any of the makeup because it's so out of date." Nick walks over and puts his hands on her shoulders.

"Hey, you look great. Let's just go out and have a nice time together." He was going to say, *for once* but thought better of it. "I'm going to check on the boys and start the car. We'll take your car if that's ok?" Nodding yes, Whitney continues touching her curls making sure they don't look too wild.

"I'll be ready in a couple of minutes." Nick goes out and makes sure the boys aren't jumping on the couch or having a food fight. Once everything is good, he yells to Whitney they could leave.

Standing in their kitchen, he waits for his wife. Whitney comes into the kitchen messing with the buttons on her jacket and keeps her head down. Walking over to her, he tips her head up and looks at her.

"Hey, stop fussing. You look great! Let's go!"

Morgan & Heidi

Driving back into town, Heidi and I talk about the plans to use the farm as a vineyard.

"Did you and Sara talk to Uncle Jonathan yet? He seems just a trifle uptight."

"Boy, it didn't take you too long to figure out your Uncle Jonathan. He is getting better, but the past hasn't been too kind to him, so it's taking him a bit to get back to his old self. He will come around, I'm sure of it. Tell me, what did you do after you left the farm?"

Bursting into laughter, Heidi responds, "Well, I went back and raided the refrigerator, which by the way we need to do some grocery shopping. You hardly have anything worthwhile to eat. Then, I caught up on my shows which are on-demand, and then you know the rest. I fell asleep until you called me. It's so quiet and comfortable in your new home. I like it."

Relieved, I ask her, "Anybody stop by or call while I was gone?"

Keeping her eyes on the road, she says, "No, but there was some guy visiting Seth and Olivia. Actually, I think he might be staying with them. I saw Seth helping him bring in some suitcases. They must have some family who came to stay with them. Hopefully, this will bring Olivia some peace after what you told me happened to her granddaughter. Any relief from her grief would be a good thing, don't you think?" Listening to Heidi, I wonder who was visiting Seth and Olivia. Trying not to seem too interested, I asked Heidi if she saw the visitor.

"I did, but just for a moment. He was walking behind Seth with a big briefcase and another office type box under his arm. I don't think it was a relation." Without warning, my stomach does a back-flip. Knowing how perceptive my daughter is when I seem uninterested, I keep the tone of my voice even.

"What would make you say that?"

Heidi hesitates a moment before saying defensively, "Mom, he didn't look like family, ok?"

Exasperated, I try another question, "Well, what did he look like then?"

Turning to look at me briefly, she says, "I'm pretty sure he was a person of color." Holding my breath for what seemed an interminable time, I then exhaled.

"It's Jackson. He must be in town." Stopping at the first western store, which wasn't too far from the diner, we browsed around the store. Heidi finds a cute pair of boots she wanted, and I tell her it would be cute if she wears them while she was here. It didn't take much to convince her, and we walked out of the store with a brand-new pair of boots. Leaving the store to head to the diner, Heidi turns to me.

"Who is Jackson, Mom?"

Frowning slightly, I laugh quietly and answer, "Jackson is Seth's brother. Before you say anything, he's adopted. They are very close in age, and in reality, they were more like brothers than some I know who actually share the same blood." Expressing herself was never Heidi's weakness, so I knew something was coming.

"So, are they still close now? Because from what I could see, they sure looked like they are cool with each other." Trying not to sound too knowledgeable, I shrug my shoulders.

"Really, Heidi, I don't know. Jackson wasn't around here much after he went to college. We actually attended the same college, but he was finishing up when I was getting ready to start. I honestly don't know what became of him after college. He came home the summer he graduated for a few weeks, and then left for an internship at a law firm in New York. Funny, I haven't thought about him in years." We were turning into our driveway, and Heidi stopped the car and turned to look at me.

"Mom, something tells me there is more to the story of Jackson. You seemed uninterested, and then proceed to tell me all about him." Nervously laughing, I try to make a joke of it.

"Heidi, I really don't know what he has been doing for the last twenty years, but there might have been some hanging out when we were younger."

Lightly punching my arm, Heidi says, "Now we are getting somewhere. So, you do know him."

We both got out of the car, and looking over the top, I say, "Yes, I do. We spent some time together in the summer before I went to college. I'm ashamed to say I don't know what he has been doing for many years, but he was a lifesaver for me during a really rough time in my life."

As we walk up to the house, Heidi smiles and says, "Well, tomorrow we will have to wander over to Seth and Olivia's, so you can catch up with your old friend." With a sideways glance, I see a devilish look on her face and realize she is being just a little sarcastic. After unlocking the front door and laying my keys down, I turn to check to see if there are any messages on the phone. Seeing the light was blinking, I realized it might be Brett who called.

Not wanting to listen to the machine while Heidi was in the room, I say, "Hey, are we still going to head down to the diner? Because I would like to get a quick shower."

Heidi runs up the steps and shouts over her shoulder, "Not before I use the bathroom. I won't take long, I promise. By the look of my hair in the car mirror, it needs a little help since I appear to have destroyed it while I was napping earlier." As soon as I hear the bathroom door shut, I go to the counter where my pen is sitting on my notepad.

Listening to the messages, I hear Tom Fraser's voice, Misty, Tom Fraser. *I've been leaving messages for Jonathan and haven't heard back. If you have a chance, I would appreciate a call back. I would like to talk with you about the sale agreement. I can be reached on 823-BANK. I look forward to hearing from you.* Another beep sounds and then, *Morgan, Seth and I were wondering if Heidi and you could stop over later? I stopped over earlier, but I saw you were gone. Call me when you get home. See ya.*

I hung up the phone and sat back for a moment. Tom must be getting impatient which is fine with me. He can wait. Maybe waiting and wondering about the outcome of the sale will make him more agreeable. I dial Olivia's number and listen to the rings. On the third ring, I hear Olivia's pleasant voice.

"Hey, Olivia, it's Morgan. You called?"

"I did. What have you been doing for the last few days? Seth and I hoped you would have time to stop over." Knowing my next words were going to send her into a tailspin, which would create a barrage of questions, I take a deep breath.

"Heidi and I went out to Jonathan and Sara's the other day and spent some time there." Waiting for her response, I heard the upstairs toilet flush and the shower start.

"You did what? Oh my, how did that go over with everyone? Jonathan was shocked, I'm sure. But how did Heidi take it?"

Smiling, and hoping my smile showed in my voice, I say, "Olivia, fine, yes and ok then better after a little while. Those words sum it up in a nutshell. Time will tell with Heidi. She is very strong-minded, and I don't want to rush her into accepting a family she's just met."

Olivia laughs out loud and says, "Are you kidding me, Morgan? I'm sure Jonathan is head over heels in love with his niece, and Sara must be ecstatic for all of you. Morgan, your family is all together finally. It must have been wonderful seeing the two of them meeting Heidi for the first time."

Smiling in memory, I say, "It was fantastic listening to the two of them talking and Jonathan looking at me with such love in his eyes. Olivia, Heidi and I are going to the diner to eat some dinner. How about tomorrow afternoon, we head over and visit. Seth and you can get to know Heidi. She told me you had a visitor come today."

Gleefully, Olivia responds, "Oh yes, Jackson has arrived, and I finally feel like entertaining again."

"Oh boy, Jackson, well we will be over. We will see you all tomorrow. Bye."

Heidi comes into the kitchen asking, "Hey, were you on the phone?"

"Yes, I called Olivia. She left a message to call when we got home. We are going to visit them tomorrow afternoon if that's ok with you?"

Smiling and giving me a small hug, she responds, "Of course it is, Mom. I want to get to know everyone here."

"Well, we will start tonight by going to the diner. I'm sure there will be someone there we can talk to. Are you ready to go?"

Looking closely at me, Heidi says, "No offense Mom, but are you going in those clothes? You have cobwebs and dirt all over you." Glancing down, I have to laugh.

"No, I think I better get a quick shower. Besides cobwebs, who knows what else might be in my hair. I'll be quick." With that, I run upstairs and get a quick shower.

Standing in front of the mirror, I look closely at myself. The years of running from one assignment to another had kept me in shape. Over the last few weeks, there hasn't been much exercising. But now my partner is here, so I'm sure we will be walking, running, or doing something active. Putting some mascara and eyeliner on with a dash of lipstick, I am ready.

As I am running down the steps, I yell, "Heidi, grab my purse and keys. I'm ready to go."

Heidi comes from the kitchen saying, "I left the light on over the oven. Wow, Mom, you look so pretty. What kind of magic did you create in fifteen minutes?" Laughing hard, I lightly punched her in the arm.

"Hey, thanks a lot. It's called taking a shower and washing one's hair. It's amazing how easy it is to get ready these days. Not too much time spent on dressing up and applying minimal makeup has made life very easy."

Grinning at me, Heidi replies, "Well it works for you, so are ready to take on the diner?" On the way, we talk about what food we are going to make to take over to Seth and Olivia's tomorrow. Heidi asks if my friend she met at the house is going to be there.

"You mean my friend, Brett? No, I doubt it. He's been very busy at the tavern. I'll have to take you there now that you are the big twenty-one."

"Well, Mom, I am going to hold you to it. Maybe we can have Uncle Jonathan and Aunt Sara meet us there some night. That would be cool, right?"

Swinging into a parking spot, I look over at my daughter and agree, "It sure would be."

Whitney & Nick

Pulling into the diner parking lot, Nick scans the lot to see how busy the diner might be.

"Whitney, it looks like we may be in luck. It doesn't look like they are very busy tonight. Probably because it's early in the week, and their busiest time is Thursday through Sunday." Nick is hoping Susie is working tonight. He wants to make sure there is nothing upsetting for Whitney. Walking into the diner together even seems odd. He realizes now there wasn't a time he could remember eating there with his wife. The diner had become his refuge from all his problems. No one judged anyone here. Everyone comes to enjoy friendship and acceptance which is always plentiful.

"It looks like we are going to have our choice of seating due to the lack of cars here in the parking lot," says Whitney. Stepping out of the car, they walk in together to find a table. Nick looks around to see who is dining there tonight.

"Whitney, I hope Susie is our server, there has been a new girl handling the late shift. We might be in luck, though, because I'm pretty sure I saw Susie's truck in the back."

Touching her curls to make sure they aren't having a field day, she puts on her best smile and says, "Nick, no worries, I'm just happy we are out having dinner together. Oh, look, Susie is coming out of the kitchen, so I'm sure we will have her wait on us. There really aren't too many people here tonight." Nick looks out the front window and swallows hard. Morgan's car is pulling into the parking lot. Nothing has prepared him for a confrontation with Morgan and Whitney. Feeling sick to his stomach, he begins sweating, and his hands start trembling. Whitney is looking at him in concern.

"Nick, are you alright? What is wrong with you? Your hands are shaking."

"Nothing. My hands have been hurting lately. It must be arthritis. Please don't worry about it. I'm so happy we are out together tonight."

Grabbing Nick's hand, Whitney squeezes it and comforts him, "Let's go and see what is on the special board. It doesn't really matter if Susie doesn't wait on us. It's a remarkable feeling for me to be here with you."

Looking at the menu board, Nick does his best to relax knowing Misty is going to be coming in. There is no reason to be getting anxious. He thought *Whitney and I are in a good place right now, and Misty is part of our past.* Hearing the door close, Whitney looks up from her menu and frowns. Misty and a young woman are walking through the door.

"Nick, I really hope you didn't know anything about this."

"About what?" She nods toward the door, and he turns and looks full well knowing what he is going to see. In a split second, he makes a decision. "Whitney, I would never intentionally put you in an uncomfortable position, but since she is here, we are going to be very civil, ok? There is no need for us to continue to avoid seeing her because I'm pretty sure Misty is here to stay. And by the way, she goes by Morgan now."

"Nick, I'm fully aware of the new person she is trying to be, however, we both know Misty is still inside the disguise she's wearing."

Morgan & Heidi

Heidi and I walk into the diner, and out of habit, I scan the room and my eyes come to rest on Nick and Whitney.

Under my breath, I say, "Great, just who I want to see right now."

Heidi turns to look at me asking, "Mom, did you say something?" Shaking my head, I steered her to a booth as far away from Whitney and Nick as possible. Sitting down, I try to keep myself calm. Then I realize Heidi has no idea who these two people are, so it really doesn't make any difference if they are here. Susie comes out of the kitchen and scans the diner for any new customers.

"Oh my, I hope all of you haven't been waiting too long."

Walking over to Heidi and me, she smiles broadly saying, "Hey, Morgan, I haven't seen you for a few days. I guess you have been busy setting up your new home. It's great you have decided to stay here in Millersville."

"Susie, it's great to see you again. You're right, I have been busy lately. I would like to introduce you to my daughter, Heidi."

With a shocked expression, Susie says, "You have a daughter? I didn't realize you were married. Oh my, how rude of me. It's very nice to meet you, Heidi."

Looking up at Susie, Heidi smiles and says, "It's nice to meet you too, Susie. I guess you have been feeding my mom for a few weeks now."

"Yes, I have been, and it's been great getting to know her. You resemble your mother a lot, but I guess you hear that often, don't you?"

Reaching across the table, Heidi grabs my hands and tells me, "Only about a thousand times, but I'm very proud to look like her. She is my hero." My eyes tear up, and I squeeze her hands. Looking at Susie, she is wiping her eyes with her apron.

"Oh my, what a moment. It looks like it's going to be a busy night. How about I bring you some drinks? Morgan, the normal unsweetened iced tea?"

"Unsweetened iced tea for both of us will be fine," I say smiling. She walks away to take care of the other customers in the diner.

Once she walked away, Heidi lets go of my hands and with a determined look she inquires, "Mom, are you planning on staying here permanently? You never said you were thinking about staying. Well?"

Struggling with how to tell her, I looked around the diner. Seeing Whitney and Nick sitting there makes me realize I need to stay here for a while. There are old wounds which have resurfaced and need to be finished with for all our sakes—none of which can be done quickly. What Heidi doesn't know is that I've taken a leave of absence from my job, and there is a very good chance I am going to be staying in Millersville indefinitely.

"Heidi, I feel like I have a commitment here. Uncle Jonathan and Aunt Sara are going to need me for some time, so that means being here is important. I know you want us to go back to Linn Creek, and I understand why. But now that you have been introduced to Millersville, can you see yourself staying here, at least for a while?"

"Mom, I don't know! Work is giving me three weeks off, and then I must go back or be demoted. I'm on the way up, so this is not an option. So, it seems I will have to make a decision in the next few days. If I could get a job here with Wawa, then I would consider it. I was told by a couple people at work that Sheetz and Wawa are very similar. So, with all my experience with Sheetz, I should be able to get a job here with Wawa."

Heidi studies my face and must see something she doesn't like because she continues, "Please don't be upset with me. You know our home is Linn Creek, and I don't know if I want to leave, even if it means you won't be there with me." Sitting quietly for a second, I absorb her words.

"I understand. Let's enjoy the time you are here and leave the future up for discussion for later. You still have several days off before Sheetz wants you back to work right?"

Nodding, she confirms "Yes, and I have some PTO available to use if I want to stay for another week. So, we don't have to talk about this now. I understand how important it is for you to stay."

Susie arrives with our drinks, and we order our dinner. One of the specials was enticing to both of us—Chicken Parmesan with spaghetti and ice cream for dessert. I watch Susie as she goes over to Nick and Whitney to take their order.

Heidi, noticing the direction I was looking in, asks, "Do you know those two people? I think the guy was here at the diner the day I arrived." The next words out of my mouth need to be carefully scripted because I am not ready to expose everything about my past, yet I know it can't wait much longer.

"He's from a local family who has lived here for a long time. That is his wife with him, and she has also been here most of her life." I could see Heidi looking over toward them, and I prepared myself for whatever my intuitive daughter was going to say.

"So, you know them, right?"

Taking a deep breath, I say, "Yes, I do. We all went to high school together."

Staring at me intently, Heidi asks, "Do they know you are back?"

Laughing a little too loud, I say, "Probably! Let's go over and say hello."

Pulling away from me, Heidi nervously laughs telling me, "Mom, I don't want to go over there to meet them. Why don't you go over there and say hi? You are the one they know, not me. Go ahead!" Feeling relief in my stomach that Heidi doesn't want to deal with meeting Nick and Whitney makes it just a little easier to get up and walk over to them.

As I begin to make my way across the diner, Susie approaches their table and I hear her begin, "Hey, it's nice to see the two of you out tonight. There are several specials on the board if you want me to go over them."

Smiling at Susie, Whitney responds, "Thank you Susie, we are happy to be here. It's been some time since we have been here for dinner. I know Nick comes here for lunch quite a bit." I notice Susie casting a quick glance at Nick, probably deciding if she should comment on just how often Nick is at the diner. She quickly takes their orders and heads to the kitchen.

Whitney is distracted, looking out the window at the traffic going by. Nick has his head down looking at his phone. Neither one of them sees me coming. Standing at the edge of their table, I clear my throat. Whitney turns and sees me with a look of complete surprise. Nick jerks his head up and quickly looks at me, and then at Whitney. It appears we are both waiting for Whitney's reaction. Somehow, this connection between Nick and I made me feel very uncomfortable. It is as though we were both standing on a precipice looking down and deciding which one of us should jump. I realize I am holding my breath.

Whitney hesitates for just a moment and then says, "Hello, Morgan. It's nice to see you again."

Smiling slightly, I agree, "It's nice to see both of you as well. There's nothing like comfort food at the diner."

Suddenly Nick regained his voice, "Definitely. We were in the mood for one of the great specials Susie always has here during the week. Are you eating here by yourself?" Whitney raises her eyebrows at her husband. I shoot him a look that says, *it is none of your business*, but still decide it is best to face it head on.

"No, actually I'm here with my daughter, Heidi. She is here visiting for a few weeks." Whitney suddenly choked on her iced tea.

After she was able to talk again, she says, "Oh my, my tea must have gone down the wrong pipe. Sorry!"

I smile and assure her, "It's ok. Don't you remember when we would go to the diner after school or after cheerleading practice and get french-fries with brown gravy and cherry 7-ups. We would be laughing so hard at each other the soda would sting our noses." Whitney laughs loudly. For a minute, we are taken back to our youth, and then the moment is lost. "Well, I better get back to my table. Heidi will be wanting to order our food."

Whitney nods and Nick says, "Well, Morgan it was nice seeing you again. If you are still here when we are finished, we'll stop by your table. We would like to meet your daughter, wouldn't we Whitney?" Keeping her expression as neutral as possible, Whitney agrees. Walking back to our table, I realize I am experiencing a calmness which surprises me, but the feeling is a good one.

Heidi has an exasperated look on her face, so I ask, "Were you getting impatient my dear?"

"Uh yeah, I'm starved."

Taking a sip of her water, she asks, "Were you friends with them then?"

Understanding Heidi's desire to know more about my life here, I cautiously say, "Yes, we were. Whitney grew up down the street from me, and Nick lived in town." Trying to see them, Heidi stands up halfway looking through the barrier that separates all the booths.

"Well, I'm not sure what you said to each other, but Whitney looks upset. Have you seen them since you've been back here, Mom?"

Knowing Heidi isn't going to take a nonchalant answer from me, I say, "Nick is good friends with Seth and Tom at the bank, so I've run into him several times during the last few weeks. Whitney stopped over and saw me a few days before you arrived." Susie arrives to take our order.

As we are finishing up the ordering, Heidi looks at me again and says, "How many other people are still living here that you knew before?"

Trying to keep her isolated from the drama surrounding my leaving here and not wanting to get into the past too much with her, I smile and say, "Most of the people I went to high school with have moved to other areas. Some people are still here, like Nick and Whitney and Susie. She went to the same school as I did, but she was younger."

Realizing too late my mistake, Heidi says, "That's weird because when we came in, she acted like she hadn't known you for very long."

"Well, you said to yourself how much I've changed. Apparently, she's just forgotten. Like I said, she was an underclassman, and I was only going to school half days my senior year." Before anything else can be said, our dinner arrives. We eat in silence because the food is good.

Heidi, between mouthfuls, says, "This is some of the best food I've eaten. We are going to come here every day to eat while I'm here. Did you see the pies displayed behind the counter?"

Breathing a sigh of relief, I laugh and tell her, "Your love of food continues to amaze me when you are so thin. If you still have room, we'll have Susie tell us about the desserts." The rest of their dinner continued in a mutual appreciation of the food they were eating.

Whitney & Nick

Nick was finishing up his steak sandwich and noticed Whitney had hardly touched her food.

"Whitney, what's the matter? You haven't eaten much of your dinner. Don't tell me you are upset because Morgan stopped at our table." Noticing the gray around Nick's temples and the lines at the corner of his eyes, she remembers again how much she loves him and how the years of turmoil and guilt had aged him. Seeing Nick and Morgan near each other again made her realize the quiet communication between the two. She truly believes they don't even know it is happening, it is so subtle.

"No, Nick. My stomach seemed to get upset after I choked on my iced tea. My acid reflux is acting up and having a meatball sandwich is definitely not what I should be eating. Morgan didn't upset me. She did make me remember the good times we had together when we were kids though. Did you know she had a daughter?"

Frowning at Whitney, Nick forces out an answer, "Now how would I know if she had a daughter? She has always been by herself or with Brett Compton. Sometimes she hangs out with Seth and Olivia, but then you know how everyone is their friend."

Smirking at Nick, she agrees, "Yes that's true, although I don't think they would call me one of their friends. Of course, they know Morgan or Misty, she is their neighbor, isn't she?"

Getting his wallet out to pay the bill, Nick looks up at Whitney and says with irritation, "How do you know where she lives?"

Figuring it doesn't matter now, she says, "I went there to talk to her. You knew about it because she told you."

Counting out the money and calculating the tip, he mumbles under his breath, "Whatever Whitney."

"Listen Nick, tonight was really nice, and I don't want to ruin it by being my old self. So, if you want to stop by Morgan's table we can." Nodding, Nick figures up the tip, and then they get up to walk over to where Morgan and her daughter are sitting.

Morgan

Finishing up what looked like her last bite of her dinner, Heidi takes a deep breath and says, "Oh my, Mom this was so good. Was this diner here when you lived here before? Because they have it down, the food is so good. It doesn't seem like diner food." A feeling of nostalgia comes over me for all of the great things about Millersville, and what strikes me more than anything is the families of this community. More than ever, I realize it is my mission to clear my family's name and make their property successful again no matter what it takes. Hearing footsteps, I look and see Whitney and Nick walking up to our table.

Nick speaks first, "So how was your dinner?" Looking at Heidi's plate, he goes on, "It sure looks as though you enjoyed your dinner. The food is good here, isn't it?"

Heidi smiles, points, and says through her laugh, "Yeah, I told Susie I need a box."

Laughing, Nick says, "Nice, it's great to see the diner busy again." With just a slight bow, he puts his hand out and says, "Hi, I'm Nick, and you are, Heidi?"

Heidi responds with her own hand out, "Yes I am, this must be your wife, Whitney." Whitney makes eye contact with me, and then shifts her attention to Heidi.

"It is very nice to meet you, Heidi." I sit back and watch the three of them interact.

Nick continues, "Heidi, what do you think of our town, Millersville? Your mom, Whitney, and I spent our childhoods in this town." Heidi glances at me, and I shake my head slightly letting her know everything was ok. She sometimes needs reassurance from me when situations are uneasy. This was one of those times.

"My mom grew up here with all of you, except for some reason, she never came back after college. I can't imagine not coming back to all my friends in Linn Creek."

Whitney coughs, and Nick responds, "Some of us wanted to move on to other cities and your mom always wanted to see the world. Whitney and I decided to stay here and raise our family."

Heidi looks over at me, and I can practically see the words crossing through her brain, *Mom, why do I feel like he is talking to you and not me?* Whitney grabs Nick's arm, and I can feel her anxiety as she tries to move him along.

"Nick, it's so nice you and Whitney were able to meet Heidi. She is my pride and joy."

Whitney puts her hand on my shoulder and says with a smile, "It was great to meet your daughter." Then looking at Heidi, she adds, "You are very beautiful. Your smile seems to brighten the room." Heidi, in her charming way, stands up and hugs Whitney.

"Thank you so much for saying that and taking time to stop and meet me. I love that the three of you were friends, and its so cool Mom is back in Millersville." We all say our goodbyes, and Nick and Whitney leave the diner. Trying to get my bearings after the last few minutes, I look over at Heidi.

"Are you ready to go? It's not too late, why don't we stop and see Seth and Olivia?" Susie is walking up to our table before Heidi has a chance to respond.

"How was everything?"

Heidi grabs her hand and says with great enthusiasm, "Susie, it was so good. I told Mom we need to eat here every night it was so good. Except this time, Mom and I will have to take a raincheck on dessert."

Gathering up our dirty dishes, she laughs, "You and a lot of other people have rainchecks. It's called your eyes are bigger than your stomach." The diner was starting to get busier, so Susie tells us she will be back with our check soon. Heidi stands up and says she needs to go to the restroom. After she left, I put my head in my hands. It is all I can do to keep myself together after watching the three of them having their conversation. I really need to figure out how I am going to navigate my past here in Millersville with Heidi.

Getting into the car, I turn to Heidi and ask, "Hey do you feel like going right home? I thought we would stop by the tavern and have an after-dinner drink. What do you think?" Heidi smiles.

"Mom, of course. I've heard you, Seth, and Olivia talk so much about the tavern. It would be great to stop there."

Wondering if Brett was going to be there, I decided it would be a great time for Heidi to experience the community feeling of the tavern. Parking close to the door, we stepped into the bar. As usual, the jukebox is playing some rock and roll song and the TVs are silent with pro football games playing. Finding stools, I look around and see Jillian on the other side working the bar. I yell out her name, and she turns with a big smile. Walking over to us, she banters with each of the customers as she passes by.

"Hey, Morgan. How are you?" Looking at Heidi, she motions with her head. "Who do you have with you?"

Putting my arm around Heidi, I say, "Jillian, I want you to meet my daughter, Heidi. Heidi, this is Jillian, Brett's right-hand person, and I heard recently a new partner." Smiling from ear to ear, Jillian went on to tell us all her ideas and how happy she was with her new role at the tavern. Heidi and I had a beer, talked to a couple customers, and then got up to head home.

"Mom, that was so cool having a beer with you. Jillian seems like a nice person, so I hope it works out for her."

Grabbing her hand across the seat, I tell her, "Don't worry, I'm sure she will make out just fine. She is very dedicated to her job, and word on the street is, she has a great boss."

Morgan & Jackson

Driving back home, I turn to look at Heidi and ask her, "Did you enjoy your dinner tonight? It sure looked as though you did by the clean plate you gave back to Susie." Laughing, Heidi rubs her stomach.

"Like I said earlier, we could eat there every night if it was up to me. The food at the diner," she pauses and puts her hands across her heart, "is divine!" Laughing together, we pulled into our driveway and park.

Sitting in the car for a moment, I turn to Heidi and tell her, "I'm going to call Olivia and see if they are around, and if so, we will walk over there. If you need to freshen up, you can have the bathroom first. All I need to do is check my hair and retouch my lipstick." Heidi hesitates to get out of the car.

"Mom, Nick and Whitney were more to you than all of you said, weren't they?"

Not wanting this to be the time I share my past with her, I explain, "Heidi, sometimes you are so perceptive when it comes to me. You are right, there is so much history between the three of us. Some good, yet there were times we struggled to stay friends. Believe me when I say, Whitney, Nick, and I have so much history together, and the outcome wasn't exactly what we all wanted."

Touching my hand, Heidi smiles and offers, "Mom, my only regret is you didn't feel confident enough to tell me about your life here. Now I'm here with you, and my desire to know everything about your past is practically bursting from my soul. Like you have always said, 'Time heals all wounds,' and I truly believe whatever happened to you here when you were young will be fixed before you leave here. That is if you leave here." Hugging her tightly, I find I don't have the voice to respond.

Instead, as we get out of the car, I quietly say to her to head up and get ready to head over to Seth and Olivia's. Grabbing my phone, I called Olivia's cellphone. After a few rings, she answers.

"Hey Morgan, what's going on? How was the diner?"

"It was great, and Heidi just loved the food. She wants to eat there every night but of course, I told her I would cook. So, what are you and Seth doing? Heidi and I were thinking about walking over."

There was some dead space on the phone, and then Olivia came back on the phone saying, "Sorry about that, I was checking with Seth. Please stop over, we have so much to talk to you about." I am distracted for a moment because Heidi begins tapping me on the shoulder pointing to her hair wanting me to ok it, I guess.

Nodding at Heidi, I get back to the conversation and say, "Olivia, what did you say?"

"Just come over."

Hanging up the call, I turn to Heidi assuring her, "Yes, your hair looks fine. Let's go. Olivia seems excited for us to stop over."

"Mom, did I take up too much time in the bathroom? You didn't get a chance to freshen up." Looking at myself in the hallway mirror,

I realize my makeup is intact and remind myself that we are just going over to Seth and Olivia. Who else was going to be there but the five of us?

"Let's go, Olivia is probably waiting at the door." Going in the back door, we find Olivia in the kitchen making some dip.

"Hey, what are you doing? Don't do anything special for us, we aren't going to be here too long. We have had a long day out at the farm and just finished dinner." Turning around, she realizes Heidi is standing beside me.

"Heidi, how are you? How has your visit been so far? It's a lot to take in right now, huh?" Heidi, being the people person that she is, goes up to Olivia and puts her arm across her shoulders.

"It's been different to say the least, but Millersville is growing on me, and it's all because of my new-found family and people like you and Seth. So, when are the drinks being served? You know I just turned twenty-one, right?" Olivia and I laugh out loud.

"Well, let's get Seth. He is the bartender. Right, Olivia?"

Grabbing my hand, Olivia assures, "Why don't you find Seth and see what he is up to. Then, Heidi and I can get to know each other."

I decided the best way to navigate Seth and Olivia's house is to go outside and go in the front door. Their house is so broken up with the rooms being uniquely staged throughout their space, so it is always easier to navigate it from the front. As I walk up on the front porch, I detect a slight smell of cigarette smoke, but looking around I don't see anyone.

Just as I'm getting ready to walk in the door, I hear, "Well, who do we have here?" I look around and can't see anyone as the sun had already set a while ago.

"Just Morgan, Seth and Olivia's neighbor." Suddenly remembering Jackson was visiting, I laugh and say, "Ok, Jackson, you can come out now. Scaring your brother's new neighbor probably wouldn't sit well with him." Standing up from the wicker chair, which was at the end of the porch, he turns to walk toward me.

"So, you must be Morgan. Olivia and Seth have told me a lot about you." Sticking out his hand, he grabs mine and pulls me to him as if to hug me. "It's very nice to meet you, Morgan." Suddenly letting me go, I lose my balance and stumble back hitting the flower stand which had a beautiful fern displayed. Catching my balance, I stand and find his face within inches of mine—so close that the menthol fragrance of his breath is mingling with my own.

"Well Jackson, that was a hell of a hello. You could have just left it at the hug, and maybe I wouldn't have a throbbing pain in the back of my leg. By the looks of Olivia's fern, we might have some explaining to do." Jackson was stunned. He was holding onto me, and I could feel his arms tightening. For a moment, I feared his mind brought back some of the same memories I had tucked in my mind and refused to surface except during the night in my dreams. Reading the confused look in Jackson's eyes, I hurriedly say, "I am trying to find Seth, do you know where he is?"

Regaining his composure, Jackson responds, "Seth is upstairs getting a shower. We can head to the kitchen where Olivia is. He should be down shortly."

Moving through the house, I answer, "The kitchen is where I just came from. We were in search of drinks." Getting ahead of him so he can't get too close to me again, I see Olivia and Heidi laughing together which was a relief.

"Hey, you two, have you started the party without the rest of us?" I ask. Through their continued laughter, I watch as Heidi's eyes travel back and forth between Jackson and me. Then, she raises her eyebrows.

"Mom, I see you have run into Jackson. Olivia said he was out on the front porch taking a nap."

Casting a look at Jackson, I reply, "Yes I have, or should I say he ran into me." Olivia quickly looks between Jackson and me trying to discern the outcome of our small encounter. Before anything more can be said, in walks Seth.

"So, I see our guests have arrived. Come over here, Heidi, and let me look at you."

Heidi literally sashays over to Seth and says in her mid-western accent, "How do you do, sir? It's very nice to see you again." Laughing and hugging her, Seth turns to me.

"Morgan, it's about time you came over to visit. Olivia was beginning to think you were mad at her."

"Oh, Seth, stop it, I did not. Morgan, he is pulling your leg. I know you have been taking Heidi around town visiting." Smiling at my dear friend, I lightly punched Seth in the arm.

"Why do you torment her like this? She is going to put a whipping on you." Jackson is smirking behind his hand.

"What are you laughing about brother?" asks Seth.

"Nothing, it's very nice hearing all this banter between friends. I've missed it terribly. So let me get all of you drinks, and we can sit and visit for a while." Looking over at Heidi, Jackson adds, "That is, as long as you are allowed to stay up."

As indignantly as she could, Heidi stands up and says, "For your information Jackson, I am twenty-one-years-old, and my curfew is over." They all start laughing, and Jackson goes about his business making drinks.

Olivia pulls me aside quietly whispering, "Hey I don't think Jackson realizes who you are yet? I've already talked to him about Abby and what we think caused her death. He wants to help us, and he has a lot of experience fighting the establishment."

Touching Olivia's arm, I reply, "There's a good chance he will figure it out tonight, but in the meantime, let's have a nice visit."

The evening conversation stays centered around Heidi and Jackson since they were the two newcomers to our little trio. Heidi entertains us with her cooking attempts while casting looks my way, all in jest, about her mom leaving her on her own.

"Honestly, my cooking experience is very limited. A boiled egg, scrambled eggs, and grilled cheese are the things I can do well—beyond those it is dicey to say the least. Mom, on the other hand, is a great cook. Our friends in Linn Creek used to call her the Iron Chef and were always asking her to cook for them." Listening to Heidi talk makes me realize how much I miss Linn Creek and my friends there.

Shaking off my thoughts, I look discreetly at Jackson. He is still as good looking as he was when he was younger, except now there is some gray speckled through his otherwise dark hair. He was always so dark from the sun; however, I could see his life had taken him inside because his skin was more the color of a golden raisin. Seth always got such a kick out of telling everyone Jackson was his brother because obviously Jackson's ethnicity was different from Seth's.

Most people would politely laugh, and then Seth would say, "No really, he is. My mom went to the Five & Dime and picked us out." Everyone would howl laughing, and then there was never a question again that Jackson and Seth were brothers.

Now, Jackson regals us with stories of courtroom theatrics and unusual cases he defended and, of course, won. Jackson and Heidi are sitting next to each other, and she is hanging on to his every word. In Jackson's way, he is making her feel important and keeping her involved with the conversation. Realizing I need to use the bathroom, I excuse myself from the conversation.

As I make my way down the hall, I notice all the family photos Seth and Olivia have strategically placed along the wall. There are pictures of Jackson and Seth when they were little and when they were older—perhaps a graduation day. A picture of Olivia as a teenager, blond curls swirling around her face as she smiles brightly at the camera, which I'm sure was held by Seth. Further down, the pictures change to showing Cissy as a little girl. Then what looks like a high school picture where Josh is smiling over her shoulder as he holds her tightly. The next is Abigail with her young smile. Standing in front of her picture, I try to imagine who she would have become if her life hadn't been cut so short. Hearing footsteps, I turn to see who is coming, and I see Jackson's smiling face.

"Morgan, are you lost? Seth and Olivia's bathroom is the next door on the left."

"I know, I was just admiring their photos." Moving to stand next to me, he begins telling stories about a couple of the pictures. He becomes quiet when he walks up to Abigail's picture and traces the outline of her face with his finger.

Turning toward me, he speaks quietly, "Seth and Olivia should not have to be grieving their granddaughter. Something tells me you know what contributed to her sickness."

Bowing my head to hide the sudden tears coming to my eyes, I tell him, "I agree, Jackson they shouldn't, and it's possible they will get some validation now that you are here. Olivia told me they talked to you about their theory. But listen, I really do have to go to the bathroom, so can we talk about it later? You are staying, aren't you?"

Just as I shut the bathroom door, I hear him say, "Yes I am!"

When I came back from the bathroom, everyone had moved to the porch. It is a warm fall night, and the porch is very inviting. Olivia has freshened up everyone's drinks, and I notice Heidi has a glass of wine sitting on the side table next to her. Smiling to myself, I thought, *my little girl is growing up, and I'm so glad we are close.* Jackson had the floor at the moment, and I watch as he works the room involving everyone in his conversation.

Suddenly, Jackson focuses his attention on me and asks, "So Morgan, what brought you to Millersville? It doesn't seem to me as being one of the most visited areas in the country, so what gives?" Feeling Seth and Olivia's eyes on me, I decide to tell as much as I can of the truth.

"In Linn Creek, I worked for a newspaper and handled their tourism department. I'm not sure if you know where Linn Creek is, but it's in the valley of the Ozark Mountains and has a huge tourism trade. People are coming to spend their vacations outside enjoying nature while listening to great music, eating great food, and seeing Mother Nature at work. I pitched an idea to my editor to find other places similar to Linn Creek on the East Coast for an article on how small towns are surviving. So, I've been on a road trip ever since and came here because of the proximity to the Jersey Shore. There are plenty of small towns getting revitalized with wineries and breweries, so I wanted to capture the excitement."

Jackson, lawyering up, says, "So you are staying for a while. I see you have made your house next door very inviting." Looking Heidi's way, he asks, "Heidi, are you visiting or are you planning on staying?" All of sudden, I heard a noise coming from Olivia. Looking over at her quickly, I realize she is bursting with anger.

"Jackson, what the hell is wrong with you? Heidi and Morgan are our guests, and you are interrogating them like they are the prosecution's witnesses. Stop it!" Apologizing, Jackson becomes less aggressive during the rest of the conversation. Heidi motions to me she is getting tired and is ready to leave.

I wasn't quite ready to go yet, so looking over to her, I acknowledged her and said, "If you want to head home, Heidi, it's fine. I'm going to stay for a little while longer." Heidi politely excuses herself, tells everyone goodbye and heads across the yard to our house.

Watching her go, Olivia turns to me and says, "Morgan, I am so happy Heidi was able to come here and stay with you. It's very important for you to have her here with you now." Realizing her mistake a little late, we both look to see if Jackson is paying attention. Thankfully, he and Seth are talking football and dissecting the Eagles defensive line which was struggling with Fletcher Cox. Olivia shrugs her shoulders and whispers, "I don't think he heard me. I'm so sorry for calling you by that name. You know you have to decide what you want to be called."

Leaning toward her, I whisper, "Hey I already have decided, and it will be Morgan." Looking over at Seth and Jackson, they are both staring at the two of us.

"What are you two over there whispering about?" asks Seth. "I swear if I didn't know any better, I would say you two are up to something." Olivia, still burnt about Jackson's interrogation of

Heidi, decides to tell Seth and Jackson that it is none of their business. The mood of the night seemed to dissipate, so I let everyone know it is time for me to go home.

"Olivia and Seth, it was a very entertaining evening, and I so appreciate all of you making Heidi feel at home. Jackson, it was very nice seeing you—meeting you I mean—and I'm sure I will see more of you while you are here."

Jackson, looking directly at me, says, "Let me walk you to the door." Realizing it probably would not be a good idea to discourage him, we walked back in so I could grab my phone and head through the kitchen to the back door.

Quietly, Jackson leans into me and says, "It was nice seeing you again, Misty, or is it Morgan now?"

Turning to look at him, I ask, "What did you just say?"

"Come on, Morgan, what did you think was going to happen when you were faced with someone who knows you as well as I do?"

Staring at Jackson, I reply, "Well apparently your sense of recognition is intensely better than most people in Millersville because I have been walking around here for weeks. No one has figured it out unless I wanted them to." Pacing back and forth, Jackson seems to be tormented with his thoughts.

"Are you kidding me right now? Misty, I spent that summer with you. Then when I came back after the law clinic I had to attend, you were gone. I knew you were attending Arizona but no goodbye or anything. Seriously, why would you do that after the summer we spent together?" Trying to keep myself together, I lean into him and hug him.

"Jackson, we had a great time that summer, and I haven't forgotten what we felt during that time. It was just not the right time to keep it going. You were starting your law career, and I was getting ready to leave for my college experience."

Grabbing my arm, he pulls me to him and says softly, "Those images replay in my head over and over again, hence why I knew it was you. Your smell hasn't changed, and it was wafting over me the whole evening. Don't tell me I'm wrong because I haven't smelled that same fragrance since the summer I graduated from college. No matter what you do to your hair, your face, or your voice, you can't hide from me."

Moving away from him, I speak quietly, "Jackson, I'm not hiding anymore. When I arrived here, my intention was to hide my identity so the community would welcome me as a newcomer, not someone they knew from their past. And then, the past becomes the present for the person."

Jackson listens, and then in an even softer tone says, "Morgan is that what you think would have happened if you had just come home? Do you really think anyone remembers what happened all those years ago? Most people can't remember what they did last week and honestly, Morgan, those events were terrible for you not anyone else." Standing on the bottom step of the porch, I look up at Jackson.

"Yes, they were terrible, but not just to me. My family, Jackson, was shunned, demoralized, and in some cases my father was demonized.

Some of the community, back then, were so small-minded yet critical of his theory about the electrical towers. Most of them didn't understand it, but instead of trying to grasp it, they took the low road." Getting emotional, I tearfully continued, "We were a well-respected farming family and within just a few years, it all changed. So, it's not just about me and what happened, it's about my family. I do remember, and remember vividly, the pain it caused my mother." Walking down the steps, Jackson grabs both of my hands.

"I didn't mean to get you upset, but now I know who Seth and Olivia were talking about earlier. It's you, isn't it, who will be helping them?"

Releasing his hands, I nod and say, "Yes, I am. There is no reason why we are attending seven-year-old's funerals. So yes, I am going to try to help them as much as possible. You lived here then, Jackson, you saw the people getting sick for no apparent reason. Your own mother was constantly battling headaches, and the doctors had no solution for her. The building she worked in was right under the towers located off the main highway in Millersville. This has been going on for a long time, and nothing has been done about it. With your help, we might be able to make a difference. So, Jackson, will you stay here and represent us?"

Smiling, in spite of himself, Jackson looks around the house where he spent most of his later years. Seth and Olivia are his family, and he seems to have made such a life for himself so nothing would stop him from helping. I hope knowing I was involved would make it more important to him to stay. Hesitating for a moment, he walks up and takes hold of my hands.

Pulling me closer, he whispers, "I will never forget the summer we spent together. Those memories are tucked in the special place in my mind for the time when all is quiet, and I can relive all of the intimate times we had. Sometimes, it feels like you are still laying there next to me. Yet I realize all of us have moved on, and our lives have taken many turns. I've been lucky or blessed, whatever you want to call it. So yes, Misty or Morgan, I will be here, and we will stop who is behind this or at least make them accountable." Leaning in and hugging him, I quietly hummed the song we always listened to when we were sitting in his car.

"Jackson, I remember as well, and you saved me that summer. You made me realize the time spent with someone can be joyous and fulfilling. I will never forget what you did for me." I turn and walk as quickly as I can while feeling his eyes boring into the back of my head. Spinning around, I wave to him and say, loud enough for him to hear me, "Hey, I'm really glad you are here. We all need you right now."

Getting inside my house, I walk into the family room looking for Heidi but realize she must have gone upstairs. Quietly laughing, I concluded the wine probably made her sleepy. Walking into my kitchen, I sit down at the counter and lay my head in my hands. Rubbing my face, I look at my reflection in the small mirror I have hanging by the door. Seeing Jackson brought back so many memories and having him in the same room as Heidi was unnerving. My past with Nick and the Jackson rescue wasn't something I was ready to share with her.

First, it was time I talked to Brett and told him who I am. It can't wait much longer because I am taking the chance of him finding out from someone else—especially now. Seeing Whitney and Nick earlier, and then spending the last few hours with Jackson had my nerves frayed. It was time for me to go to bed and recharge my mind for tomorrow.

Hearing a truck coming, I look outside and see Brett's truck coming down the road. Looking at my watch, which confirms it's past 1:00 AM, I decide he must be coming over after the tavern closes. Going to the front door, I turned the light on so he would know I was still up. Then I hang my pocketbook up on the hook under my sweater and hurry in and go to the bathroom. Just as I am coming out, he is pulling into my driveway. Opening my front door, I walk out to the porch and wave to him. Watching him get out of his truck makes me realize how happy I am to see him. Instead of waiting for him to come up to the porch, I ran down to him.

"Brett, it's great to see you." Proving my gratitude, I reached up and hugged him.

He tips my head back and with the longest kiss, he sighs and says, "Morgan, I missed you. It feels like it's been forever since I've seen you, but it was just a few days ago."

Smiling up at him not wanting to let go, I say, "I know!" Staying there within the comfort of his arms, I laid my head on his chest and listened to his heartbeat. In that moment, I know this feels like home. It was time. I had to tell him tonight.

"Let's go up and sit down on the porch, and I'll get us something to drink." Walking up he grabs my hand which brings another smile to my face. Brett gets situated in a rocking chair, and I head in to get us some wine. In the kitchen, I poured each of us some wine knowing it was time to tell him.

Whitney & Nick

Earlier, on the way home from the diner, Whitney was very quiet. Her head was turned as if the passing landscape held her in some kind of trance. Pulling into their driveway, Nick shut off the car. No one moved as if they were held there together in anticipation of some kind of doom. Nick touches her arm and Whitney jumps back as if she has been burnt.

"Whitney, I don't mean to scare you, but we are home now. Do you want to go inside, or do you need some time alone?"

Whitney shakes her head and tells him, "No, Nick I don't need time alone. Please, don't sound so concerned, everything is fine. It was so surreal having Misty stand at our table talking to us as if we were sitting at the lunch table twenty years ago. The only difference is Misty would have been sitting there with you, and I would have stood on the outside looking in." Getting out of the car, they walk toward the house. Putting his arm over her shoulders, Nick stops her at the door before going in.

"Whitney, you are right. It was surreal having her stand there, but what you are wrong about is you belong across the table from me now, not Misty. We have been trying to shut out the past for so long and honestly, without much success. Now, with time, we will finally be ok with it. She is here to stay, and all of us need to accept who we have become not who we were. Then, maybe we could somehow be friends again. All of us!" Smiling up at Nick, Whitney stands on her tiptoes and lightly kisses her husband.

"We have all changed, and I hope for the better. My demons concerning the past are mine to extinguish, and I will. Each day, I am feeling better. Let's go inside and check on the boys, then I'll get us an after-dinner drink, so we can talk some more."

The boys start asking them questions as soon as they enter the door.

"What did you have to eat?"

Nick Jr. lightly smacks his younger brother, Preston, scolding him, "Stop asking so many questions. Who cares what they had for dinner? You should be asking if they had any of the great desserts. Dad, at practice the other day some of the players were talking about how good the desserts were at the diner."

Smiling at his oldest son, Nick says, "Nicky, we didn't have any dessert. However, we did see an old friend while we were there. She was there with her daughter eating dinner." Nicky sits on a kitchen chair backward and leans on the back of the chair.

"Is it someone I know? Preston and I know most of yours and Mom's friends." Looking over to see what Whitney is doing, Nick sees she's getting a couple of glasses out and reaching up high to get the bottle of Jameson down. Seeing her struggle, he walks up behind her and reaches for the bottle. Suddenly, feeling her body pressed up against him makes him understand why things happened as they did. He couldn't resist Whitney's softness and her all-encompassing love for him. Feeling a tightness, he suddenly steps away and sets the bottle on the counter. As he moves away from Whitney, he feels her eyes on him but answers his oldest.

"You wouldn't know her. She just moved back here recently, and her daughter is here visiting. Your mom was her neighbor, and all of us went to high school together. She hasn't been living around here for a long time."

Listening intently, Nicky looks over at his mom and speaks to just her, "Hey, Mom, this must have been so cool reuniting with your friend. What happened, how come you haven't told us about her before? If you were neighbors, you must have had a great friendship." Trying to keep her composure, she looks over at Nick and he shrugs his shoulders.

"We were best friends and spent most of our waking hours together. But Nicky, things happen between friends which sometimes can't be taken back. This isn't something you have experienced yet, but something tells me you won't escape this frustrating fact. Your dad and I are just happy she has been able to relocate here so that we can rekindle our friendship."

Nicky looks at Nick and Whitney and rolls his eyes, "Really Mom, all my friends are so cool. We are BUDS!"

Smiling at Nick, Whitney gathers up all the plates and cups from the boys' dinner and yells, "Preston, it's time for you and Nick to get your showers and get ready for bed. Don't dilly dally because it's getting late."

After the boys get showered and go to bed, Nick pours a finger of Jameson for each of them to drink. Sitting at the counter together, they toast.

"Whitney, I really had a nice time tonight. We need to get out together more often."

Taking a sip of her drink, Whitney smiles tentatively agreeing, "Nick, it was nice tonight, and I enjoyed your company."

Thinking about his words, Nick hesitates for just a moment before adding, "It was a little unsettling when Morgan came to our table, but I don't think she meant to interrupt our time together. Let's be honest, we were both interested in meeting her daughter."

"Yes, we were Nick. Heidi, is her name, right? She stayed at their table, and the conversation with Morgan at our table seemed strained."

Trying not to get aggravated, Nick quietly says, "What did you think it was going to be? Both of us approached her separately, and I'm sure your conversation was the same as mine. Neither one of us left feeling good about ourselves. So, let's be honest, Whitney. Did you think it was going to be an old home week between the three of us?" Sipping her drink, Whitney remains silent for a few moments.

"No, I didn't, but you know, Nick, if we had been in sync with each other, we would have gone to see her, but instead we went separately. Unfortunately for all of us, the visits became a guilty trip for you and me. Morgan, on the other hand, lashed out all her pent-up feelings." Nick stands and goes over to Whitney and pulls her up. Holding her close, he looks at his wife of twenty plus years.

"She's home now, and we need to embrace it. This is our chance, Whitney, to make amends. Find a place in ourselves where we forgive and forget." Shrugging her shoulders, Whitney leans down and picks up her drink finishing it in one swallow. Reaching up and pulling Nick closer, she kisses him with a long-lost passion which has been quietly dormant in her. With surprise, Nick kisses her back.

Then Whitney pulls away and says, "I love you, Nick." Then she walks away and heads up to her room.

Morgan & Brett

Sitting together on the porch with glasses of wine, our conversation is very general. I know Brett was curious as to what I had been doing for the last few days. Steering the conversation, I ask how things are going at the tavern. For the next several minutes, Brett tells me of his decision to make Jillian a partner. Listening to him, I realize how much he thinks of Jillian and what a generous person he is.

Wanting to be closer to him, I get up and move to sit on his lap. Looking at him, I marvel at the intense feeling I get every time he is with me. Stopping him in mid-sentence, I lean down and gently kiss him. His response was to slowly gather me in his arms and rest me in his lap. For a moment, I can feel a gentle longing for a deeper capture in his arms.

Prolonging the kiss, I move my hand inside his shirt to feel his skin. I lay my head on his chest and hear his heartbeat quicken and feel his hands caress me. Tracing his lips with my fingers lightly and sliding them down his neck feathering his skin, I feel shivers ripple through his body. Continuing down his chest, I stop only for a moment for my lips and tongue to fondle his nipples, which are now erect. Groaning, Brett scoops me up and takes me inside.

Between kisses, he asks me, "Where?" Finding it very hard to speak, I pointed down the hall to the guest room. Some semblance of control enters my mind as I decide that it is better to be downstairs than in my bedroom next to Heidi's room.

Pushing the door open, we struggle with our balance. Then laughing, we fell on the bed—me lying beneath him. I look into his eyes and see them change to a deep blue burning with passion. His hands are exploring my body, and passion for him overwhelms me. Shivers move up and down my body as his hands leave each part of me yearning for his touch again. Pulling me up, he lifts my shirt up moving it over my shoulders. Nipping my shoulder, he moves his mouth downward and explores my breasts with his tongue, converting the inside of me into deep pangs of excitement.

Working his shirt off, I scatter kisses all over his chest feeling him quiver with anticipation. Desire fills his eyes, and he kisses me. Then, I feel his tongue enter gently into my mouth. Moving my hips so I can feel his need for me intensify, I work my hands to his belt and look at him for confirmation. Suddenly, we are stripping the rest of our clothes off, and the hunger in his eyes sends my yearning for him into deep passion.

Slowing down his excitement, he becomes an expert in ecstasy. His hands and his mouth transport me to the threshold of euphoria, and just when I think there is no greater enchantment, he enters me. I am immersed in an explosion of intoxicating pleasure. The sensation and feeling now so intense our bodies writhe together in harmony until I cannot take it any longer and release. Feeling Brett shutter, I held him tightly stroking his back lightly. Still wrapped in one another's arms, we lay quietly gently touching one another. Turning on my side, I lay my head on his chest and together we fell asleep.

Just as I drift off, I hear Brett whisper, "I love you, Morgan."

Morgan

The sunlight is sending its rays through the curtain. When I hear Heidi moving around upstairs and the toilet flushing, I realize it is time to get up. Brett appears to have never moved during the night because his arm is still lying across my body. Sliding slowly away from him so as not to wake him up, I headed down the hall to the downstairs bathroom.

Splashing cold water on my face, I stare at my reflection in the mirror remembering the night spent with Brett. Rubbing my arms, I notice some bruising along my bicep. Smiling to myself, I remember how intense we both were and looking a little closer at myself, I see the pink rash from his whiskers along my jawline. Going back into the bedroom, I quietly gather up my clothing and slip back out and head upstairs.

I make it to my bedroom, and just as I am opening the door, Heidi says, "You're up early, Mom. Were you sitting downstairs for a while before you got dressed?

"I actually slept downstairs last night." Looking closely at me, Heidi knows better than to ask her mom why she slept downstairs. She knows I will tell her soon enough.

Heading downstairs, she turns and says, "Well, I will get the coffee ready, and I'm in the mood for waffles, so I'm going to see if you have everything to make them." Turning the corner, she practically knocks Brett over. "Oh my God, Brett, you scared me. What are you

202

doing here?" Then she noticed Brett's attire, and her mouth opened in silence, *Oh*.

Realizing Brett is standing before her shirtless and in his boxers, she immediately turns away and says, "The bathroom is down the hall on the right. I think Mom has fresh towels and washcloths in there if you want to take a shower." Smiling appreciatively, Brett walks down the hall and shuts the door to the bathroom quickly. Heidi shoots a smile in my direction, and it all but says, *Now I know why my mom was downstairs so early.*

Now alone, I am able to get a quick shower. I look at myself in the mirror and realize I had better put some makeup on to cover the whisker burn I have on my chin and cheeks. Fixing my hair and making sure my face was in good repair, I headed downstairs to my daughter and her inquiring eyes.

Hearing pots and pans clanging, I walk in asking, "Do you need any help with the waffles?" Moving to where she is standing, I lean over her shoulder to look at what she is whisking.

"Stop inspecting Mom, I know how to make waffles. It was more of a problem finding where you keep things. I thought it would be set up something like our kitchen at home, but it looks like you had something else in mind." Laughing, I moved to get a coffee cup out and pour my coffee.

"Heidi, I really haven't been living here very long and with all of the things going on with Uncle Jonathan, it's been hard to get settled. Literally, I just moved in a few days ago, and then you arrived. So, Lord only knows where I might have put anything." Sitting down at the kitchen table, I watched her maneuver the waffle iron which I didn't even know was here. Hearing footsteps, I look over my shoulder and see Brett pausing at the doorway. Motioning him in, I smile and say, "Brett, did you find everything you needed for your shower? Putting extra towels in that bathroom was something I did do when I moved in here."

Turning around from working the waffle iron, Heidi says with just a touch of sarcasm, "Well by the look of Brett, I would say he found everything." Smiling at Brett, I point to the chair next to me at the kitchen table. Before sitting down, he walks over to where Heidi is working.

Tapping her on the shoulder as he looks over at the batter she is dipping onto the iron, he says, "You know if you add a little bit of vanilla, it makes waffles so much better." Looking up at Brett, Heidi had a quick retort but saw the smile on his face and started laughing.

"Brett, it definitely does. That's why I always add it to waffles and pancakes." Laughing with her, the awkward moment which could have been fueled was extinguished, leaving everyone talking and enjoying the relaxing atmosphere of the morning.

After having great waffles, we talked about Heidi's plan over the next few weeks, the tavern, and Brett's announcement of making Jillian a partner.

"Brett tell us more about the partnership you and Jillian are going to have. I think it is great news."

Heidi claps her hands and says cheerfully, "Oh my, Jillian must be over the top with happiness. She is such a nice person." Shaking his head, Brett proceeds to tell Heidi and me all of the great attributes of Jillian and his relief that she agreed to take on more responsibility.

"Now I will be able to leave the bar on a Saturday night and not have to go back to close up and count the money. We will actually be able to have some kind of schedule where we both can enjoy our personal lives more." Heidi asks Brett some questions about the tavern and the clientele, who I'm sure was in anticipation of stopping out there since she was now twenty-one. While enjoying their conversation, I realize I keep hearing a dog barking. It seems like the dog is nearby because there is an echo.

Excusing myself, I walk to my front door and look out the side windows. A van is sitting across the street with tinted windows. Opening the door to walk out on my porch, I see the van begin to move slowly toward the house. Immediately, I recognized the van as the same one I saw coming down Brett's street when I was riding by his mom's house the other day taking Heidi for a ride around the area.

Staring to see if I could see the person behind the wheel, I started to walk out toward the street. Hearing the van speed up quickly, I raised my hands to implore the driver to slow down. Just as it approaches my position, the van slows suddenly, and the window rolls down. Dark hair and sunglasses look at me, and then he waves. Turning away quickly, I find myself feeling uneasy, my stomach flipping over with trepidation. Walking slowly up my front steps, I hesitate at the door. Looking down the road, I suddenly feel the atmosphere shifting. I knew wickedness had arrived. Opening the front door, I walk right into Brett's arms.

"Morgan, are you ok? You look rattled. What happened while you were outside?" Hugging him tightly, I walked back into the kitchen. Turning to him, I find myself wondering, *what exactly is going on right now?*

"Brett, the van riding by my house right now is the same van I'm pretty sure was going by your mother's house the other day. It also was parked at the diner tonight when Heidi and I went there for dinner earlier. I don't know who it is, but I have this feeling of foreboding."

Frowning and moving to stand at the sliding glass door, Brett stares out at the scenery before him. He walks out, hesitating for a minute, then sits down at the patio table.

"Morgan, when I was at my mother's house the other day, there was a phone call. Her phone is in the foyer, and I had just stepped back inside from the front porch after watering her flowerpots when I heard it ring. I heard it echoing and realized the ringing was coming from outside. When I first got to her house, there was a van parked out front. The same dark van that has been riding around the neighborhood and back and forth in front of your house.

The voice on the phone was ominous and threatening. I've been kicking myself for it ever since, but when I took the call, I didn't think to check the van at the same time. But when I hung up and checked out the window, the van was gone. I know the caller was the same person in the van. At the end of the call, I asked if there was a message for my mother." Feeling an uneasy sensation, I continue to listen.

"Go on," I hear myself say Brett hesitates for just a moment as if he were contemplating whether or not he should share the next bit of information. It was obvious the call upset him and that he cared for me, but something or someone was holding him back from easily sharing the next bit of information.

"He said to me, 'Tell Elizabeth, Carl knows what you did.'" I could barely control my facial expression. Bursting out an expletive, I calmed down slightly not wanting to appear upset about what was said by the caller.

"What in the world does that mean?" Shaking his head, Brett once more was lost in thought. Watching Brett struggle with his thoughts, I realize if this conversation continues, the role I've been playing will come to an abrupt end. Despite feeling not ready or maybe simply not wanting this to be the moment I tell Brett, it becomes obvious I need to do it before more time passes and we become closer.

"Brett, I need to talk to you about something. It is way overdue. You know the farmer your stepfather Jack was involved with all those years ago? Well, he was my father." Brett seems as though he is in a trance.

"Brett, please say something. I know this is a shock." Shaking his head as if he can't believe what he is hearing, he looks at me with doubt and something else which made my heart twist—despair.

Finding his voice, Brett quietly says, "Morgan, I'm not sure why you are saying this. How is it possible the Jenkinses are your parents?

You just came to Millersville a couple months ago. Your name is Morgan Kiernan not Morgan Jenkins."

Understanding his confusion, I continue, "Honestly, Brett it is hard to explain without it seeming far-fetched, but my real name is Misty Jenkins. I became Morgan Kiernan when I left Millersville twenty years ago. My father is Carl Jenkins, and Jonathan Jenkins is my brother." Getting up and pacing around the deck, Brett continually shakes his head in disbelief.

Suddenly, he stops and says, "Oh my God. Now it is all starting to make sense. This is why Seth and Olivia have become so friendly with you. They know who you are, don't they?" Sitting with my hands in my lap, I shake my head yes.

"Please don't be mad at them, Brett. I swore them to secrecy. You are their best friend, and that has not changed. If anything, they are so happy we have become close."

Brett turns to me and with a quiet anger, he speaks, "Morgan, why would you lie about your identity? Why wouldn't you just come here and be who you really are?" Standing up and feeling myself getting emotional, I grab his hands and hold on to them tightly.

"Brett, because I became Morgan Kiernan for a reason. Misty Jenkins ceased to exist when she left Millersville and went away. I came back here as Morgan Kiernan, and no one but a few people know who I am. This is the way I want it to be. There are reasons which I can't explain right now, but I will soon, and then, hopefully, you will understand." The entire time I'm talking, I can see the confusion in his eyes.

Then with a dawning of realization, he lets go of my hands and angrily says, "Morgan, you knew my stepfather, Jack, didn't you? You just said your father is Carl Jenkins. What exactly was your father doing, causing Jack to spend so much time with him? Tell me Morgan, why did you really come back here? Something tells me it's not entirely about seeing your brother. You were more than a little interested the day I took you to my mothers to visit. You knew she was Jack's wife, didn't you?" Moving past him, I stand at the railing looking at the flowers I planted around the deck lost in my thoughts. "Morgan, answer me, you knew."

"No, Brett I didn't, and if you would calm down for a moment you would realize why. Your last name is Compton not Callahan. Every time you talked about your stepfather, you used his first name. I didn't realize who your mother was until I was there talking with her. She mentioned my father's name when we were there in the solarium with the piano. If you think back, you will remember my confusion. I became very quiet, and it was shortly after we left. The next visit, however, was quite different. It became a fact-finding visit for me. Your mother and I were getting to know each other better, and I wanted to know how much she actually knew of Jack's agenda." I trail off there. There was no reason to tell Brett anymore of the events that happened on that day. Jackson's investigation into Elizabeth Callahan will not be hampered by Brett possibly warning her.

"Please, Brett let's go inside to talk. There is so much more to this than whether or not I knew who your mother is." Nodding and walking past me, Brett sits down at the kitchen table. Following him,

I wonder how he will process his feelings for me now that he knows who I am. Turning away from me, Brett stares off in the distance. Several minutes go by in silence.

Suddenly, he looks at me and says, "Morgan, I refuse to call you Misty. Why did it take you so long to tell me? We made love last night. Love, Morgan, do you hear me? I love Morgan Kiernan. Except you are Misty Jenkins, and I don't know who she is." Leaning down, I take his face and kiss him.

"It's going to be ok. I am Morgan. Please give me time to explain everything to you."

Jackson, Seth, & Olivia

Jackson comes downstairs to see what is on Seth's agenda for the day. Walking into the kitchen, he sees Olivia standing at the sink where it seems she is concentrating on something outside.

"Hey, what is so interesting out there? Did Seth leave you on your own today, or is he what you are looking so intently at right now?"

Turning quickly, Olivia smiles and tells him, "I was just looking over to Morgan's house." Standing next to her, Jackson's eyes scan the area, and then come to rest on Morgan's back deck. Sitting on the deck with her is a dark-haired man. As he is taking in the view, he sees Morgan lean down and kiss him.

"Olivia, who is the man with Morgan right now?"

"Oh, that's Brett Compton, he owns the Town Tavern. Don't you remember him? He was good friends with Seth."

Frowning slightly, Jackson shakes his head and recalls, "I knew most of Seth's friends in school, I don't remember him at all."

"That doesn't make any sense. I don't know why you don't remember him." Pausing for a moment, Olivia looks lost in a memory before beginning again, "Now that I think back, Brett moved away for a while, and he didn't go to high school with you and Seth. He went to private school, so Seth only spent time with him during the summer." Getting a cup of coffee and sitting down at the kitchen table, Jackson stirs his coffee slowly.

"Olivia, if Seth became friendly with him after school, then it explains why I don't know him. I had already left to work under the intern program at the law firm. Seth and you are still good friends of his?"

Olivia goes to the refrigerator to put the creamer away, and turning toward Jackson she confirms, "Yes, we are, it seems like we have become better friends in the last couple of years. Brett is transforming the tavern into a nice and friendly place to hang out. We will have to go there while you are here Jackson."

Taking a sip of his coffee, he laughs confessing, "Olivia I stopped there before I came here yesterday. I met a pretty bartender who seemed interested in who I was."

Olivia giggles and says, "That was Jillian. She and Brett run the tavern most of the time. If either one of them is not there, then you know something is afoot. Seth and I go there quite often. We met Morgan there." Walking back over to the window, Jackson looks over toward Morgan's house. Seeing they have gone inside, he turns to Olivia.

"Liv, I know the grief flooding this home is not like the devastation Cissy and Josh are feeling, but I also have seen the sparkle leave your eyes and the slump in Seth's shoulders. So, with Morgan being the person I need to talk to about Abigail's death, I am going to be spending a lot of time with her. And if so, why Olivia? Tell me, what does she know which is so powerful?"

"Oh my, Jackson you have no idea. I don't know how to tell you why. Just realize she is going to be your most important ally, and in the end, the two of you will find out why Abigail died." Reaching for Jackson, Olivia whispers, "Jackson, I know you remember the summer before you went to law school. Think back! Then you will understand why Morgan is so important to our life." Jackson stands back from Olivia and squeezes her arms.

"My dear Liv, nothing will ever erase those images from my mind. Rest assured, I already know who has become Morgan."

Jackson leaves Olivia and decides to take a walk around his old neighborhood. Seeing so many of the houses in disrepair made him realize the area had fallen to bad times. He begins to wonder if what he is seeing has any direct impact on his plan to destroy those who hurt Abigail. Something tells him these houses were standing empty because of the inability to live comfortably and healthily. This was going to take more thought, so he turns back toward Seth's and decides it is time to do some more research.

Ray

Meanwhile, the driver of the dark van pulls into the local drugstore and parks. He needs to make a phone call. Looking around at the people walking in and out of the pharmacy, he realizes the size of the job he has been given. *What is the chance I am going to be able find Misty Jenkins by herself when every time I get near her, she is busy with someone? Today was the perfect opportunity to scare her. What does she do but burst out of her door, and I wave!* The company is getting impatient with him and has been very explicit. No one is to be hurt. There is so much at stake with all the new towers planned for the area and the feedback from one of the community leaders has been very positive. They plan to put the first towers on her family's farm. The company was so close to completing the deal with Jonathan Jenkins, and then Misty Jenkins appeared back in town. If she continues her father's work, there is a serious threat to the company's plans.

Jack Callahan was supposed to finalize the plans twenty years ago. It was back then the company was canvasing the area trying to determine the viability of the project. It consisted of rural areas—wide open areas of farmland with hungry farmers wanting to discontinue their family legacies and sell out for the big money was exactly the contagion they needed. Now, twenty years later, he is spending time worrying if Misty Jenkins was ever going to be alone. This wasn't a productive way to begin his day. Putting his van in gear, he decides it's time to see his contact to convince him to put a little urgency behind his planning. The problem is that the only thing he knows about his contact is the sound of his voice and that he is feeding information to someone with power at the bank. Taking what little information he had, he decides to scope out the activity around the outside of the bank.

The arrival of Misty Jenkins back in Millersville and her reconnection with her brother has put a halt to the project. The company is asking for an update within four weeks, and it currently isn't looking too good for the completion of the towers. It is time he talked to the individual in Millersville who the company had monitoring the situation. The company had strongly prohibited him from reaching out to this contact, however, the time had come for him to find out exactly what was going on with Jonathan and Misty Jenkins. Their land has a value on it that has no limit.

Sitting down on a bench, he watches the comings and goings of the people in Millersville. *The people are friendly*, he thinks. They're always stopping and asking how he is, making small talk when they don't even know him. He sees a man walking into the bank who is constantly scanning his surroundings and appears much more skittish that the rest of the friendly folks in town. Feeling a sense that this might be his contact, he hurries to get inside the bank recognizing this is a chance he may not get again Seeing the same anxious man who he thinks is his contact talking to one of the customer relations advocates, he overhears him asking if someone named Tom is available.

Walking over to the plaque which lists the top executives of the bank, he scans for the name Tom. After all the board members' names is the list of the top management of the bank. Tom Fraser is listed as *Vice President of Development/Commercial/Residential Finance.* A well-dressed man walks into the lobby from the back offices and shakes the contact's hand, talking animatedly to him while leading him back to his office. The familiarity of the two of them made him uncomfortable. Leaving the bank, he tells himself to pay more attention to his contact and see what he is up to.

Nick

Nick is in Fraser's office waiting impatiently. Apparently, there is an irate customer in the lobby, and Tom is needed to diffuse the situation. Looking around the office, Nick notices all the different community plaques and photos hanging on the wall. Standing up to get a closer look, he realizes most of them are taken during the early days of Tom's career. A photo catches his eye, and he sees Tom with his arm across the shoulders of a young boy. Looking closer, he realizes the boy standing next to Tom is Jackson Palmer, Seth's younger brother. Reading the caption at the bottom of the photo causes a frown to cross Nick's face. It read, *People's Award, Jackson Palmer, Great success in his future.*

Nick wasn't Jackson Palmer's biggest fan. He never cared much for Seth's younger brother, but he tolerated him for Seth's sake. It had been several years since Nick had seen Jackson, and thinking about him now still irritated him. Sitting back down in the chair, he leans his head back and closes his eyes. The arrival of a memory takes him back to the summer of his senior year.

I left for Michigan shortly after graduation for first-year football camp. The couple of months leading up to it were horrible. Misty wanted nothing to do with me after my betrayal of her with Whitney. What in the world possessed me to screw around with Whitney?

Then, Pandora's Box opened. Whitney couldn't wait to ruin Misty's life with me and yet now, looking back, Whitney tried to be a good wife. She tried even when we lost the baby who drove us to marry. Both my actions and my treatment of Whitney were shameful. After our first son was born, things got a little better which led to our second son entering the world. Then financial problems and Whitney's drinking started to eat away at what was a very shaky relationship to begin with. Her paranoia and guilt put a wall up between us that neither of them was willing to climb. Years of arguments, misunderstandings, and lack of empathy for each other changed both of us. Hearing the door open jerked him out of his reverie, and he stood up to meet Tom Fraser.

"Nick, it's good to see you. We have a lot of catching up to do. I honestly thought you would have stopped in here before now." Moving to sit back down, Nick finds himself slightly annoyed.

"So, tell me Tom, did you forget how to use the phone or are you willing to go out on a limb and tell me you just didn't feel it necessary to get in touch with me?"

Standing behind his desk, Tom fiddles with an eraser replying, "I have a few things to tell you as well, and I don't think you are going to be so cocky afterward." Motioning his hand to go on, Tom sits down. "Jonathan Jenkins is giving us some problems. His wife, Sara, and his sister, Misty, are giving him grandiose ideas about what the farm can become. You know Misty, don't you Nick?"

Frowning, Nick angrily says, "You know damn right well I know Misty, so what's your point? What are they telling Jonathan to do?"

Getting up to look out his window, Tom begins, "Word on the street is they are considering converting the land into a vineyard. He continues to postpone the signing of the agreement saying there are elements to it which need to be changed. Every time I call there,

Sara says Jonathan is busy and can't come to the phone. I have tried to talk to Misty, but she won't return my phone calls. Surely, I don't need to emphasize to you, Nick, the Board of Directors is very annoyed and becoming impatient." Tom turns to look at Nick before continuing, "This is not going to be good for either one of us if this sale isn't completed. So, whatever you have left in your arsenal you need to use to influence this family. They may need help in deciding what will be the best route for them to pursue."

Putting his head in his hands, Nick mumbles, "Time is supposed to heal all wounds, not this one." Lifting his head and staring at Tom, he says more directly, "You know you have a lot of nerve even asking me to do any more to help you. Your minion who is driving all around Millersville is getting too obvious. Everywhere I look, his van is going by or is parked somewhere, which believe me, is not what I call discreet. All of this must come to an end. I can't influence any of the Jenkinses and least of all Misty. The bank will have to manage this on their own. All this cloak and dagger stuff being facilitated by your man in the van has to cease." Tom comes around to the front of his desk and sits down on the edge crossing his arms.

"Nick, I understand except it really doesn't matter what you feel, does it? You will be a part of this for as long as we need you, or we can make those loans you've been skipping payments on come due. It's your choice, you can continue to help us seal this deal or else we will have to handle those loans as we see fit. Neither one of us want it to get to that now, do we?" Trying to keep his anger at bay, Nick stands up abruptly.

"You know, Tom, I rue the day we became involved with each other. Unfortunately, for me, I really didn't think there was any chance Jonathan would be able to work the farm again, but I was wrong and apparently so were you. However, it seems to me my role has become more important, and there should be some good faith reciprocation between us. Plus, I have a sneaking feeling someone else is pulling the strings on this deal, so if you want more cooperation from the Jenkinses, then I think you better tell me exactly what is going on."

Moving back around his desk, Tom Fraser looks at a paper on his desk and spins it around so Nick can read it. What Nick sees on the paper gives him the chills. *Who in the world would have ever thought they would want the Jenkins farm?* Trying to keep his emotions off his face, he slowly turns the paper around to face Tom again.

"Wow, I had no idea! Now it all makes sense why the bank has been so intent on sealing this deal. Except, how do they plan on getting approval from the Township?" Tom doesn't feel comfortable revealing too much to Nick Darlington. Nothing he had done so far would involve him beyond no return, but if Tom tells Nick exactly what is going on, it all changes. Not knowing which way to turn, Tom decides to trust Nick.

"Nick, you realize the Jenkins farm has ground that is mostly clay. There is a small portion of it on another road not too far from their homestead that has sandy soil, and this is the parcel the bank is willing to section off the deed for Jonathan to use. Our customer is very interested in the main part of the farm. The issue he has with the agreement is Jonathan's milking parlor is part of the land the customer wants to buy. So, if Jonathan wants to continue to milk, he will need to rebuild. His wife and sister are influencing him to change his farming method. Unfortunately for my client, there is a population of bog turtles located in the old irrigation pond which we have recently found are a protected species of turtles." Nodding as if he understands, Nick is wondering why the electric company wants Misty's family farm.

Tom continues, "This project has been in the works for over twenty years. They were working with another contact trying to initiate a push with Misty's father to hand over his methods of detecting stray voltage, but there were complications which made the company withdraw their efforts. Unfortunately for Jonathan Jenkins, they were watching and waiting for his failure, so they could re-establish their contact and finalize their original plan." Nick is getting irritated with Tom for his continued diatribe of the company plan without saying exactly what they were after.

"Tom, get to the point, what does the electric company want with the Jenkins farm?"

"Nick, I'll tell you what they want. They want to install massive electrical towers connecting all of South Jersey with North Jersey, so they will be able to cut the electrical costs and in turn, increase the kilowatt charge extended to the consumer." Nick swallows tightly, alarmed by Tom's comments.

Misty's dad had spent the last part of his life fighting the electric company trying to prove the stray voltage dropping from the old towers was detrimental to animals and humans. In the end, he died trying, or at least this was the consensus among the old timers of the community. Nick knows now why Misty came back here. She plans on finding out what happened to her father and doing whatever she can to stop more stray currents from harming our community.

"This is why you have been asking me to intervene for you all this time? The feigned friendship and then the subtle threats have been all about purchasing this land for the electric company's greed. What is in this for you? Tell me there is good reason for you to sell out your community." Nick stands, walks to the door, and turns toward Tom Fraser. "Tom, I really don't know how you can sleep at night knowing what you intend to do to the Jenkins family." Coming to stand next to Nick, Tom motions around his office.

"I've been serving this community for over twenty-five years, and what do I have to show for it? A title, a large office, and a measly pension which doesn't amount to anything, let alone stand a chance of sustaining Mrs. Fraser's tastes and her feeling of importance in the community. So yes, Nick I do have sleepless nights, but it isn't about hurting my community with giant silent killers, it's more about what I am going to do with all the money which will come my way when this deal is solidified." Sitting back down at his desk, he looks at Nick. "I think we are done here Nick. Just remember what I said. They will severely frown on your lack of cooperation, and if I were you, I would follow along just like you have been. Don't get a conscience now!"

Nick finds himself at a loss for words not believing what just came out of Tom Fraser's mouth. Standing up, he quietly leaves the office and heads back home. Suddenly, he feels the need to see Whitney.

Ray

Deciding to wait to see when his contact exits the bank, the driver of the van sits down on a bench not too far from the bank's front door. Leaning his head back and closing his eyes for a couple of moments, he enjoys the warmth of the sun on his face. Hearing someone clear their throat, he opens his eyes to a beautiful young woman with sun-kissed skin and eyes the color of a tropical sea.

"Excuse me sir, but do you mind if I share this bench with you? I'm waiting for my aunt and uncle to come, and from here, I will be able to see when they arrive."

Sitting up tall and straightening his jacket, he says, "Sure miss, be my guest."

Sitting down, the young woman extends her hand and states, "Hi, my name is Heidi."

Before he could stop himself, he tells her, "My name is Ray."

"Well, it's very nice to meet you, Ray." Together they sit on the bench watching the people of Millersville wander by. Ray decides to find out a little more about his bench visitor.

"Heidi, you have a strong mid-western accent. Are you from around here?"

"No, I'm not but my mom is, and we are here visiting. Ray, are you from here?" Wondering how to answer her question, he quickly decides to pick a place.

"Actually, I live in New York City."

Giving him a truly genuine smile, Heidi responds, "Wow, so cool. I have always wanted to visit there. It looks like such a great city. I love musicals and plays, so it would be impressive to see something on Broadway like Wicked or Mama Mia."

Smiling back at her, he replies, "Well, you really aren't too far from there. It only takes a couple of hours to get into the city. Maybe you and your mom could take a road trip and catch one of those plays. I bet one of them is running in one of the many theaters on Broadway." Out of the corner of his eye, Ray sees a man in wheelchair coming toward them. As the man is approaching, Heidi turns and sees him. Jumping up from the bench, she walks toward the man.

"Edmond?" Edmond looks up at the young woman talking to him. Trying to figure out if he knows her, she continues, "I'm Morgan Kiernan's daughter, Heidi." Watching Edmond's expression turn from a visage of miserableness to one of curiosity with a hint of a smile made Heidi press on. "You befriended my mom when she first came back here. I have been wanting to meet you." Edmond puts his brake on with a flick of his wrist. Staring up at the young woman, he motions with his hand for her to stoop down so he could look at her on his level. Heidi, realizing right away, kneels down, and with a glance at Edmond, lays her hands on his legs.

Edmond smiles and replies, "Well, my dear, aren't you a spitting image of your mama? It's so nice to meet you. I do have to talk to your mama because she has been very neglective. In all our conversations, a daughter was not brought up, so make sure you tell her Edmond is a little put out by her lack of truthfulness." Heidi frowns slightly and wonders how much Edmond knows of her mother's story. Taking a chance, she speaks quietly so the stranger still sitting on the bench wouldn't overhear.

"Edmond, do you know my mother's story? She told me about staying at the Hotel and all the conversations she had with you. There is so much I'm sure she wanted to tell you but couldn't due to the circumstances surrounding her at that time." Edmond is listening to Heidi talk and thinks back to when Morgan and he would sit on the bench outside the Hotel. Morgan's constant help to get him up and down all the stairs in the Hotel would be something he would never forget. Her selflessness when he couldn't work his chair, or his legs wouldn't cooperate was priceless.

"Heidi, my dear, I spent some time with your mother, and her story is hers to tell. Someday she'll let me know what that story is, and I can't wait. Something tells me, it will be one I will never forget, but you and I both know it's her story. It's been very nice meeting you, and please tell your mom I said hello." Realizing the conversation was over with Edmond, Heidi exchanges her goodbyes and goes back to sit down. Ray is still sitting there but seems preoccupied with the front of the bank.

During the conversation Heidi was having with Edmond, Ray was keeping his eye on the front door of the bank. Suddenly, his contact bursts through the door looking angry.

Trying not to cut his conversation short with his newfound acquaintance, he apologetically says, "I'm sorry, Heidi, time gets away from me sometimes. I must run, but it was nice meeting you."

"Sure, my aunt and uncle should be pulling up at any moment. It was nice meeting you as well. Maybe I will see you around."

Ray doesn't want to appear in a hurry, so he extends his hand and offers, "I'm sure you will." Heading toward the bank door, he quickly comes up with an idea and rushes into the bank looking worried. Seeing a customer relations advocate, he walks quickly up to her.

Recognizing a customer in distress, she says, "Sir, can I help you?"

"Yes, you can. I was supposed to meet clients here, and I am running late. I don't see them anywhere here. Could they be in the back with someone?" Coming around from behind the counter, she motions to the back offices.

"The only person who has been in the back this morning was Nick Darlington, but he left a few minutes ago." Ray bows his head as if in defeat.

"It looks like I must have missed my clients. It was spouses looking to purchase some land from a friend of mine. I was going to take them on a tour of the area. Oh well, I'm sure they will contact me." Turning to leave, he smiles. Some things are so easy. In a matter of a few seconds, he found out who the contact was. Now he can put a name to the face.

Heidi

Heidi sees Aunt Sara and Uncle Jonathan pulling up to the curb. Walking quickly toward them, she thinks about the conversation she had with the gentlemen called Ray, and more than anything else she thinks of meeting Edmond. Understanding more about her mom after talking with Edmond, it becomes obvious. Heidi knows there are things she didn't know about her mom's past. Edmond is a quiet soul but intense about his feeling for Heidi's mom. Morgan must have impacted Edmond's life in the short time of arriving here. Sometimes you find the most interesting conversation with the most unexpected people. In Linn Creek, it was so normal to wander along the street and talk to strangers because they were enjoying the same things you were.

Getting into the car, Heidi greets her aunt and uncle and they are off to the outdoor market she has been dying to go to. Her focus is buying some of the fresh vegetables Aunt Sara was telling her about. Her aunt also informed her that apparently, raising your own cows so the beef is fresh and homegrown is popular right now. Knowing her mom was raised on a farm, having a steak dinner will be high on her list, so Heidi decides to get a couple of steaks to pair with the fresh vegetables as well. She continues putting the whole menu together in her head as her aunt begins talking.

"Heidi who was the person you were sitting with when we picked you up? He didn't look familiar to me or Jonathan."

The three of them pull up to the market, and getting out of the car, Heidi looks at her aunt replying, "You know it would be crazy if I did know him since this is the first time I have been here. Yet, you know, Aunt Sara, this guy seemed as though I knew him, he was so friendly."

Grabbing Heidi's hand, Sara responds, "Heidi, Millersville is like that. People are so friendly, so it doesn't surprise me what happened to you today. Just remember not everybody is as they seem."

Laughing and squeezing Aunt Sara's hand, Heidi replies, "Don't worry I am a big girl, and he truly was a nice guy. There weren't any alarm bells going off in my head." After grabbing everything she needs and getting introduced to the owner, Heidi leaves with her aunt and uncle heading back to her mom's house altogether.

On the way back, Heidi asks Sara, "Do you think my mom is going to stay here? I know how important family is to her, and she seems to be so happy now. I thought we had a great life in Linn Creek, but seeing how she is now, I wonder." Taking a minute to answer Heidi, Sara looks over at Jonathan. Noticing he is staring intently at the roadway; Sara realizes this answer is going to be hers and hers alone.

"Heidi, you did have a great life, and you should be very proud of what you and your mom have there. But your mom never forgot her family here. When she was younger, it was just too hard for her to navigate all the memories which reside in this community. Now enough time has passed, and she has matured. She realizes there was unfinished business here, and it was important for her to come home."

Listening intently, Heidi inquires further, "Why now? What made her want to come back now and not before?" Jonathan has remained silent until now.

"Heidi, I can answer a lot of your questions." Sara quickly looks at him with raised eyebrows. Jonathan continues, "Your mom has always been about family, and when she felt it was necessary to leave here, I know it had to be devastating. You ask why now. Her family needed her. I needed her and have always needed her but could never tell her. When I finally realized, it was too late. Thankfully your mom was smart enough to keep tabs on what was going on at home, and she knew it was time."

Looking out the window watching the landscape go by, Heidi listens to her uncle. She knows first-hand how important family is to her mom. She just always thought she was all the family they needed. Now looking at her aunt and uncle, she realizes there is so much more to her mom than she understood.

"Uncle Jonathan do you mean the farm? Is that why you are glad mom is here now?"

Glancing over his shoulder quickly before turning his eyes back to the road, he says, "Yes, it's about the farm. I was planning on selling the farm before your mom came back home. Now we—your mom, Sara, and I along with you—are coming up with another plan which will save a lot of the farm but sell a portion of it so we can have enough capital to implement your mom and Sara's plan."

Pulling up to the house, Aunt Sara suddenly adds, "Jonathan look, if I didn't know any better, that looks like Jackson Palmer sitting with Olivia." Getting out and opening the door for Sara, Jonathan stands with the two of us.

"Well, I'll be damned, Jackson has come back to Millersville." Annoyance shows in Sara's face.

"Of course, he's here. Why wouldn't he be? Seth and Olivia have just buried their granddaughter. You're making it seem like such a surprise Jackson is here."

At that moment, Jackson yells over, "Hey you two, come on over."

Jonathan touches Sara's arm and encourages her, "You go ahead over. I'm going in to talk with Morgan for a minute. We'll all head over shortly."

Walking toward the house, Heidi turns and proudly states, "Uncle Jonathan we are family, so together we can do almost anything." Jonathan smiles and follows her into his sister's new home.

Nick

Nick heads home from the bank still steaming about his conversation with Fraser. He finally got to see the real Tom Fraser who he definitely did not care for much. All this time helping him keep an eye on Jonathan, and lately Misty, was because he was in cahoots with the electric company. The faceless man named Ray had taken to following Misty which was freaking Nick out. Fraser didn't care about the land being used to improve the rateables. All of the meetings and phone calls were all a front to what was really being planned for the land—huge electrical towers, the exact ones that Misty's dad was fighting to stop all those years ago. They were lying in wait for Jonathan to fail, so they could swoop in and buy the land for pennies on the dollar. Remembering the paper Tom turned for him to see gave him chills. The investors wanted to take all of the Jenkins' property and install the new towers that were starting to show up in different parts of the county. But it was worse than he ever expected. They were going to install a new substation on the property. Morgan's father will be turning over in his grave knowing his land was used in such a way.

Nick was just about home and knew he couldn't involve Whitney in any of this. If she knew how far in debt they were, she would go ballistic. This was his problem, and he needed to find a way to fix it and still come out clear of any hold Tom Fraser or the bank had on him. Pulling into his street, he sees a van parked in front of his house. Briefly, he wonders if it was someone visiting

Whitney but shakes the thought away knowing Whitney very rarely had company.

Tapping his garage door opener, he waits for it to open enough to pull into his garage. Once inside the garage, he puts down the door and heads inside to see his boys. As he opens the door to the kitchen, he hears Whitney talking to someone. Figuring she must be on the phone, Nick steps into the kitchen. Sitting at his table was a dark-haired man who is having a conversation with his wife which seems to be amusing her. In a split second though, he notices Whitney pushing back her hair, tapping her long fingernails on the table, and tapping her left foot which told him one thing—she is very uncomfortable. Stepping into the room, he puts on an expectant look.

"Hey Whitney, I didn't realize we were having company. I would have made a better effort to get home sooner."

Trying to hide her nervousness, she looks at Nick and says, "It's fine Nick, Ray just stopped in to see you. I knew you would be home soon, so he decided to wait. You didn't tell me your college buddy was in town." Following her lead, Nick goes toward Ray motioning him to stand up. Realizing what is happening and not wanting to show his hand yet, Ray goes along with the ruse.

"Hey Ray, I had no idea you were going to show up here today. What gives? I thought our plan was to meet sometime next week." The two of them shake hands and stiffly give each other a man hug, and then Ray sat back down. Nick takes his normal position leaning against the counter.

Ray speaks first, "Nick, I know we had a plan to meet next week, but something came up today which made it important for me to be in Millersville. So here I am!"

Continuing the ruse for Whitney's sake, Nick asks, "How long have you been in town? I thought I saw the van you are driving around yesterday."

Smiling as if in agreement, Ray says, "Yes, I actually was in town yesterday driving around. Saw how beautiful Millersville is, and the small diner has delicious food as well. Today I had some time to kill before heading over here, so I sat on one of those nice benches you have lining your main street. It was a very pleasant experience. I met the most fascinating young woman named Heidi." Looking directly at Nick, Ray continues, "You know who I mean? Dark hair, eyes that remind you of tropical water and skin that was touched by the sun like a peach. Familiar?" Whitney quickly glances at Nick to gauge his reaction. Understanding the anger she could see in his eyes, she stood up to move next to him.

Taking the lead, she says to Ray, "I believe who you saw was our dear friend Morgan's daughter, Heidi. But then you already know her name, don't you?"

"Well, of course I do. She was so friendly and welcoming."

Frowning and squeezing Whitney's arm tightly, Nick speaks, "I'm sure she was very nice, but as far as I know, she just arrived here in Millersville." Getting up and standing next to Whitney, Ray puts his arm around her shoulders.

"Honestly, she was so informative. I told her I would see her again soon." Taking Whitney's hand, Nick walks her away from him.

Keeping a neutral expression on his face, Nick asks, "Ray, how come you got here so early? Like I said, you were due next week. Then, showing up here and making moves on my wife is not cool man." Whitney looks between Nick and Ray wondering exactly what is going on. Nick seems happy to see him, but she knows her husband. His eyes are strained, and his hands clenched by his side.

Apparently, he wants her to go along with whatever was going on in front of her, so she smiles and says, "Nick, yes, I was quite surprised to see Ray standing at the kitchen door. He scared me to death. You conveniently forgot to tell me he was coming, so you can imagine how unexpected it was when he showed up."

Ray puts on a show of indignation whining, "Why, Whitney, I thought we had a nice talk with each other. You were so inviting when I showed up at your door." Sharing a look with Nick, Whitney realizes this is her chance to actually help Nick with this quandary he has found himself in. Something isn't right about this person. She was almost sure his name probably wasn't Ray, and she was positive he wasn't a college buddy. So, following Nick's lead she goes along with Ray's comment.

"Of course, any friend of Nick's is a friend of mine. I'm sorry for my reaction when you came to the kitchen door, but I very rarely have visitors here. However, now that you're here, why don't I get us something to eat." Moving around in the kitchen gives her an excuse to get away from Ray. "Nick why don't you and Ray go out in the garage and talk. This way I can have the kitchen to myself, so I can get something put together for us."

"Thanks Whitney." Nick puts his arm around Ray and tells him, "Hey buddy, let's leave Whitney alone so she can create her magic." Nick heads toward the door which leads out to the garage. Looking over his shoulder, he smiles at Whitney to relieve any doubts she might have swirling around in her brain about their visitor. He couldn't have her find out about his involvement in the Jenkins' project.

Once the two of them are out in the garage, Nick turns angrily to Ray and says in a stifled shout, "What the hell are you doing here? You aren't supposed to be standing in the same room as me, least of all show up at my house and talk all friendly to my wife. Our contact is to be strictly over the phone, and even then, only when you have an update. So how did you find me?"

Ray says through a smirk, "Do you really think I am an idiot? All these months I have been taking directions from you to keep an eye on Jonathan Jenkins. Making sure any sign of rejuvenation in the farm's appearance was reported. Then his sister shows up. What the hell! I was told this was going to be a cake walk. Nothing but following around a washed-up farmer to make sure he stayed that way. Now you want to know how I found you. Instead, you should be asking me what is happening. There are people spending inordinate amounts of time and money out there, and it looks to me he has gotten a new lease on life. So, my advice to whomever you are working for is to initiate Plan B because Plan A is obsolete." Nick takes a step toward Ray.

"You have no idea what you are talking about. Jonathan Jenkins is a washed-up farmer who is in way above his head. So, whatever you think is going on you are mistaken. How about you continue what you have been asked to do and are being paid for and let the rest of us worry about the Jenkins project. As for his sister, I will take care of her. You need to keep focused on your part in this, but your new acquaintance, Heidi, is off-limits. Stay away from her, do you hear me!"

Stepping back and putting his hand up as if to ward off Nick's words, Ray responds, "Oh my! Awful protective of Heidi, aren't we? She seems very smart and looks like a young woman who can take care of herself. What are you one of them guys who prey on young women?"

Pushing Ray back, Nick grits through his teeth, "Shut up, you don't know what you are talking about. Just leave it alone."

Just then, Whitney comes to the kitchen door and says in a cheery voice, "Hey you two, food is ready. Come right in because I don't want it to get cold."

As she backs away from the door, Nick says to Ray, "When we finish eating, you are going to politely excuse yourself and leave here. And by the way, don't ever come back here to talk to me. Just do what you are being paid to do."

———— • ————

Later, after Ray leaves, Nick tells Whitney he needs to go into the office to get some paperwork. Whitney wants to talk about their visitor, but the look on Nick's face tells her otherwise. So, relaxing, she decides to catch up on a series she is watching on Netflix. Backing out of his driveway, Nick looks carefully around his neighborhood making sure Ray's van is nowhere to be seen. He realizes it is possible Jonathan has gotten a rebirth with Misty back in town. It looks like he better take a ride there and see what is going on for himself. Tom Fraser definitely appeared rattled when he saw him last.

Turning at the light, he notices Brett walking with Jillian, his bartender, down the street toward the bank. Seeing Brett made Nick burn with jealousy knowing Misty was spending more and more time with him according to Seth. The need to know what and how she is doing overrides the lecture he knows would be coming whenever he finally asks Seth. Knowing it was probably not a good idea he turns down her road. Getting closer to her house, he sees Seth, Sara, Heidi, and JACKSON! *What in the world is Jackson doing back in town?* Then, realizing why, he feels like such an ass. Of course, Jackson is here because of Abby.

Pulling up to Seth's place, he rolls down his passenger window and shouts, "Hey everyone, what's going on today?"

Seth walks over to the car and leans in to respond, "Nick, what's happening? I guess you saw Jackson is here. He got into town last night, and Olivia really feels good about him being here."

"Wow, Seth this is great for the two of you to have your brother here with you during this difficult time. Let me get straightened up here with my parking, and I'll come in and say hello."

Stepping back, Seth turns to look over to Morgan's house to see if he could see any activity. Nick steps out of his truck and walks around to Seth. Standing together, he follows the direction of Seth's view and sees Jonathan and Morgan walking out the back door and sitting down at her patio table. Their heads are leaning toward one another as if they were in deep conversation. Thinking back to his previous conversation, maybe something was brewing at the Jenkins farm. Turning away from the image at Morgan's, Nick and Seth walk up toward the house.

"Hey Jackson, it's so nice to see you again, man! How long has it been?"

Smiling, he replies, "Hey man, it's good to see you too! How is your family? Your kids must be so grown up now."

"Yeah, they are. Nicky is going into high school next year, and Scottie is going to be in seventh grade. They both play football, and Whitney wants Nicky to take up golf in high school for his spring sport."

"That's great to hear. It figures they are good athletes with your genes running through them."

Sara interrupts and says to Nick, "Have you met our niece, Heidi? Nick swallowed thickly. Regaining his composure, he put his hand out to take Heidi's hand.

"It's very nice to see you again, Heidi."

Heidi, being polite, says, "Aunt Sara, I met Nick and his wife, Whitney, at the diner." Seeing how uncomfortable Nick is behaving, Seth wants to turn the conversation in another direction and motions toward his house.

"Here comes Olivia." Nick, needing to move away from Heidi, walks up to Olivia and gives her a hug.

"Hey sweetie, how are you doing today? You are looking very pretty today and a little happier as well."

Hugging Nick back tightly, Olivia says genuinely, "Thanks for noticing Nick. I am feeling better today. Every day gets a little better, and Jackson being here has really helped."

At that moment, Jackson and Seth join the two of them. Nick wonders how long Jackson is going to stay knowing he has a big practice out of New York. Figuring it was none of his business, he listens to the conversation going on around him. Glancing back over to Morgan's, he sees Jonathan and Morgan are still talking. Turning back to look at Olivia, he sees her staring at him. Subtly shaking his head in the negative, he says he needs to head out and makes his leave. Watching him go, Olivia squeezes Seth's hand nodding toward Morgan's. Jackson, as always, is observing all that has gone on since Nick arrived. Tucking this information in his mind, he suggests going out to dinner to Seth and Olivia.

"Hey, you two, how about I take both of you out to dinner later? And not to the tavern! Don't give me a look Olivia, I just want to take you to a nicer place where we can talk without yelling over the rest of the people. Is there still the restaurant at the golf course?"

Seth smiles and answers, "Thanks Jackson we would love to. The restaurant is still there, and I believe there will be live music there tonight." Grabbing Olivia and twirling her around, Seth tells her, "Get dressed in your cutest outfit because we might be cutting the rug later tonight." With dinner decided, they all go inside.

New Chapter

The evening was proving to be a warm one, so Olivia dresses in one of her summer dresses and grabs a denim jacket in case it becomes cooler in the later evening. Knowing the group that she was with, they would be staying late.

Brett had just left Morgan's when Jonathan, Sara, and Heidi got back to her house from their trip to the market. Brett was on his way to the tavern and was very upset about having to leave. Sara and Heidi walk over to Seth and Olivia's while Jonathan stays back at Morgan's. Walking into Olivia's kitchen, Heidi sees Seth at the kitchen table reading a book.

"Hey Seth, Sara and I wanted to visit with you and Olivia. Are we interrupting your relaxation time?" Putting the book down, Seth smiles at his visitors.

"Come on in and sit down. Sara, it's nice to see you. What are you ladies up to?"

"Mom and Uncle Jonathan are over there talking. Sara and I wanted to see what you and Olivia were up to."

"Well, you just caught us. Jackson, Olivia, and I are heading out to dinner. If your mom and Jonathan can break away from their conversation, you are all welcome to join us."

Sara replies, "Thanks Seth, but Jonathan and I have had a busy day, so we are going to head home."

Heidi laughs and says, "I'm always up for a good time so let me talk to Mom and we will get back to you." With that, they get up and make their way back over to Morgan's.

Jonathan came in off the patio. Looking over at his sister, he watches her and wonders what her next move is going to be. Everything Morgan does is calculated. Not in a bad way. Her mind works differently than most people. Every action requires a response, so seeing her struggling right now made Jonathan realize something had happened.

"Morgan, I am pretty sure Brett Compton's truck was turning out of your driveway when we came down the road," Jonathan says with all the subtlety of any big brother inquiring about his sister's relational affairs.

"You are right. He was here for quite a while today."

Jonathan looks at me and says, "What happened Morgan, how long do you think you can keep this up?"

Walking back up to the house, I say, "I know, and it came to an end today. I told him who I was, and he is struggling with the whole idea that I am Misty Jenkins and not Morgan Kiernan. So, I'm not sure if the relationship we have will be coming to an end or not, but right now, we need to talk about what is going on with the bank." Having said this, I can see Jonathan quantifying how much Brett really means to me so he would know what to say, or rather what not to say, next.

"Morgan wait. Sara and Heidi went over to Seth and Olivia's. We need Sara here to be part of this conversation about the bank." Heading to the door, he sees Sara and Heidi walking back over.

"Jonathan, you know there is no point in milking again. Please tell me you are on board because honestly Jonathan, you and I can't go through this again. This is good for the farm."

Reaching Seth's back door, Jonathan turns to me and says, "You know Morgan, I have done a lot of thinking about everything, and it makes a lot of sense what you and Sara are proposing, but it's going to be difficult to turn a profit at first. Have either of you thought about how we are going to make money during the first few years? You do realize that grapes don't produce right away."

With my hand on Seth's back door, I sigh and tell him, "Jonathan, yes, I know. This is why we have to go back to the bank. Having enough capital to start the winery and buy grapes from somewhere else is imperative. So, we need to converge as a group and discuss our options before anyone goes to the bank." At that moment, Heidi opens the door.

"Mom, Seth, Olivia and Jackson are going to dinner, and we are invited. Are you up to joining them?"

Looking at Sara, I realize Jonathan and the two of us have a lot to discuss, so I look at her and say, "Heidi, go ahead and go. The rest of us have some things we have to discuss, so I can't join all of you."

Ray

Ray left Nick Darlington's house smiling. Finally, a face with the voice connects a lot of the doubts that are swarming around his mind. With the money from this job, Ray can pay off all his debts and become legitimate. No more surveillance for the people who are taking advantage of the lesser in the world. As he pulls into town, he finds he really wants to go by Misty Jenkins' home again. Turning at the light, he drives out toward her house. Slowing down, he sees several people standing outside of the house next door. Seeing Misty and her brother standing a little away from the rest of them slightly worries him.

After observing the activity around the Jenkins farm, Ray concludes there is definitely something going on that probably isn't going to fit into the plans of his bosses. The backhoes and dumpsters are definitely an indication of a cleanup in the works. This is just one more reason he needs to get out of this job as soon as possible. Driving past, he looks around and sees someone he thought he would never see again. Jackson Palmer was standing talking with Misty's neighbors. *What was he doing here?*

Thinking back to his early days of surveillance, he became involved in a huge EPA case. Jackson Palmer was the EPA's counsel. His techniques and ethics were always teetering on illegal, but he always got the win. Ray remembers the run-in he had with him, and he knew that day he never wanted to go up against him again. Coming to the end of the road, he decides it probably wouldn't be a good idea to do a U-turn and head by there again, so he turns left.

Jonathan, Sara, & Morgan

Around my kitchen table, Jonathan, Sara, and I continue our discussion regarding the possibility of turning the farm into a vineyard. Meanwhile, Heidi is hanging out with Seth, Olivia, and Jackson having dinner.

I remind my brother, "Jonathan, you have most of the equipment needed to get the fields ready. We just need to decide how many acres we want to utilize. However, I get the feeling you want to keep the calves you have. It's a possibility, but we both know the amount of work we will be required to do with the winery, and honestly if we pursue the vineyard idea, you won't be milking cows anymore. It will be raising them until they are ready to be bred, and then we would have to have a buyer ready to take all of them." I look over at Sara hoping she would interject something to help Jonathan come to grips with the prospect of never milking again.

Jonathan frowns slightly and begins, "Morgan, don't you think we better make sure we will have a prospective buyer for the grapes and an expected yield? Then we can decide the acres needed. Besides I need to do some extensive research on growing grapevines."

Sara taps her husband on the arm and tells him, "Sometimes you amaze me. Haven't you been planting and growing corn, hay, and soybeans on this ground for the last twenty years? How different do you think it's going to be? We will find out what soil count is needed, and we will fertilize accordingly." I smile to myself. Sara was always so practical, and her personality belied her enthusiasm for something

246

she believed in. This idea of having a vineyard was growing on her, and I could tell she is totally on board.

"Jonathan, I talked to Uncle Anson, and he still has connections out in California who will send us some young vines to plant which have a fast yield. I also talked to Jolene at Donatella Winery. She is very intrigued and will help us get started with the understanding that we sell her the first yield of grapes. Her husband, Scott even offered to help us prune when it's time. They have been doing it for several years, and their winery is very successful."

Getting up from the table, Jonathan starts pacing the kitchen. Watching him, I can see the turmoil of the thoughts running through his mind.

Coming to a standstill, he turns to me and inquires, "What are we going to tell the bank? If I must renegotiate with Tom Fraser on the number of acres split from the farm, I need to do it as soon as possible. He has been leaving numerous messages on my phone, and I haven't called him back."

"Jonathan, come back and sit down. You're making me nervous pacing back and forth. The agreement was for you to keep fifty acres to farm, so we will go back to them and ask them to revise the proposal. There is still a lot to be reviewed in the agreement, and I am going to ask Jackson to look over the agreement before you sign your name to it. He is going to be staying here to help Seth and Olivia find out if there is an environmental reason Abigail contracted leukemia."

With a look of disgust and an irritating tone to his voice, Jonathan declares, "Really Misty, you aren't going down that road again. Have you been feeding Seth and Olivia a bunch of foolish ideas of electro-magnetic fields hurting our environment?" Pushing back my chair, I stand up, and with my hands on my hips, I try to get myself under control.

"Yes, Jonathan I have been, but they are not foolish ideas, and you know it! What happened to you?" With my voice raised, I continued, "You know as well as I do there is a good chance something wasn't right at their house. Seth and Olivia told us repeatedly the week she died that she always got a little better when they traveled. Every time they were home for an extended amount of time, Abby would get sicker and sicker.

Now I can't go down to Cissy's house with Dad's rods and check to see if there are EMF rays surrounding the house, but I know I'm right. The old electrical towers are on the other side of the tree line by their home. This is why Jackson is staying. So, I am going to ask him to help us with the sales agreement for the farm. He has the experience and the legal clout to question the bank and their client as to why they want the farm so badly. We both know there is more to all of this than Tom Fraser is letting on. His puppeteer is having him dance on a string doing their bidding."

After watching the two of us express our strong opinions, Sara must have decided that she was going to claim her own bigger role in the bank problem as she interjects, "Hey you two, why don't you take a breath and let me talk for a minute? My role in the sale of this farm has not been huge, however, I believe everyone has a part. How about I visit Tom Fraser? I can possibly pull information from him the two of you may have missed."

Laughing out loud, Jonathan says, "Really Sara, what exactly do you think you are going to see or hear that Misty and I have not?"

Trying to hold the disdain, I suddenly feel for my brother. I put my hand on Sara's arm trying to comfort her as I begin, "Don't listen to him, it's a great idea. Having you go to the bank will throw Tom Fraser off so much he might just let his guard down. So why don't you call there now and see when he is available? Today would be great but highly unlikely due to his busy schedule." Flashing a look of thanks to me, Sara dials the bank number and asks if Tom Fraser is available.

When she is put on hold, she turns to me and whispers so that only I can hear, "You know watching you and Jonathan battle each other with your expressive eyes and body language has been entertaining. Jonathan would be mad if I told him, but he was acting just like his dad. First words out of their mouths are negative. Then they change their tune after time."

Before I can offer my agreement, Sara pauses to listen to the phone, and I move in closer so that I can hear the voice on the line begin, "Mr. Fraser is out of the office for the rest of the afternoon, however, I will let him know you called." Giving the woman on the other line her number, she and Sara exchange goodbyes, and Sara looks at the two people she loves the most.

"Ok, you two, let's come up with a game plan."

Smiling broadly, I say, "That a girl. We are going to win this battle of wits with Mr. Tom Fraser, guaranteed."

Jackson

As they wrap up their dinner together, Jackson listens to Seth and Olivia talking with Heidi. His thoughts circled back to the other night when Morgan and Heidi were over. It amazed him how quickly he figured out who Morgan was and thinking back, he now knew his feelings for her were quietly dormant, but now all he can say is *Wow*. Heidi is a whole other issue. Her laugh is infectious, and her personality is a bright light in what was a sometimes-dark world. He decides he will get to know her better, and he has a feeling he is going to be in Morgan's company a lot in the next few weeks. Hearing his brother and his beautiful wife laughing spontaneously and enjoying their time with a person they just met made Jackson smile.

Thinking about tomorrow, he decides it is time for him to have a serious talk with Morgan about exactly what her dad was into before he died. Listening to Olivia discuss the towers and the harm she felt was coming from them was very serious and slightly unnerving. Seth talked about it in a much calmer manner, yet he also had the same view and concerns about the towers. Morgan seems to be instrumental in how Seth and Olivia feel, and it was Jackson's job to figure out how serious these accusations were.

On the ride home, Heidi talks about her home in Linn Creek. Jackson admires the enthusiasm and passion she has for her hometown. It reminds him so much of her mother. When they pull into Seth and Olivia's driveway, Olivia asks Heidi to come in, so she can show her some of her cookbooks.

Across the yard, Jonathan and Sara are walking toward their truck. Noticing that they are about to leave, and that Heidi is preoccupied with Seth and Olivia, Jackson recognizes he should be able to talk to Morgan uninterrupted. Moving quickly across the yard, he comes to Morgan's deck and hesitates.

Knowing Morgan was Misty Jenkins brought so many memories to his mind. He was unsure how to approach her, but he needed to talk with her about the death of his niece. Olivia was adamant Morgan had information to give Jackson. Finally, taking the last few steps, he knocks on her door and leans against the door jamb to wait.

Looking around her yard, he can see her personality in all aspects of her deck and the yard beyond—flowers and gazing balls along with ornamental grasses waving along the edge. Birds are chirping and finding water in all the bird baths she has scattered around the yard.

———— • ————

Hearing a knock at the door, I call down, "I'll be right there." Within a few minutes, I was downstairs and shocked to see Jackson standing at the door, but I quickly covered my surprise with a smile. "Well, hello Jackson. I wasn't expecting anyone, least of all you. I was getting ready to walk over to Seth and Olivia's to see all of you. Is there something wrong?"

"Nothing is wrong. They are having a great time. Heidi is entertaining them, and it's nice to hear them laughing and talking.

I wanted to talk with you alone." Stepping back, I motioned him to come in.

"Please have a seat. Would you like something to drink?"

"No, thank you. I just want to talk to you. Olivia has assured me that you have information that will help us figure out if there were outside forces contributing to Abby's death. I need as much information as you can give me, and I know from your past this could be painful. After listening to Olivia talk about Cissy and Josh's house and the towers in the area, coupled with her feeling better when she was away from the house, it all points in the wrong direction."

Sitting back in my chair, I do my best to smile though I am certain it appears quite sad, and I begin, "You are so right Jackson, it is painful. But it's been a real problem in this area, and I've come back to Millersville to try to educate the community and hopefully get the attention of the electric company. My dad was way before his time, and most of the community thought he had lost it. Nothing was wrong with his mind other than he was obsessed with proving there were electromagnetic fields surrounding all of us."

Grabbing my hand, Jackson says, "You left out something. He believed those electromagnetic fields were harming us, in some cases killing us. Well Morgan, I have the reputation, clout, and connections to make the electric company listen. Now the hard part comes, and I want to make sure you are truly ready to do this. It could bring out the dissenters from before because believe me we will be making waves. We must find other people suffering from the effects of EMF."

THE SILENCE IS BROKEN

Feeling dread with a tingling of excitement, I get up and lean down and give Jackson a hug.

"Jackson, you have no idea how happy and scared I am to finally do something about this. It has been silently killing people for many, many years and no one knew or if they did, they were scared or didn't care enough to speak up. The people who do know are making way too much money to change their methods and make people safe. So, I don't care what it takes, we will find the people responsible. We will find those who are sick with life-threatening and chronic diseases and have them come forward." Jackson stands up and takes me into his arms.

"You need to know, Morgan, if we begin, I will not stop until we prove your father's theory was valid, the electric company makes the towers safe or finds a safe alternative, and the victims and their families are compensated." His arms are strong and his scent so familiar that, for just a moment, I am transported back to that summer. Stepping from his embrace, I look up at him.

"Jackson, I am so grateful you are here to help us finally put an end to the suffering of those in Millersville who are and have been innocent victims of a known, silent killer."

Reaching for me one more time, Jackson squeezes my hand and says, "Morgan, I am determined to find my brother and his wife an answer for the sorrow they are feeling every day and to tell my niece exactly what happened to her daughter." Moving away, I sit back down at the table.

"Jackson, if you have time tomorrow, come over. I have the day free." Sitting down across the table from me, Jackson's look becomes intense.

"I have time now if you can talk." Looking over to Olivia's, I can see Heidi at the table laughing and talking.

"Ok, Jackson, let's get to it."

"First, Morgan. What is going on with Jonathan and the farm? Seth and Olivia were telling me the bank is involved now. Are they planning on bailing him out of his debt or what?" Not wanting to sound derogatory about Jonathan, I quickly think of a way to explain what is happening with the farm and how the bank has become involved.

"The bank gave him a proposal to buy off part of the farm and leave enough for him to farm small. Dairy farming is a thankless occupation in today's market unless you are milking a thousand cows. Milk prices have been on a rollercoaster since 2014 with the low being $12 in 2020. Fluctuating up and down for years, milk is now bringing almost $28.00 per hundredweight. In dairy farming, milk is your product. Corn and hay are grown to feed the animals not to sell. There are other crops they can plant to turn a profit. Unfortunately, the caveat there is, you have to farm a large amount of land. The average size farm only has enough ground to use for crops to feed their animals.

The point is, Jackson, farming has too many unknowns. It relies on Mother Nature being its biggest fan, and we both know what a crap shoot that is. So, Sara and I feel strongly Jonathan should not go back to milking cows. We are working on a plan to turn the acreage into a vineyard." Jackson listens intently, and when I pause in my story, he begins to speak quietly.

"Morgan, I get it, but why do you think the bank is so interested in the farm? From what I remember when studying the area for a paper I wrote in high school, most of the ground is not going to perk. Building a big development there would cost a ton of money with all the excavation, preparation, and infrastructure which would have to be done. Also, having the barns and other buildings standing empty and deteriorating also lends to some discrepancy in the basis of their interest. It doesn't look like a good investment to me, so there has to be something else that has generated this attention. We need to figure out what they truly want with the land."

Thinking back to my earlier conversation with Jonathan and Sara, I answer, "Jackson, I'll be honest, Jonathan has delayed calling back the bank partly due to my dismissive attitude with the agreement. There are obvious conditions which are wrong, and then too many parts of it look suspicious. But I'm ashamed to say a lot of it is legal ease which is confusing, and we don't understand it."

Grabbing both of my hands across the table, Jackson smiles and adds reassuringly, "Morgan, my dear, I'm here now and they can throw all the legal jargon they want at us. We will nail them to the wall if they are doing something underhanded. Just get me the agreement, so I can go over it tooth and comb. Then we will go back to the bank with our demands and what will become the future of the Jenkins farm."

We sit and talk for another hour about all the possible reasons the bank is in this at all. I confide in him that Sara will be making a visit to Tom Fraser, wondering if he thinks it is a good idea or a waste of time. He agrees her visit could not hurt, and on the other hand, could even be a good move. Exactly what I thought, and it is nice to hear it is Jackson's view as well.

Elizabeth

Elizabeth is wondering why Brett has not been by lately. He usually comes over to see her often, and it had been a few days since she had seen him. She also wonders if he is still seeing Morgan Kiernan. She knows being away for so many weeks has made it difficult to keep tabs on what he was doing. The last time he visited was very disturbing. Leaving as she had on holiday was just what she needed to keep Morgan from pursuing what she found on the day of her visit. The unique container was taken from the Jenkins property after the events of so many years ago. Jack insisted on keeping the canister for nostalgic reason, but it gave Elizabeth the creeps.

So, after Morgan left, Elizabeth put it away. Elizabeth remembered the look on her face when she discovered it. Devastating! It was as if Morgan knew where the canister came from. That look is what Elizabeth couldn't stop replaying in her mind. Elizabeth couldn't help but think to herself, *this is not good. What was I thinking when I hid it in that drawer?* After Jack died, there were less and less dinner parties, eventually even her lady's luncheon was reduced to once a month. In the past, the house was always busy with guests visiting or company executives invited for dinner. Now the guest bathroom has become just another room to clean. So, it was the perfect hiding place.

Then Brett brings a woman into her house. A woman who wanted to look at the flowers and play her piano intruding on her perfect solitude. Morgan's look made Elizabeth uncomfortable. Hazel eyes became dark brown with some kind of emotion when Morgan was questioning Elizabeth about the piano. Elizabeth wonders, *how could I deny her request to come again and walk through my flower garden? I should have never agreed to her askance. What am I going to do about this now that she found the canister?*

Jack was supposed to shut down the Jenkins man from finding out the intention of the electric company. Instead, he became friends with the man, so completing the plan never happened which didn't work into Elizabeth's plan for Jack's career. Thinking back to that time, she can remember being so angry with him. The discussions which occurred everyday about how much the two of them were talking and sharing stories. She knew Jack lost his direction with the task the company had given him. He knew what the job entailed, but the friendship he developed with Carl Jenkins was deterring him from completing it. She knew that if he had pursued the path laid out before him, they would have been set for life.

But no, everything went to hell that summer, and she felt it was time to take things into her own hands. Jack decided he needed to take a break, and he went on an extended trip. This only made it easier for her to execute her plan without involving him. But now she was stuck with this canister that Jack left with her. Originally, it was to be Jack's constant reminder of his relationship with Carl Jenkins. Now, it was Elizabeth's constant reminder of the guilt she felt, and she could never get rid of the canister for fear someone would see it and start asking questions. The canister had engravings on the side which depicted the farm in its early years. There would be a lot of explaining to do if Brett ever found out about it, especially now Morgan has put her eyes on it.

Turning to go back inside the house, she grabs a glass of iced tea and sits down at her table to go over all the mail she hadn't been able to look through. Seeing a small envelope with unusual handwriting on the front, she gets her letter opener and slits the top of it open. Pulling out a card, she flips it over. There, in a childlike scrawl, *we know what you did to Carl.* She drops the card like it burned her hand. Trying to keep her control, she picks up the card again by the corner and really looks at the writing.

So many thoughts raced through her mind. *Who was behind this? So many years have passed, and most people have forgotten all about Carl Jenkins. His family fell apart after his death, the farm became un-profitable under his son's management, and the daughter has never come back to Millersville. Who could possibly care now after all these years?* Suddenly her phone rang, scaring her for a moment.

Getting up and hurrying down the hall to the phone, she grabs it and somewhat breathlessly says, "Hello." Hearing nothing, she re-peats herself.

Then, she hears a whisper, "I guess you got your card. Did you like the message?"

Elizabeth grips the phone tightly and responds with as little fear as possible, "What do you want?"

"We just want to let you know we are here and watching."

Breathing quickly, Elizabeth asks, "Watching what?"

The voice on the other end speaks louder, "She's back!"

Responding quickly, "Who is back?" Hearing nothing, she asks again, "Who is back?" Realizing they had hung up, she put the phone back in its cradle. Going back to the kitchen, she sits down and puts her head in her hands asking out loud, "Who was behind the whisper and why are they watching me and why would they be telling me someone was back?" She could feel herself getting alarmed. Calming herself down, she decides to call Brett. Maybe talking to him would be calming. Getting up, she goes to the phone again and dials Brett's number.

"Hello, Mother, how are you!"

"Brett, I need to see you. If you can, get over here right away. I received a very disturbing phone call. Can you come over?" Hearing his mother's distress, he realizes it is something he needs to address right away, especially after the phone call he intercepted before she had arrived home. Telling Jillian, he had to leave and assuring her he would be back within a couple of hours, he jumps into his truck and heads to his mother's.

Pulling up to her house, he sits in his truck for a moment gathering himself before facing her. He contemplates whether or not the earlier phone call was something he should tell her about, or is it possible there is more to this so sitting back and observing might be the better avenue? Frowning to himself, he wonders why his mother was getting these calls, and he prepares himself for some disturbing revelation. Beginning his walk up to the front door, he sees his mother standing on her front step.

"Brett, thank God you got here as fast as you did. I am so afraid they might try to call again." Taking her arm, walking her back inside the house, and seating her at the table, he then grabs himself a chair.

Turning it around and sitting down with his arms folded on the back of the chair, he begins, "Mother, I have no idea why someone would be harassing you. If there is something you need to tell me, now would be the time to share it. Those people who continue to work the neighborhood looking for trouble need to be stopped. This is a nice area, and you are telling me something very disturbing, so what gives Mother?" Looking at her son, she realizes he has no idea what lies behind the perfect façade she maintains.

"Brett, I don't know. They were so invasive on the phone, and it scared me. It seemed as if they were standing right outside the door with the tone of their voice. They whispered to me on the call telling me someone is back. Who in the world were they talking about?"

"Mother, I'm sure it was just a crank call. You are overreacting to this phone call which is exactly what they wanted to accomplish. Calm down and tell me everything said." Bowing her head, she can't help but feel like she is being sent a message. Someone from long ago has arrived, and they aren't planning on letting her forget what happened. Looking at Brett, she appears to have calmed down.

"You know, you are probably right about a crank call. I don't know why I got so upset. I'm sorry I dragged you away from the bar during your busy time."

Leaning forward to be able to look her in her eyes, Brett states matter-of-factly, "Mother, it's no problem, I will always be here for you. This has apparently shaken you up severely, so again, what else did they say?" Hesitating, not wanting to show Brett the note, she tilts her head away from Brett so there would be no eye contact.

Then she begins, "Earlier when I got the mail, there was an envelope addressed to me with no return address. The handwriting was crudely scrawled, you know childlike…"

"Mother, what did it say? Let me see it." Knowing in the next few minutes she is going to be asked a dozen questions, which were going to be extremely hard to answer, she takes a deep breath.

Getting up and walking out to the hallway table, she picks up the note, turns, and senses that Brett is already walking toward her.

"Let me see it, Mother." Handing the letter to Brett makes her feel as though she is handing herself a death sentence. Looking down at the note in his hand, Brett reads the childlike, handwritten note and a chill goes down his spine. He looks at his mother doubting her for the first time in his life. Quickly, Elizabeth tries to think how she is going to manipulate the next few minutes.

"Mother, who is Carl, and why would they be telling you they know what you did to Carl? Would you like to tell me why this note got you so upset?" Walking back to the kitchen and sitting back down, Elizabeth folds her hands and looks at her son.

"Brett, I'm going to tell you a story in which you play a part but weren't a willing participant. The Carl in the note is Carl Jenkins." Brett frowns, trying not to let his mother know he is aware of who Carl Jenkins is or at least who his daughter is.

"Now I remember. Carl Jenkins was the farmer that Jack was involved with when I was young. He became obsessed with the man, didn't he?"

Leaning back in her chair, Elizabeth continues, "Yes, he did, and I couldn't stand it. There wasn't a day he didn't go over there and spend hours with the man. At first, it was just occasionally because I believe Carl didn't want Jack around the farm. Then a friendship was born, and it was then Jack went every day. He even participated in the birthing of a calf." A tentative smile appears on Brett's face.

"I remember Jack telling the story. The mother cow was having problems birthing the calf, so Mr. Jenkins, Charlie, and Jack pulled the calf, right?"

Nodding her head, Elizabeth agrees, "Yes, and that single event bonded Jack and Carl Jenkins. The problem was the electric company wanted Jack to come up with a solution about Carl Jenkins' theory about the electrical towers."

Brett raises his eyebrows and asks, "What kind of solution were they expecting?" Realizing she is treading in dangerous territory, she continues to tell the story.

"The company wanted Carl Jenkins to stop his visits around the county stirring up the citizens with stories of serious health consequences of the electromagnetic fields being fed by the towers. He had become suspicious of the high rates of sickness and disease for those who lived in proximity to the towers and gathered evidence to support his suspicion. It got so bad a consortium of people banded together to try to stop the construction of new towers out on Highway 77." Listening to his mother speak, Brett tries to hide his emotions. He contemplates his next words carefully.

"Mother, tell me what exactly did you have to do with this solution? The note says they know what you did to Carl. Before you say you don't know, there has to be some reason why they sent the note to you."

Brett is doing his best not to show he is reeling with despair. Trying to process what he had just found out from Morgan, and now his mother is telling him something he was sure would change the outcome of his feelings for both his mother and Morgan. Looking at her son, Elizabeth decides to tell Brett as much of the truth as she could. There are parts of this story that would go to the grave with her, but for the sake of Brett, she needs to tell him something.

"Brett, you know how much I care about my reputation here in Millersville. I've always held myself to a certain standard, and that meant money was very important to me. Jack's relationship with Carl Jenkins was threatening that very thing, and I was terrified of the outcome. The company was becoming more demanding and was making visits to the house wanting to know what was going on because Jack had stopped reporting on the situation. So, I took over the reporting behind Jack's back. The company was calling the house so much that it was easy to tell them whatever I could find out." Brett can't help shaking his head in disgust.

"Mother, what did you think you were going to accomplish by doing this to Jack?"

Controlling her emotions as best she could, she responds, "Our standard of living was not going to survive if he was to get fired, and the electric company wanted Jenkins shut down, so I did what I had to for you and me." Standing up from the table and walking over to the sink to get a drink of water, he stares out the window toward the immaculate yard with all the show stopping flowers.

"Mother, we could have lived differently. To my recollection, you weren't happy, and I know it for sure because you made life miserable for me growing up. There was never anybody good enough to come over to hang out with me, and I rarely asked to do anything or have anyone over because I was ashamed of how perfect my house was. The only person you really tolerated was Seth, and I'm not sure why, but you were always happy when Seth came over. Now thinking back, it was those times when you and I talked the most. There always had to be someone else with us for us to talk to, and it was Seth. So, tell me Mother, what was it about Seth that made you so happy?"

Hearing Brett describe his childhood and teenage years was hurtful. Elizabeth never believed she treated her son with anything else but respect and devotion. She wanted nothing else for him but to become successful and well-respected in his town. This talk about Seth was unnecessary. Seth was Brett's friend, and she felt she understood their need for companionship. Seth helped Brett develop his confidence and his understanding of girls.

"Brett, I'm not sure why you are saying these things. Seth was and still is your best friend. I was delighted when Seth was around because you were happy. I couldn't bring the smiles and laughter to your life, but Seth could." Getting up and walking over to Brett, she put her hand on his arm. "Brett, nothing has made me happier than to see you turn into the man you are today. I did what I needed to for your success. I love you the only way I know how, and that is to give and support you in whatever way I can." Brett turns and looks at his mother.

"There is something I need to tell you. Recently, I have learned Morgan is related to Carl Jenkins." Elizabeth sways and quickly catches the chair and sits down.

"What? Morgan is related to the Jenkins farmer. How is that possible?"

Pulling her out of her chair and staring into her eyes, Brett grits through his teeth, "She is his daughter. Jonathan Jenkins is her brother. She remembers Jack and his visits to the farm, and I'm sure she remembers a lot more, but I left before she could tell me. So how about you tell me, Mother. What exactly happened between you and Carl Jenkins? And don't tell me nothing because I won't believe it." Putting her head in her hands, she wonders how life became so difficult. Looking up at Brett and trying to smile, she grabs his hands.

"At first Jack stopped once a week. Then, as time went by, Jack visited Carl almost every day. In the beginning, I didn't pay much attention to what Jack was doing. I knew how important his job was, and I was enjoying all of the perks of his position. Eventually, I realized Jack was talking with Carl about his theory concerning the stray voltage of the old towers around the county. There wasn't much interest on my part, because again, all I cared about was all the luncheons and dinners we were invited to." Brett frowns, and Elizabeth can see his expression changing to disgust or maybe it was disappointment.

Continuing, "Jack became obsessed with everything going on at the Jenkins farm. His conversations were changing almost being admirable of the man. Suddenly, the company started calling asking for Jack. I was continually leaving messages for him to call back, but apparently, he was ignoring them. One day, I received a call from Jack's superior asking if there was something happening that he needed to know about. For weeks, I deterred them to cover for Jack. A couple of months later, I decided to ingratiate myself in Jack's career by intercepting the calls from the company. This is when I realized what their plan entailed, and nothing Jack was doing was helping them achieve their goal." Brett put his hands up to stop Elizabeth from continuing.

"So Mother, what exactly were they trying to achieve? It doesn't make any sense to me why Jack was so interested in this one dairy farmer. What could he possibly be doing? I know my time at home during this time was limited due to my exile to boarding school. But when I was home, I distinctly remembered Jack's involvement with Mr. Jenkins, and it was more than a business visit. So please continue."

Wondering how to come out of this conversation in a stronger light in Brett's eyes, Elizabeth starts again, "His visits were becoming so frequent and much longer in duration. So, one day I asked to go with him. He was very hesitant at first, but after some thought, he agreed. After a few days, we planned to go, and I didn't want to visit someone new without a gift. Jack didn't want me to bring anything. He said they were not the kind of people who would expect a gift from a first-time visitor. Explaining to him it went against everything I believed in, he lamented and suggested I bring my peach tea. Knowing how Jack felt about me taking something, I realized his suggestion of the tea was a good one. So, making a fresh batch we went over.

We arrived just before lunch, and Carl was still in the field working. Heading up to their back door, which to be honest, I just couldn't fathom doing, but Jack insisted it was the door to go. He opened the door and yelled, 'Mrs. Jenkins.' A few minutes went by and then a woman came to the door. Brett, she was nothing like I expected. Her hair was done, she had on a colorful dress with sturdy but attractive shoes. She wore pale pink lipstick, and her eyelashes were tipped with just the hint of mascara. Her expression, however, was not welcoming at all. But then, something came over her. A slight smile suddenly came to her lips, and she opened the door to let us in. You know, Brett, now thinking back that smile is very similar to Morgan."

"Mother, please tell me what all this has to do with the phone calls and visits you are getting from men in dark vans. Plus, you have yet to explain the note you received."

Getting up and moving to the windows looking out at her beautiful flowers, she proceeds, "After a few months went by, Jack's superiors were at the end of their rope. So, a plan was developed to impale Carl Jenkins' ability of testing stray voltage of the local towers." Realizing she is moving into dangerous territory; she comes back to sit down and puts her head down on her arms. Knowing his mother and her need for comfort in trying times, Brett sits down with her and puts his hand on her arm.

"I know this is extremely hard for you to tell me about this." Looking at his watch, he realizes it is getting late, and he needed to get back to the bar to relieve Jillian and get ready to close. "Unfortunately, my time is limited now, but believe me, this is not over. We will continue this conversation, but for now, you have a reprieve. Just know Mother, I firmly believe you and Morgan's family are connected somehow, and I'm going to find out how." Leaning down and giving her a small kiss on the cheek, he leaves. Elizabeth watches him leave, and then breaks down into tears.

Jonathan & Sara

Jonathan and Sara go home from Morgan's house, and after some chores, they decide to sit out in their backyard and have a cocktail. Sara is so excited about this simple time together that she changes her clothes and puts on a little makeup. It has been years since they sat out back. The sunsets are spectacular, and she missed having this time with Jonathan. Just the fact he suggested it is proof he is feeling better about things. She goes out to clean off the chairs and lights a candle while Jonathan goes down to the barn to see what else was done with all the cleanup going on over the last few days. Seeing the progress, he smiles to himself with the realization there is a chance they would be successful again.

Walking up to the house, he quickens his step knowing Sara is excited about sitting out back. For a moment, he wishes his mother and father could be here seeing the changes on the farm and knowing their daughter had finally come home. No matter what happens, he feels in his heart he and Misty will be fine. Coming around the corner of the house, Jackson sees his wife, sitting with a glass of wine admiring the landscape. His heart swells with happiness and just a little sadness for all the time they lost immersed in the farm and its slow deterioration.

"Hey, you look beautiful tonight. It makes me so happy to see you like this. It's been way too long."

Smiling and standing up to hug her husband, Sara says, "Jonathan, it's great. We haven't sat out here much looking at our view. Isn't it beautiful? This is our land, Jonathan. We are not going to let go of all of it. Part of this land will be buildable, and we are going to sell it. Then, we can start a vineyard. Here, I got you a glass of wine, sit and enjoy yourself. Remember sometime in the future, those will be our grapes making the wine. So, sit tight while I get the cheese tray I made for us to nibble on."

Sitting down and sipping his wine, he thinks back to his wife and when he first met her. Sara was the quiet but very intelligent girl who blended into the crowds unnoticed. During their junior year, he had an English class with her, and she sat in front of him. He saw her personality shine when it was her turn to speak to the class or read a passage from a book. She had a way of becoming the character in the book, and hearing her voice change with the emotion of the words was so enjoyable.

After spending time with her in class, he tried to talk to her during other times of the day. Most of the time, she became her quiet version, but one day he saw the strength in her rise to the surface. There was a girl who accused a boy of forcing her to have sex when they were in eighth grade. She didn't come forward with the information until they were juniors. The student body was split down the middle with those who believed her and those who believed the boy. The whole town became involved in the controversy, and lives were irrevocably changed during those horrific days.

During an assembly, Sara stood up and talked to the student body about friendship, truth, and the power of our words. Her speech was so empowering that several weeks later the girl came forward and said she had lied. By that time, the family had left the area, and the boy was at college. Thinking back to those days, he realized how the power of words can influence someone either positively or negatively.

But on this particular day, Jonathan could still see her up on stage waving her arms and motivating us all to be better people. When Sara cared about something, she was a formidable woman. He knew she was the best person to go to the bank. The emotions Misty and he carried on their shoulders inhibited them to speak calmly, and this agreement desperately needed to be changed. Turning his attention back to Sara, he puts his glass up in a toast.

"Sara, this is to more nights like this, and may the view be row after row of grapes."

Brett

After leaving his mother's, Brett feels the need to drive around for a little while before heading back to the tavern. He suddenly finds himself on Morgan's street. As he comes around the bend by her house, he sees the dark van sitting across the street again. Slowing down, he quickly turns into her neighbor's driveway, so he can watch what is going on with the van. No sooner did he pull in than the van started to pull out.

Backing out of the driveway quickly, Brett follows the van. Keeping a good distance back so he wouldn't be noticed, he continues to follow the van as it is moving toward town and eventually all the way through town and out toward the country. Continuing his surveillance, he realizes they are heading toward the Jenkins farm. Staying a considerable distance behind the van, he decides he needs to call Morgan.

———— · ————

"Hey, are you alright? I just saw a dark van outside of your house again, and I am following it right now." I immediately sat down at my kitchen table hearing these words through the telephone.

"Brett, you don't know how happy I am to hear your voice." Hearing no response, I continued, "I had no idea the van was sitting out there. Where are you now?"

He takes a moment to respond before saying, "Morgan, he is riding by your dad's farm and for some reason, he has pulled over close to their property, and I am idling not far from him." I hesitated for a moment on the phone. *What was this van doing out by the farm? Could this be another play by the bank? This van has been conducting surveillance for the past week around the whole area but especially around here.* Now it's moved toward the farm.

Realizing I have been silent for too long lost in my thoughts, I say, "Brett, it could be dangerous. I think you better be sure the guy doesn't know you are following him." I can hear the engine cut off as he pauses again before answering me.

"Morgan, I really don't know, but this same van was parked in front of my mother's house earlier, and I'm pretty sure whomever it is has called her as well. Since then, they have been in front of your house watching, and now they are watching the farm. What is it that ties all this together?"

Frowning into the phone, I responded, "Brett I honestly don't know. I came back here to clear my family's name and find out what happened to my father. Why would this person be interested in all of us?"

Brett, sounding frustrated says, "I really don't know but I'm going to find out. Random people have been harassed by this person, but now I believe there is a link which ties all of this together. Please lock your door, and when business slows down at the tavern, I would like to come over and talk if that's ok?"

Smiling to myself, I, as calmly as I can, reply, "I can't wait. I will be waiting for you!"

Morgan & Jackson

Sitting back and relaxing a bit after the phone call with Brett, I go over my day. The confession to Brett was hard, but I feel like the world has been lifted from my shoulders. In time, he will understand why I came back to Millersville the way I did. If I had arrived as Misty Jenkins, there would have been too much gossip which would hamper the end result. Now the Jenkins farm will prosper, and my family will survive our ugly past.

My thoughts flick to Jackson, and I find myself wondering how important it is he came back for Seth and Olivia. Thinking about Jackson made me smile. It was so great to see him again after so many years. It didn't surprise me that his canny observations led him to his declaration of my identity. A flood of memory washed over me.

I had met Jackson when I thought I couldn't feel any worse. Whitney, my best friend, had slept with Nick. Around the betrayal was a circle of intent, planning, and deceit by Whitney and a lustful betrayal by Nick. It devastated our long-trusted friendship, destroyed what had been a deep and committed love, and tore my heart into pieces. The love of my life succumbed to his immediate wanton fascination while love and friendship were replaced with lust. Nothing could stop the avalanche of hurt.

Then Jackson came home from college. It started as a favor by Seth. Jonathan and Seth had been friends for as long as I can remember. There were times I would try to hang around with the two of them, but Jonathan would dismiss me quickly. He never understood how much I wanted to be part of his world, and Seth never said an evil word to me. He was so nice, and as a young girl, I had a huge crush on him.

I was heading to college orientation in midsummer, and Jackson had just graduated from the same university I was going to attend. Seth knew what had happened and thought it would help if there were one thing which could be made smoother in my life during that time. I didn't know it then, but at Seth's nudging, his brother, Jackson, agreed to come over to visit me. He would try to help by turning the direction of my thoughts to the wonderful experiences the University would offer and all the ins and outs of college life.

After several hours of conversation and getting to know each other, he asked if I would go to dinner with him the following evening. We were talking and laughing until the restaurant closed for the evening. For the next several weeks, we spent time going to the lake to swim or picnic in one of the fields that looked over the farm. We would drive back there and park under a huge oak tree. No one ever knew we were there because you couldn't see it from the road.

Before we knew it, there were only a few days left before Jackson would have to be heading up to New York to begin his internship at a prominent law firm. So, we decided we would spend the last few days together doing all the things we loved to do. First to have breakfast at Susie's Diner, go to the Lake for a morning swim, enjoy the afternoon with a picnic in the field, and then the evening in the company of the setting sun. We did this every day during his last week.

On the last day, we talked about our plans for the future, and he told me of his aspirations of becoming one of the greatest EPA lawyers. I quietly told him of my desire to become a journalist moving around the country writing stories which touched the soul. After eating breakfast at the diner, we headed to the lake for a swim. The lake was perfect when we arrived. The geese had not taken yet to the sky and were still basking in the morning sun. We both had worn our suits under our clothes and slung shirts and shorts over a branch as we raced one another to the water.

After a refreshing swim and skipping rocks, we left to stop at Olivia and Seth's to pick up sandwiches, cold drinks for the afternoon, cheese and crackers, and wine waiting there for us—all of which Jackson had prepared ahead of time. We headed back to the farm and found the perfect spot under a canopy of oak trees. Pulling a blanket from the car, Jackson laid everything out.

We spent the entire afternoon talking, walking in the fields, and exploring the woods. We were so busy laughing and enjoying the discoveries we made we didn't anticipate the arrival of the sunset until its colors began to paint the sky. Sitting down and eating all the goodies we had brought, Jackson poured us some wine. Between the beauty of the sunset and the wine, the evening had begun to make me feel euphoric. Feeling Jackson's arm around me was so comforting, and I found myself leaning into him.

Unexpectedly, he turned and kissed me. He pulled me closer, our lips still blended, and wrapped me in his arms laying us together on the grass. Leaning over me, he gathered me beside him. I felt the tenderness in his touching as his fingers slid gently through my hair. Looking up at me, he smiled, and a feeling of desire swept through me. I raised my lips to his and kissed him. His eyes met mine and shivers of desire cascaded over me. I moved my hands down his chest skimming his nipples. My desire heightened further as they responded to my touch.

Working my way down, I slid my hands over his ribs feeling the ripples of his muscle. He pulled my shirt over my head, and with just a flick, my bra was gone. Then kissing my neck, he flipped me over and moved me beneath him. Feverish anticipation took over as my fingers released the buttons on his shirt. It felt open. Tenderly, my fingers caressed his nipples, and he gasped. I looked into his eyes watching as they darkened with desire. I helped him slide off his jeans and realized looking at him how strong and desirable he was to me at that moment.

From that moment, I was lost in my longing for him. Every touch burned with the intensity of the passion we both felt for each other. Knowing my own body's response to him, I raised my hips to meet his. I could feel him hard, pushing against me.

Looking into my eyes, he whispered, "Misty, I want you so much, but I can stop anytime you want me to." Wanting him and knowing he wanted me, I explored his body—stroking and touching him, glimpsing his expressions of ecstasy and getting braver. Wanting to have him move, I pressed hard against him, and he looked at me. In a hushed tone, he asked, "Are you ready for this?"

Touching him, lost in euphoria, I whispered, "Yes." Slow and easy, he entered me. When he began to move inside of me, the feelings racing through the center of me were nothing I had ever felt before. After, we lay together in each other's arms thinking separately about our futures.

Morgan & Brett

I realize thinking about the past won't get me anywhere, and my heart feels I am getting more connected with Brett. After the other night, our relationship moved to another level because I had told Brett the truth. I am not sure where it is going to end up, but he is coming over later after the tavern slows down. I am hopeful the revelation of my identity isn't going to be too much for him to accept. Feeling a little melancholy, I decided to go up and take a long bath.

Going upstairs, I begin filling the tub with bath water. Waiting for it to heat up, I walk over to look out my front window. I notice headlights moving slowly toward my house. As the vehicle gets closer, I recognize the van that has been becoming a nuisance to the area. I hurried back to shut my bath water off, run downstairs, and out the front door. Waving my arms, I ran down close to the road. The van pulls over and stops.

The driver rolls down the window and says, "Miss, are you ok? I saw you frantically running out of your house."

Keeping my composure, I say, "Yes, I wanted you to stop. You have been riding all around our community, sometimes very slowly, and people are wondering why." With a smile that didn't reach his eyes, he takes a chance with a very obvious question.

"I'm actually looking for Misty Jenkins. Do you happen to know her?"

I decided quickly to say, "Yes, I know her. What do you want with her?"

Obviously thinking he had some kind of advantage, the driver says with a small smile, "Let her know *a friend of Nick's* is looking for her. Also, when you go in to call Nick, make sure you let him know I stopped by to see you. Have a nice evening."

He then pulls away from the curb. I watch his taillights going down the road. Well, what an interesting turn of events. Turning back toward my house, I think about what he said, A friend of Nick's. Then, the comment of stopping by to see me which means he knows who I am.

Well tomorrow, I will have to make a visit to Nick and see what kind of people he calls his friends. Something tells me there is so much more to Nick Darlington since I left all those years ago. Seeing him with Tom Fraser and their familiarity with each other makes me wonder what the connection is. His rise to stardom in this town should have ended a long time ago. His run at Michigan was short-lived with the knee injury, and then having to come back to Millersville and face everyone must have been hard. Stepping back into the house, I hear the phone ringing upstairs. Running upstairs, I grabbed it just in time. It's Brett.

"Hello," I say breathlessly.

"Morgan, I wanted to know, would it be ok to head over after the bar closes? It's going to be at least another hour. We suddenly had another wave of people come in." Smiling to myself, I think, *Brett, the most gracious, polite guy even now with his emotions reeling.*

"Of course. I'll be waiting." Hanging up, I decided it was time to pamper myself. I have plenty of explaining to do, and I hope Brett's feelings for me will be enough to overcome the shock of my revelation. Stepping into the tub, I lay back feeling the warm water enveloping my body. Closing my eyes, I think how stupid it might have been to run out to the curb waving my arms like some kind of maniac. The driver didn't seem like any person Nick would be friendly with, but either way, he was going to have a lot of explaining to do after the conversation that took place tonight.

Finishing my bath, I step out to dry off and hear my back door open.

"Shit, I forgot to lock my back door," I reprimand myself. Hurrying to my bedroom, I threw on a robe and walked down the steps quietly.

Suddenly, I hear Heidi's voice yell, "Mom are you here?" I let out the breath I was holding and continued down the steps.

"Hey Heidi, I just got out of the tub. Did you have a nice visit with Seth and Olivia?"

Opening the refrigerator door, I say through a laugh, "I did, Olivia was showing me all her family recipes. Did you talk to Aunt Sara to see whether Tom Fraser called her back. Heidi, you should have heard your Aunt Sara, she was plotting and planning what she was going to tell Tom Fraser when she goes to meet him."

Laughing, she replies, "That sounds like her. Did Tom Fraser get back to her?" Sitting down at the kitchen table, Heidi takes a drink of her iced tea.

"Yes, he did, she's meeting him tomorrow at 10. Jonathan was skeptical and didn't have many positive things to say, but it didn't seem to deter Sara." I begin shaking my head, wondering what it will take to convince Jonathan the bank is not working in his favor. Sara is going to try to find out exactly what their intentions are and inform them the percentage of available acreage for their development plan is going to decrease.

Realizing Jonathan probably isn't going to have time to call Anson, I decided I'll call him in the morning. When I spoke with him earlier, he had shared so much information with me about the startup of a winery, and the first thing he said was to make sure we had enough ground for the vineyard. Methodology and the chemistry of making wine were forthcoming along with the shoots of his best grapes for us to plant. The wealth of information in his mind is there for us to tap into whenever we need help. He was intrigued by our plan and wanted us to send him a picture of the fields we will convert.

"Heidi, I'm going to go up and get dressed, and then we can plan what we want to do tomorrow. My plan was to take you to the beach, but I would rather do it toward the end of the week. Maybe we can get a place to stay for one night, so we can see the sun rise over the water."

Smiling at me, Heidi says, "Nothing would make me happier than to go to the beach. It will be so cool to see the ocean." With a look of surprise, I am confronted with the fact that Heidi has never seen the ocean.

"Ok, we will come up with a plan and head down there on Friday." Then, so only I could hear, I add, "There will be plenty of time to worry about the guy in the van."

Jillian & Brett

Jillian and Brett finally stand next to each other for longer than a minute.

"Boss, I think we are home free. The last few stragglers just stumbled out, and no one is passed out in the bathrooms."

Brett smiles and replies, "Jillian, this has been a hell of a night. Every time I looked up, the door opened, and more people came in. I think this may have been a record sales day, and if so, we are on our way. We should try to introduce new IPAs every month and rotate out the less popular brews. Then, up the quantity of whatever is the best seller. Once a few months go by, we can plan on keeping the three most popular brews and just bring in one IPA each month."

"Sounds good, Brett," she answers, stifling a yawn. "I'm beat, and my feet are telling me to sit down and soak them, so I'm going to head out. There isn't too much left to do except lock up, so you should head out as well." Together, they lock up and leave the bar.

Brett wants to see Morgan tonight. As he walks out to his truck, he sees parked next to his truck is the dark van that had been driving by his mother's house. Walking up to the window, he stands waiting. When the window doesn't roll down, he bangs his knuckles on the glass. Slowly the man lowers the window.

"Can I help you? We are closed for the evening," says Brett.

"I think you can. I'm looking for a woman named Misty Jenkins. Someone told me she was back in town, and I need to see her."

Frowning, Brett motions the guy to get out of the van. Stepping out and leaning against the car, Ray repeats himself, "I'm really trying to find this Misty Jenkins, and I've run up against a dead end everywhere I turn."

"Really?" says Brett. "Maybe that's a sign Misty Jenkins doesn't want to be found. I've seen you riding near my mother's house very slowly, and some weird occurrences have been happening there. Suspicious phone calls, messages left for my mother to hear, as well as nasty notes left for her to view while trying to enjoy her morning coffee. You wouldn't have any knowledge of this would you?"

Ray sticks out his hand, "Hey, I'm Ray, and you are?" Shaking his hand, knowing full well Ray knows who Brett is, he goes along with the farce.

"My name is Brett Compton, and I own this fine establishment behind me. Yet I'm curious what is so important causing you to ride all around town looking for this woman. So, tell me, what you are here for?"

Realizing he is in a corner, Ray thinks quickly and answers, "You know man, I really don't think it's any of your business. I will be on my way now. It was nice talking with you." With that, he turns around and gets back into his van. Brett watches as he backs out and turns to leave the parking lot. Waving his arms, he walks up to the window. Ray rolls it down halfway.

Brett says quietly, "I don't want to see you riding by my mother's house or Morgan Kiernan's ever again. If I do, I will ensure the police department is aware of you and your harassment." Giving a sinister smile, Ray rolls up the window and pulls away. Brett stands there watching him leave and feels the impact of what his mother had told him earlier. This guy might be the company representative, and all of the stalking he has been doing was to find out if Morgan or Misty was here again.

Getting into his truck, he turns toward Morgan's house.

Morgan & Heidi

The next day dawns hot and humid, typical of Millersville in the summer. I thought about the night before when Brett came over. He seemed distracted and jittery. We talked until late. I really wanted him to stay, but he wasn't quite ready to forgive me. It was getting late, and we were both tired of the conversation. Feigning sleepiness, we say our goodnights. At the door, Brett leaned down and kissed me so sweetly I can almost still feel his lips on mine. Hugging him tightly, I kissed him again before he turned to leave. Afterward, I went to make coffee for the morning. As I stood by the coffee pot, I remember looking out the window at the darkness of my yard, envisioning my future and feeling strongly that Brett would be in it.

Refocusing my attention to the day ahead, I hear Heidi start the shower. It always makes me grin whenever the shower is turned on. You can hear it whistling through the water pipes. The shower at our home in Linn Creek was the same way, and it was my notice not to flush the toilet because it made the water scalding in Heidi's shower. Figuring I might have some time to kill tomorrow, I decide what my plan should be when I talk to Nick.

Busying myself with breakfast, I wonder what Nick could possibly be doing associating with someone like the guy in the van. If it is true, and he is a friend, then Nick had fallen far from his expected success. Hearing Heidi on the steps, I put Nick out of my mind. Turning away from the counter, I see my daughter practically skipping through the kitchen doorway.

"Well, aren't we chipper this morning? What has you so jovial this early?" Smiling and giving me a quick hug, Heidi spins around, and then sits down.

"Mom, I woke up this morning realizing how great a time I am having here with you. Spending time with Aunt Sara, Uncle Jonathan, Seth, and Olivia has been so enjoyable, and I feel like I belong." I hugged her shoulders, and then turned to start making the eggs.

"Heidi, I am so happy you feel this way. I had some doubts about your acceptance of your newfound family, but nothing makes me happier than to see you interacting with Jonathan and Sara. It's hard not to like Seth and Olivia, plus you get the added enjoyment of getting to know Jackson." Breakfast is ready. We start to eat, and Heidi fills me in on her plans for the day.

"Aunt Sara is going to be at the bank right at 10:00. She is going to let me know when she is finished, and I'm going to meet her to do a little shopping. I want to buy a new bathing suit for my first time at the ocean—feeling the salt water on my skin and jumping in the waves," she says with a few giggles. "Mom, believe me when I tell you, I was shocked when she asked me to help her. It seems Aunt Sara wants to change her look." Standing up to clear our dishes, I turn to put them in the dishwasher and see movement outside my window. Jackson is walking up the back deck.

"Heidi, Jackson is about to knock on the back door. Can you go open it for him?" Walking quickly over to the door, Heidi swings it open just as Jackson puts his hand up to knock.

"Gosh Heidi, you scared me. Were you two spying on me out of the kitchen window?"

"Really Jackson, it's hard not to see you walking onto my deck when my kitchen window is right over it," I chuckle. Moving to take a chair at the table, Jackson motions with his hand.

"So, what do you two ladies have on your agenda today?"

Not wanting to tell either one of them I was going to try to see Nick, I say, "Well Heidi is going shopping with Sara for some new clothes, and me, well I don't know what I am going to get into. Why?" Casting his eyes toward Heidi, he subtly shook his head no. Realizing he wants to talk to me privately, I turn to Heidi. "Hey, why don't you run over to Seth and Olivia's and see if they want to have a cookout tonight? Fall is right around the corner, and then we won't be able to be out too long at night." Hopping up, Heidi is out the door before I can say what time. Sitting down at the table with Jackson, I look at him calmly. "What's going on Jackson? What is so important you couldn't say it in front of Heidi?" Jackson is tapping his foot which, if I remember correctly, is a sign he was agitated.

"Morgan, I need you to tell me everything you know about what your dad was doing all those years ago. Seth and Olivia have told me their suspicions surrounding Abby's death, and they also told me you can give me more information. Before you say anything, I want you to know that I will represent you in any legal proceedings. All we need is enough evidence to prosecute the electric company. Therefore, anything you tell me is under the client-attorney privilege." Stunned for a moment, I just stared at Jackson.

"Are you telling me you would help me seek evidence to discover, as I and others believe, there was a negative impact of the stray currents."

"Yes, I am, and why do they continue to utilize the old towers when people are getting sick or dying like little Abby. I can't stand by and watch my brother and his wife grieve for their granddaughter or watch Cissy and Josh's marriage crumble because of the unbearable sorrow of losing their only child. So yes, Morgan with your help we are going to do something that should have been done a long time ago." I walk around to where Jackson is sitting, pull him up, and hug him tightly.

"My father deserves to have his legacy restored, the truth be known about the electric company, and the truth of the dangers of electromagnetic currents emanating from towers. So, what do you need me to do?" Jackson holds out his hand.

"Let me have your phone. I am going to download a voice recorder for you to use. No matter where you are if something comes to your mind, I want you to record it and send it to me. This way I can start compiling all the information. Leave it to me to sort through it and prove a case." Just as he finishes explaining, Heidi comes bounding up the deck steps bursting into the kitchen.

"Mom, Olivia wants to know what time and what you want her to bring. Seth said something about getting crabs to eat. I didn't want to tell him not to, but Mom you know how I am about fish," she says as she rolls her eyes.

Jackson starts laughing, adding, "What's the matter Heidi, have you never had crabs before?"

"No, I haven't, and I don't think I want to start today."

Standing and walking over to her, Jackson drapes his arm over her shoulders and tells her, "Heidi, you don't know what you are missing. Let Seth cook up some crabs, and you'll ask him to do it every weekend. He douses them with Old Bay and other spices which make them delicious."

Smiling at the look on Heidi's face, I volunteer, "Why don't you and Sara see if you can pick up sweet corn, and we will cook it in the steam pot."

Heidi grabs her head yelling, "Oh my God, I almost forgot. Seth said you should look in the garage on the bottom shelf and there is a big pot there with a basket and burner. He told me the people who used to live here cooked crabs all the time. Seth always borrowed his stuff whenever he and Olivia wanted to cook crabs."

Jackson starts cracking up saying, "This is so like him to borrow a pot from his neighbor."

Standing up from the table, I motion to the two of them instructing, "Let's go out and see what we can find. If Seth says it's out here, then I'm sure it is." Walking into the garage, I flip the light on, and sure enough, there are shelves all along the back of the garage. Right where he said is a big stainless-steel pot with cooking gloves lying across the lid.

"Heidi, run back to Seth, and tell him I found it. I'll leave it on the deck for him to get, or he can cook them over here if he wants to. Oh, and I don't care what time, I'm going to be here all afternoon. There is someone I must see this morning, but it shouldn't take too long."

After Heidi leaves the garage, Jackson touches my arm reminding me, "Morgan, please be sure to record everything you can think of from when you were young. Even the smallest thing may be important. You were with your dad a lot whenever he was visiting people and evaluating their homes." Pulling me to him, he softly kissed my forehead before continuing, "I have never forgotten that summer and I hope you remember it as fondly as I do. We could have taken on the world together then, and we didn't. But understand, we will now, and we will win."

Looking up at him, I say with a smile, "Jackson, I remember, and you are right we could have taken on the world, but I appreciate what you are doing for me and especially for Cissy and Josh."

"Morgan, if those towers are as old as I think they are, there must be stray current leaking out of the coils. If we can prove it, it will help us build a case. We need as much information from the community possible which means getting out there and asking questions. Find out who is sick with what, why, and how long." Thinking to myself about Jackson's determination and finally understanding how intense this would be, I find it hard to express my gratitude. This is going to be instrumental in proving what the electric company is doing concerning the towers.

Frowning, I turn to Jackson and ask, "What makes you think after all this time they are going to pay attention?"

As if immediately understanding my dismay, Jackson replies, "Morgan, you haven't been around me for the last twenty years, but I have made it my life's mission to fight for those who are standing against the companies who disseminate, use, and transmit hazardous and toxic radiation, chemicals, and waste that contaminate the air, soil, and water and are capable of causing death or injury to life. My experience is so vast that it will be more than they can handle," he pauses to add a smile before continuing, "and yes, I am that good."

Whitney

Whitney wakes up late and listens to the noises of her home wondering who is still there. Getting her bearings, she realizes Nick and the boys were doing an early morning run. Realizing her bladder was about to bust, she hurried to the bathroom. Sitting on the toilet, she wonders what the day will bring her. She really wants to see Misty today, and somehow, she is going to make things right. All the years of battling through the guilt and the betrayal of their friendship are eating her alive. If her marriage is going to survive, she has to talk to Misty, and it has to be today. Too much hurt and time has passed. Somehow, she needs Misty to understand how sorry she is for seducing Nick, and ultimately taking him away from her. It would be better for everyone if she went over to Misty's before Nick and the boys got back. Nick would try to stop her, and she was determined to finish what she had started so many years ago.

Putting a few last-minute touches to her hair and makeup, she hurries down the stairs to leave. As she opens the garage door, she notices Nick's college friend driving by rather slowly. Waving tentatively, she gets in her car and backs out. Thinking back to Ray's visit, something just didn't seem quite right. Nick was overly friendly and that was not his way at all. Anyway, she hopes Ray doesn't come around again. One visit from him was enough for her, that's for sure.

Putting Ray out of her mind, she heads over to Morgan's. Slowing down so she can pull into the driveway, she is startled when the garage door goes up and standing inside the garage is none other than Jackson Palmer.

———————— • ————————

I try to hide my surprise because parking, getting out of the car, and marching up my driveway is Whitney Darlington.

Mustering the best smile, I can, I walk toward her and greet her, "Whitney, what brings you by today?"

Before Whitney has a chance to answer, Jackson suddenly is at my side saying, "Whitney, right? My goodness, I haven't seen you in years. What have you been doing with yourself? Are you married, have kids?"

Staring at Jackson as if he had just lost his mind, I nervously laugh and remark, "Jackson, Whitney is married to Nick, remember?"

"That's right, how could I forget? Well, Whitney regardless of all that, how have you been?" Whitney looks like she is thrown through some kind of time warp.

When she finally gets her wits about her, she responds, "I've been good. Our boys keep us busy with sports. Honestly, they keep me going all day long, between school and practice there is very little time just to be, if you know what I mean." I stand off to one side listening.

Finding an opportunity to interject, I ask, "So what brings you by today?" Taking a deep breath, Whitney looks in her pocketbook and finds the envelope with all the pictures and hands them to me.

"I found these in a box Nick had stored away. I thought you would like to have them. Morgan, I feel it's important for you to see these pictures. When I saw them, it brought back so many memories of my best friend when we knew we were going to take on the world. I know so much has passed between us, and the last memories were horrible, but I'm hoping well, you know what the old adage is 'Time heals all wounds.' Nothing would make me happier if we could just give each other the time of day. I'm not so delusional to think we could go back but at least, could you try to forgive me?"

I wonder how much it took for Whitney to finally come over. Knowing her, she stopped and started more than once. I've got to give her credit—this was probably one of the hardest things she has ever done, and the least I can do is try.

"Whitney, I'm sure this was very hard for you to do, and I want you to know I appreciate the effort. When I get a chance later today, I will look at them. This looks like it's been away somewhere dirty. Were you cleaning out somewhere? Is that how you found them?"

Whitney laughs and replies, "No, actually I saw Nick climbing up in the garage putting the box up in the rafters. After he left, I got a ladder out and grabbed it, so I could look at what was so important that he was hiding it. When I saw what it was, I decided right then it was important for you to see the pictures. Never again will I put you in a position where you feel you have to leave your home. Honestly, I really hope your plan is to stay here permanently." Jackson has maintained his silence watching us struggle with old memories and the desire to regain some semblance of friendship.

But when the silence lingers just a little too long, he offers, "Morgan, it should be like walking down memory lane when you look at the pictures. You and Whitney were always together getting yourselves into mischief. Don't forget, I was just a few years older than the two of you. Sometimes I would hear Seth talking to Jonathan who was constantly complaining about the two of you."

Whitney laughs out loud and comments, "Jonathan couldn't stand us hanging around him, right Morgan?"

Smiling at Whitney while looking at the pictures, I say, "Back then he complained about everything especially when it had something to do with me. Jonathan sometimes forgot he was my older brother and not my dad. He became so bossy especially after Mom got sick, and he didn't like Nick hanging around." Everyone gets a little quiet, but then the awkward moment passes, and small talk ensues for the rest of her visit.

Nick

Nick and the boys arrive home and realize Whitney is not there. Getting the boys herded to the showers, Nick pulls his cellphone out and calls her. After several rings, he hangs up and decides to text her.

Nick: Hey, we are back home, the boys are in the shower, just wondering where you are.

Hitting send, he stares at his phone waiting for her response. His phone dings.

Whitney: Ran out this morning to run an errand. I ended up stopping at Morgan's house. Be home soon.

Staring at his phone, he isn't sure if he read the text correctly. Rereading it, he swallows tightly. *What the hell was Whitney doing at Morgan's?* Something told him it is not good. Hearing his boys goofing off in the bathroom, he goes down the hall to oversee their shenanigans. An hour goes by and still no Whitney. The boys are comfortably sitting in their beanbag chairs watching a movie on Netflix, so he tells them he will run into town to get some donuts.

Driving toward town, he turns to go down by Morgan's house. Slowing down somewhat, he looks to see if Whitney's car is there but only seeing Morgan's car in the driveway. On a hunch, he pulls into her driveway and parks. Getting out of the truck, he sees Jackson standing out on Seth's patio looking over toward him. He waves and walks up to Morgan's front door.

———— — • — ————

As Nick approaches my door and is getting ready to knock, I open the door and as pleasantly as I can, I begin, "Well Nick, this must be my day. First Whitney, now you. So, what do I owe for all these visits from the Darlingtons? Never mind don't answer that, just come in because I need to talk to you." With a surprised look, Nick comes in and stands in the hallway looking toward the kitchen. Seeing the direction of his eyes, I ask, "Have you had breakfast?"

Shaking his head, he replies, "No, the boys and I went for a run this morning, and when we came back, Whitney wasn't home, so I texted her and she said she was here."

Laughing quietly, I say, "So that's why you stopped here. Well, you missed her by fifteen minutes. She was here for a little while, and then said she had somewhere to be." Watching Nick's face and wondering what was going on in his mind, I decided it is time I minimized some of my anger. "Nick, would you like something to eat? I have bacon and potatoes already made, so it would only take a minute to whip up some eggs."

Moving the rest of the way into the kitchen, Nick looks at me as if trying to read my expression. He watches me cracking eggs into a bowl, whisking to make them scramble, and moving back and forth in the kitchen. Feeling Nick's eyes continue to watch me, I wonder if his thoughts were moving in the same direction my own were. The domesticity of the situation is unnerving, and realizing that, I turn around to look at Nick.

"Nick, this is what we missed because of what you and Whitney did, and it took years for me to chase the images from my mind.

Nothing prepared me for the hurt and agony I felt from the deceit and betrayal by the two of you. I believe that coming back here and seeing what has become of the farm and the people I care deeply about helped me to heal and finally forgive. Something, until recently, I didn't believe was possible."

Watching Nick's facial expressions as I speak makes me feel as though he has been enduring his own form of suffering all these years. Nick felt for all of them.

"Morgan, we can't change the past, but it would be great if we could somehow be friends again. Whitney feels the same. She has done nothing but talk about your friendship since you have been home." Nodding, I finish getting breakfast and put a heaping plate of eggs, potatoes, and bacon in front of him.

"Nick, let me ask you something. A guy is riding around the area as if he is looking for me. He went by here recently, and I ran out to wave him down." Nick has a weird expression on his face but motions for me to continue. "When he finally pulled over, I asked him what his business was in the area, and he said he was a friend of yours. If that is true, why is he riding all around and not just coming to your house and hanging out there?"

Nick hesitates as if he is trying to be strategic with his words before answering, "I don't know Morgan, what did he say his name was?"

Walking to the refrigerator to put the eggs away, I turn toward him replying, "Ray. It was strange, he seemed like a person you wouldn't be friends with."

Again, he took a little too long before finally saying, "Morgan, I heard about this guy riding around, but I have no idea why he would say he was friends with me. There is no one I know by that name. Do you remember what kind of vehicle he was driving?" Listening to Nick, I recognize his tone sounds defensive.

Trying to figure out what might be causing this tone, I respond, "I think it was a dark color van. Besides what difference does that make? It's more about why he is stalking certain areas of the town. I'm not the only one who has been seeing him drive slowly by their homes."

"It probably is nothing Morgan."

Turning back to the sink, I slowly say, "No Nick, it is something, and I don't believe you. You know why I don't believe you? Because this so-called friend of yours that you don't know, well, he knows me. And I don't mean Morgan Kiernan. I mean Misty Jenkins. So, if you see him again, I suggest you get to know him and find out exactly what he wants with Misty Jenkins." I finished cleaning the dishes.

Standing up and walking up to me at the sink, he touches my arm, "Hey, thank you for breakfast and the conversation. There is nothing for you to worry about, I will handle our neighborhood stalker. It was nice spending time with you." At that moment, Nick must feel his phone buzzing in his pocket because he starts digging around to pull it out.

He answers it saying, "Hey Whitney. Are you back home already?"

Because Nick was still standing close enough, I heard Whitney reply, "Nick, I stopped by Morgan's house and saw her and Jackson. Then I ran some errands. I'm back home now, where are you?"

Hesitating for a moment, he says, "Actually, I was looking for you and stopped at Morgan's house where, apparently, I just missed you. I'm heading home now, so I'll see you soon."

Whitney's tone changes ever so slightly as she responds, "I'll be waiting." Putting his phone away, he looks at me and smiles.

"I better be on my way, but I must tell you this was perfect. We needed to begin a dialogue between us. Sometime in the future, I hope we can all sit together and discover a way to begin a friendship." Looking at the man I thought I was going to marry; I wonder if his suggestion would be possible.

Jackson

Jackson walks back over to the house and sits at the counter in the kitchen drinking coffee and thinking. The last couple of times being with Morgan made him realize how much his life may have been different if he had stayed in Millersville. *Our decisions can cause a chain reaction in many people's lives,* he thought. Now, being here with her and meeting Heidi inserts a nagging thought in his mind of their time together.

He couldn't stop thinking of Heidi's age and found himself constantly looking at her. If he had stayed in Millersville, life would have turned out differently. His career certainly would not have been the same, and Morgan could have been a big part of it. No sense in overthinking that now. He is here now, and so is she. Now, she needs him again, and this time he wouldn't let her down. Pulling out his notebook, he writes down some notes.

Morgan's dad believed stray currents were dropping from the antiquated electrical towers in the area. The environment along with other outside influences turns the stray current into electromagnetic fields which attack the weakness in our body and mind. So many residents who are exposed to the towers subtly find their body's defenses weakened, and they struggle to stay healthy. Morgan's dad was so sure certain areas' exposure was more significant than others, and history has shown the impact of disease has been immense. Now the controversy was beginning again because of little Abigail's death. It was touching his family now, except now he has the expertise to prosecute the people who are responsible. It will take a lot of work, and a hell of a lot of luck, but with Morgan, Jonathan, Olivia, and Seth maybe luck will be on their side.

Writing a to-do list is first on his agenda. His talk with Morgan this morning will give her a chance to think about the past and record anything that comes to her mind. Also, he needs to talk to the townspeople and see if there have been any unusual sicknesses affecting people in the area. He will need Seth and Olivia to help with this because they have lived here and know people in the community. It is essential for these people to feel comfortable talking to someone familiar to them. Opening his laptop, he begins his research determined to find information—determined to help his family and his friend.

Seth & Morgan

After Heidi had come over with the invite for later, Seth decides to take a run. While running, he thinks about his daughter, Cissy, and her husband, Josh. Each day they seem as if they are getting stronger, but he wonders if it's a façade they are putting up to keep everyone from discomfort when they are around them. As he nears his house, he sees Nick backing out of Morgan's driveway. Nick never sees Seth as he speeds away from her place, so Seth decides to check in on Morgan. Walking up her driveway, Seth wonders what Nick was doing there. He is about to find out.

Stepping on her deck, he knocks on her sliding glass door. While waiting for her to come to the door, he looks toward his house to see if anything or anyone was moving. He thought he saw Jackson's light on when he left this morning. Hearing footsteps, he turns back to the door and sees Morgan walking toward him.

———— • ————

"Well, hello, Seth, what brings you by this morning?"

"I was doing my cool down, and thought I saw Nick's truck leaving here. Just doing my neighborly duty and checking in on my favorite neighbor. Really though, is everything ok?" Motioning for Seth to come in and sit down, I grab two bottles of water out of the refrigerator.

"Here Seth, you look like you need some water. As for Nick, he stopped here because he thought Whitney was here."

With an incredulous look, Seth replies, "What in the world would Whitney be doing here?" Walking back into the hallway, I grab the envelope of pictures.

Handing the box to Seth, I explain, "She brought these pictures over for me to look through. Something led her to believe that my seeing these pictures would help the three of us forgive and forget. Today, I tried my hardest to listen and keep my emotions in check when she was here talking with us."

Seth raises his eyebrows and questions, "Us? Don't tell me Heidi was here when Whitney showed up."

Laughing nervously, I assured her, "No it wasn't Heidi, she was over at your house visiting Olivia. It was Jackson."

Slightly annoyed, Seth asks, "Jackson, what in the world was he doing over here so early this morning?"

Realizing Seth is irritated, I take a second before answering, "Jackson is going to represent us. All we need to do is get enough evidence and prove my dad was right. He wants to talk to me more about my dad and wants me to start recording notes, anything and everything I can think of, even the smallest thing. I'm sure he will tell you and Olivia the same thing when you get home. Jackson will help us find the people responsible for all the loss and pain we and many others have experienced. Will it bring back Abby or my dad? No, it won't, but at least we will have made their suffering and deaths have not been for nothing."

Walking to the door and looking out, Seth pauses for a moment softly saying, "Morgan, when your dad was doing all of his research, we laughed at him. I am so ashamed now because if I had listened to your dad then and Abby now, she might still be alive. Morgan, we have to be sure Jackson is going to be committed."

"Jackson cares, Seth. It has nothing to do with his ego. It has all to do with family and the right for individuals to be safe and free from environmental contamination in their surroundings. He is determined to pursue the truth of the perils of the towers on the health of those exposed, and the electric company's continued use of old towers exuding electromagnetic fields. His goal is to expose their efforts to deceive the community and bury evidence of the devastating harm caused by exposure to the fallout from the towers."

"Well, in that case, knowing my brother, he will not stop until he can gather the testimony, evidence, and documentation to substantiate his case." Pausing briefly, he adds with a snort, "I guess I need to tell Olivia to expect Jackson's stay in Millersville to be much longer than we originally thought." Together we laugh. As the laughs subside, Seth's face becomes serious, and he vows to stand beside his brother in his resolve and dedicates himself to their pursuit.

Hearing the door close, I look, and Heidi walks into the house briskly.

"Hey Seth, Olivia wants to know if you got lost on your run. She has been keeping breakfast warm for a while now. Oh, and Mom, we are eating around seven tonight, so…" Heidi trails off and stands up very straight and begins in a different voice, "we have to get the crabs done by then Olivia said."

Seth laughs, "Oh my Heidi, if that doesn't sound exactly like my wife."

"Well, it should because I repeated it precisely as she said it."

After Seth leaves, Heidi and I finish cleaning up the kitchen and sit down for a minute.

Heidi smiles broadly and says, "Mom, Aunt Sara was leaving for the bank this morning at 9:00. It's almost 10:00 now, so she should be starting the meeting any minute. I hope she can get through to Tom Fraser. Uncle Jonathan says he is impressed with himself."

Shaking my head, I encouraged her, "You know Heidi, Sara will do great, but Uncle Jonathan is right. He can be difficult and quite arrogant. This is why we thought it would be good for Sara to go there." Standing up to look out the window, I see Olivia and Seth sitting on their patio. "Heidi, it's important this project with the bank and the farm work out for us. Jonathan and Sara need this to happen, so they can regain some kind of respect in the community. The vineyard is such a good idea and there is no one better than Sara to pitch it to the bank. I have extreme confidence in her."

I allow myself to become lost in thought before beginning again, "Hey what are your plans for the rest of the day? I need to go to the farm to do a few things, but I don't want to leave you alone." Standing up to move next to me, Heidi puts her arm around me.

"Mom, I think I'm just going to hang out here. Sit and catch up on all my Netflix shows, it will probably take the whole afternoon to do, so take your time. I will be right here when you get back." Hugging each other, I then headed upstairs to grab my pocketbook and a notepad.

Sara & Fraser

This morning is going to be important for Sara. It is her visit to the bank to meet Tom Fraser. Taking extra time with her hair and putting on makeup helps to give her some confidence. Hearing Jonathan rustling around in the kitchen, she walks downstairs. As soon as she gets to the bottom of the stairs, she hears a whistle. Jonathan is whistling in appreciation, and Sara can feel herself blushing.

"Oh Sara, you look fabulous, honey. You have always been so pretty, but now, babe, you have left me speechless. Tom Fraser doesn't have a chance." Smiling and relaxing, Sara walks over to get her coffee. Moving to the table to sit down, Sara pulls out the notes she has written.

"Jonathan, can you sit with me for a minute? I want to go over my game plan. Tom Fraser needs to be put at a disadvantage somehow, and I plan on making headway with this intention of ours." Reading over her notes, Jonathan sits back and looks at his wife.

"Sara, it is perfect, just be yourself. He will be so surprised when you show up to the meeting. One thing about Fraser is he loves to talk about himself. Get him talking about the farm, his ideas, and note anything that seems unreasonable. Once he says something about the number of acres they want to buy, then you can start the conversation about the vineyard." Frowning slightly, Sara stands up from the table and dumps her coffee into the sink.

"Jonathan it will be fine. I've put a lot of thought into this and believing in us. This land and family means nothing will deter me today." Looking at her watch, she says, "I better get ready to go. The plan is to get there early before he has a chance to get involved in some other customer's issues."

Smiling and standing to hug his wife, Jonathan whispers in her ear, "Sara, I know you are the best person to do this for our family. Morgan and I believe it will all work out for the best no matter what happens today."

Later, Sara drives into the bank parking lot, shuts the car off, and lays her head back on the headrest. Closing her eyes for a moment, getting her thoughts together, and if she was going to admit it, more courage as well. At home in her kitchen, with Jonathan and Morgan's support and encouragement, her bravery scale is off the charts. But now, with the moment upon her, it is different.

Sensing her nerves stirring up things in her stomach, she decides it is now or never. *There is no sense in sitting here any longer*, she thinks. Stepping out of the car, she straightens her skirt and leans down to check her makeup in the side-view mirror. Seeing everything in place, she walks into the lobby and confidently asks to see Tom Fraser. The customer service advocate working this morning was Sara's neighbor's daughter.

Smiling, the young woman says, "Hello Mrs. Jenkins, if you don't mind me saying so, you look beautiful this morning."

Finding herself blushing slightly, she smiles at the young woman and says, "Thank you. If you can let Tom Fraser know I'm here, that would be great." Slipping out of her cubicle, she motions to Sara to take a seat and acknowledges she will let Tom know Sara is here.

While Sara is waiting, she looks around at the portraits adorning the walls in the lobby. The bank president's photo is quite large, but what strikes her more is the portrait of Tom Fraser. His expression captured by the artist is unusual for a portrait to hang in a business lobby. It is as if while posing, he was looking at a memory he had lost and found again. It seems odd to Sara for the artist to have captured this when painting Tom. Hearing her name, she looks and sees Tom walking toward her. Standing quickly, she extends her hand.

"Tom, it's so good to see you again. How long has it been?" Tom lets go of her hand and puts his hand under her elbow to lead her back to his office.

As they are walking, he says, "Sara, it's been quite a few years since I've had the pleasure. You look great, but then you always did have a sparkle about you." Opening his office door and leading her inside he continues, "So what brings you in this morning? I was so surprised when I saw your name on my calendar." Making herself as comfortable as she can, Sara clasps her hands in her lap and looks across the desk at Tom.

"Tom, I want to discuss the sales agreement the bank has drawn up for our property. There has been a new development which I would like to discuss with you today. I'm sure you are aware of

Misty's arrival here in Millersville. It was probably such a shock for you the day she arrived here with Jonathan."

Trying to maintain his composure, Tom responds, "Yes it was quite a surprise seeing her sitting across from me. Actually, she sat right where you were. Now tell me about these new developments." Sara knows Jonathan and Morgan are united behind her on this plan and she can almost feel their energy in the office.

This image gives her the confidence she needs to begin, "Well Tom, as we both know, several wineries have found great success in our county. Now one of the biggest obstacles they are facing is having the acreage to grow grapes. This is especially true of the wineries that just opened recently. Our family has done some exploration into whether the soil content at our farm is conducive to successfully growing grapes. The last and final report has come back from Rutgers, and our soil has all the qualities of growing a good crop." Listening intently to Sara, Tom is also thinking to himself, *this cannot be happening." Is she telling me they want to cancel the whole deal?*

With a fake calmness that he doesn't actually feel, he asks, "Exactly what are you telling me, Sara? Does your family want to pull out of the agreement? Because I would have to advise you, it wouldn't be a good idea." Knowing the conversation was going to lead in this direction, Sara is prepared.

"Tom, no one is proposing pulling out of the agreement. We need to modify the acreage defined in the agreement which will stay in our ownership. The amount of land needed to have a vineyard is slightly larger than the bank initially offered. We will have our law-yer contact you with the new parameters, and then we will be able to meet again." With that, Sara stands up and puts her hand out to shake Tom's hand.

Noticing a slight hesitation in Tom, Sara softens her stance some-what and adds, "Tom, as long as the bank is willing to work with us, this will be a win-win for both parties involved. We see the vineyard as a way to renew farming with different crops. It also would be aes-thetically pleasing to the buyers of the new subdivision. It would be nice to have a winery as a neighbor."

Shaking her hand, Tom smiles and answers, "Sara, it was great to see and talk with you. I look forward to hearing from your lawyer. One word of caution though, make sure this doesn't take too long. There are several investors anticipating a huge return on developing the ground. We wouldn't want any of them to become uneasy about the money they are going to spend on this development."

Opening the door to leave, Sara turns and comments over her shoulder, "Message received. We will have something for you within a few days. Thanks for taking the time to see me today." Tom follows Sara out to the lobby walking her to the door.

When they reach the door, he touches her arm and says smugly, "Sara it was my pleasure." Sara opens the door to bright sunshine and hesitates on the step to find her sunglasses. Suddenly, she feels someone come up. Glancing up from her bag, she finds herself look-ing right at Nick Darlington.

"Nick, you surprised me. Let me get out of your way, I was fumbling for my sunglasses."

"Sara, it's fine. How have you been?" Not really wanting to engage in conversation with Nick, she moves off the step of the bank and stands on the sidewalk. Noticing the traffic is backed up, she wonders if there has been an accident. She feels some kind of trepidation worrying about home. Knowing old habits die hard, she shakes it off.

"Nick, I really have to get back to the farm, is there anything I can help you with today?"

Taking her arm and moving her off to the side because people are trying to get by them, he says, "No not really, I just wanted to know how all of you were doing now that Misty was home. It was quite a shock for Whitney and me, but we are working through it." Stunned for a moment, Sara isn't sure how to respond. Looking around to see if anyone is listening to their conversation, she lightly taps Nick's arm.

"Nick, do you realize not everyone knows Misty's back home? You know, she wants to be called Morgan. She wants to take it slowly, and the anguish she has experienced throughout her lifetime has made her somewhat wary which is understandable, don't you think?"

Bowing his head, Nick mumbles, "I know. Don't think it hasn't been a constant rerun in my mind for the last twenty years. Almost ruined my marriage, but you know, Sara, Misty's return has become some sort of renewal for Whitney and me. We, along with Misty, are healing, and it's been a long time coming. Please give my regards to Jonathan." With that, Nick walks away. Sara hurries along the sidewalk heading back to the bank parking lot. It seems imperative she gets home as soon as possible to talk to Jonathan and Morgan.

Brett

Brett got to the tavern early today to do some paperwork that was lingering and needed his attention. Finishing up and walking out to the main bar, he looks around his bar. It was amazing how much has changed since he took ownership of the place. Jillian is a big part of the tavern's success, and he realizes what a great decision it was to make her part owner. Now to get to the real thing that was bothering him—his personal life was proving to be somewhat difficult and not for a lack of trying. Morgan has become so important to him except recently it has become challenging. Thinking about it, he pulled his phone out and called her.

———— • ————

After several rings, I grab my phone answering, "Hey Brett, how are you?"

I hear what sounds like a sigh of relief and then he says, "How are you feeling today after everything we talked about yesterday?" I know Brett is upset. The more I think about the last few weeks, remembering the visit to his mother's house and finding the canister, the more uneasy I become. There is something not right with her, and I am determined to find out what it is. My father's canister showing up in her bathroom is leading me to believe she had more to do with her husband Jack's work life than she let on. Now, though, I need to talk to Brett. The feelings I have for him are becoming so strong, but my mind won't let me come to terms with his mother. It's too suspicious to let go.

"Brett, I'm fine. The bigger question is how you are really doing today. I know you have had a lot thrown at you over the last couple of days. We will have to get together soon to talk. There is so much more I want to tell you."

Sighing again, Brett responds, "Morgan, I'm managing. Nothing is more important to me right now than understanding why you thought you couldn't come back as the same person you left as, but I'm sure you have your reasons. Let's try to spend some time together later today."

Sara

Sara pulls into her driveway and parks. Sitting in the car rehashing the last hour and a half brings a slight smile to her face. She did it. The plan was for her to talk to Tom Fraser and inform him of the new developments regarding the future of the farm. Something tells her Morgan and Jonathan are going to be so happy with her report of the meeting. It wouldn't have surprised her in the least bit if Tom had already called Jonathan.

Getting out of the car, she turns and looks at the farmyard. Huge excavators were still sitting in the yard like quiet giants waiting to stir. Standing for a moment, she enjoys the smells of the farm. Gone are the odors of cow manure, the noise of the milking machine, the fumes coming from the tractors, and best of all, the groans of Jonathan as he walked into the house each morning. Now, new sounds would be coming. Sara smiles to herself and walks into her house.

Setting her pocketbook down, she stops and listens. Realizing it was unusually quiet, she decided to go upstairs and change her clothes, so she could go to the barn. She figures Jonathan is sitting in the milkhouse. While changing, she hears someone pulling into the drive. Looking out the window of her bedroom, she sees Morgan getting out of her car and walking to the back door.

Hearing the door slam, she steps out of her bedroom and yells downstairs, "Morgan, I'm up here, come up. I have so much to tell you about my visit with Tom." Listening to Morgan opening the refrigerator, presumably to pour herself some cold iced tea, makes Sara smile and believe the future is bright. She is so happy Morgan is here with all of them, and together they are going to change the outcome of the past years.

———— • ————

Walking up the stairs, I realize how nervous I feel wondering how Sara made out with Tom Fraser. Stepping into my brother's bedroom seemed almost sacrilegious. Old habits die hard. His room was always off-limits to me, and it was hard to forget his anger when and if he caught me in there.

Sitting down on the chair by the door, I look at Sara and intensely ask, "Well, how did it go? Please tell me everything." Sara laughs at my question or maybe my fervent desire to know everything about her morning as she takes a seat on her bed.

"Morgan, I was so nervous leading up to the meeting, but I stayed focused, and hopefully you will believe it was successful. Tom was polite and attentive at first, telling me how surprised he was to see my name on his appointment calendar. Once I started discussing the property agreement and our desire to change our land from a farm to a vineyard, his demeanor changed. He immediately thought we were going to attempt to cancel the deal with the bank until I assured him that we were requesting for the agreement to be revised."

Frowning, I say, "I can hear him now with his smooth banker's lingo. He is so sure this agreement is close to being signed, and the more I hear about his attitude, the surer I am he is into this much deeper than just being the banker."

Sara nods and further explains, "He seemed stunned when I told him we were going to want more acreage and even more surprised when I explained why." Standing up and sitting next to her on the bed, I touch her arm.

"Sara, you did a great job today, and I'm positive you handled it perfectly. How did you leave it?"

Smiling broadly, she says, "I told him our attorney would be sending in a new proposal outlining our plan. On the ride home, though, I realized I didn't even know who our attorney was. So, I would say that should be our first priority."

Hugging her lightly, I say, "No worries, Sara. We have Jackson to represent us now. We will sit down with him soon and get his take on the situation. His experience is broad, but his specialty is in environmental law, however, don't worry about his ability or his desire to help us."

"Morgan, it was nice seeing Jackson earlier. I didn't realize he was back in town." Then, lightly tapping her head, she gasps, "Oh my, I am not thinking, of course, he would be here visiting Seth and Olivia. It's because of Abby."

"None of us have seen him in a long time, or at least I haven't. Somehow, I don't think he came home often from different things he has said. The great news is he has decided to stay for a while." Before continuing, we both heard the door slam. Hopping up quickly, which made Sara laugh, I headed out of the bedroom to go downstairs.

As we were walking downs the steps, Sara whispers, "I don't think he would get mad about you being in our room." Giving her a look and smiling, we headed into the kitchen. Jonathan is leaning against the sink eating an apple.

"Hey, you two, what's going on? Sara, how was your meeting? I've been outside working and cleaning up, but I kept looking to see when you got home. So, tell me, what happened?" Sitting down at the table, Sara repeats what occurred at the meeting with my input on Tom's real plan.

"Morgan, is Jackson going to represent us? I didn't realize you had been talking about this with him. Does he know who you are? Did you tell him?" Understanding the tone of his voice, I realize he is still hurt by my absence of all those years. Regardless of his feelings now, we have much larger things to conquer.

"Of course, but even with all the years that have passed, he already knew. The outcome is good because he is going to represent us to the bank as well as help us find out what happened to Dad."

Sara sits back and watches the two of us working with each other. At the mention of Dad's name, I noticed her eyebrows pinch together with deep interest—like she had her own suspicions about his death and was waiting to hear what we had to say. I'm sure it was devastating for her as well losing him when we did.

She listens to us go on for a little while longer before interrupting, "What are you two talking about regarding Dad? We all know he died suddenly from a heart attack." Visibly irritated, Jonathan pushes his chair back, scraping the floor.

He looks at his wife and says dryly to me, "I think you should be the one to tell Sara your suspicions since you are the one who seems to doubt what happened to Dad was not an accident. It was time I got back to work." Casting me a dirty look, he kisses Sara, and out the door he goes.

Sara and I sit in silence for a few minutes, and then I begin talking, "Sara, you remember how Dad believed stray current was dropping from the old towers and turning into electromagnetic fields. Before you met Jonathan, Dad became obsessed with wanting to check everyone to see if they were keeping their body in the right zone. It became embarrassing to all of us but especially Jonathan. He didn't believe there were any stray currents drifting down from the towers. When the cows got sick, he blamed our father, saying he was so obsessed with taking care of the community that he stopped being a good farmer. This, in my opinion, is very far from the truth. People were getting sick, and I'm not talking about your common cold or the flu. They were dying of cancer, blood disorders, brain tumors, and the list goes on and on."

Sara listens, twirling her spoon in her coffee before interrupting, "A lot of what you are saying I know, albeit after the fact. However, all of this makes more sense to me than you know. When I first met Jonathan, you were still in middle school, and we were seniors. Jonathan and I didn't get serious until near the end of the year and spent most of the summer with each other. During the next few years, we were inseparable, and I saw how he and your dad related to each other, which wasn't good most of the time. It was a constant discussion between us, and the more time went by the worse it got. You were having the best time living your life and hanging out with Nick. Then your mother got sick, and the whole thing with Nick and Whitney happened."

At the mention of Nick, I shake my head adding, "Well we know how that worked out, don't we?"

Sara continues, "Yes, we do, but it isn't why you came back, is it? I know how hurt you were then, but now look at how much you have accomplished and the woman you have become. Nick and Whitney have built a life and have a family here, and I believe it was all in an attempt to try to move on, to assuage their guilt."

At this last comment, I have another moment of realization that it is time to finally let it go, especially after the last few hours. Having spent such a personal time with Nick made me finally understand the anger, the hurt, and most of all the shame. I loved him more than was possible, or so I thought.

"No Sara, I came back to restore our family's reputation and get the farm back to its glorious state. Believe me, I knew Nick and Whitney were going to be here for me to deal with, and as hard as it's been, I believe we all might come out of this whole again. What I want to tell you about is Dad's belief. There was something going on in our community. Do you remember Jack Callahan? He was the salesperson who constantly stopped here to talk to Dad. It became almost comical to Jonathan and me because Dad never let any salesperson spend too much time here. Jack Callahan and Dad almost became friends. He came by here almost every day with some excuse for stopping.

During this time, Mom was starting to deteriorate, so when she became so paranoid about Jack, I believe dad ignored it. After Mom died, Jack's visits became even more intrusive, and I truly believe there was more than just a curiosity or friendship bringing him around the farm. His wife, Elizabeth, was constantly sending her special tea for dad to drink and inviting him over to their house." Sara listens and nods every so often. I can tell by the way she scrunches her face that my sinister version of the memory was making her rethink what she once believed.

"Morgan, I remember Jack, and he was here a lot, but I don't remember there being anything suspicious going on. I do remember; however, how annoyed Dad became when Charlie, Jack's friend, came over. He had an aura around him that said keep away. Jonathan didn't care for him either, and we talked to Dad about it."

I perk up, "What did Dad say? Did he agree that Charlie seemed shady?"

Sara thinks for a minute before replying, "You know, Morgan, Dad brushed it off as paranoia which we were carrying from Mom. Honestly, after that conversation, I decided to stay out of the Jack Callahan saga. The only thing is Jack's visits became more frequent, and a couple of times, he brought his wife with him. I never could figure out why she came with him. Most of the time she sat in the car, although one day, I do remember her walking around the property."

Knowing Sara was still unsure of my account of the past, I decided to take a chance and tell her about my visit to Elizabeth's, Brett's mother, and Jack Callahan's wife.

"Sara, you know I've been seeing Brett Compton for some time since I've been back in Millersville. A few weeks ago, I went with him to visit his mother, and you'll never guess who his mother is. Elizabeth Callahan."

With a shocked look, Sara gasps, "Elizabeth Callahan, as in Jack Callahan's wife?"

Laughing bitterly, I say, "Yes, the one and only. She was married before, which explains Brett's last name. He really wanted his mother to like me, so we went there a couple of times. One time, I went over by myself after she had invited me to come and tour her garden. She realized how much I appreciated flowers and beautiful landscaping. The visit was going fine, although there were a couple of times that she became somewhat interrogating. She seemed to have an unusual interest in my background. I found myself telling her snippets of my life without revealing my real identity. There was a moment when I was admiring her grand piano where I mentioned how our family was musical because of our mother."

Sara responds quickly, "Oh my, what did she say when you said it? The reason I'm asking is she knew how musical Mom was because I overheard Dad telling Mom Elizabeth wanted to come and listen to her play." Frowning but continuing, I tell her the rest of the story.

"Elizabeth appeared to become somewhat uneasy, so I knew it was time for me to leave. Before leaving, I asked to use the bathroom, and she said the guest bathroom was right off the conservatory which is where the piano was located. Sara, you can't imagine what this bathroom looked like. It was as if I had entered a spa. Everywhere there were bath salts, bath bombs, lotions, potpourri sachets, fresh flowers and chocolates, and a beautiful, uniquely designed vanity. I honestly felt like crawling into a hot bath right then and there. Instead, I took care of my bloating bladder. When freshening up, I saw my hair and decided to look for a brush and hairspray because my hair was in dire need of repair. You'll never guess what I found hidden in one of the drawers of the vanity."

Sara turns to me and inquires, "What could you possibly find that would mean anything to you or us for that matter?"

"Sara, I couldn't believe my eyes, but in one of the drawers was the canister my grandfather designed for Dad. It didn't seem possible, but I checked inside it on the underside of the lid and sure enough, there were my grandfather's initials." Standing up, I walked to look out the window toward the field where my dad was found dead. I turn back to Sara and quietly continue, "I need to find out why Elizabeth Callahan has my dad's canister and why it appeared as if it had been hidden. Something is not right about her role in the relationship between Dad and Jack. She knows something I'm sure of it. Brett recently told me of someone harassing his mother on the phone leaving cryptic messages.

So, now you know Sara. My dad didn't die of natural causes, I'm sure of it. With Jackson's help, I'm going to find out what happened to him and make those involved pay for what they did. This goes much deeper than we know, and it ties back to the electromagnetic fields silently destroying the health and lives of the people of our community."

Sara stares at me with sympathetic eyes. I feel like I can see her considering the difficulties I faced making the decision to leave right after losing my mother. She knew all the heartache and humiliation that followed me around that summer had hardened me enough to leave. She knew the only good thing I had in that time was Jackson. I grew up that summer, as if one day I was a teenager and the next day a woman. Sara saw me through it all. After a moment in her thoughts, my sister-in-law comes and stands next to me.

Touching my arm, she whispers, "Morgan, I know how hard this is for you, coming back here and reliving all the memories. At least Jackson is here. He always did have a way of bringing a smile to your face. I remember how you slowly changed. It was as if Jackson had put some kind of spell over you. At those times, you would drive up the lane and sit for hours. Meanwhile, Nick was constantly riding by slowly trying to catch you outside so he could talk to you. Jonathan put a stop to his shenanigans, but he always threatened to show up.

I distinctly remember one weekend. It was right before Jackson was leaving for New York. He was so sweet. He called me to see what kind of wine you might like. Said he was going to make the day special for you. You know, now that I think about it, you were so much happier after that weekend. You were constantly smiling, and Jackson was calling all of the time. Anyway, back to Jackson of today, did his wife come with him? I haven't heard you mention her."

Giving Sara a quick hug, I say disgustedly, "Who Katrina? She isn't going to lower herself and stay with Seth and Olivia. She and Olivia do not get along at all. Katrina is a narcissist. She doesn't see herself like the rest of us do. Olivia told me a few years ago she had texted Katrina about why Jackson and Seth's relationship had deteriorated over the years. Her response was that it was all Olivia's fault—never once acknowledged all the work and time Seth has spent helping their mother, brought up things she felt were done to her by Olivia, which by the way Olivia doesn't remember any of them, and went off on Olivia saying there was no going forward with the brothers until these so-called issues were resolved.

Olivia and Seth basically divorced themselves from Jackson and Katrina, but with the death of Abby, it appears Jackson has figured it out. He has led me to believe he is staying here indefinitely, which puts his relationship with Katrina in question. I haven't asked Jackson what is going on at home because it really isn't any of my business, but if I was a betting person, I would bet Katrina and Jackson are no longer a couple."

Sara shakes her head with a look of repulsion and says, "Thank God you and Jonathan have come to terms with your relationship. I really don't know how much more Jonathan could have taken. Everyone knows how we change as we grow up. We get married and start families understanding those people are our world and nothing will deter us from being their champion. Siblings go through the same events, but there is something inherent in them which reverts to their childhood. Competition between each other, favoritism by a parent, success in school or sports, and then fast forward and those same feelings are present. Except now, now it's a competition with careers, homes, and unfortunately children, in some cases grandchildren. So, do we except the sins of our generation when our children and grandchildren are the ones who suffer? I don't think so. Thankfully, you came home when you did."

Looking at Sara, I feel vindicated. I want the best for Jonathan and Sara and Seth and Olivia. They are all my family, and at night when I close my eyes, I see my dad and mom working in the fields, milking the cows and providing a good life for Jonathan and myself. With the farm sale pending and the weight of the decision to sell falling solely on Jonathan, I needed to come home and be a part of the solution. Because that's what families do, we support each other no matter what.

Smiling at Sara, I reply, "Well I couldn't agree with you more. As a unified group, it looks like we may have a better plan for the farm. Between the three of us, we will get Tom Fraser and the bank to come around to our way of thinking."

Leaving Sara and heading back home, I find myself driving to the tavern. I need to talk to Brett. Pulling into the parking lot, I notice Nick's truck along with Whitney's car. Great, I wasn't in the mood to deal with either one of them, but it looks like I have to.

Morgan

Taking a deep breath, I push open the door and walk in. Memories assault me with the smell of old stale cigarette smoke and roasted peanuts. Smoking had been banned from the tavern for years, but smoke seemed to have embedded itself into the wood. Brett had done every possible cleaning technique to remove the smell, but once you are away from it for a few days, the impact of the smell hits you as soon as you come back in. Scanning the bar looking for Brett, I see Jillian looking my way. Waving, I headed in her direction.

"Hey Jillian, looks like you have a crowd today."

Looking back at the bar, Jillian turns and says through a laugh, "You could say that. It picked up just a few minutes ago. Are you looking for Brett? He was here for a little while this morning but left to go buy supplies." Grabbing an empty barstool and sitting down, I wonder what I should do.

"Jillian, did he think he was going to be long? I'll wait if you have an idea when he might get back."

"Listen Morgan, let me text him and see what his ETA is, and then you can figure out your plan. In the meantime, I can get you something." Realizing it's almost noon, I made a quick decision.

"Hey, just get me the lowest percent IPA beer you have. Thanks." Waiting for Jillian to get me the beer, I look across the bar and see Nick and Whitney playing darts. Jillian comes back and puts the beer down.

"Hey Jillian, let me know when Brett gets back to you. I saw a couple I know over there playing darts. That's where I'll be, ok?" Turning her head to look at who is playing darts, she quickly looks at me.

"You know Nick and Whitney Darlington?"

Laughing a little harder than expected, I say, "Jillian, you have no idea. But the answer to your question is yes, I do."

With that, I walk around the bar toward Nick and Whitney. I notice different people smiling and nodding in a way that tells me I am a familiar face to them. Coming up to Whitney, I noticed an empty barstool next to her. Sliding into the seat, I see her head turn slightly watching Nick play darts.

Tapping her lightly, so I wouldn't startle her, I say, "Hey Whitney."

Whitney turns quickly with what seems to be her resting bitch face and then catching herself, she smiles tentatively saying, "Oh hey, Misty, I mean Morgan. I'm sorry, I just can't get used to calling you by that name, but I'll get used to it."

Laughing quietly, I reply, "You know Whitney, it took me awhile to get used to it too, but I've had twenty years. On the other hand, I chose the name and you have only had a few weeks to use it." Seeing Nick standing up bullshitting with the other couple they are playing against, I continue, "I need to get some beer for the crab feast we are having later today over at Seth and Olivia's. When I walked in, I saw you and Nick over here, so I thought I would come over and chat for a minute." Whitney smiles broadly.

"Morgan, I'm so glad you did. Nick and I were just talking about how we all should try to spend some time together. You know, just hang out and talk. The only condition, which I think we all agree on, is there can be no mention of the past. We need to move on. Wouldn't you agree?"

Touching her arm, I agree, "Whitney, you have no idea. I have spent so many years wrapped up in anger and agony. Constantly replaying that night over and over in my mind until it made me sick, wondering if you were happy and secretly hoping you were not. It took so much energy and wasted days of time." Hearing someone walking up, I stop talking. Looking past Whitney, I see Nick slide onto his stool.

"Hey Morgan, what brings you into the bar so early today?"

Whitney interrupts, "She stopped into get beer for the crab feast they are having tonight over Seth's."

Nick smiled, adding, "Wow, Seth is actually having a crab feast? He has always talked about having one but never did. You must have some powerful influence over him if you actually got him to do one."

Smiling to myself, I keep my facial expression under control and say, "It's all about Heidi. She told Seth it was all she heard about the Jersey Shore, so he decided to give her a real South Jersey dinner— corn on the cob, jersey tomatoes, and crabs."

Whitney continues her smile and says, "I didn't realize Heidi had never been here before. Even when she was younger, she never visited? How old is she now?"

"Whitney, Heidi just turned twenty-one, and it's so nice for us. We both like to go to wineries, and now she can partake instead of drinking soda. Visiting here has been great for her being able to finally meet her family. Now that she is here, I have been driving around Millersville showing her all our landmarks and the farm. It's important for her to see what my life was like before she came into mine." Whitney looks between her husband and me with her lips quivering slightly.

"Twenty-one years old. Really! Do either one of you think this is a little odd?"

Nick comes over and puts his arms around his wife, saying calmly, "Whitney, relax! Don't get paranoid. Remember what we talked about." Looking at me now, Nick says, "Whitney and I are working on our relationship. Trying to give each other a chance to speak without the other one jumping to conclusions. We even talked about spending some time with you, so the three of us can get something back of our friendship."

Getting ahold of herself, Whitney turns to me and quietly says, "Morgan, it's great your daughter came to see you. If you don't mind me asking, when did she turn twenty-one? You know we lost a baby. It would make me feel better if I knew when our child left this world another child arrived. I just want to know if that was the case." Realizing what Whitney was doing, I decided it was time.

"Whitney, Heidi's birthday was just a few days ago. It wasn't until recently that I heard about your loss, and I'm so sorry. It wasn't long after I arrived at college. For some reason, I never got morning

336

sickness, but when my waistline was changing and my 'friend' hadn't come, I realized something was wrong. Having a small baby while going to college wasn't easy, and it was a rough four years, but we survived."

Noticing the looks between the two of them, I decided to take the high road and continue, "Whitney, in the next few days, it would be nice if you wanted to spend some time with Heidi. She is staying here in Millersville for quite a few weeks. Honestly, I'm trying to get her to stay permanently, but you know how that goes." Seeing Nick squeeze Whitney's shoulder, I lean in and whisper to her, "Whitney, it doesn't matter anymore what happened in the past. It's about all we have now and to be thankful."

Looking over at me, Whitney smiles and whispers, "You're right. I sometimes still have trouble with the loss of our child, but my boys mean everything to me. So, you are right, I am thankful." Moving to stand between the two of them, I put my arms around both their shoulders.

"Well, let's come up with a time you can both come over. Heidi loves company. As a matter of fact, why don't I call Seth and see if it would be fine for you guys to come to the crab feast? That is if you don't have anything better to do." Nick and Whitney look at each other with the unspoken communication husbands and wives have together.

Nick speaks first, "That's a great idea. Do you want me to call Seth? He's used to me inviting myself over to his house. Olivia has a standing plate for me some weekends, especially if Whitney is doing something with the boys for the day." The smile on Whitney's face doesn't quite meet her eyes, but I know it's going to take time.

"Nick, if you want to call Seth, great. I'm sure Olivia will be good with it." Seeing Jillian motioning me over, I stood up. "Hey, it was great talking with you both. Nick, you better make sure you bring beer. You know Seth, getting crabs and all the other fixings may be too much for him, so beer might be forgotten." Nick laughs, and I let them both know we would see them later at Seth's.

Walking over to Jillian, I chided myself for the stupidity of inviting Whitney and Nick over to Seth's. He's going to think I have lost my mind. Reaching the other side of the bar, I see Jillian put her hand up to wait a second. Sitting down on an empty stool, I wait for Jillian to come over to me. Feeling a rush of air on my neck, I turn to see who came in the door. Brett was walking in scanning the bar. As his eyes move around, they land on me. Smiling briefly, he walks over to me.

Leaning down, he puts his arms around me and whispers, "It's great to see you, Morgan. I'm so sorry I've been distant. It's been a lot to take in." The intense feelings I have for Brett come rushing in.

Turning toward his face, I kiss him tenderly, "Don't say anything, just know I've missed you." Lifting me up off the stool, he hugs me tightly.

"Let me check with Jillian and see what's going on, and then I'll be back, ok?" He heads over to where Jillian is serving customers. I watch as he interacts with customers and even leans over to kiss an older woman on the cheek. Looking at the woman, I realize she looks familiar. Trying to place her face, I watch Brett talking with Jillian. He is attentive when someone is talking to him, dipping his head close so he doesn't miss one word. Jillian is very animated talking and using her hands to describe something. It appears Brett might be staying for a while to help out, so I grab my phone and text Olivia.

Me: Hey, I hope you don't mind, but I've added three people to the crab feast tonight. I saw Nick and Whitney and I blurted out an invitation to them, and now I want to ask Brett to come. Nothing like having someone invite guests to your party. Let me know.

I hit send and Brett starts coming back over to me.

Leaning over the bar so he can talk to me without everyone around me hearing him, he says, "Morgan, I have to stay here for a while to help out Jillian. She just told me there is a bachelorette party coming in here later." I feel my phone vibrate. Looking down I see Olivia sent me back a thumbs up.

"I figured something was going on. Jillian's hands were telling the story. Do you think you could break away from here before the party gets here? Olivia and Seth have crabs, and I was hoping you could stop by and join me there." Brett quickly looks around the bar and then turns to me.

"I'm pretty sure I will be able to make it. Jillian needs some help right now getting out of this backlog, but there will be a window of time when I can scoot out of here."

Smiling I touch his cheek and say, "Great! Text me when you are on your way. Seth said he was shooting to have the crabs done by six. There will be a few people there, but you'll know everyone." I give him a quick kiss and add, "I'll see you later."

Elizabeth

Over the last few weeks, Elizabeth returned to her normal schedule after being away for a couple of months. This morning there was a doctor's appointment, lunch with her friend Marcia, and hopefully a visit with Brett. His behavior when she first got home from vacation was different than normal. He seemed distant until she started getting the phone calls. Then he seemed more suspicious than anything. Thank God those had stopped. After telling him all the events of the past, I knew it was going to be tough for him to start the conversation again. She stood by her decision not telling Brett the full truth. The company needs to stay away from her and Brett. She noticed the van was still riding by frequently and slowing down, watching the house, but as long as the guy in the van didn't stop at her house, she didn't care how many times he rode by. It was time, however, to make an impromptu visit to Tom Fraser.

Grabbing her pocketbook, she heads out to her garage. She goes to the spare refrigerator to grab a bottle of water. Opening the refrigerator, she notices there are some jars of her tea that had been made before she left for vacation. Making a mental note to take them into the house later, she gets into her car. Watching the garage door go up, she scans the driveway and the road. Seeing the area is clear, she backs out. Once she puts the garage door down, she scans her rearview mirror again and sees the dark van riding slowly by. Throwing the car in park, she steps out of her car and walks toward the road. The van stops and the window rolls down.

"Elizabeth, it's so nice to see you. Are you going out for a drive?"

"Well, I was planning on it, but you seem to be riding by my house constantly, and I have had enough of it. I believe you are behind the obscene phone calls I have received, and any claim that this is a popular road is preposterous. So, what do you want?" Ray steps out of the van and leans on the door with his arms crossed.

"Elizabeth, there is no reason to get upset. We are concerned about the recent developments at the Jenkins farm and the company wants to make sure you are still on board." Reaching back into her car for her phone, she turns back to Ray.

"I told them when Jack died my participation in this project would be over." Ray laughs and reaches back into the van for his phone.

"Would you like me to call our boss, and yes before you say anything, he is your boss too even if it's been a long-distance relationship. You do know there are people around here who have been watching your actions since Jack died."

Putting her phone back in the car, Elizabeth turns and looks at her visitor responding sternly, "So threatening is your plan of attack? I've been up against a lot worse people than you. Call your boss and let him know I'm finished with all of this. Also, remind him, he will continue to protect me because I did his dirty work all those years ago. The fact is whatever is going on now is not my problem. The next thing you should be doing is getting back into your van and leaving me alone."

Looking around making sure there aren't any other cars coming their way, he grabs Elizabeth's arm tightly and says, "My opinion is you need to keep your wits about you and your mouth shut. Jonathan Jenkins' sister is back in town, and suddenly things are looking up for the Jenkins family. So, you may want to be done with this Elizabeth, but it's just getting started. There will be no being done with this. You are right smack in the middle of it again, except this time, it will be final. We will take control of their land no matter what because the alternative is unacceptable."

Struggling with his hold on her arm, Elizabeth motions with her free arm waving her hand up in the air and turning on her temporary captor, her eyes blazing as she roars back, "Do you honestly think a plan which was hatched twenty years ago is still worth pursuing? All of us have now figured out it was not successful, so the utilization of Jack and the recruitment of me has become an expired mission. Jack is gone, and I really don't want to relive those last days of Carl Jenkins' life. So, tell your boss to get someone else to do his dirty work because I'm out and out for good. I've spent the last twenty years trying to forget my role in the company's plan."

Ray knew when it was time to fold, so letting go of her arm, he leans against his van and stares at Elizabeth explaining, "I'll leave for now, but rest assured, I will be back, and you will help us again. You and Jack were part of this plan! And as the upstanding community member which you were, it was a perfect fit. Now with Jack gone, all of our attention is on you. So, you see this isn't going away." Furious and feeling cornered, Elizabeth looks at her visitor.

"I did my part. Somehow the failure of acquiring the Jenkins' property doesn't seem like my problem anymore."

Ray laughs and answers, "Oh my, Elizabeth, don't you understand that once you are part of the company there is no retirement date? See you soon." With that, he gets into the van and pulls away. Elizabeth sinks to her knees and leans her head against her car.

Suddenly fear quickens through her, and she says aloud, "What in the hell am I going to do now?" Anger wells up inside of her, and then fear sets in. Standing up, Elizabeth lets out a scream. *Who did these people think were coming here after so many years demanding I participate again in their plan? Nothing would make me work with the company ever again. They can figure out how Jenkins' property will be theirs for the taking without my help.* Walking back toward the house, she feels her phone vibrate in her pocketbook. Taking out her phone, she sees it's Brett calling.

Gathering herself together and not wanting to decline the call, she takes a deep breath and says, "Hello. Brett, how is my favorite son today?"

Laughing, he says, "Mother, I'm your only son, but I'll take the compliment. I realized earlier we hadn't talked for a day or so, and I wanted to make sure everything was all right after our conversation. I have more questions for you, and it's important to me to understand all of the past."

Frowning slightly, she responds, "Brett, I'm fine. I know how busy you are, and my day has also been busy with this and that. I know you are uneasy about our conversation. Come over later, and we can talk some more." Hesitating for a moment, Brett tries to read his mother's tone. Something was off, but realizing it was useless to pursue that line of conversation, he goes along with her.

"Mother, I know you struggle with not having a full day of socializing, but I'm glad you are feeling good about things."

"Oh Brett, there is just a lot to do after being away for so long. Now that I am back home, I notice things I didn't pay attention to before I left, so I have a lot of work ahead of me." They continue to make small talk, steering clear of the previous conversation. Brett says goodbye saying he needs to get to the tavern. Sitting down on her front step in relief, Elizabeth bows her head and closes her eyes. *This has to end. The company could not possibly think I would participate in anything they had planned. All of this was supposed to be over years ago.*

Brett

Things were slowing down at the bar, so Brett told Jillian he was going to get out of there. Giving her some last-minute help, he grabs his keys and heads out. Jumping into his truck, he realizes he needs to get something to take to Olivia and Seth's. His mother would have a heart attack if she thought he would go somewhere empty-handed. Knowing the normal thing for him to bring would be alcohol, he decides to stop and get some flowers instead. Hoping the flower shop downtown was open, he parks in front and sees the lights still on. Running inside, he grabs a bunch of flowers for Olivia and at the last minute decides to grab another for Morgan.

There are so many feelings running rampant through his mind about Morgan. His unease about her real identity, the connection to the guy in the van, and worst of all his mother. Paying for the flowers, he gets back in the truck and starts out toward Seth's. Driving over, he thinks about the past few months. Meeting Morgan had felt like a falling star, a flash of bright light penetrating his mind, and the sense of wonder his heart felt was overwhelming. Over the last couple of weeks, something had changed. Now he knew why there was something about her that was off. Tonight, being with his friends was the best medicine for his psyche, and the next chapter to Morgan's story was going to have him in it.

As he turns onto Seth's street, he sees more cars than expected. He finds a parking spot as he wonders who has been invited to this BBQ. Walking up to their house, Brett notices Nick's truck and wonders what he is doing here. Bracing himself for the environment he is entering and understanding all the personalities he is about to face gives him strength. He might not have been a part of all of the participants of this group in the past, but he had made his mark in this town which stands up for itself.

As he gets closer to the house, he glances over to Morgan's house and sees through the front window, Morgan and Nick standing together. Watching the two of them together and noticing the tilt of Morgan's head toward Nick gives him an uneasy feeling. Shaking it off as stupid, he heads around back to Seth and Olivia's patio. Seeing Seth walking toward him, he quickly considers how much time he had spent at the bar recently which has caused him to not be able to catch up with his friends.

Shaking Seth's hand and pulling him close for a hug, Brett says through his smile, "Hey Seth, it's great to see you. How have you and Olivia been holding up?" Seth acknowledges Brett's comment with a shrug of his shoulders.

"We are doing our best to stay strong for Cissy and Josh, although Olivia has her moments. Right now, I'm grateful for our friends with tonight being a testament to my gratitude. Friends and family enjoying food, drink, and camaraderie. Come on, let's join everyone." Olivia comes out of the house and sees Brett and Seth. Blowing a kiss to both of them, she hurries over to the makeshift bar Seth has set up.

Setting down wine glasses and a couple of bottles of wine, she turns to look over at Morgan's house and wonders what is taking her so long to come over. Looking at the rest of her guests, she sees Whitney talking with Jackson and realizes Nick is missing as well. Whitney catches her eye, and before she can turn to go back in to get more items, Whitney is standing in front of her.

"Olivia, I saw you looking around. If you are wondering where Nick is he is over with Morgan." Staring at Whitney trying to gauge her comment, Olivia can't help but feel annoyed at Nick and Morgan. *What are they doing?*

Realizing Whitney was waiting for her to respond, she says, "No I really wasn't looking for anyone. I just want to make sure there are going to be enough seats for everyone." Sensing a movement out of the corner of her eye, she turns and sees Morgan and Nick walking toward them.

ANNE ELDER

Morgan & Nick

Sitting down at my makeup table before the barbecue, I begin my makeup routine by applying some moisturizer and eye cream. Taking a minute to look closely at my face, I cringe at the sight of wrinkles forming under my eyes and the slight formation of marionette lines near my mouth. All in all, though, I felt pretty good about my visage. Finishing up the rest of my routine, I stand in front of my closet and peruse the clothing I brought with me for the trip. Most of my clothes were still hanging in my closet at my home in Linn Creek. Finally settling on an embroidered black skirt and a top with open shoulders, I grab my black sandals and stand before the mirror. My legs and arms were still tan from the hot summer sun of New Jersey. Not too bad. Grabbing a pair of hoops and my bracelets, I walked downstairs. As I hit the bottom step, I heard footsteps on my front porch.

Glancing quickly out the side window, I see Nick standing before the door staring. What in the world is he doing here? He and Whitney should be over at Seth and Olivia's for the barbecue. Realizing he wasn't going away; I opened the door.

"Nick, what are you doing here, and where is Whitney? Is there something wrong?" Nick seems dumbstruck. "Dammit Nick, say something." Shaking his head as if he is in some kind of trance, he looks at me.

"Morgan, I'm sorry. You just look so pretty, and it took me back. Really, I didn't mean anything by it. Can I come in?" Stepping back, I opened the door wider and invited him in.

"Let's talk in the kitchen. I was about to head over to Olivia's." Grabbing a chair, I sit down and look at Nick as I continue, "So apparently whatever you need couldn't wait until we were over at Seth's." Watching him shaking his head gives me an uneasy feeling. What could he want to talk about or do for God's sake? "Nick, what is going on with you?"

Finally, Nick begins talking, "Morgan, you're coming back here has brought all of those memories back for both Whitney and me. We have never forgotten, but now we are talking about it and honestly, and I think that is worse. Before, I drowned myself in my own guilt, and as for whatever Whitney was feeling, I didn't care because I blamed her. Now, though it seems like we have become closer in our relationship. Maybe it's because we have come to terms with the role, we all played in those fateful days leading up to the prom. Except it's so painful, almost like it was happening again. All those days I drove to the farm asking Jonathan if I could see you, and then the rest of the summer hoping I would catch a glimpse of you somewhere in town." Listening to Nick talk, I can't help but feel some compassion for him and Whitney.

"Listen, we all need to move on. I plan on staying here in Millersville, which means we are going to see each other a lot." Touching his arm, I go on, "You know we were good friends, the three of us, and forgiveness is something God would want for us.

We will never be happy as individuals if we don't forgive and forget. Believe me when I say I've been trying to forget for a long time, and now we have the chance to forgive." Sitting there looking at Nick, I know that Nick, Whitney, and I will come to terms regarding our relationship, and somehow it will all work out, so I add, "Right now, we need to focus on forgetting the past and embracing the future where we have all hopefully evolved into better people."

Nick walks to the window and looks out as he responds, "Morgan, I've done things which aren't depicting an upstanding citizen, and at the time, I felt there was no choice. Now, I have become all wrapped up in your return and my relationship with Whitney, and I don't know what to do with all of it. I haven't been able to stop thinking about you since Whitney and I saw you at the bar. Whitney was upset when we went home. She couldn't stop talking about how old Heidi was and the fact she was born when you were away at college. When you said you had her during your first year there, that really threw her for a loop." Staring at him, I am hoping he is not going to start interrogating me about who Heidi's father is because, honestly, I don't know.

Finding my voice, I say, "Whitney admitted herself that she was interested because of the loss of your own child. What else could it be?"

Laughing bitterly, he says, "Morgan, doesn't it seem coincidental to you at all? We were together right before the prom, and the prom is in June." I begin feelings myself becoming irritated.

"Oh, yeah that's right! Was that before or after you slept with Whitney? Somehow this continues to be thrown in my face, and when I came back here this was what I didn't want to hear about, least of all from you. Did you not hear anything I just said? We can't keep going around and around about this because it will not help our psyche, especially if we are trying to forgive. Do you remember the night you stood on my porch when you found out who I was? I told you then I was over it. Yet here we are again with you expressing your confusion and hurt. So, get to the point, Nick. What are you asking me?" Getting up from his chair and pacing around my kitchen, the play of emotions is running havoc over his face as I just sit and watch.

Quickly coming and kneeling before me, he grabs my hands and asks, "Morgan, is Heidi my daughter?" Pushing him back, I stood up and moved to stand at the sliding doors looking over to Olivia and Seth's house.

Keeping my emotions intact, I turn around, look at him, and blurt, "Holy Mary, Mother of God, are you kidding me right now? Is that all you can say after everything? You must really think highly of yourself if you feel as though one time would be the consummation of my daughter. Sometimes, I wonder what goes through your mind when you get around me because the things that come out of your mouth are unbelievable. I don't know what business it is of yours or Whitney, who Heidi's father is, so my suggestion is to let go of any fantasy you might have." The next few minutes are quiet, and Nick continues looking outside. I busy myself getting the food out of the refrigerator for Olivia's barbecue.

Walking over to him, I touch his arm and say, "Let's go over to Olivia and Seth's. Whitney has to be wondering where you are, and neither one of us wants any kind of drama." He turns and looks at me.

Touching the side of my face, he quietly says, "Morgan, no matter what you said earlier, I will continue to work on building our friendship and whether you want to admit it yet, Heidi has a dad. So, it might be good for you and her to make an attempt to identify who her dad is. I don't know what went on with you that summer, but I know for sure you weren't with me."

"No kidding Nick. We know it wasn't you because you were having a relationship with Whitney. I really don't know how this is any of your business anyway. Heidi's father is my bWe better get over to Olivia's house before both of us say something that will destroy what little bit of headway we have made since I came home."

As Nick and I are walking over to Olivia's, I can't help but feel disheartened about my conversation with Nick. He apparently felt the need to unload his guilt and wanted me to help ease his attempt to make things right between Whitney and me. Scanning the yard, I see Jackson standing at the bar making a drink, Whitney talking to Olivia, and Seth standing with Brett. Looking back at Whitney and Olivia, I notice the two of them have focused their attention on me and Nick. Smiling and breaking away from Nick, I walked up to the two of them.

"Hey, you two, what has you both looking so intense?"

Whitney casts her eyes downward, but Olivia seems slightly angry as she answers, "Morgan, I was wondering where you were, and Whitney told me you were with Nick." Raising her eyebrows in question, I find myself struggling to respond.

"Whitney, I'm sorry if you were worried. Please don't be. Nick was pleading his case to me about you and I regaining our friendship. I told him to let things be and everything would work out." As soon as the words are out of my mouth, I feel Brett standing at my shoulder. Wondering how much he might have heard; I scanned his face trying to read his expression. Seeing a shadow pass over his eyes, I know he is confused.

Reaching up to give him a quick kiss, I softly say, "Hey stranger, it's great to see you." Brett gives me a quick hug. Olivia takes over and tells everyone to get whatever drinks they want and then motions to Seth to start the water for the crabs.

"Morgan, would you mind helping me get the appetizers set up inside?" Stepping away from Brett, I grabbed Olivia's hand, and we headed into the kitchen. No sooner do we get inside than Olivia turns to me half shouting, "Morgan, what the hell are you doing? Nick and you, alone, in your house. Do you realize how that looks to everyone?"

Frowning, I agree, "Yes, I do, but the everyone is Whitney, and I can assure you, she has nothing to worry about. Nick is lamenting about his relationship with Whitney, me, and some kind of guilt about something he has done that doesn't fit his upstanding citizen badge." Olivia gives me a quick hug.

"Morgan, I'm sorry for being angry with you. Whitney seems resigned to the mess of the relationship she and Nick have, but you being back home has amplified her despair. How is everything going with Brett?" Leaning back against the kitchen counter, I cross my arms and close my eyes for a moment.

"Olivia, I had to tell him. We have become so close and emotionally connected. It wasn't fair to either one of us for me to keep deceiving him." Olivia immediately comes over and hugs me.

"Oh my, how did he take it? He's here, so am I to assume he is ok with it?"

Laughing nervously, I reply, "Not exactly, but he is working through it with my help. There is so much more I need to tell him, and it will come in time. For now, he needs to understand my thought process of why I didn't tell him and swallow the fact that you and Seth did know."

Frowning, Olivia says, "Morgan, I'm sorry. Brett has been a good friend to Seth and me, and we love supporting the tavern. However, we were so distraught hearing Jonathan's despair during the time you were gone. It became our mission to find you, and in the end you came home. So, I hope Brett can forgive us." Hearing the door open, we both jump and turn to find Jackson standing there.

"Geez Jackson, you startled me," I say. Smiling broadly, Jackson moves into the kitchen area and pulls out a chair at the table.

"My apologies. What has caused the distress I see on both of your faces? If I overheard correctly, Morgan, you have a difficult task ahead of you. There is more at stake now." Olivia opens the refrigerator to start getting out the cheese and pepperoni trays and all the dips.

Looking over her shoulder with suspicious eyes, Olivia asks, "Jackson, you sound so ominous. Have you found out something?" I sat down with Jackson at the table and stared at him.

"Please tell. I knew you were investigating, but I didn't realize you had found anything." Jackson stands up suddenly and goes to stand at the door.

Looking at the two of them, he motions to the outside before beginning, "I will keep this short due to the activity outside. The so-called friend of Nick's who has been riding around the neighborhood has made a mistake. I've been following him very discreetly, and he made a visit to Brett's mother's house where he seemed to have been harassing her. Now, I can't fathom what reason he would have for harassing Elizabeth Callahan, but something is amiss, and I will find out what."

Knowing the conversation, I just had with Olivia as well as the earlier conversation with Nick, I am already feeling uneasy, but now I am even more unsettled after hearing Jackson's report. Who is this guy, and why is he even in our community?

"Jackson, please use all your resources and find out what is happening."

Moving to stand with both of us, Jackson puts his arms around us and says, "Listen, I don't want the two of you to start worrying about this more than needed. I am going to find out everything, but in the meantime, let's go out and have a great feast. Olivia, you two have outdone yourselves again." Gathering up all the items we need, we all head outside.

The Callahans

Seth goes around the side of the house with his crab boiling pot and starts filling it with water from the outdoor spigot. As he is walking there, he sees Jackson sitting in a chair nearby. Tapping Jackson's shoulder, Seth motions for Jackson to follow him.

"Jackson, I have hardly had a minute to talk to you today. But now that I think about it, your car wasn't here much today."

Grabbing the pot to hold it, Jackson responds, "No I wasn't here earlier. There was something I needed to do, and it took a little longer than I thought. Seth, how well do you know Elizabeth Callahan?"

With his eyebrows raised, Seth says, "Brett's mom? Why?" Jackson sets the pot down on the ground to fill it the rest of the way up with water.

"Seth, you know about the guy riding around our community. Well, he found his way, a couple of nights ago, in front of Morgan's house, and then today, he was found in Elizabeth Callahan's driveway. I don't know what he is up to, but I am determined to find out." Seth motions for him to pick up the other side of the pot, and they start walking back.

"Yes, I know, and it's been disturbing, especially if he is contacting Morgan and Brett's mother. As for Elizabeth, I've known her for years, well at least as long as I've been friends with Brett. But really knowing her, honestly, I can't say. She's Brett's mother, so when I was over there or hanging out with him, she was there, but I must tell you she was aloof, and that is being kind." They make it to the burner. Setting the pot down, Seth lights the burner.

Seeing Olivia coming from the house, he yells, "Hey Olivia, bring out the old bay seasoning and vinegar. Jackson and I will grab the crabs from the garage refrigerator." Olivia acknowledges him and does an about-face, and heads back into the house. Jackson and Seth head to the garage and continue their conversation.

"Seth, did you know Brett's father? I remember him when we were growing up. But he was always traveling and a passing glimpse of him was all I ever had." Opening the refrigerator and pulling out the bushel of crabs, Seth looks up at Jackson.

"It was his stepfather, Jack Callahan. He spent a lot of time out at the Jenkins farm. Jack Callahan was someone Misty and Jonathan didn't care for. I can remember Jonathan telling me he had to finish up milking in the morning a lot of the times because his dad was visiting with Jack Callahan. It started to become difficult for me because even though Brett went to a private school, I also had a relationship with Brett because of the proximity of their house to us." Together they carry the bushel out of the garage and head to the burner. Olivia is standing and monitoring the pot with the vinegar and old bay seasoning sitting on the side table.

"Hey, you two. Thankfully you have arrived with the crabs because the water is starting to boil. When are we supposed to put in the seasonings?" Lifting the pot and instructing Olivia about how much to put in, Jackson and Seth start adding the crabs to the pot. Once they are all in, they all step away. Jackson and Seth join the rest of the group as Brett walks over to everyone.

"Jackson, it's been a long time," Brett says with an extended hand.

"Yes, it has been. How are doing these days, Brett?" Before Brett can respond, Morgan appears.

———————— • ————————

"Ok, what is going on here? It seems there are a lot of males staring at a boiling pot. So, tell me Olivia, what is wrong with this picture?" Laughing, Olivia high-fives me.

"I hear you, my friend." Casting a glance at Brett, she says, "I'm so happy you were able to break away from the bar to come and enjoy some crabs." Brett puts his arm around me and leans down to give me a quick kiss.

"I wouldn't have missed it. Morgan stopped in the bar this morning to make sure Jillian would be able to take over tonight." Pulling me, a little closer, he smiles and says, "It's been a busy few days, so this is good, very good."

The next couple of hours were fairly uneventful, and Nick and Whitney seemed to enjoy themselves. At one point, though, I felt Brett looking at me deep in thought, and it made me wonder how he was doing.

Olivia stands and motions to me it is time to clean up the food, so together we gather all the dirty serving dishes and throw away all the used paper plates.

Walking into the house together, Olivia quickly says, "Morgan, don't say anything, Whitney is coming up with more dishes." Turning around to hold the door open for her, Whitney steps into the house.

"Olivia, everything was so good. I haven't sat and eaten crabs for so long." Looking at me, she continues, "It was great being with old friends."

Scraping off the food into the trashcan, I agree, "It was great today, and I'm glad Nick and you were able to come. It's an important step for all of us in our healing."

Brett steps into the kitchen, saying, "I have to run back to relieve Jillian for an hour or so, but I can swing back around."

Olivia smiles and says, "Sounds great. We will still be hanging out because I saw Seth and Nick getting wood together. We must be having a bonfire."

Touching Brett's arm, I offer, "Hey I'll walk you out." Brett nods and we both walk out. "Text me when you are heading back, so I can let you know if Heidi and I are still over here."

With a slight tip of his head, he says, "I'm going to tell everyone I'll see them later. But Morgan, you and I need to talk later. There are certain things that you need to clear up for me."

Morgan & Whitney

Brett is becoming apprehensive about everything, and it shows every time we are together. Soon, I am going to tell him of the events leading up to my leaving, and hopefully he will understand why I left. Heading back to the party, I see Nick and Whitney talking with Heidi. Coming up to them, I hear Whitney asking Heidi if she is planning to stay in Millersville. Heidi sees me and hesitates, looking to me for help.

"Honestly, Whitney, Heidi and I have not talked about it. She hasn't been here very long, and she has work waiting for her at home so staying long term will need some planning." Heidi gives me a thankful look.

Turning back to Whitney, Heidi goes on to say, "It really has more to do with my mom and her plans. If she decides to permanently move here, well I would have to find work here. My mom and I have never been far apart, and I want to keep it that way." Nick is touching Whitney's arm to signal her to stop asking questions. Whitney brushes his hand away and focuses her attention back on Heidi.

"Don't you have other family and friends in Linn Creek who will want you to come back?"

Throwing a dirty look at Whitney, I start to answer but hear Heidi say, "Whitney, I thought you knew. It is just me and my mom. I do not know my father. My friends will just have to take a road trip and come see me. Anyway, I can fly back there when I want to hang out because we still have our house there. Right Mom?"

Smiling at Heidi, I assure her, "Yes, we do! There is no plan on selling or renting it out at this point. If we both stay here long term, then we will have to figure something out. Until then, I want to focus on our time here in Millersville." Putting my arm around Heidi, I continue, "The unknowns facing all of us have become anthems in our mind, and God gives our life new meaning." Heidi smiles and pulls me just a little bit closer.

"You all know my mom, don't you? I mean she grew up here and so did both of you, right?" Watching Nick, I see him flinch slightly and then shrug his shoulders as if to say, here it goes.

He puts his arm around Whitney, which I view as a unified front, and says, "Yes, Heidi, we did grow up here, and your mom, Whitney, and I were friends. We spent many days together when we were in high school. Your mom and Whitney were best friends from grammar school all the way through high school. They lived right down the street from one another."

Whitney looks as if she is going to burst into tears. My heart skips a beat seeing her distress. Tentatively touching her arm, I gently pull her into my arms. Feeling her body convulsing with the years of guilt trying to empty the misery occupying her soul, I look at Nick.

Nodding, he moves toward Heidi and suggests, "Hey, how about we leave your mom and Whitney alone for a minute? Let's go over and see what Seth is up to. He looks like he is setting up beer pong." Heidi at once loses interest in what is happening in front of her.

"Let's go, Nick. I need to tell you beer pong is my sport, and you need to be ready to play your best game." Laughing, the two of them walk away. Taking Whitney's arm, I walk her to the patio chairs under Seth's oak tree.

"Whitney, we are away from everyone. Please calm down. All this guilt you are carrying must end." She is trying to talk to me between the hiccups and sniffling.

"Misty, oh my, can I call you Misty?"

Not wanting to upset her anymore, I say, "Yes you can. I will always be Misty to you, Whitney. Please try to get yourself together. We can talk later."

Getting herself together, she looks at me, "No it must be now. I cannot do this anymore. Misty, I have turned into a person who walks through everyday playing a role that does not fit what I dreamed my life would be. I'm constantly wondering now what path God will take me and asking Him to help me to push away the evil thoughts floating through my mind.

When I look at myself in the mirror, I see this person I do not know anymore. The anger and guilt I have felt for all these years has eaten into my soul and controlled every aspect of my life. You were my best friend. My best friend, Misty, and I betrayed you terribly. My life with Nick has not been the best, but I feel as though now we might be getting closer."

Wanting to interrupt her from talking, I motion with my hand to stop, shaking her head she goes on, "Misty, I know you were scared to come back here. There is so much history here, and the last part was so awful for you, and for that, I am sorry. Yet really, what does saying you are sorry mean if nothing changes for either one of us? Nothing would make me happier than for all of us to be friends again and turn our past into a positive future."

Knowing there is still a long way to go for the future to be bright for all of us makes me a little sad. Time will tell how we all will fare during the next few days. Things were intensifying, and with Jackson's last discovery concerning Elizabeth, I'd bet Brett and my relationship would be tested to its limit.

Smiling at her, I say, "Whitney, I am not going anywhere, and hopefully neither will Heidi. We will have time to get to know each other again. Neither one of us is anything like we were when we were teenagers. Life experiences have changed both of us. Let's get back to the party." Leaning toward her, I whisper, "Go inside and fix your makeup. Olivia's tool bag is in the closet next to the shower. I'm sure she won't mind if you use it." We both stand up and at the same time reach to give each other a hug.

"Well, this is a start," says Whitney. Whitney heads into the house, and I walk over to where the guys, Heidi and Olivia are standing around the fire.

Nick saw me first and immediately asked, "Is Whitney ok?"

"She will be. Olivia, she might need to use something out of your tool bag if you do not mind."

Seth laughs loudly, "Olivia's tool bag?" Looking at his wife, he asks suspiciously, "Why do you have a tool bag?"

Sending Seth an exasperated look, Olivia says, "Really Seth, it is my makeup bag. Every woman's tool bag, which we constantly update, not like men who still use the first screwdriver they ever had."

Looking at me, Olivia nods and heads into her house. The five of us remained standing around the fire, and suddenly everyone got quiet enough that the crackling of the fire was the only sound. Trying to be discreet, I look at Jackson under my lashes wanting him to look at me, so I can let him know I need to talk with him alone.

Heidi lightly punches Nick in the arm teasing, "Hey, so do you want a rematch in beer pong, Nick? I do not want to destroy your record by having you beat by a woman, so…?" Right as Nick responds, Jackson moves so he is standing next to me and quietly agrees we need to talk.

Seth volunteers, "I'll take you on, Heidi. If we can get another taker, we can have teams. Jackson, Morgan, either of you want in?" I hear the back door slam and see Whitney and Olivia walking out.

Jackson says, "You know, Seth, I have my pride, and by what I saw earlier, Heidi might kick your ass." Olivia laughs as she walks down the path to the fire pit.

"Oh my, Heidi, please win." Grinning from ear to ear, Heidi puts her arm around Olivia.

Heidi practically sings, "I will if I have a good partner."

Before Olivia can reply, Whitney takes a deep breath and shocking us all she says, "Heidi, I'll be your partner. Ask your mom, I was damn good when we were in high school."

Smirking, Heidi retorts, "Wow Mom, you were playing beer pong in high school. Weren't you underage?"

Looking around the group for help to no avail, I respond, "Yes, we were, but you know the old saying, 'Do as I say not as I do.' Thanks a lot, you all, for having my back." Tapping Heidi on the arm, I encourage, "Whitney will be a great partner, so I hope you both teach those guys a lesson." With that, they all move to the table and set up their cups. Understanding the effect this was going to have on Whitney and Nick as well as Heidi, I walk over to Olivia and Jackson.

Noticing how dark it is becoming, I look at my watch and see it's getting late. Hoping nothing is amiss at the tavern, I decide to text Brett and see what his ETA is.

"Olivia, it's starting to get dark, do you want to turn on your outside lights? Tell me where the switch is, and I will go turn it on. The restroom is calling me. You know, too many beers, and the bathroom becomes your friend."

Olivia cracks up laughing, and says, "You got that right, my friend. The switch is right by the back door. Jackson and I will be right here by the fire pit watching Heidi and Whitney take those men down." Smiling at the two of them, I set out for the house. Walking through the back door, I see the switch and flip it up. Glancing out the door, I see all the patio lights come on. Hearing the familiar text alert, I looked at my phone and saw Brett texted me.

Brett: Morgan, things are crazy here with the bachelorette party and Jillian needs help. I'm not sure if I will be able to come back until very late, but I really want to talk to you. Is it ok if I come over later?

Thinking for a moment about how to respond, I text back.

Me: Brett, listen stay there if you must. Everyone will be out of here in the next couple of hours and Heidi and I will be going home. How about meeting sometime tomorrow, for breakfast?"

Looking at my phone, waiting for his response, I realized the bathroom really was calling me because I could feel my bladder screaming. Sitting down on the toilet, I hear my text notification.

Brett: Ok. I wanted to come over tonight, but I understand if it will not work for you. Text me tomorrow when you get up, and we can come up with a plan. We really need to talk, ok."

Finishing with my toiletries, I walk back out to the kitchen. Looking out the door, I see Jackson and Olivia in deep conversation. Knowing I needed to be part of it, I quickly texted Brett back.

Me: Hey that is fine. We do need to talk, so I will call you tomorrow.

I hit send and wonder if I should have said more. Pushing the door open, I walk down the path toward Olivia and Jackson.

Olivia walks toward me grabbing my hand and whispering, "Morgan, Jackson has so much to tell you. He is on to something, and it is about Brett's mother."

Swallowing tightly, I think about my text messages with Brett. This is not going to end well. Knowing how determined Jackson can be reassures me, but the impact it's going to have on Brett, possibly

Nick and Whitney, and most of all, Jonathan, Sara, and I is haunting my thoughts every day. If Jackson finds out what happened to our father, and it implies Elizabeth or Jack, I do not know how Brett and I will survive.

"All of us need to sit down together, and it looks like Seth might be losing in the beer pong game. Not necessarily a proud moment, but Heidi is kicking their asses. Whitney is getting aggravated, and we all know how competitive she is, right?" Jackson and Olivia look at one another and shake their heads in agreement. We sit together for a moment, and then Jackson speaks quietly.

"Morgan, there is something amiss with Elizabeth Callahan. I've done some quiet investigation and she was known to be very involved in her husband's career. Jack Callahan was not known for his finesse, and word on the street is during his career he became the electric company's henchman." Stopping Jackson, I try to hide my surprise.

"Jackson, he came over to our house all the time. At first, he was so friendly and said all the right things to my dad. Talking, farming, and milking were the conversations when he would randomly stop over. Everyone thought he was so nice and interesting. It wasn't until much later later when he became so attentive with what dad was doing to help the community. After several months, it became obvious, he was more invested in Dad's other activities than what was going on around the farm.

This is when Mom started to feel threatened whenever he was around. Eventually, she stopped joining their conversations and continually expressed her distress over his visits to Dad. We all knew how she felt about Jack, and it became even more clear when he brought his army friend over, Charlie. Let me tell you both, he was an evil person. His eyes were dead and showed no emotion whatsoever." There was an intenseness in Jackson which I had never seen before. He was pacing back and forth rubbing his hands through his curly hair.

"Morgan, all those things happened because he was trying to find out what your dad knew about the effect of the stray voltage falling from the electrical towers. You do realize that if your dad were still alive and had time to prove his theory, the electric company would have had to pay millions of dollars in damages. Money drives people to do things which may border on being criminal, and from all I have uncovered, there is a strong possibility Elizabeth is as criminal as you can get."

Stunned, yet feeling validated, I begin to think about the conversation needing to take place later between Brett and myself. Nothing could prepare me for whatever Brett's reaction would be, and I know my face portrayed my anguish. Olivia watches the play of emotions moving across my face and realizes the turmoil I am feeling.

Touching my arm, Olivia looks between Jackson and me and says, "Well this is going to be interesting. Isn't Brett supposed to be coming back here tonight?" Standing, I look over toward my house.

Continuing my gaze, I quietly respond to Olivia, "Brett will not be coming back tonight. The bar is busy, and Jillian needs help. My reprieve, however, will only be tonight. He said it could wait until tomorrow."

Jackson stops pacing and says, "What could wait until tomorrow?" Feeling uneasy knowing Jackson isn't going to understand my feelings for Brett or the impact of telling him who I really am is causing me to hesitate. Glancing at Olivia, she nods and smiles as if to say it would be ok. Sitting down and folding my hands in my lap, I look at Jackson.

"Jackson, Brett just found out who I am and is sure there is something more going on. All this time he thought I was a woman visiting the area who decided to stay. This same woman met his friends, Seth and Olivia, and moved into the house next door. Beyond his most-recent introduction to Heidi, he did not know much more about me until yesterday. However, his friendship is important to me, and now you are telling me his mother may be complicit in the death of my father." Jackson stands quietly listening to me, and I can see his mind working.

"Morgan, life can be hard, and some people have it harder than others. Right now, in this family, we are fighting with what God has laid out for our life's plan. Cissy, Josh, Seth and Olivia are trying to understand, but none of us want to face the horrible events bestowed on us. But we are made of strong stock, and our faith in God is unbreakable. Palmers are strong people, and you, Morgan, are strong as well.

This is going to be difficult for you, but nothing is stopping you from telling him how much you care for him if that is the case. My exposure to Brett has been brief. Seth and he were friendly, and I knew him, but he was Seth's friend, so I made it a point to keep it that way." Olivia became quiet, and I felt for her. Her and Seth have developed a strong relationship with Brett, and if what Jackson knows is true, it could jeopardize their friendship. Knowing the two of them, they were going to do their best not to fault Brett for his mother's actions.

Keeping her voice low not wanting everyone else to hear, Olivia asks, "Jackson, do you have a plan to validate the information you have found? The last thing I want is for false allegations against his mother affecting Brett's business. The tavern has done so well since he took over, and it has become a great place for our community. The clientele has changed since we were young and all for the better. He doesn't put up with too much nonsense there, and as a result, it made a mark on our community as being one of the must-see places in our area."

Jackson puts his arm around Olivia and says reassuringly, "Do not worry about this, Olivia. All we are doing right now is guessing, and none of what I have found has implicated Brett. His mother is the one who's past we need to look at more. It is possible she played a bigger part in her husband's career than everyone originally thought. Whatever her role was then and now, you can be sure I will find out. Something tells me there is more to Elizabeth Callahan than meets the eye." Joining the rest of the party, Olivia, Jackson, and I put our conversation away for now to enjoy the rest of the night with everyone.

Abruptly, Heidi lets out an, "Oh yeah," and we look over to the four of them still playing beer pong. Heidi grabs Whitney's hand and dances around Nick chanting, "That's right, we beat you and Seth." Twirling Whitney around, Heidi continues, "Whitney, we beat them. You were right, you are good, and you can be my partner anytime." Whitney quickly looks at me, and I smile and pump my fist.

"You go girls! Way to beat these guys!"

Running over to me, Heidi throws her arms around me exclaiming, "Mom, this is so much fun. I'm so glad I'm here and have gotten to meet all your good friends. Hey, you all come over here, it's time for a group hug and a picture. Nick, you have the longest arms, so here is my phone." Seeing Jackson standing back, Heidi spins around, "Jackson, get over here and stand with my mom." Jackson hesitates for a second then moves himself next to me.

Nick holds Heidi's phone up and says, "Ok, move in a little closer." Jackson moves to stand behind me and Seth moves behind Olivia. Waiting for Nick to maneuver Heidi's phone seems like several minutes instead of just a couple of seconds with Jackson standing so close to the back of me.

Feeling nervous, I impatiently say, "Nick, can you snap the picture?"

Smiling Nick turns to look at me and says, "Ok everyone, say cheese." The wonderful thing about the new phones is you can snap a bunch of pictures in a matter of seconds. Nick steps away looking at Heidi's phone.

"Oh damn, Heidi, I need your password." Heidi steps out of the group and grabs her phone.

"Ok, oh my God, look at these pictures, they are so good. Mom, come here and look." Standing next to her, I see the photos. My heart swells with something I can't identify. Nick is standing behind Whitney and the two of them are smiling with feigned happiness while Seth and Olivia are smiling with a sadness only those close to them can see. Heidi has such a contented look on her face with her eyes sparkling and her great smile that I can't help but wonder what she was thinking. And then, Jackson's hands are on my shoulders, and his face is hovering close to mine smiling with joy of friendship and a hint of something else.

"Well, this is a picture worth framing," Olivia exclaims. "Look at all of us, we are a pretty good-looking group. Jackson, I never realized how photogenic you are. You and Morgan are definitely cheesing." I can't help myself, I burst out laughing and can't stop. Everyone looks over at me.

Heidi speaks first, "Mom, are you ok? Why are you laughing so hard?"

Trying to control myself, I sputter between laughter, "I don't know what came over me, but something did, and apparently it must have been my own joke because the rest of you are looking at me like I've lost my mind."

Jackson puts his arm around me and whispers, "It's the stress releasing, no worries." Leaning into him trying to let him know I agree while also getting myself together, I apologize to everyone for my outburst. The moment is over.

We finish up our drinks and help Seth and Olivia clean up from the night's festivities by putting all the cushions in the garage and putting out all the tiki lights. As I am walking back from the garage, Whitney comes from the side of the garage.

"Morgan, wait. I want to talk to you for a minute."

"Damn Whitney, you scared me. What's going on?" Clasping her hands in front of her, Whitney motions me back into the garage.

"Morgan, I overheard Olivia talking to Jackson about some guy who has been driving around the neighborhood and sitting in his van watching your homes. She seemed really upset, and I swore she said you confronted the guy. Tell me you didn't?"

Wondering where this is going, I respond, "Whitney, he was bothering all of us with his constant riding by so when he drove slowly by my house the other day, I ran out to him. Why are you so concerned about this? Has he been driving near your house as well?" Whitney hesitates to answer and looks around to make sure no one else is in earshot of her response.

"Morgan, I think this guy was in my house the other night. He said he was a friend of Nick's from college and happened to be in town, so he stopped by. Nick came home and seemed very uncomfortable about him being there."

Getting a sick feeling in my stomach, I ask, "Whitney, what was his name?"

Leaning against the garage as if in support of herself, Whitney looks at me and says, "Ray." Stunned for a moment, I try to gather my thoughts together.

"Ray was his name. Are you sure, Whitney?"

"Yes, Morgan, I'm positive, and I'm sure he was not a college buddy of Nick's. Now I don't know what to do. Nick and I are finally moving in the right direction and accusing him of lying to me about this guy, Ray, would not be good. I have a bad feeling about this, and I don't know who else to turn to, believe it or not." Listening to her, I quickly think about what to say next. This confirms Nick knows this guy who has been tormenting all of us. Now it becomes a decision of how much to tell Whitney. I can tell by her expression she is doubtful of her husband's relationship with this person.

"Whitney, I'm positive he is the same person I ran out and stopped. He told me he was a friend of Nick's, and he was looking for me, well, you know, Misty Jenkins. What I don't understand is why Nick is friends with someone like this guy or what in the hell he would want with me." Whitney's facial expression is so full of sorrow, so, I touch her arm. "We will figure it out. Let's keep it between the two of us for now. I'm sure Nick will have an explanation. We better get back to the party. Olivia will be wondering where we are when she is doing her dishes by herself." Together we hurry into the house and help Olivia with the cleanup.

Elizabeth & Fraser

The morning comes with quite a chill. Fall is coming. You could feel it in the air. The sun is rotating at a different angle, and as a result, it takes the days longer to warm up. Elizabeth knows it is a matter of time before all of the years of deceit and evil explode around her. It is time to do some damage control, and it needs to start with Tom Fraser. Reaching for the phone, she calls the bank and asks to speak to him. Hearing the ringing of the phone, she impatiently taps her nails on the table.

Come on, Tom, answer the damn phone. Hearing the beep in her ear for the voicemail makes her want to throw her phone at the wall. Whatever happened to people answering the phone instead of letting it go to voicemail, so it could be screened. She could just see him sitting there listening to her voice.

"Tom, this is Elizabeth Callahan. I need you to clear your schedule today. There are issues we are facing that need to be resolved immediately. Please call me as soon as you get this message." Hanging up the phone, she continues to tap her nails. Talking to the empty room, she pondered her options. "If he doesn't return my phone call by this afternoon, maybe I should go right to the source of my aggravation which is Morgan Kiernan, who I now know is Misty Jenkins for Pete's sake."

She retrieved the canister from its new hiding place. Opening up the lid, she sees the remnants of the tea leaves used on the day she lost her soul to the company. Panicking, she takes the canister to the sink and runs water into it, washing out any residue that remained. Sitting down on the small settee by the tub, she puts her head in her hands questioning all of her choices all those years ago. *Why in the world did I cooperate with them? How could I sacrifice my son's well-being and his chance for success? Did I really think it wouldn't come back to haunt me?* Her desire to be so important in this small town seems so ridiculous to her now. She closes her eyes and thinks about that day.

———————— • ————————

Jack was hurrying through breakfast and downing cups of coffee. The mornings had been the only real time they had together where the couple they once were seemed evident. Somehow, this day was going differently, and after a few minutes he said there was an appointment he needed to get to. Watching him leave the driveway, Elizabeth thought back over the past two years of Jack's time with Carl Jenkins, and it suddenly hit her. Jack was heading over to the farm. Carl was probably getting ready to come in for breakfast. The anger that welled up inside of Elizabeth almost took her to her knees. She hated this farmer for his integrity, honesty, and determination. His desire to help his community was unrealistic, but he kept pursuing a solution.

Carl Jenkins turned her husband into this person who wanted to learn to milk a cow, drive a tractor, bale hay during a hot summer day, and worst of all, support Jenkins' drive to stop the stray current from dropping into his community. Jack's career was going to be over and with it, Elizabeth's standard of living—no more dinner parties with the politicians of the area, cancelled lunch appointments with the ladies of the country club, looks from the townspeople as if she was one of them now. And in her mind, the contempt Carl Jenkins and his wife had for her, as if she was some kind of piranha, was enough to put her over the edge. This was the moment. Elizabeth felt it was time for her to take matters into her own hands as the company was disgusted with Jack's performance and beginning to look to her for a solution to this problem of Carl Jenkins.

During Elizabeth's travels abroad, she came across Wolfsbane and realized the danger of the plant. Contact with the plant could slow the heart and cause heart failure if the exposure was significant. A plan began to formulate in her mind. In the past, she sent her peach tea with Jack to share with the Jenkinses, and Jack told her Carl kept it on his tractor and sipped from it throughout the day. It made him laugh because Carl always drank it right from the jar.

For the next several days, Elizabeth made sure new jars of tea were sent with Jack when he went to his so-called appointment which was always out to the Jenkins farm. He came home sunburned and so light-hearted. She knew there was so much more happening in his days than he told her. With gloves on, she rubbed the jar surface with wolfsbane, concentrating it around the rim. Knowing Carl would be drinking it out of the jar was all the better. Thinking about all the phone calls from the company and the demands they were throwing at her, Elizabeth had to do something. So, she kept sending them, and Jack kept assuring her how much Carl appreciated the tea. It took several weeks, but one day, while eating dinner, Jack received a phone call. After a few minutes listening, he put down the phone and without saying a word, walked out of the house. Elizabeth followed him outside, and as he was getting into his car, he turned and looked at her.

"Carl Jenkins is dead. Are you happy now?" Closing the car door, he backed out of the driveway and left.

———— • ————

Remembering his words brings chills to Elizabeth even now. It seemed to be the only way to save Jack's career. The company wanted Carl Jenkins to stop. Jack would not or could not do it, so more drastic measures were needed. It was time, though, for the rest of the participants to take notice. Grabbing her purse, she goes to the garage.

Starting her car, she sits there and considers that today may be the end of it. Brett already knew about Misty who is now Morgan, Carl's daughter. And the company is exhibiting some muscle with Ray lurking around every corner. Elizabeth's goal is to keep as much away from Brett as possible to try and salvage some kind of relationship with him. She feels his disappointment in her is already on high alert, and that all began with Morgan Kiernan. If she had not come back, none of this would have been uncovered. Morgan's suspicions are leading her toward the truth, and Elizabeth knows she needs to stop Morgan from finding out what really happened to her father. Putting her car in gear, she backs out of the garage and heads into town. Finding a parking spot near the bank, she swings in and parks. As she is getting out of the car, she hears her name called.

"Mrs. Callahan? Elizabeth?" Looking over her shoulder at who called her name, she sees Morgan standing on the sidewalk.

———— • ——

I call after Elizabeth, and when she turns to face me, she looks over-heated. She then turns back to her car, pushes the lock button on her key, and continues hesitantly toward the sidewalk, so I follow behind her.

Concerned, I offer again, "Elizabeth are you alright? You are looking flushed. Do I need to get you water?" Embarrassed, she leaned on my arm.

"Morgan, can you help me over to the bench, so I can sit for a moment? I don't know what came over me."

Getting her settled on the bench, I leave to get the water. We are sitting right near the bank, so walking inside, I ask the teller if there is a water dispenser. Following her point to the corner of the lobby, I see it and hurriedly get Elizabeth a cup of water. Deciding to get myself a cup, I turned awkwardly with the two cups and my pock-etbook fearing there would be no water left in the cups by the time I got back to Elizabeth. Just as I am trying to maneuver the door, Fraser is suddenly at my elbow.

"Morgan, let me get the door for you. Also, I can take the cups of water from you. Where are you going?" Not wanting to engage in too much conversation with him right now, I point to where Elizabeth is sitting.

"She felt faint, so I helped her to the bench and offered to get some water." We could see Elizabeth with her head between her hands leaning down as if she felt faint again. Tom picks up the pace, and we quickly give her some water. A couple of minutes go by, and she seems to revive herself.

"Tom, did you get my message? I need to talk to you, and it cannot wait." Watching Tom through the corner of my eye, I see him frown, and hesitate to speak. Elizabeth says again, "Tom did you or did you not get my message? We have a mutual acquaintance who needs assistance, so I would like to go to your office if you could so kindly help me." Turning back to me, she adds, "Morgan, thank you for your assistance. It is much appreciated. Tom will help me now." Getting up from the bench with Tom's help, the two of them walk into the bank.

Taking a seat on the bench, I lay my head back and think about the last few minutes. I begin replaying in my mind starting from when I first saw Elizabeth get out of the car. She stepped out quite confidently, and her stature faltered when I called out her name. It might make sense she was surprised to see me but not to the extent of feeling faint and needing to sit down. Something was going on with her, and the tone of her voice when she spoke to Tom Fraser was nothing less than threatening.

Realizing the time, I got up and started back to my car and head back home to see if I can talk with Jackson. We need to go over the sale agreement and revise the acreage that would remain in Jonathan and Sara's possession. Plus, Jackson is looking into whether there is an environmental reason that would stop them. On my drive back home, I think about Brett and the impact all of this is going to have on him. Something tells me his mother is going to be implicated in the death of my father.

Pulling into my driveway, I wonder if Heidi has risen yet. Last night was a lot of fun, and it was really late when the party ended at Olivia's. Walking around the house to go in the sliding glass door, I hear voices. Turning the corner, I see Heidi, Jackson, Seth, and Olivia sitting at the table drinking coffee.

"Well look at what we have here. Is this the new brain trust of our neighborhood? All of you look so serious."

Heidi speaks first, "Mom, we are discussing the outcome of the beer pong tournament. Seth wants to recap the game in case there might have been a chance for him to WIN!" We all laugh, and Jackson gets up and pulls in another chair for me.

Olivia touches my arm, asking tenderly, "How has your morning been? You left early."

Smiling at all of them, I offer, "It was an eventful morning. Elizabeth Callahan needed my help."

Seth was the first of them to exclaim, "She what?"

Jackson shoved back his chair inquiring, "You didn't say anything to her about the visitor she had, did you?"

Giving him a dirty look, I say with offense, "Of course not, she got overheated or something and almost fainted. I was right there, so I helped her to the bench that was nearby. It was weird, though, she seemed fine when she stepped out of the car. It was as if hearing my voice threw her into some kind of fainting spell. It goes on from there. I went into the bank to get her water, and who helped me with the door but Tom Fraser. He walked with me to Elizabeth. The conversation between the two of them didn't make any sense to me."

Everyone speaks at once, "What do you mean?"

Taking a sip of my coffee, I continue explaining, "You would have to be there. It was like watching the principal reprimand a student. There is definitely some kind of dynamic between the two of them which is peculiar to say the least." Equally unsure of what to make of this exchange, Seth and Olivia stand up with their coffee cups and announce they are going to head back home to get some things done. Heidi informs me she would be taking a long soaking bath, so the bathroom upstairs would be out of commission for the next couple of hours.

Jackson looks at me, and says simply, "Morgan, something is up with Elizabeth Callahan. The fainting spell you saw, I'm sure was the fact you were occupying her thoughts, and then you appeared. In my experience there are criminals in all hierarchies of our society, and Elizabeth Callahan is no exception." Debating whether or not I should share Whitney's conversation, I get up and stand at the railing. Ultimately, I decide to tell him because there is more at stake now, and this isn't some high school secret between besties. Nick participates in this somehow, albeit not a willing accomplice.

Unfortunately, there will be casualties and relationships destroyed when Jackson finds out the truth. Even Heidi won't escape the tragedy—either her real father will be an accomplice to her grandfather's

384

death, or he will be the man bringing justice to her grandfather. I have no way of knowing for sure, and it will continue to be locked away in my mind. Heidi seems to think it isn't that important to her because her life has always been whole. She will know when she is ready, and until then, we are going to keep things status quo.

"Jackson, I need to tell you about a conversation Whitney had with me last night. She followed me to the Seth's garage when I was putting away the chairs and she definitely seemed agitated."

With a small laugh, Jackson leans back in his chair saying, "Come on Morgan, Whitney seems agitated or upset most of the time. What makes you so concerned about this time?"

"Maybe it was the urgency in her voice and her body language that led me to believe she was scared. This person, who we now know is named Ray, was at her house the other night acting like he was a friend from Nick's college days. During the time he was there, she said Nick was trying to act the part, but she's sure Ray wasn't a college friend. The two of them went out to the garage, and Whitney could hear Nick's voice getting loud. She couldn't understand anything being said, but she was sure Nick was very upset.

"Jackson, this guy is the same person riding around bothering everyone and also the person you saw with Elizabeth Callahan. There is some kind of connection between all of them, Nick, Ray, Elizabeth, Tom Fraser, and whomever they are working for whether directly or indirectly." Jackson listens to me attentively with a thoughtful expression.

Leaning forward, he says sternly, "Later today, I'm going to pay a visit to my old friend, Tom Fraser and see how the landscape has changed in Tom's life."

———— • ————

Elizabeth makes it to Tom's office without any other episodes. He has left her sitting there while he makes his way back to the lobby to get her some more water. These notes, phone calls, and now a visit from Ray—the company's muscle is disturbing, and she is sure Tom is wallowing right in the middle of it. He returns with the water.

"Elizabeth, are you feeling ok? No more fainting spells, please. If you need me to call someone for you, I will happily do so. Or better yet, I can take you home and let Brett know to come for your car."

Putting her hand up to stop his incessant chatter, she says, "Tom, please shut the door, and then shut your mouth. We have a problem which we are going to figure out a solution to today." Shutting the door more aggressively than needed, he comes to sit behind his desk.

"Elizabeth, if we have a problem, I was not aware of it. So, if you can speak calmly and respectfully, I will see what can be done to help you."

Bursting out with laughter and then becoming very arrogant, she starts talking, "Tom, stop the bullshit. You and I both know we work for the devil, and he has come calling again. Your involvement in the company has been going on as long as I've been involved, and all of this has to come to an end. The Jenkins farm has been in the company's sights since Jack worked for them twenty years ago. Now everything has changed.

All of the time wasted by the company at my expense is exhausting, ridiculous, and unacceptable. None of you could come up with a plan to get Carl Jenkins to stop his obsession with proving stray voltage was killing people. Yet I did, and unlike the rest of you, I actually went through with it. Now all these years later, you still haven't been able to get your hands on their property. Sending your henchman to scare me is not going to work. I will go right to Morgan Kiernan, who I know you realize is Misty Jenkins, and tell her everything."

Listening to Elizabeth, Tom decides it is time to push this agreement to a conclusion before all involved are found guilty of the illegal tactics used to change the narrative of the Jenkins family. From the death of Carl Jenkins, Jonathan's failure as a farmer, the destruction of the family's reputation, and now with Misty returning, the company is pressing to get the agreement completed and signed by Jonathan.

"Elizabeth, I think we better sit down and talk intelligently about just how deep we both are in this scheme to take over this family. So, before you run off and tell Morgan Kiernan everything and have us all put in jail, let's come up with a plan. Tell me what is going on and who has been harassing you?"

Shaking her head in frustration, Elizabeth slaps her hands down on his desk and shouts, "You damn well know who it is. He is working alongside you and whomever else you have under your thumb.

Sometimes I wonder why all of you were so weak when you decided to do the bidding for the company. It's been over twenty years since we were recruited to do their dirty work. Tom, you know as well as I do what it takes to do what they asked, and can you look in the mirror? Because I sure as hell can't. So, it needs to be completed once and for all."

Pretending to hear some activity out in the hallway, Tom excuses himself. Walking out of his office, he uses this ploy to give him some time to figure out his next move. Watching his co-workers manage an unruly customer, he wants to find the courage to walk out the door and never look back. His career started out so well—giving customers their dreams, helping young people buy their first house, and finding money for the local businesses who might have fallen on hard times. All of these things were accomplishments he should feel good about. Instead, he felt used and defeated. Walking toward the unruly customer, he motions to his coworker that everything is fine, and he would handle it. Finding a quiet spot in the lobby, he takes the customer there.

After dealing with the customer, he heads back to his office and opens his door quickly to find Elizabeth on the phone with Brett. Listening to her conversation, he becomes aware of the fact that Brett knows more about the project than he was comfortable with. Motioning to her to hang up, he paces his office watching and listening to her. Elizabeth watches Fraser moving around his office like a caged animal. Finishing her conversation with Brett, she hangs up the phone and walks toward Tom.

"Stop pacing, Tom, you are making me nervous. What is your plan? Because I am getting tired of all of this and want it to end." Giving her a look, Tom sits down at his desk.

"Elizabeth, I want you to go home and relax. No one will be coming to your home threatening you anymore. However, remember this, the company is not going to let you forget your commitment to them, and because of your past actions, I would suggest you continue to find them in your favor. This will only end badly if you don't follow my suggestion."

Having enough of his condescending attitude, Elizabeth stands and moves toward the edge of Tom's desk where she lays her hands down.

Looking at him, she says, "Tom, we both know our actions of the past have sealed our fate, but I will be damned if my life will have a bad ending due the incompetence of this group of amateurs you have gathered." Walking to his door, she turns adding, "My suggestion is to get the company to back off on the Jenkins deal for a time and let the return of Misty Jenkins become old news."

Leaving the bank, Elizabeth decides to take a ride by the Jenkins farm and see for herself what is happening. Turning onto their road brought back so many memories, and she could feel a chill run down her spine. Coming up over the hill, she suddenly stops and pulls over. There are dumpsters and heavy equipment along with several men working and cleaning up debris. Moving ahead slowly, she notices Jonathan Jenkins and Morgan sitting on the back of a pickup truck talking. Not wanting to appear as though she is slowing to pull in, she accelerates and drives past.

She had been hoping Brett had been wrong. Telling Tom that she was going to Morgan Kiernan was an empty threat. Seeing Morgan Kiernan with Jonathan Jenkins confirmed Brett's revelation. Nothing else made sense. *Why would she be here having what looked like an animated conversation with a stranger? How dare she come back here falsely trying to hide her identity?* Recalling the most recent conversation with Tom, Elizabeth realizes he never blinked an eye with her threat of telling Morgan Kiernan—the threat of telling Misty Jenkins. That son-of-a bitch already knew Morgan Kiernan was Misty Jenkins and stood there calmly listening to her.

Nick & Whitney

Nick drives home from the bank in a daze. All these years, he thought Tom Fraser was someone with a good business sense but still had compassion for his community. It was apparent with all the forgiveness he had shown Nick throughout the years. There were so many times Whitney and he couldn't make their mortgage payment and other times Tom would approve home equity loans to help them get out of the hole they were sitting in.

Today was not the Tom Fraser he had been friends with for the last twenty years. Something had happened, and Nick couldn't fathom the change in Tom. He literally said he would sell out his community for money. Nick knew better than anyone that prestige, money, and popularity did not make someone happy.

Thinking about Whitney, he knew she would be very upset when he told her about Tom, and it would only bring up old arguments about money. He vowed he wouldn't cover up and hide things to make her feel secure anymore because he finally realized he wasn't there for her anyway. She handled everything with the boys when he was only being part of their sports journey. Recently, she and the boys have even been committed to going to a big church.

The lead pastor is a young, charismatic, and powerful speaker, and the church is so welcoming to everyone. The boys are involved in the youth group and have been asking him for a couple of weeks to come with them. He knew deep down Whitney wouldn't ask him to go. She was recovering, but he knew the hurt was deep down, and it was going to take some time before she realized he was there to stay. Morgan was in his past. It took some time to figure it out, but Whitney loved him. She was the mother to his boys, and their life was going to get better. He would figure out how to pay their debt. Tom wasn't going to dictate the rest of his life like he had for the last twenty years.

Pulling into his driveway, he sits for a moment in the truck looking at his house. It is as if a light had suddenly come on in his mind. Looking closely, he sees their roof is getting worn in some places and his windows really need to be replaced. Thank God they bought a home with aluminum siding, so it could be painted every few years. He vows to ask Whitney her opinion on the paint color. Later, he would call a couple contractors he knew to get pricing on a new roof and windows. Getting out of the car, he is more energetic to get inside than normal.

Opening the back door, he yells, "Hey, is anyone around?" Walking into the kitchen, he hears the boys in the family room with the TV up loud watching some kind of action movie. Moving toward the bottom of the stairs, he hears Whitney upstairs singing. Looking back at the boys, he sees they are absorbed in the movie, so running up the stairs, he hears her singing becoming louder and realizes it is coming from the bathroom where she is taking a shower.

Leaning against the door, he listens to his wife singing a song he was sure she heard at church. It brought a smile to his face knowing Whitney was healing. Life with Whitney happy was a good life, and he was going to do everything he could to make her happiness last.

His feelings for Morgan needed to be kept tucked away and not brought out anymore. There is no going back twenty years to rekindle something that he had destroyed.

Nick goes into their bedroom and lays down on the bed with his hands behind his head. Listening to Whitney finish up her shower, he wonders if she would want to go out later or have a quiet night at home. Hearing the bathroom door open, he keeps his expression neutral knowing she is going to be surprised to see him. Whitney walks into their bedroom and feeling good, drops her towel and starts to put moisturizer on her body. Hearing a sound, she turns and sees Nick lying on the bed.

"Oh my God, Nick. What in the world, are you trying to give me a heart attack? I didn't even know you were here." Swinging his legs over, he stands up and tentatively walks to his wife.

"Whitney, there is nothing more captivating than seeing you naturally and comfortable in your own skin. I realize things haven't been the greatest between us, but now you and I have moved to a new time, and it means so much to me to see you now as you are. Together we have been through so much, and I feel things are changing." He leans down and kisses her shoulder.

Feeling her body shiver, he wraps her in his arms and whispers, "We will be ok. Together we will be stronger and better." Stepping away from her, it is evident she is overwhelmed. He moves to the door and turns back to look at her.

"Whitney, I know it's hard to hear this now, but you are as beautiful as you were that day at the lake. Please understand the battle I have fought, but know in the end, we will survive. We just have to believe it."

Jackson

Sitting at the desk Olivia and Seth had set up for him, Jackson reviews his notes. Morgan's memories of her father's actions during her youth were invaluable to his case. Now, it's time to talk to all of the players in this saga and find out what roles were taken. Someone became the fall guy for the company, and he was sure it was Elizabeth Callahan. His immediate thought is the resident stalker was the muscle, and if his gut is correct, Tom Fraser is the brains. Looking down at what he jotted down before going to bed last night, it became obvious there had to be someone close to the family giving information to the rest of them.

Making a quick decision, he grabs his car keys and heads out. Realizing he couldn't just stop in to see her, Jackson stops in the driveway and walks back into the house. Seth is walking out the back door with some kind of lawn ornament.

"Hey Seth, I was wondering if you would take a ride with me. There is someone I want to go see, and I may need some interference." Seth turns and looks at his brother. Seeing the determined look in his eyes, he motions to the lawn ornament.

"Sure Jackson, give me a minute to hang up this for Olivia. Then I can go with you. By the way, where are we going?"

Hesitating for just a moment, Jackson smiles and says, "I want to make a visit to Elizabeth Callahan's, and I need you to pave the way for an introduction to your friend."

Seth raised his eyebrows and responded, "A friend of mine? Elizabeth Callahan is not a friend. She is Brett's mother. My knowledge of her is limited at best. Most of the time I was hanging out with Brett, she was in her office or out with her woman's garden club. Jackson, I honestly don't know very much about her."

Smiling devilishly, Jackson reassures, "Seth, my dear brother, all I need is an introduction. I will do the rest. All I want to do is talk to her on her own turf. Don't worry. It will be fun." Together they walk out to Jackson's car.

"Well one good thing out of this trip is I can ride in your new car," Seth says with a laugh. "I have been admiring it since you got here, Jackson. This car must have cost you a pretty penny."

"Seth, just get in will you. I really need to talk to Elizabeth Callahan. Something tells me she knows a lot more about Morgan's father, and I will bet my car that it is not good. My brother, you will get the ride of your life because I believe Abby's death has started an avalanche, and we are going to be at the bottom picking through the pieces. There is an evil lurking among our community, and it stands like a silent killer over all of us, and my plan is to extinguish it."

Backing out of the driveway, Seth puts his hand on Jackson's arm and says, "Wait here for a minute, I need to go in and tell Olivia that you and I will be out for a while. She gets nervous when I am gone for too long. Ever since Abigail's death, she doesn't like to be alone. It's gotten better lately, but I still want to let her know."

Watching his brother run inside to his wife, Jackson feels a surge of love for him, which surprises him but makes him smile. Coming back to Millersville and staying was something he surely didn't think was possible when thinking about his future, but now nothing had become more important. Subtle things are happening. None of them make sense individually, but put them together, and a thought is taking shape in his mind. Snapped out of his thoughts with Seth's closing of the car door, Jackson puts his car back in gear, and they are on their way.

On the way over to Callahan's, Seth begins to question Jackson on their impromptu visit.

"What is it you are trying to find out today? Elizabeth isn't a person who you can just stop in and see without notice. All I'm saying is be prepared."

Smiling at his brother as he downshifts for the stop street, Jackson replies, "Seth don't worry. This is right up my alley. I've coaxed more than my fair share of confessions out of guilty people, so rest assured, something useful will come out of our visit today."

Frowning slightly, Seth retorts, "Jackson, do you think Elizabeth is guilty of something that has to do with Abby's death, or is this about Morgan? Because as far as I know, Brett's mother doesn't have any idea who Morgan is, so without revealing her, I don't know what you are going to find out from Elizabeth."

Slowing down in front of the Callahan house, Jackson pulls to the curb and parks. The two of them get out of the car and walk up to the front door. Jackson is scanning the front of the house looking for any movement. Seeing the curtain flutter, he is sure Elizabeth is aware she had visitors.

Touching the ring doorbell, they wait a minute or two and then the deadbolt moves, and the door opens......